BOOKS BY NEAL ROBERTS

IN THE DEN OF THE ENGLISH LION
A Second Daniel
The Impress of Heaven
A Dragon in the Ashes
All the Men as Mad as He

ALL THE MEN AS MAD AS HE

Book 4 of
In the Den of the English Lion

BY NEAL ROBERTS

Hamlet:
Ay, marry, why was [Hamlet] sent into England?

Gravedigger:
Why, because he was mad: he shall recover his wits there; or, if he do
not, it's no great matter there.

Hamlet:
Why?

Gravedigger:
'Twill not be seen in him there; there the men are as mad as he.

FREE DOWNLOAD

DEDICATION

To Myra, Adam, Gigi, Mom,
the rest of my extended family, and
Hicksville Comets '68 – '71

ACKNOWLEDGMENTS

First and foremost, to my good friend and correspondent Brenda James, who alone deciphered the code in the dedication to Shakespeare's sonnets and who, together with William Rubinstein, began the long and arduous—but fascinating—task of introducing the true bard to the world. To a new friend and foremost investigator of the true bard, Dr. John Casson, co-author of the compelling new book *Sir Henry Neville Was Shakespeare: The Evidence*.

I'd also like to extend my heartfelt thanks to my treasured wife Myra, to Gigi, to the ever supportive and lovely Jennifer Nagler, Uncle Jack, the Donovans, Good Cousin Barbara (think screenplay), Nadine Rabinowitz (who first brought Mrs. James's work to my attention), John O'Donnell and his friend Alistair Clark, who's a doctoral candidate at Merton College, Oxford (for improving the Queen's Latin), Mom, my wife's mother Lily, and all the other relatives and friends who've lent their time, and their moral and literary advice and support to this project. To Dr. Jeffrey Laitman for his advice concerning the progress and treatment of pre-eclampsia; any mistakes are solely my own.

To my editor, Martin Jones, I extend my sincerest thanks. To my ever-faithful reader and proofreader Laurel Busch. To my publicist Samantha Williams of Aurora Publicity, for her continuing Herculean efforts in dragging the recalcitrant niche of historical fiction into the 21st century, and to her associate, the world's most patient up-and-coming cover designer, Melody Barber.

Finally, many thanks to my good friend, the talented photographer Jeffrey Loeser, who took the photo appearing on the back cover of this book, and in so doing accomplished the extraordinary task of making me look presentable.

PRINCIPAL PERSONS
OF THE STORY

ELIZABETH, BY THE GRACE OF GOD, QUEEN OF ENGLAND,
FRANCE, AND IRELAND

NOAH AMES, barrister, advisor to HM
MARIE AMES, his wife by remarriage
JESSICA, LADY SAINT IVES, his daughter
JONATHAN HAWKING, BARON SAINT IVES, his son-in-law
ARTHUR ARDEN, barrister, his friend
ESTHER, his cousin
BETH FERNANDEZ, cousin to Noah Ames
STEPHEN RODRIGUEZ, elder son of Marie Ames

SIR HENRY NEVILLE, HM's Ambassador to France
LADY ANNE NEVILLE born KILLIGREW, his wife
DAVID "CHEERFUL" KILLIGREW, his wife's nephew

LORD SHEFFIELD, a neighbor
LADY SHEFFIELD, his wife
CONSTANCE, their spicemaid

GARDNER, Senior Yeoman of the Guard
FRANCIS, Yeoman of the Guard
CHESTER, Former Jailer of Cambridge Castle

THOMAS, Lord Grey

SIR JOHN FORTESCUE, Chancellor of the Exchequer

HENRY BILLINGSLEY, knight, HM's collector

CUTHBERT BENNETT, barrister
TOBIAS BENNETT, barrister, his identical twin

BARNSTABLE, Southwark constable

WHAT-GOD-WILL KNOTT, cathedral constable

BUCKLEY, knight, of the Wardrobe
TELLER, his assistant
RALPH, another assistant

AUGUSTINE PHILLIPS, manager, Lord Chamberlain's Men

JACOB, assistant at Drapers' Hall

The Cecil Faction

ROBERT CECIL, LORD KEEPER OF
THE PRIVY SEAL, First
Secretary of State
FRANCIS BACON, Queen's
Counsel

THE LORD ADMIRAL
ROBERT SIDNEY, knight
JOHN LEVESON, knight, cousin
to Sir Henry Neville
WALTER RALEIGH, knight,
Captain of the Yeoman
Warders

The Essex Faction

ROBERT DEVEREUX, Earl of
Essex
GELLY MEYRICK, his principal
attendant
HENRY CUFFE, his secretary
CAIM, his footman

HENRY WRIOTHESLEY, EARL OF
SOUTHAMPTON, friend to the
Earl of Essex

FERDINANDO GORGES, knight,
Captain at Plymouth

CHARLES PERCY, knight
JOSCELINE PERCY, knight, his
brother

CHAPTER 1

LONDON, ENGLAND
AUGUST 31, 1600

AFTER MIDNIGHT, cloaked and cowled all in black, the conspirators quietly converge on the courtyard outside a little church adjoining a cathedral. Though some of the dark figures approach through the stone arch to the west and others from sleepy London town to the east, they assemble single-mindedly, facing each other in a tight circle.

Esther awaits their arrival crouched in a dark corner at a safe remove. She shudders with cold, looks down at her costume, and vaguely wonders how she could be wearing nothing but a thin night rail. She vaguely recalls retiring to her room at the Ames's house, but nothing after that. The chill deepens to the kind of bone-chilling cold that comes just before a ghost appears. And it seems already to have spread to the conspirators.

"God, it's flippin' freezin' out 'ere!" blurts one of the conspirators, chafing his sides. "Didn't anybuddy tell the Good Lord it's summertime? Mebbe He'd send us some heat."

Another conspirator, much taller than the first, snarls at him. "What makes ye think God would do *anythin'* for the likes o' you? Not bloody likely, after tonight," he muses. "Keep it down. We can't afford to be seen or heard out here." He points in Esther's general direction. "Here they come."

Esther nearly gasps aloud, but then realizes that he's pointing not to her, but to two tardy conspirators approaching together from the east. Both are short. One is plump, the other thin.

The tall conspirator quietly addresses those already arrived. "If any o' you gentlemen ain't got the stomach for it, just leave it to me. I'll take care of 'em both meself if I need to. *Christ,* it's cold!"

Esther's shuddering so hard, she wonders that her teeth haven't chattered, and prays they don't start now.

"'Ey," says the tall one, roughly greeting the newcomers as they come close enough to hear. "Took yer sweet time about it."

"We had to await an opportune moment to get away," says the plump newcomer, in a far more cultured voice than that of his inquisitor. "You wouldn't want our new friend here accidentally revealing anything by disappearing out of turn, would you?"

"Nah. He wouldn't reveal anythin' *by accident*," says another of the early arrivals as the newcomers join in their circle.

"What's *that* s'posed to mean?" asks the thinner of the newcomers. "I got away quick as I could!"

"Word has it," says the tall one, "that the Tower Guard's caught wind of what's goin' on. You two wouldn't know 'ow that 'appened, now, *would* ye?"

The newcomers seem startled and defensive. "Well, they didn't find out from us!" the plump one protests.

The tall one steps toward them menacingly. "'*Course* they didn't," he says sarcastically, glancing about at the other early arrivals, as though to assay his support. "Naaah! Weren't *you*!"

With the word *you,* the other conspirators thrust the newcomers to the center of the black circle, which swallows them whole. Blades flash in the moonlight, and the tall one stabs each of the newcomers in the abdomen. The others quickly join in a murderous frenzy, cutting them all over their bodies: neck, belly, back, legs.

The victims gasp in protest, too surprised to do anything but raise their hands to no avail, and gape in horror at their own butchering. Blood flows freely to the ground.

Esther feels the urgent need to cry out, to call for help, but finds that all she can do is whimper in horror.

"No, no," the victims repeat in disbelief. When the assailants step back into their former circle, the victims look briefly into each other's eyes and collapse to the ground in horror, the thin one motionless.

The plump one squirms in agony a few moments. "You bastards will pay for this!" he grunts. "Wait till my brother—"

"Yer brother'll be *joinin'* ye in just a bit," says the tall one, and stabs him in the throat, silencing him at once. Blood spurts over the pavement. "Give 'im my best wishes for all eternity."

With the mention of eternity, the other assassins recoil in horror from the bloody scene, as though they'd forgotten that the stain of evil will follow them past the grave.

In the blink of an eye, killers and victims disappear from Esther's view.

Though Esther's now standing at precisely the same spot where she formerly crouched, it's suddenly become an overcast winter's day, and she's dressed in the new cloak Mistress Ames just bought for her. But she's still so very cold—what she's come to think of as *unnaturally* cold.

She's surrounded by pandemonium, a scene filled with armed men loosely organized into two opposing groups, though neither side wears any sort of uniform.

One group, with the little church at its back, appears to be comprised of gentlemen with their swords drawn. At its center, a tall thin man with dark reddish hair and beard pleads with them to avoid fighting.

The opposing group stands athwart the stone archway, defending it— or perhaps blocking the swordsmen from passing through. It's a poorly armed contingent, with most members lacking so much as a sword, instead wielding pointed sticks and partisans to keep the swordsmen at bay.

Immediately before the arch stands a tall young blond man with his back turned to Esther. As he exhorts the pikemen to avoid bloodshed, an opposing swordsman runs him through from the rear, inflicting a ghastly wound. The blond man's head jerks backward as his torso moves forward with the blow. He falls dead to the ground, his face still out of Esther's view. She whimpers to think it might be David Killigrew, with whom she's fallen deeply in love.

"Esther!"

———————— ⇒◦⟨⟩◦⟜ ————————

"ESTHER! WAKE UP, DEAR!"

A woman's mature voice comes to her from somewhere outside this horrible reality. She feels herself being shaken. "Wake up, dear." It's the soothing voice of Mistress Ames.

With great effort, Esther expels the bloody scene, and opens her eyes.

She's relieved to find herself in her own bed. Mistress Ames is seated next to her looking quite worried, while everyone else in the house crowds the doorway of her room, looking anxious and rumpled in their bedclothes. The pale glow of dawn seeps through the windows.

Mistress Ames's only daughter, a raven-haired beauty on the cusp of womanhood, breaks the silence. "Why is it so *cold* in here, Serjeant Ames?"

4 | NEAL ROBERTS

"Yes," adds her brother of nearly the same age, "one could hang meat in this room with no fear of spoilage."

Serjeant Ames looks to Mistress Ames's eldest son. "Stephen," he says in his most serious voice, "please escort your brother and sister back up to their rooms." He turns to reassure the younger ones before they're led off. "Everything will be made clear to you later. Meanwhile, *don't* mention this—especially the *cold* – to anyone outside the family."

The two youngest moan in complaint, but turn to go. While they'd clearly like an explanation now, they know better than to resist when Noah speaks in his serious voice.

Stephen steals a parting look at Esther, and reluctantly escorts his younger siblings upstairs.

Marie places her hand on Esther's forehead. "You feel warmer now." She lifts the blanket to feel Esther's bare feet. "Much better now," she says with relief.

For his part, Noah is also relieved to see that her feet are perfectly clean and unbruised, proving that she hasn't been sleepwalking, as his daughter Jessica was wont to do in childhood, much to her father's alarm.

A FEW MINUTES later Esther is sitting up in bed. Though the late summer's warmth has quickly returned, she holds a small bowl of hot water in her hands, given her by Mistress Ames. Esther dutifully sips it from time to time while Marie looks on from her perch on the bed.

Noah has dressed hurriedly and now stands by the bed uncertain what to do. He'd planned on seeking out Sir Walter Raleigh this morning, but he's concerned about his young cousin's health, although to all appearances she's as robust as ever. He's also troubled by the visions that came to Esther in dreams she's now recounted twice.

Both deadly scenes were set at precisely the same location, but Noah cannot discern anything else they might have in common. They took place at different times of day; one on a night in fading summer (much like the one that's just passed), the other in winter's harsh daylight.

Perhaps they were just dreams. After all, the girl probably has ordinary dreams sometimes, the same as everyone else. But, even if she does, he doesn't believe these dreams were ordinary, not even for her.

Marie turns to him. "There's no reason for you to remain here, dear. Esther is feeling just fine." She turns to the girl and asks, "Isn't that right, dear?"

Esther, who's taking a sip from her bowl, smiles wanly up at Noah, and turns to Marie. "Yes. Thank you so much for all the care you've given me. Both you and Serjeant Ames." Her pretty face breaks out into a broad smile.

"Yes," says Noah. "I may as well go."

"Noah," says Marie hesitantly, "may I speak with you a moment first—in your study?" She takes a parting look at her ward, kisses her on the forehead, and follows Noah to the study, where she leaves the door open a crack, so she can hear if Esther calls.

"I suppose," says Marie once they're alone, "that there are several sites in London fitting Esther's description of the place where those terrible events took place."

Noah shakes his head confidently. "No." He raises his index finger. "One only."

"Are you quite certain?" she asks. "It's long been common practice in England to erect a small church adjoining a great cathedral."

"So I've learned," replies Noah. "The little church is run by the parish priest, the cathedral by the bishopric."

Marie nods. "But how can you be sure which church she saw?"

"By the *gate* she mentioned," he says.

"But London has several gates."

Noah shakes his head. "In London, only one little church adjoining a cathedral overlooks a city gate." He hears a horse-drawn cart pull up somewhere nearby, but takes no heed of it.

Marie arches an eyebrow quizzically. "Which gate?" she asks.

"Ludgate," he replies. "It's overlooked by Saint Gregory's Church by Saint Paul's Cathedral. The events in Esther's dreams took place—if *ever* they took place, or ever *shall*—in that little square between Saint Gregory's and Ludgate. I've forgotten its name, if it even has one."

There's a sudden pounding at the front door.

"Serjeant Ames!" says an urgent voice outside. "Serjeant Ames! 'Tis I, Arthur Arden. Please come to the door, sir, if you can hear me!"

Startled, Noah races to the door. He opens it, and the chill of early morning sweeps in. Outside stands Arthur in his barrister's robes, overcome with anxiety.

"What is it, Arthur?" asks Noah abruptly. Then, hoping to put the young man at ease, he adds: "Have you time to come inside?"

"Much as I would like to see everyone, sir," says Arthur hesitantly, "I'm afraid we're losing time. I've made a rather grisly discovery which

I expect will be of concern to you in your duties at the Tower. Come, sir. Please take a seat up front with me and I'll tell you along the way what I've found."

Noah kisses Marie, who watches as he climbs up to the driver's bench. He turns to Arthur with concern. "What have you found?" he asks.

Arthur shakes the reins and the cart begins to move. "Two corpses, I'm afraid. They appear to have bled out on the pavement before I arrived a short while ago. I'd had trouble sleeping, so I'd risen early to go pray."

"*Where* were you going to pray?" asks Noah.

At first Arthur appears mystified by the question, almost defensive, but then evidently realizes it's not as irrelevant as first it seemed. "I was heading for Saint Gregory by Saint Paul's."

Noah's mind starts to buzz. "Is that where you found the bodies?" asks Noah, mindful not to let his suspicions get the better of him. To avoid the appearance that he had foreknowledge of the crime, he adds, "Were the bodies *inside* the church?"

"No, sir. I hadn't a chance to enter before I found the bodies outside, on Bowyer's Row."

Bowyer's Row. "That's the square by Ludgate?"

"Aye, sir," says Arthur, "you've passed through there many times, I'm sure, though—not to pray, of course."

Noah answers quickly to save Arthur from the awkwardness that all Christians seem to feel in referring to Noah's Hebrew faith. "Nor to buy an archer's bow," he says. "Of course, I've passed through there many times. I just never learned the street's name. How were the victims dressed when they died?"

"All in black, sir, though they're so covered in blood, it was hard to find a clean place on their clothing to confirm that."

As Bowyer's Row comes into view, they find it deserted, still covered with a fine, icy mist that obscures the ground. The corpses, partly obscured, appear as two heaps of bloody black rags carelessly discarded onto the pavement.

Noah wonders what it all means. Why would Esther have seen this crime, in particular? Does it have some connection to her? He wonders whether the crime or its solution might not affect her in some way. Perhaps if the crime is solved, it will reveal something helpful to her. Perhaps if he *fails* to solve it, she'll somehow suffer injury. Or, conversely, perhaps it's *meant* to go unsolved, and he might injure her by solving it. Either way, he feels precisely the same as he does whenever such questions are raised by Esther's strange gift. Completely befuddled. Fortunately, he has no choice but to plod on.

Noah looks to Arthur. "Have you been here before, I mean so early in the morning?"

"A few times," says Arthur reticently, as he slows the horses down to assure a safe approach to the west end of Saint Gregory's.

"Is there always an icy mist like this?" asks Noah.

"Sometimes in late autumn," replies Arthur, drawing the cart to a halt. He gazes toward the eastern horizon. "As you can see, the rising sun strikes Saint Gregory's, which casts its shadow over this courtyard." He pauses a moment and shakes his head. "But there's usually no such mist at this time of year. It's just too warm."

Noah silently wonders whether it's so cold now merely because Esther was here. He shakes his head, dismissing his own thoughts. She *wasn't* here physically, as shown by her unsullied feet. In what sense *might* she have been here? Though he tries his best to dismiss such thoughts as mystical nonsense, he can't help but locate the corner where Esther, or her spirit, might have cowered in wait for the conspirators. It shows no sign of her former presence … but for the icy mist.

He clears his head and follows Arthur to the first of the two bodies lying in the square. As they reach the nearer one, Noah observes that it's slight of frame and surrounded by a pool of glistening blood. The face looks familiar.

Arthur's been watching Noah, and evidently discerns the look of recognition. "I've seen him, too," says Arthur. "It took me till I was nearing your house to remember where I'd seen him."

Noah shrugs. "Where?"

"If I'm right," says Arthur, "he's one of Her Majesty's wardrobe servants."

Noah bends down for a better look. He remembers this man's face only vaguely, as he would that of an actor who's appeared many times upon the stage, always in the guise of someone's servant, his few spoken lines always self-effacing, always strictly in keeping with his supposed trade—a face meant to be looked at, but not seen. As for any information to be culled from the grievous wounds, Noah will need to attend the examination to be conducted by the coroner, who'll no doubt show up at any moment.

Arthur has already moved on to the second blood-drenched body, this one a bit stockier than the first. As Noah approaches, he asks Arthur,

"Did you recognize this one, as well?"

Arthur responds by mournfully pointing his chin at the man's face, half of which is visible. The other half is pressed firmly onto the pavement, as though the victim, having settled down here for an awkward night's rest, mistook the street for a pillow. Noah squats by the victim for a better view of his face.

"Do *you* recognize him?" asks Arthur.

Noah sighs. "How could I forget someone who's risked his life to save mine own, however long ago? This is one of the Bennett twins." As he says those words, he remembers Esther's retelling of the last words heard by this victim, the import of which was that his brother would soon follow him in death. Noah wonders whether there's anything he can do to avoid that prophecy's coming true, as he has no idea where the other Bennett twin might be found. "I saw them together just a few days ago," says Noah, "when they left London as part of Lord Essex's retinue."

"That was short service," Arthur says bitterly.

Noah points to the knife in the victim's hand. "Let's make sure to recover that, once the coroner's through with it." Arthur nods silently.

On impulse, Noah walks to the corner where he imagines Esther stood as she watched the murders, and turns to take in precisely the perspective she had in her dream.

A hearse clops up to the scene unbidden.

Noah glances toward Ludgate, wondering which blond man will die of the cowardly thrust foreseen by Esther. Or perhaps it already befell some poor bastard on a winter's afternoon long ago. Or perhaps, perhaps … *perhaps*. Such wild conjecture exasperates him. He sighs.

It all seems so much madness.

CHAPTER 2

NOAH PACES ABOUT the library at the Neville's home in the Lothbury section of London. When Sir Henry walks in, Noah collapses in a chair and remarks to himself that his friend has gained weight since returning to London mere weeks ago.

"Good to see you, Ames!" says Sir Henry, heartily at first. But then he regards Noah dubiously. "You look as though you've seen a ghost. What's happened?"

Noah sighs. "I've stopped in on my way home from a murder scene," he says apologetically. "I'm afraid your relative Arthur Arden found two bodies butchered at Bowyer's Row quite early this morning."

"Anyone we know?"

"Arthur and I think one was a wardrobe servant to Her Majesty."

Sir Henry arches an eyebrow. "And the other?"

"One of the Bennett twins."

Sir Henry cocks his head. "One of those identical twins who rode off with Lord Essex when he was released from confinement a few days ago?"

"Yes, those were they. You'll recall, years ago, during the Lopez case, I was spirited away from Guildhall by a group of young barristers, with Essex's men in hot pursuit. The Bennetts were among my saviors."

Sir Henry's face flashes with recognition. "The 'jesters'! Of course!" He lowers his tone. "And now you've lost one. My deepest sympathies."

"The Bennetts were a quiet pair," says Noah, who rises and resumes pacing. "They seemed to have little interest in politics, other than to defend the Queen—and me—in that one instance. Shortly afterwards, they disappeared, reputedly up into Cheltenham, but no one's really sure *where* they went. Just a few weeks ago, they were seen in the company of Essex's men, trying to steal Walsingham's correspondence from Burghley House."

"Oh, they fought alongside the dwarf in that fracas?" asks Sir Henry.

Noah's heart aches at the mention of the dwarf; a good soul who'd fallen among thieves and paid with his life. "Monk, they called him," he says earnestly, as though the mere mention of his name might serve as some small memorial. "Yes, the Bennetts fought alongside him—in the most dubious of causes—although I strongly suspect Essex had no idea what they were doing. As you'll recall, Essex was still under house arrest at that time. Right now, my immediate concern is to find the surviving Bennett twin."

"Do you suppose he's in danger from his brother's murderer?" asks Henry.

With some regret, Noah quickly decides it's not yet time to confide in Sir Henry that Esther "saw" the murder take place and "heard" the killer announce that he would kill the surviving twin. It would take too much persuading for Sir Henry to take it seriously, and there's insufficient time at present.

"One must so presume," says Noah. "The twins were inseparable." He resumes his seat. "I came here to ask if you would help in the matter. I hope you won't deem it presumptuous that, before coming here, I sent a note to our old friend Constable Barnstable telling him I'd be here."

"Not at all," says Sir Henry, snickering at the rhyming name, "but why would you tell *him*? His bailiwick is Southwark. That's a far cry from the murder scene at Bowyer's Row."

Noah squirms in his chair. "There's nothing to indicate that the Queen's safety is at risk. Her Majesty may not wish me to investigate at all, so it seemed presumptuous to notify the Tower Guard before consulting with her. Instead, I asked Barnstable to seek out the constable having jurisdiction over Bowyer's Row and to accompany him here, if possible."

"Still," muses Sir Henry, "the victims did consist of one of Her Majesty's servants and a member of Essex's retinue."

Before Noah can reply, there's a knock at the library door.

"Come!" shouts Sir Henry.

Walker, the Nevilles' footman, enters, nods familiarly to Noah, and turns to Sir Henry. "There are two gentlemen at the door, sir, asking to speak with Serjeant Ames."

"*Are* they gentlemen?" asks Sir Henry dubiously.

"Hardly, sir, judging by their mode of dress. At least one appears to be of the local constabulary. The other?" He shrugs.

Sir Henry turns to Noah. "Would you prefer to meet with them alone, Ames?"

"I'd like to speak with Barnstable privately. Perhaps I might accompany Walker to the door and confer with Barnstable, while Walker escorts the other to the parlor to await me. Then, with your permission, Sir Henry, I'll bring him in here and we can chat together."

Sir Henry smirks. "I shall await you here," he says, selecting a book from the shelf and depositing his ample girth in a soft chair.

Walker leads Noah to the front door and admits the two constables into the foyer. Barnstable's familiar face is a bit more careworn than when Noah last saw him. "Constable Barn-Stable," says Noah, being careful to pronounce the name in the unrhyming manner preferred by its owner, "thank you so much for escorting this gentleman here."

Noah turns to the other constable, whose haughtiness appears to have frozen his mouth in a permanent moue of distaste. His black attire is correspondingly severe. The man is plainly a puritan, one of those ill-favored reformers of the Church of England dedicated to eradicating from that institution any remnants of humanity; no stained glass, no music, no mirth of any kind.

Having had no intercourse with puritans, Noah strains to recall what little he's learned of them from others. He's chagrined to realize the sum total of his knowledge comes down to two points: First, puritans are generally detested by those who aren't puritans and, second, some puritans have strange names.

Noah leans in toward the man. "Constable—?"

"Knott, sir," says the constable, bowing perfunctorily. "What-God-Will."

Noah is momentarily speechless. "I beg your pardon?" he says at last.

His confusion seems to have provided the constable with a welcome opportunity to grimace in condescension. "My full name, Serjeant Ames, is What-God-Will Knott. My father thought a given name ought to be a source of humility, rather than pride, you see, and so chose my given name as a source of mild amusement."

Noah finds it difficult to avoid smiling, but bows politely. "I take it your name betokens a puritan faith, sir. Perhaps you are of eastern Sussex?"

"I am, sir," replies Knott. "And you are a *Jew*, are you not?" Knott glances at Constable Barnstable, the apparent source of this evidently distasteful intelligence.

"I *am* ... Knott," replies Noah, letting the ambiguity hang in the air like an unspent sneeze. "Please await me in the parlor. I'll be there presently."

"This way," says Walker, who bows and escorts Knott away.

As soon as they're out of sight, Constable Barnstable earnestly draws Noah out of the house through the doorway. A light breeze wafts through the leaves, providing the early afternoon with wholesome relief after this bloody morning.

Barnstable leans into Noah earnestly, keeping his voice down. "Knott is 'cathedral constable' ... at Saint Paul's, suh."

"Then why did you bring *him* here? These crimes took place out of doors, on Bowyer's Row."

"Aye, suh, but it's right next to the cathedral ... as y'know. The cathedral constable also investigates things that happen outdoors on the cathedral grounds."

Something still makes no sense to Noah. "But he's a puritan, Constable Barnstable. How on earth did he secure employment by the bishopric?"

"He was chosen by the lay vestry, suh, not the bishop. But that's not why I wanted to talk with you privately, suh."

"No?"

"No." Barnstable looks down at his feet, abashed. "It's rather that I don't *like* 'im, suh. Don't *trust* 'im, neither. Only met him twice, but both times ..." His voice trails off and he sneers in disgust.

"What's the matter with him?"

"He seems interested in only one thing, suh. Can't seem to get it out of his head."

"And what's that?"

Barnstable, by his expression, is lost somewhere between disgust and confusion. "He's always guessin' 'bout what people do ... in private, suh."

Barnstable is apparently awaiting some sign of recognition on Noah's face, but all Noah can do is motion for him to continue.

"Between the sheets," the constable hints, a little more specifically. "Especially"—he makes an odd thrusting motion with his hand—"buggery, suh ... which he deems quite common."

Noah's taken aback, fully aware that the good constable is not wont to jest in a matter so serious as a murder investigation.

"*Buggery?*" Noah repeats doubtfully. "Well," he says indulgently, "surely there was something in your conversation to suggest the topic. No?"

Barnstable shakes his head vigorously. "No, suh. He finds a way to insert it—what am I saying?—to bring it up—*gawp*! It comes up in *every* conversation, no matter how immaterial. You'll see." He looks over his shoulder, as though eager to extricate himself from the topic.

Noah finds a half crown in his pocket, and palms it into the constable's hand. "Thank you for warning me of this man's morbid preoccupation. I only wish I'd known before you brought him here. He's liable to be more hindrance than help."

"Sorry, suh," says Barnstable. "Wasn't time, or I woulda talked to ye first."

"Don't fret, constable," replies Noah. "If he becomes a nuisance, I shall see him removed from the case."

"Thank you, suh," says Barnstable. "I've no doubt you could do it."

Noah watches the constable ride away, wondering whether the powers-that-be would truly remove a solemn puritan from a murder case on the word of a heathen Jew, however highly placed.

He reenters the house alone, shuts the door behind him, and ambles off to the parlor. To his chagrin, however, there's no sign there of Constable Knott or anyone else. He turns about just as the diminutive Lady Anne marches straight into him. Noah turns to apologize, though blameless in the collision, but, before he can speak, Lady Anne's keen stare pierces him through, her green eyes darkened to set them off sharply from her fair skin and roan hair.

As Lady Anne has always been such a welcoming figure, and so obviously fond of Noah, he's alarmed by her sudden change in aspect.

She stabs his chest with her finger. "I want that insolent prig out of my house at once!" she says with unaccustomed severity.

"You wish *me* to remove someone?" asks Noah innocently.

Lady Anne glances about demonstratively. "Are we not alone, Serjeant Ames? Is there someone else here who cannot be seen, perhaps?" She places her hands on her hips and observes him impatiently.

Her reference to someone who cannot be seen reminds Noah fleetingly of Esther, but he expels the thought. "No, m'lady. I ... you *did* mean Constable Knott, did you not?"

"Certainly Knott! I mean *certainly*!" She's a bit flustered. "Whom else would I mean? You'll find him in the library, worrying Sir Henry like an Aberdeen terrier."

"I shall see to it at once, m'lady!" Noah bows smartly and hurries off to the library, where he finds the constable, hands joined behind his back, hovering over the seated Sir Henry, as though engaged in legal examination.

Noah closes the door as he enters, to avoid their voices carrying to

Lady Anne. At the clack of the door, Sir Henry looks to Noah hopefully.

"Constable Knott!" says Noah. "At last I seem to have caught up with you."

Knott releases Sir Henry from his gaze, and drops his hands to his sides. "Sir Henry and I were having a nice chat."

"Oh?" says Noah, arching an eyebrow. "On what topic?" Sir Henry's eyes flash in mute warning, but Noah's question is already out.

Knott turns on Noah sharply. "Serjeant Ames, you *yourself* frequented the Inn of Glaucus, did you not?"

Noah has no clue what he's being asked about, but for the constable to demand an answer from him at all is wholly impertinent, and he seizes the occasion to gain the upper hand, replying with a question of his own.

"Why are you here?" he demands sternly.

"Why," says Knott, "you *summoned* me here."

"No, I didn't. I asked you to wait in the *parlor*. But I did ask you to come to this house. Why do you suppose I did that?"

The constable is flustered, just as Noah had hoped. "To discuss your discovery of dead bodies on Bowyer's Row, of course."

"Not my discovery. Master *Arden's*," says Noah sternly. "And is *that* the topic of discussion between you and Sir Henry?"

Evidently catching on that he's being upbraided, Knott tries to turn the tables on Noah. "I have it on good authority," he says, "that your Master Arden frequented the Inn of Glaucus years ago."

Noah allows his irritation to show. "You forget yourself, Constable. I asked you to await me in the parlor. Instead, I find you gone from there, having drawn the ire of Lady Anne—that most gracious of hostesses—and now find you in the library, riddling our mutual host with questions." He shakes his head in admonition. "This business shall progress no further at this time. Please inform Walker where you may be found … although I doubt I shall require your services further."

"You? Require my services?" Knott frowns. "Sir, I serve the Bishop of London."

"And I *the Queen of England*!" says Noah sternly.

Though the constable is patently crestfallen and his face red, he raises his chin in bested pride.

Noah opens the door and gestures for the unwelcome visitor to leave. "Good day, Constable!" The constable proceeds through the doorway at a deliberate pace, obviously hoping to come up with some suitable riposte to cover his retreat. Noah adds, "Kindly leave the way you came. And I trust you shall go *directly* the way you've been told this time."

The constable takes a single step into the hallway and turns back as if to speak. Before he can utter a word, Noah slams the door in his face.

"Ames," says Sir Henry drily, "you still possess that uncanny ability to make new friends wherever you go."

Noah turns to him dourly. "Not a friend I'd care to have," he muses.

"Thanks for removing him from the house," says Sir Henry, "but I doubt it will be so easy to exclude him from the *case*."

At that moment, the door opens a crack, and a beaming Lady Anne appears and invites them to dinner.

NOAH FORGETS HIS troubles for the moment, as he dines on a delicious pumpkin soup (his favorite) accompanied by game hen served in its own gravy.

"That was delicious," he says as they finish, bowing in his seat to Lady Anne. "Thank you so much for the invitation." But now that he's eaten, all at once he's overcome with fatigue.

Lady Anne cocks her head and smiles prettily. "Why, all the blood has drained from your face, Noah. You seem not quite yourself."

Noah smiles apologetically. "I was awakened early this morning, m'lady."

Her eyes widen sympathetically. "I do hope you were not awakened by worry."

"No, madam," he assures her. "It was rather my niece Esther who'd had an awful nightmare and awakened us all with her protestations."

Noah sees that the mere mention of Esther has aroused Sir Henry's interest. "Quite an exceptional girl," Sir Henry remarks, turning to his wife. "I'd expect Noah has also been disquieted by the unpleasant discovery that brought him here."

Lady Anne purses her lips and says, "Which no doubt also brought that scoundrel of a puritan here. Well," she says, rising from her place at table, "I shall leave you two to solve the affairs of the world."

Noah rises. "I hope that my business has not chased m'lady away from such a pleasant dinner."

Lady Anne waves away the thought. "Not in the least. Noah, you are *always* welcome at our home. Isn't that right, Sir Henry?"

"Most assuredly," mumbles Sir Henry as Lady Anne departs, leaving the two men alone in the dining room. Henry pours himself a cup of his favored sherris sack, and mutely inquires whether Noah would care to partake.

Noah shakes his head. "Where the devil is this Inn of Glaucus that Knott was going on about? I seem to recall hearing of it long ago, but can't quite conjure the place or time."

"You once resided quite near it," muses Sir Henry. "It's entirely plausible you never went in, however, as you had ample reason to keep out."

"*I* resided near the Inn of Glaucus?" says Noah skeptically. "When?"

Sir Henry takes a sip of sack. "During the Lopez case, back in '92."

"I resided at Gray's Inn for a good many years," says Noah, "and can recall several local inns, but none by that name. Where was it located, relative to my quarters?"

Sir Henry snickers. "Next door."

Noah's confused. "Do you mean Mountjoy's Inn, where Doctor Lopez kept rooms?"

Sir Henry seems to be enjoying this little guessing game, but it's beginning to irritate Noah.

"Nearer still," mutters Sir Henry, taking another sip. Evidently noticing Noah's consternation, he adds, "'The Inn of Glaucus' was a jocular name Anthony Bacon gave to his quarters at Gray's Inn, in the building adjacent to yours. Remember? One of Anthony's friends even took it upon himself to fashion a little wooden sign saying 'Inn of Glaucus' for display on the landing leading up to Anthony's rooms. Oh, but Bacon never allowed it to be displayed."

Noah searches his memory. "I remember hearing of it, but never saw it. Wasn't Glaucus a figure in Greek mythology, a fisherman who was transformed into some sort of sea-god, or some such thing?"

Sir Henry smiles. "You're recalling that from Eton."

Noah shrugs. "I suppose so. Who can recall where one first hears such nonsense?"

Sir Henry shakes his head. "That's the *fisherman* Glaucus," he says. "No, Bacon's imaginary inn was named after rather a different Glaucus, also from Greek mythology." Sir Henry refills Noah's cup and sits back.

"Oh?"

"To place matters in context," Sir Henry begins, "1592 was rather a momentous year for several in our circle. It was the year Mistress Ames lost her husband in a murder that both you and I witnessed (but Lord Essex did not), and the year your daughter Jessica returned to your life, having been widowed the year before. It was also the year when *you* awoke from the long emotional torpor that followed the death of your first wife.

"But it was also a watershed year for Anthony Bacon, as he returned to England from his long self-exile that followed hard upon the death of his father, the Lord Keeper of the Great Seal. As you'll recall, Anthony was a sickly fellow, afflicted with the stone, as well as gout even worse than mine own, that would pitch him into paroxysms of agony at the most unpropitious times. It made travel most difficult for him. For twelve long years, Anthony had been exhorted by his mother's letters (and to a lesser extent by those of his brother Francis) to return to England and secure his rightful place at the Queen's court.

"Francis meantime had qualified as a barrister, but he'd met with no success in seeking a place in Her Majesty's confidence. Francis naturally hoped that Anthony's reputation for international espionage could secure them both places at court. However, quite contrary to Francis's efforts, Anthony has never exhibited the slightest interest in currying Her Majesty's favor. To this day, he has never attended at the Queen's court—despite numerous invitations—and those rather resembling *commands*."

Though loath to interrupt Sir Henry's tale, Noah asks, "Why did Anthony Bacon return to England after twelve years' absence? Did he run out of money?"

Sir Henry nods. "That had a great deal to do with it, but there was something even more urgent. Anthony had caught wind that one of his former associates by the name of 'du Plessis de Mornay,' was coming to England, and Bacon was afraid du Plessis might reveal that Anthony had been convicted of buggery at Montauban-de-Picardie, in France. Public knowledge of the conviction had been suppressed by none other than King Henri the Fourth, but du Plessis had knowledge of it."

"Sorry for the interruption," says Noah, "but curiosity got the best of me. I'm fully attendant upon your history now, Sir Henry."

Sir Henry smiles. "In early January 1592, Anthony's supporters heard of his intended return to London and secured rooms for him at Gray's Inn. The lease commenced on the first of January—a bit early, but, as you know, there was (and is) no telling when the winds will favor a jaunt across the South Sea from Calais to Dover. One can be delayed for days, or even weeks. If Anthony had arrived prior to commencement of his lease at Gray's, the only place where he could have stayed was his ancestral estate of Old Gorhambury House in Hertfordshire, or what was left of it after much had been sold off to pay his bills abroad. And the problem with Gorhambury was that someone resided there whose very presence was anathema to him, namely, his mother.

"While the Gray's Inn rooms were yet vacant, others availed themselves of the place when they wished to avoid being seen by anyone in London, except perhaps by a few preoccupied, stodgy old barristers."

Noah snorts at the disparaging characterization of a class of men that could readily have included himself.

"No offense to present company," Sir Henry assures him.

"None taken," replies Noah. "In fact, I *didn't* notice any unusual comings and goings at the time, so your description suits me well."

"In fact," says Sir Henry, "I could share an illustrative tale of a pair who occupied Anthony's rooms before he took possession."

"I'm eager to hear," says Noah.

Sir Henry seems suddenly conscious of the servants clearing away plates, cups, and the remaining food. He summons Walker. "Once our places are clear," he says, "please see that Serjeant Ames and I are undisturbed."

CHAPTER 3

SIR HENRY PLOPS his gouty foot onto a chair in a manner that would never have been countenanced by Lady Anne, were she still here at table. When they're alone, Sir Henry leans earnestly toward Noah.

"I'll tell you a true tale of the Inn of Glaucus. It's about a young couple who fell in love at Gray's Inn at Twelfth Night festivities in that same year of 1592.

"As seems ever to be the case, our two lovers first espied each other across a crowded room. They fought the urge to approach one another until all remaining festivities had come to an end, bringing the Christmas Season to a close, till all prying eyes had gone home, and the lovers could slip quietly out a rear door together. As our lovers are to remain anonymous, what names shall we assign them?"

"Romeo and Juliet?" suggests Noah.

Sir Henry beams at him, as though his volunteering those two names was some sort of masterstroke.

"Very well," says Sir Henry, "Romeo and Juliet they shall be. Twelfth Night that year was uncommonly temperate for early January, and there was a full moon, so they strolled together hours on end about the perimeter of Gray's Inn Fields, discussing everything of import in the life of the mind: family, religion, poetry, and plays, finding that they agreed upon nearly everything.

"It was only the subject of political faction upon which their views diverged. Yet, so smitten were they by their newly forged bond that their love seemed eternal, such that nothing merely temporal could stand in its way. It seemed to them that their paths, though quite separate until that night, had been fashioned by destiny to bring them together for the very purpose of falling in love.

"It was well after midnight by the time they wearied of walking further. As Romeo knew where to find the key to Anthony Bacon's vacant rooms, he retrieved it and admitted himself together with the fair Juliet.

"Now, perhaps I should blush to reveal that the tug of destiny was so strong between them that Juliet succumbed to Romeo's ardent advances with little resistance—indeed barely the faintest hesitation—and all thought of restraint was shied to the wayside. They left the rooms separately before dawn to ensure they would depart unseen, exchanging oaths of love and a promise to meet there every night thereafter at midnight, so that the rooms might serve as a secret place where they would share their passion forever.

"Of course, both Romeo and Juliet realized that the rooms would not remain vacant for long. Once Anthony would inevitably arrive (which turned out to be in the first week of February), they knew they'd be ejected from their little Eden, and forced to find another trysting place. Nevertheless, for those first few weeks of their romance, the rooms were a heavenly respite to them. Every night, each would bring the other some new piece of literature and some delectable bit of cheese, a baked ware, or perhaps an unfamiliar form of spirits that they could experience together for the first time, and so enhance their love.

"To complicate matters, as with the theatrical characters of Romeo and Juliet, their love was forbidden, and could never be brought to light. Because of circumstance and hidebound attitudes, marriage was forever forbidden to them, and mere discovery could cost them their very lives. Nevertheless, for a few months after Anthony took occupancy of his rooms, our lovers retained their mutual devotion."

Sir Henry takes another sip of sherris, and sighs as though loath to move on from the lovelier part of the tale. "But, as their search for another Eden widened, they were reminded on a daily basis of the inevitable frustrations of their love. Their flowering sense of idyll wilted and began its inevitable decay. They found it impossible to replicate their original trysting place or the warm feelings it bred. Their sense of occupying a universe all their own gradually gave over to a sense of isolation. The risks attendant upon discovery, which had originally reinforced their feelings of togetherness, now drove them apart. What if they were discovered? Their places in society would be forfeit, as might their very lives.

"Under this untenable burden, they began to bicker over politics, of all things, as it was the only topic that ever divided them. And after half a year, they broke off their affair.

"For many months, they were both miserable. As is the way of grief, eventually each became but an hourly thought for the other, then a daily, then a weekly. And now, although they cannot help but see each other in passing from time to time, nothing remains of their love but the occasional pang of loss."

Sir Henry's voice has drifted off and he now gazes at the horizon as though touched to the quick by his own tale.

For Noah's part, he's unsure whether the tale is ended.

Sir Henry turns to him. "How does our tale make you feel?"

"'Tis a very sad tale of love," replies Noah. "Tragic really, but all the more common for being so sad." After a respectful interval, he poses the question on his mind. "But how does this provide any inkling into the mythological Glaucus?"

Sir Henry sighs and sits up straight. "The Glaucus that gave the inn its name was an ancient king who staunchly rejected the influence of Aphrodite, the goddess of love, refusing even to allow his champion stud horses to mate with the mares."

"If not with mares, then …?" Noah's voice trails off, as he realizes that Glaucus must have allowed his studs to mate only with other males.

Did Anthony Bacon suppress the jocular name of his quarters because it suggested that *buggery* was taking place there? Is that why Constable Knott found the place of interest? What else could Anthony have meant by applying such a name to his quarters at Gray's?

"We all knew," says Noah, "that for twelve years Anthony Bacon had completely rejected his mother's admonitions to return home—or at least to curb his expenditures. I suppose," he ventures, "that by naming his quarters the 'Inn of Glaucus,' he might merely have been thumbing his nose at his mother. You know, 'We don't give a fig for women's advice here.'"

Sir Henry smiles. "A plausible explanation, I suppose, but by choosing the Glaucus metaphor to make *that* point, Anthony would have been placing his mother—most inappositely—in the position of an erotic female goddess. Hardly maternal." He shivers. "And not a notion that would readily come to mind if you knew his mother."

"But that would leave only—"

Sir Henry nods. "*Buggery*, I'm afraid."

Noah inquires gingerly. "And our Romeo and Juliet?"

"Both men," says Sir Henry. "But, do you suppose their star-crossed love was any less sincere for that? Or its aftermath any less painful?"

"I doubt it," says Noah. "But do you call it 'love'? Can a man truly *love* another man?"

Sir Henry smirks. "Don't you love *me*?"

"Of course," says Noah, "but—can a man love another man in the same way as he does a woman?"

"I've given that a good deal of thought, and the nearest answer I can come up with is: It doesn't matter."

Noah nods. "I suppose if love's real to the lover, it's real enough. But I still don't understand why Anthony would acknowledge such a predilection. Since Her Majesty reinstated the statutes of her father Henry the Eighth many years ago, buggery has again become punishable by *death*."

Sir Henry takes a swig of sack. "And it wasn't merely Anthony who was known for such practices, hence the jocular rechristening of the whole building, or at least of the upper storeys."

"I'll take a bit of that sack," says Noah queasily, "if the offer's still open."

Sir Henry pours Noah a large cup and slides it over to him.

"So, Constable Knott was questioning *me* of buggery?" says Noah, his blood beginning to boil. "Why that little—"

"A mere shot in the dark, I expect," says Sir Henry dismissively. "But have you forgot his mention of Arthur Arden?"

Noah takes a long draught of sack. Although cloyingly sweet, its calmative effect takes hold almost immediately.

"It cannot be true," declares Noah.

"I have no idea whether it's true of Arden," replies Sir Henry, "but surely you realize, Noah, that you hold in high regard *many* men who've found solace in such practices."

"I do?" asks Noah, nonplussed. "Pray, do not tell me their names, as I would have no choice but to—"

Sir Henry arches a skeptical eyebrow. "*Arrest* them? That would make you no better than Constable Knott."

The warmth of the sack spreads through Noah's chest, and he shakes his head. "It's a serious crime in the statute books, but prosecuting such practices would be—"

"*Beneath* you," suggests Sir Henry. "Indeed, it would be entirely outside your ken and care. In all the time I've known you, you've ignored any suggestion of such practices, though you've known of them."

"Why would Arthur Arden engage in such practices?" asks Noah into his cups. "Indeed, why would *anyone*?"

He looks up at Sir Henry, who seems to be slowly drawing him toward an uncomfortable conclusion.

"Men search for love, Noah. They keep searching until they find it."

"Oh, but surely a handsome, strapping young fellow such as Arthur could find any number of willing young women."

Sir Henry's eyes dart about in obvious concern that they not be overheard. He leans forward confidentially. "While men no doubt seek out sexual relations, Noah, what they're really searching for is even more elusive: *love*."

CHAPTER 4

NONSUCH PALACE
SURREY, ENGLAND
MICHAELMAS EVE
LATE SEPTEMBER 1600

NOAH AND THE DIMINUTIVE Lord Robert rush through the halls of Nonsuch Palace in muddy boots, lightning flashing in every window they pass.

"Blast this soggy weather!" Lord Robert huffs, sloshing along. "On Michaelmas Eve, too. A fine appearance *we'll* make. At least the celebrations won't begin until evening." Thunder rumbles through the hall.

Noah asks, "Did Her Majesty's urgent summons provide any inkling into the matter of concern?"

Lord Robert regards him skeptically. "No, but I should have thought the calendar would tell you, Serjeant."

Noah nods. "As Lord Essex's royal patent on sweet wine expires tonight (and with it his income), I expect it has something to do with that. But Her Majesty has known for such a long time that this day was approaching that I thought that the urgency of her summons might portend some other matter, perhaps of more general concern."

Lord Robert grumbles. "This is how Her Majesty equivocates in matters of conscience. No doubt it provides her great comfort to send her senior counselors darting about in a downpour."

As they turn the final corner, they find the stately Lord Steward standing athwart the closed doors to the Throne Room, his upraised arm calling them to a halt.

"Boots," he intones impassively.

Lord Robert raises a skeptical eyebrow. "Are we to understand, m'lord, that Her Majesty now wishes to receive her attendants in their stockinged feet?"

The Lord Steward sniffs, ignoring the question. "You gentlemen will please allow the grooms to attend to your ... appearance." He points to their muddy boots. "And please remove those at once, before you muddy any more of the hallway."

They remove their boots and hand them to the grooms, who escort them to a side chamber used for preparing guests to appear in the Royal Presence.

Some time later, cleaner and less winded, the two stand once again before the Lord Steward at the Throne Room doors. Evidently satisfied with their appearance, the Lord Steward knocks twice on the door, which opens from within.

There on the Throne, in all her royal splendor, sits Queen Elizabeth, looking more than usually fatigued. Standing before her in mid-sentence, and evidently trying her patience, is Sir Henry Neville. Lord Robert and Noah stop immediately inside the door and wait to be summoned.

"... and so, madam," resumes Neville, "it is essential, if I am to complete my embassage with any hope of success, that the Exchequer provide me with the portion of the expenses originally agreed upon."

The Queen turns to Sir Henry with evident irritation. "*Agreed upon*, Sir Henry? Does a prince *bargain* with her subjects, to coax them into amicable agreement?"

Sir Henry blushes. "Why no, madam," he replies obsequiously. "I meant only that such was the Crown's assurance when I was appointed ambassador to France."

She casts her gaze aside and shakes her head disapprovingly. "If that's what you meant, then that's what you ought to have *said*." She sighs with fatigue and leans back on the Throne, regarding him sternly. "You seem extraordinarily protective of your own funds, Sir Henry. While I shall authorize the Exchequer to make the necessary disbursement, I cannot warrant he'll make it immediately. Just now, there are many other demands upon him ... upon *us*, rather." Her expression changes to one of disappointment. "Had you exerted greater effort in your embassage, you might have brought home from France a tidy sum that would readily have supported the disbursement you seek."

Sir Henry's face reddens, and he bows humbly. "Indeed, madam. It is with the most profound shame and regret that I have come home with nothing to augment the Crown's treasury. But King Henri of France was adamant that he cannot begin repayment of Your Majesty's loan until the Spanish have been expelled from northern France and his military expenses can be commensurately reduced."

"Well," she perks up a bit, "at least we shall have the pleasure of your company at court for some weeks."

"At your pleasure, Majesty. As ever, I shall come at your call."

The Queen smiles wanly at him, and glances at Lord Robert and Noah. "Remain with us, Sir Henry, whilst this next order of business is broached." She beckons Lord Robert and Noah.

As Noah approaches the Throne with Sir Robert, he's dismayed to find the Queen's fatigue palpable. She's so very tired. Though summer is not quite ended, she looks as though she's just survived a dreadful winter.

"Gentlemen," says the Queen, "I regret summoning you here in such foul weather, but Lord Essex's income ends tonight, and I find myself unsettled in choosing the most just course." She indicates an open letter atop a small table beside her. "I have recently received an item of correspondence from his lordship which, although it began as a letter of affection," she continues with indignation, "ended as nothing more than a plea for money. Although I am not wont to be swayed by flattery, his lordship makes the point that his income from the patent on sweet wines which expires tonight is his *only* source of money and his *only* hope of keeping his creditors at bay. Lord Robert, what do you advise?"

Lord Robert bows. "Your Majesty knows my view only too well, I fear, and wearies of my voice in the matter. The Earl of Essex has long and repeatedly forfeited any claim he once had to the Crown's thanks. His most recent outrages are fresh in memory, foremost being his reaching a forbidden armistice with the Irish rebels. Yet, I urge Your Majesty not to forget the earl's *earlier* transgressions, including his participation in the English Armada expedition in direct disobedience of Your Majesty's instructions, and needlessly exposing himself to danger during the Islands Voyage expedition. Whatever military contributions he has made pale by comparison to this parade of horribles. I urge Your Majesty to allow the earl's patent to expire, or to renew it and assign it to another of Your Majesty's subjects; I personally have no desire of it and would not accept it if offered." He bows.

The Queen nods gravely. "You may rest assured, Lord Robert, that I have mulled over *all* of Essex's considerable transgressions many times over this past month." She turns to Henry. "And what would *you* have me do, Sir Henry?"

Sir Henry hesitates. "Having been removed from domestic affairs for a year, Your Majesty, by your leave I would first wish to hear what Serjeant Ames has to say on the matter."

The Queen smiles wryly. "And so it seems 'tis not only *I* who have come to value Serjeant Ames's views. Serjeant Ames?"

Noah bows, giving himself a moment to couch his recommendation as persuasively as possible. "My view of the earl's conduct is in complete agreement with Lord Robert's. I, too, believe he long ago forfeited any expectation from the Crown. The offenses recited by Lord Robert are serious indeed, but I must confess I am most concerned with *two* offenses that I have heard Your Majesty sweep aside." All eyes are on Noah. "I was informed by Lord Burghley, God rest his soul, that in the Privy Council the Earl of Essex had the temerity to draw his sword in anger against Your Majesty. I have discussed this with Lord Robert, and he and I agree that anyone else who had done so would have been marched to Tyburn by the remainder of the Privy Council and paid with his life. Lord Essex's invasion of your closet before Your Majesty was properly attired is also of great concern."

The Queen regards him askance. "But why *those* two transgressions especially? He meant no real harm upon those occasions, Serjeant."

Noah shakes his head dubiously. "No matter, madam. He behaves as one entitled to disregard the sacred boundary surrounding Your Majesty, as though Your Majesty were a commoner and he an elder kinsman."

The Queen smiles wearily. "Kinsmen need not be *elder* to act so boorishly, Serjeant Ames, so long as they're *male*."

"Yet, I propose that all men are *not* the same, Your Majesty. I surmise you were never subjected to such treatment by either your father or your brother, may they rest in peace, and they were both *kings*. If anyone were to feel entitled to ignore Your Majesty's wishes, it would have been they."

The Queen nods, granting him the point.

"Your Majesty," says Noah, "if I may draw an analogy learned in such a lowly place as the stables. Though most horses won't bite, when one *has* bitten we would be remiss in failing to take precautions against his biting again. And foolish *indeed* would we be to conclude that one who's bitten twice won't bite a third time. Lord Essex has bitten Your Majesty's hand repeatedly. So long as he is at liberty, he is a threat to your person and your reign."

"Surely," says the Queen, "you do not recommend banishment or further imprisonment?"

Noah looks to Lord Robert and sighs. "Such counsel has been over-ruled in the past, Majesty, and I expect would yet be unwelcome. No, I rather counsel something else." He looks to each of his listeners to be sure of their undivided attention. "Your Majesty knows that the earl supports forty knights and other gentlemen, both at table and with lodging."

The Queen scowls to hear it. "What need has he of so many armed men in his retinue? Why would he need even half that number? Or even one-*fourth* part? Indeed," she says, "why so much as *one*? He needs only enough money to feed himself, his wife and children, and to shelter and clothe them all."

"After tonight," says Noah, "he'll have not even *that*, and his creditors will continue to hound him. *If* he were a commoner, Majesty, I expect he would be grateful for such an income and wish no more. But the earl is no commoner. He has been bred as a leader of men. Without men to follow him, he's not even so *much* as a commoner. He's *nothing*. For an earl to accept consignment to the boneyard at sixty is one thing, but his lordship is barely thirty-five, still in the prime of life, and will feel unbearably frustrated unless he's afforded at least some hope of a future. It is my recommendation that Your Majesty assign the patent to a trusted person (not me) with instructions to pay Lord Essex some fixed portion of the income, say, one-fourth part, with the remainder going to the Crown. The grant of such a stipend might be made contingent upon the earl ridding himself of some portion of his retinue. In such manner would he be forced to marshal his assets and satisfy his creditors by paying his bills in timely manner. Then ... should Your Majesty be pleased by the earl's conduct at some time in the future ... you could consider, at Your Majesty's discretion, increasing his portion."

"Do you plead once again for the earl?" asks the Queen wryly. "You have done so once before, as I recall, and saved his hand."

"*Blast* the earl!" says Noah, a bit more stridently than he would have wished. He bows apologetically. "I do not trust him, madam. My care is for Your Majesty alone." He becalms himself and sighs sadly. "Your Majesty will recall that a pair of malefactors lodging with Lord Essex's friend m'Lord Southampton attempted to poison your royal person mere weeks ago."

The Queen nods. "Only to be dispatched by your own hand, Serjeant," she says, "for which you have our enduring gratitude."

Noah detects something arch in her expression, as though she suspects it wasn't really he who did the varlets in. "That attempt took place even before the earl was released from custody," says Noah. "When the earl returns in a few weeks' time, London will be a powder keg, and we would do well to avoid striking a spark."

The Queen frowns. "A powder keg? How so?" she asks.

Noah glances sidelong at Lord Robert and Sir Henry. "With Lord Essex's supporters already crowded into Drury House and exhorting him to lay claim to what they deem his lordship's 'rightful place' at Your Majesty's court, there's no telling what they'll do. I have *seen* Lord Essex, Majesty, and he is desperate already. The more his hope dwindles, the less the spark needed to ignite the powder." Noah takes on a weighing demeanor. "A Crown that provides him with nothing maintains no means except *force* to control his impetuous conduct. But, a Crown that affords him enough to maintain himself with dignity can readily persuade him to … mind his manners."

The Queen looks down at the floor, as she does when thinking hard. "I gave him a good deal of money when I appointed him to lead in Ireland. Has he squandered it?"

To Noah's relief, Lord Robert chimes in. "If I may. What Your Majesty did was—quite generously—to forgive a substantial portion of Lord Essex's indebtedness to the Crown. While that surely diminished the sum of his debts, it provided him nothing in the way of actual money to spend."

The Queen turns to Lord Robert. "Is your counsel the same as Serjeant Ames's, then?"

Lord Robert glances toward Noah, then to the Queen. "Majesty, the grant of patents has always been the Crown's most discretionary power. Patents are usually granted as a reward to those who've shown extraordinary devotion to the realm. In that regard, I would not—for an instant— propose to substitute my own judgment for Your Majesty's. However, patents *have* been issued by English Sovereigns in the past for *various* purposes, and it would not surprise me to learn that such purposes included the Machiavellian one now proposed by Serjeant Ames." He briefly bows to Noah to show that he uses the term favorably. "The proposal is certainly worthy of consideration."

The Queen seems disappointed. She looks to Sir Henry, who mutely tilts his head and raises his eyebrows as though to say that Noah's proposal is not all bad. She rises from the Throne heedless of her subjects' genuflections and begins pacing, her face growing gradually more stern.

"No!" she declares at last. "I know in my bones that I'll regret acting out of fear. An unruly horse must be abated of his provender that he may be the easier managed." She turns to the Lord Steward. "M'Lord Steward, has Sir Henry Billingsley left the palace?" Billingsley, a haberdasher by trade, is known to be one of Her Majesty's chief tax collectors and a trusted surety.

"I saw him conversing but a moment ago with the Exchequer, madam," replies the Lord Steward. "I shall try to detain him before he departs." He bows out.

Lord Robert hastens to speak, evidently anticipating that the Queen is about to assign Essex's patent on sweet wines to Billingsley. "The Crown has never been ruled by the calendar in respect of patents, Your Majesty, and there is no particular urgency to the matter, except from the earl's perspective. I suggest we contemplate this and other possibilities over the coming weeks."

"Lord Robert," says the Queen, "did you not just express your doubts about Essex's loyalty? And did Serjeant Ames not just inform me that his lordship is a hazard to my reign?"

"Your Majesty's memory is perfect as regards our advice," says Lord Robert.

"Then how is it," she asks, "that you advise the Crown to confer its favors upon such a person while being under no obligation to do so?"

Before Lord Robert can respond, the Lord Steward breathlessly marches in with Billingsley in tow. Billingsley's eyes dart about, evidently assaying the Queen's visitors and their likely dispositions toward his own interests. He bows low, awaiting Her Majesty's pleasure.

"Rise, Billingsley," she says, and resumes pacing. "Do you recall our discussion of some weeks ago in which we foretold that you might soon be charged with collecting royalties upon the patent in sweet wines?"

"I recall it well, Your Majesty." He glances about, eyes pausing a moment on Sir Henry Neville. "At that time, the patent belonged to the Earl of Essex. Has the issue now been decided, Majesty?"

"It has," confirms the Queen. "With some small reluctance, we have decided to allow Lord Essex's patent to expire tonight, to issue a new patent having the same scope and a new term and, in a month or so, to entrust *you* with responsibility to make collections of the sweet-wine merchants. Until further notice, all royalties shall be paid to the Exchequer, after the deduction of your customary costs of collection, of course. Have you found someone yet to aid you in such duties?"

Billingsley smiles. "I have several good men to choose from, Majesty." He hesitates, as though a minor detail has just occurred to him. "I expect I will need the new patent to be in my name—to instill confidence in the sweet-wine merchants that I am authorized to make such collections."

"Of course," replies the Queen. "Lord Robert will see to it."

Lord Robert bows, though with some hesitation.

Billingsley rubs his palms together, blatantly relishing the prospect of handling more of the Crown's money. Noah can't help but wonder how much Billingsley will retain as "costs of collection."

The Queen dispatches Billingsley and appears about to dismiss those remaining, when Noah speaks unprompted.

"There remain two other matters, Majesty," says Noah, removing a paper from his pocket and unfurling it before the Queen. "First, before coming here, I was summoned to Essex House to attend a sermon the day after tomorrow."

The Queen looks at Noah incredulously. "A sermon, of all things?"

"Yes, Majesty. I am led to understand that m'Lord of Essex will remain in town only for that day and then return to the country for several weeks, as Your Majesty has advised. Shall I send Lord Essex my regrets?"

"Perhaps he's trying to convert you to the national church," the Queen replies humorously. After a moment's contemplation, she adds, "Meet with him. Find out what he's doing. But speak not a word of what has transpired here today in respect of the patent, except—and only at need—to say that the matter is under consideration. Was there something else?"

Noah nods. "The murders that recently took place on Bowyer's Row by Saint Paul's."

"Yes, those discovered by your Master Arden," says the Queen. "Another church matter?"

"Just so, madam. As it is far from certain that these crimes signify any threat to the Crown, I was wondering whether Your Majesty nonetheless wishes me to investigate."

"Do so," says the Queen, a dubious note in her voice betraying her uncertainty as to why Noah felt it necessary to ask. "The Crown is concerned with *all* plots laid in the kingdom, whatever their purpose."

"In that case, may I decline the proffered assistance of Saint Paul's constabulary?"

She scowls good-naturedly and shakes her head. "You should accept such assistance as they will provide, Serjeant. As you yourself once taught Lord Essex, one can never have too many friends."

Though disappointed, Noah smiles, his mind grasping for other ways to be rid of Knott and his single-minded interference.

The Queen seems lost in thought for some time. She looks up at last, evidently surprised to find that her visitors have not left. "Go now. All of you. And thank you for your good counsel."

As Noah bows out, he can see that the Queen remains in her melancholy reverie, making no motion toward leaving the Throne.

CHAPTER 5

ESTHER BASKS IN the late morning sunshine streaming through the kitchen window as she awaits Serjeant Ames's return from a place of unimaginable splendor called "Nonsuch Palace." She can barely conceive the glory of even a single visit to the Queen, and is amazed to think that they have become commonplace in Serjeant Ames's life.

Unable to keep still, Esther goes to the full-length glass in the hallway to admire the new frock purchased only yesterday "to show her off to best advantage." She wonders in passing how her admirer David "Cheerful" Killigrew would react to her resplendent attire.

She'd felt free to don the dress this morning because Serjeant Ames had promised (well, not *promised* exactly) that she could accompany him on today's visit to the home of an unnamed person of great renown—unless the visit were to be reginally countermanded, a possibility she has refused to contemplate. In any event, Serjeant Ames is expected at any moment, and will let her know whether the Queen has consented.

A bustle of activity across High Holborn catches her eye through the parlor window. Workmen are gathering in the field, carrying measuring standards, pegs, and twine, as though preparing to survey the land in preparation for a new building. But Esther's view is soon obstructed by Serjeant Ames himself, who appears on horseback and glances cursorily at the workmen before rounding the corner onto his own property.

From her perch in the kitchen window, Esther watches the Serjeant dismount and hand off his beautiful black horse Bucklebury to the stableman. She waves to Serjeant Ames excitedly through the window, and is greeted with a weary but fond smile. A moment later, the Serjeant swings the door open and spies her new dress.

"Esther!" he exclaims as he enters. "You are a vision! What ever is the occasion?"

"Don't you remember, sir? I am to accompany you this afternoon to visit a person of great esteem!"

"Why, yes, I do recall," he says, "but you rather appear dressed for an *evening* occasion."

She twirls to show him the dress from all sides. "Do you not think me pretty enough?"

The Serjeant scowls at her skeptically. "Pretty enough? My dear, you'd be more than pretty enough in a scullion's smock. It's just that … well, I expect nearly everyone else at the sermon will be a *man* and, in the frock you now wear, you'll attract a great deal of attention, perhaps unwanted."

Esther waves off the thought. "Oh, I've been gazed at by men all my life. That's nothing new. Did you say we are to attend a 'sermon'?" An unwelcome image seeps into her mind of pews filled with frowning old men in dowdy clothing, singing woefully off-key.

"Well, yes, a sermon of sorts," says the Serjeant. "I expect that any religious service will be brief, however. The sermon will no doubt be a bit longer, and the discussion longer still. But, see here, you needn't attend if it's not to your liking."

"Will we be welcome there, even though we are not … not …?"

"Church of England?" he chuckles. "They're well aware we're not Church of England, yet we have been invited by name."

"They know *my* name?" asks Esther.

"Well, they know *mine* and, when they see how charming you are, I expect more of them will be speaking *your* name aloud than mine."

There's a creak of floorboards in the hallway, and a new voice chimes into the conversation.

"Where are you taking her, Father?" asks Lady Jessica as she enters the kitchen.

"Why, Lady Jessica!" says the Serjeant. "How are you, my dear? It's been weeks since I've seen you!"

Lady Jessica crosses the kitchen, reaching her father in two graceful steps so elegant that Esther cannot help but admire them.

Jessica offers her father her hand while her husband, Jonathan, Lord Saint Ives, enters the kitchen.

"Father," says Lord Jonathan, "how good to see you! How fares Her Majesty?"

"Her Majesty is well, m'lord," says Serjeant Ames, bowing lightly, "if a bit wearied by … a few of her more wayward subjects."

"A few?" asks Lord Jonathan pointedly. "Or *one*?"

The Serjeant smirks. "One. Yet—one who leads others astray."

"I see," replies Lord Jonathan, obviously catching a meaning that entirely escapes Esther. He looks Esther up and down, and inhales noisily. "I must remark, Esther, that you are stunningly beautiful in your new frock."

"Thank you, m'lord," says Esther, presenting herself with a formal curtsey. She turns quickly to Jessica as though she's forgot something far more important. "And how fares my lady's condition?"

Lady Jessica blushes at the mention of her pregnancy. "Esther, we must not discuss that with gentlemen present!"

"Oh, but please do," says Serjeant Ames. "We are so hopeful of you, my dear."

"Things progress nicely," she says demurely.

"That's wonderful!" says Serjeant Ames. "Don't you suppose it would be prudent to bring your Aunt Beth into the picture?"

Jessica frowns, and brushes a bit of imaginary lint from her dress. "Premature, I should think."

Esther wonders what that cool remark portends, as Jessica has always been quite fond of her Aunt Beth.

Serjeant Ames, too, appears a bit uncertain. "I have every confidence that you'll consult Beth in due time, my dear." Turning toward the window, he shifts his head one way, then the other, as though to peer up High Holborn, which is quite impossible from the kitchen.

"What is it, Serjeant Ames?" asks Esther.

Noah turns back to them. "As I was riding down the lane, I noticed some surveyors at work across the way. I couldn't tell what they were doing."

Jessica smiles at her father, as though suppressing a joyous secret, and glances back questioningly at her husband.

"*What?*" says Lord Jonathan in evident exasperation. "Not an hour ago, you insisted I make no *mention—*"

Before Jonathan can finish, Jessica stands excitedly on tiptoe and lovingly takes her father's face in her hands. "We're building a town home across the street, Father. We're going to be neighbors!"

Noah is dumbstruck. "A town home? Why, that's wonderful, my dear! I'm so pleased. And Marie will be, as well." He turns to Esther. "Well, what do you think, dear? Your cousins will be a hop and a skip away!"

Esther jumps and claps her hands. "And I shall play with my new cousin so often, he'll tire of me!"

"Hold on there!" says Jonathan. "Your new cousin could be a little girl! But, either way, I'm sure the child shall never tire of you."

As though remembering something forgotten, Esther touches Noah's arm. "Are we forgetting our appointment?"

Noah becomes suddenly serious.

"What is it?" asks Jonathan.

"I've been invited to a sermon at Essex House this afternoon."

Jonathan turns serious, as well. "To that den of iniquity?" he asks.

Noah smiles wanly. "I shall take Esther along for protection. Well, I'm delighted at all this good news. Now, if you'll pardon me, I need to clean up after the long ride from Nonsuch Palace."

"Did you mention Essex's invitation to Her Majesty?" asks Lord Jonathan.

"I did," says Serjeant Ames. "She urged me to attend."

Esther blurts out, "Has anyone seen Cheerful?"

Suddenly all eyes are downcast.

At last Lady Jessica asks sympathetically, "When did you last see David, dear?"

"It's been two whole days now," says Esther. "It's not like him to disappear without talking to me first."

"I'm sure he'll turn up any day now," says Serjeant Ames. "He's as hard-headed as all the young people in this family."

⟶∘❦∘⟵

Forty-Five Miles West-Southwest

"THERE THEY GO!" says David, pointing down the hill at two men and two women on horseback approaching an inn known as the "Hind of Brakenhale." Spying their quarry's leisurely pace, David turns to his companion Chester. "Doesn't look much like an abduction, does it?"

"I was just thinkin' the same thing, suh," Chester replies.

"Let's get out of sight and circle back to the rear of the inn," says David. "Once they've entered and stabled their horses, we'll come up on the blind side of the stables."

As they turn about to take cover behind the hill, Chester looks nervously at David. "You're certain we can't be seen there from inside the inn, suh?"

"Lord Saint Ives was here a year ago," says David, "and has given us his solemn assurance that that spot cannot be seen from indoors. That should be enough, don't you think?"

"I s'pose. Still, suh, it's broad daylight."

"That's when they'll least expect to be confronted."

"But it won't work unless we surprise 'em," says Chester, adding apologetically, "Don't like you goin' in alone, suh."

"Let's take up our position."

A few minutes later, their quarry enters the inn. One of the men re-emerges, stables the horses, and reenters.

David and Chester pull up to the blind side of the barn, where Chester begins his count to two hundred. When he's done, he turns again to David. "Are ye certain ye want me to wait here, suh?"

"Stick to the plan," says David.

"I can handle meself, y'know."

"I know it well, Chester."

"What about the lady of the house, suh—the innkeeper?"

"An honest woman, by Lord Jonathan's account. I'll try to locate her and send her out to you first without being detected." Concealing both pistols on his person, he dismounts. "Once you've got her, come to the rear window and proceed as planned."

David ambles up to the rear door, doing his best to impersonate a poor traveler in need of sustenance (just in case he's seen), his handsome blond mane tied tautly into a knot beneath his cap. Without knocking, he opens the door a crack and peers inside.

It looks dark indoors, but he reminds himself that such is always the case for one standing out of doors on a bright day. There's a soft, fearful noise inside, like a dog's whimper. But it can't be a dog, for any dog would already be barking in protest of David's unbidden entry.

He gently urges the door open wider and cautiously juts his head inside. It's a dark kitchen, deserted but for a woman securely bound to a chair, a kerchief tied tightly over her mouth to prevent her from uttering a word. Her eyes betray her fear of David, which is no surprise, as she's just been bound up in her own establishment, has no idea who he is, and is entirely subject to his whim. A few light footfalls creak above his head. Someone's upstairs; perhaps all of them.

He kneels before the bound woman and inches close to her ear. "I am sent by the Guard of the Tower of London," he whispers. "Are you Jane Nightwork, the proprietor of this establishment?" Her eyes go wide and her head bobs up and down.

"I'm going to untie you now, but you must be extremely quiet until this whole affair is quite finished. Are we of one mind?"

Once again, her head bobs up and down excitedly.

David takes out a sharp knife, cuts the kerchief, removes the rag that's been stuffed inside her mouth, and drops it to the floor. His knife makes short work of the remaining rope, and he shies it quietly into a corner.

He extends his hand to the frightened woman. "Please rise," he whispers, "and step outside. There's a man on the other side of the barn. He would greatly appreciate your cooperation, as it will help him to secure employment. You will cooperate with him, will you not?"

"Yes," she croaks.

He nods, as though confident of her agreeable intentions, when he's not at all. "How many people are in the inn?"

"Four," she says dourly. "Two ladies, under some form of loose restraint. And two blockheads that I'd like to give a piece of my mind to. Dull-witted they are, but strong and armed. One's got a pistol, and the other a sword. Be careful, suh. Oh!" she says abashedly as though something important just occurred to her. "Please don't break the window upstairs. I just put it in. It's glass, and cost me a blessed fortune."

Though David is unsure he can accommodate this request, he nods his assurance and adds his most winning smile, which seems to have the desired effect. "Now please go to the opposite side of the barn, and be sure not to be seen." He watches as she makes her way, staying close to the house, and disappearing around the corner.

AS THE WAY to Essex House is straight down Chancery Lane, Esther and Serjeant Ames decide to walk.

"Serjeant Ames, would you be kind enough to tell me something of Lord Essex before I meet him?" says Esther.

The question brings Noah back from a bout of woolgathering.

"Certainly, dear. For many years, the Earl of Essex was Her Majesty's favorite. Through his repeated disregard of her preferences, and even of her direct commands in matters of war, Essex has spoiled Her Majesty's affections for him, perhaps beyond repair. This past year, he was put on trial for dereliction of duty, and found guilty. As a result of his conviction, Her Majesty placed him under house arrest for many months, from which he was released only a few weeks ago, with orders to absent himself from Her Majesty's court."

"So *you* are admitted where *his* way is barred?" she asks innocently.

The Serjeant's eyes flash apprehensively. "Yes, Esther, but you must never mention that again. It's a terribly sore point for him, as you might imagine."

"And now," asks Esther, "what is he doing?"

"Well, you'll see for yourself in a few moments, but I am concerned that the men with whom he's surrounded himself are bound to urge him to forbidden forms of protest against Her Majesty. Things are very tetchy, and becoming ever more so."

As they reach the Strand, Essex House comes into view, where they find their way barred by a young swordsman. They come to a halt before him. He greets Serjeant Ames with a bow, and tips his hat to Esther, his demeanor vaguely familiar.

"I'm Caim, Lord Essex's footman," he says. "Who's callin', suh?"

Esther is stunned by the familiar ring of the man's baritone voice, but she can't quite place it.

CHAPTER 6

DAVID CREEPS UP the staircase with a cocked pistol in his left hand, and his sword in his right. He reaches the landing, and listens for voices. Just as he's about to despair, behind a closed door to his right he detects a casual conversation between two men and at least one woman. Possibly *two* women, but the voices run over one another, so he can't be certain.

He takes two steps that bring him to the door, and swings it open on a large room with a glass window to his left and a stove on the far wall.

The two men inside reach for their weapons. The one on David's left goes for his pistol, the one on his right for his sword.

"Don't bloody move, or I'll shoot!" shouts David, aiming his pistol at the pistolier, and pointing his sword toward the swordsman. His brash entry has had the desired result; they're afraid and inclined to obey him.

"Uncock that pistol and shy it gently toward my feet!" he shouts.

The pistolier obeys without hesitation, throwing his hands up, and shrinking into the wall behind him. He appears about to piss himself. "We'll do what you want. Just don't shoot!" he cries.

The swordsman looks with disdain upon his compatriot and receives David's next glare. "You!" David shouts. "Draw your sword between your thumb and forefinger and let it drop to the floor. Then kick it over here—gently."

"Whu—" is all the swordsman can say.

"Thumb and forefinger," David commands. "Now!"

"I will, suh. But"—says the swordsman, red-faced—"what's a fore-finger?"

David can barely believe such ignorance. "Your *index* finger, you idiot!" he says.

The man shrugs pathetically.

"Your *pointer*!" says David in exasperation.

"Oh," says the dullard with embarrassment. Between thumb and forefinger, he dutifully draws his sword from its scabbard and drops it to the floor with an audible thump. He kicks it along the floor toward David and backs up to the window.

With his adversaries unarmed, David risks a glance at the women. They're both quite attractive: one seasoned and a bit haughty. That would be Lady Sheffield. The other is much younger: Constance, Lady Sheffield's spicemaid, with whom David has lightly dallied once or twice.

Despite the tension in the room, Constance coos at him admiringly, "Oh, David. I knew you'd come for me."

Lady Sheffield reacts with a silent but ostentatious rolling of the eyes.

The unarmed swordsman is practically leaning against the glass window, which won't do at all. The plan requires David to toss him out of that very window to the ground below, where Chester awaits, but David has given the lady of the house his solemn promise that he'd try not to ruin her new window.

"Take a step in my direction!" David commands.

"This way?" asks the swordsman with visible worry, awaiting an answer before daring to take a step that might go wrong.

"Yes," says David. "One step. Toward me. Now turn about, and open the casement all the way."

"Like this?" asks the man.

David nods. "Yes, that's right." After a moment's hesitation, he says, "Now, jump out."

The man falls to his knees pleading in horror. "I'll slay meself jumpin' from such a height, suh!"

"No such thing!" replies David testily. "I'm sure you jumped from trees higher than that when you were a lad. Just keep your knees bent. Now turn 'round!"

The man does so, and gazes down through the window. "There's a man down there," he observes, and turns to David to see whether his objection is valid.

"He's my man," says David. "He's *supposed* to be there! Now *jump!*"

Near tears, the swordsman declares piously, "Let my death be on your conscience." He jumps out. In a moment, there's a thump. "Aaaaow! Blast! I *told* you I'd hurt meself. I'm gonna need some help gettin' up off the ground."

David turns to Lady Sheffield. "If I may borrow your spicemaid a moment, m'lady?"

"'Twouldn't be the first time," Lady Sheffield says insouciantly.

"Miss Constance," says David, ignoring Lady Sheffield's graceless remark, "would you please take that pistol from the floor, empty its powder out of the window and toss the pistol out afterwards?"

"Oh, David," says Constance breathily, "that's diabolical!"

While David wonders what she means, Constance picks up the fire-arm and empties its powder out of the window, smiling at him all the while with a saucy leer. As someone sneezes violently outside, she tosses the powderless pistol through the open window. It lands with a meaty thud.

"*'Ey!*" shouts the man below. "Insult to injury!"

"Shut up, ye blighter," says another voice below the window. It's Chester, come to gather his quarry. "Walk this way. Come on. You can do it on yer own. Don't be such a baby about it."

The unarmed pistolier turns to David fearfully. "Are ye gonna make *me* jump, too?"

"No," says David. "You'll enjoy the luxury of walking down the stairs. Slowly. I'll have a pistol at your back the whole way, so don't try anything funny. Now, march!"

———— ⟫∘⟪⟫∘⟪ ————

ESTHER SITS IN a pew in the packed chapel at Essex House. There are at least sixty men in the congregation. The sermon drones on, a tedious talk devoted to an old work called *Utopia*. Esther catches little of it as, unbeknownst to Serjeant Ames, she feels impelled to glance repeatedly at the footman who admitted them to Essex House and who's taken a seat a few rows back on the opposite side of the room.

She searches her memory for a place where she might have seen him before, thinking back to her journey to London through Wroclaw, Dresden, Leipzig, Dusseldorf, Bruges. Though they met many English, this man was not among them. Ah, perhaps it's just her imagination. No matter how often she looks at him, she finds she can place neither face nor voice.

During one brief glance, she detects a glint in his eye that might signify he recognizes *her*, though that seems unlikely, as she arrived at the Ames's house only a few short weeks ago. She chalks his expression up to her imagination. Men she catches looking her way often have a glint in their eye. Some might call it a leer.

After a while, she loses track of him by the simple expedient of fall-ing asleep, nodding off at the point where the sermoneer (if that's what he's called) discusses the possibility that men can live peaceably with one another without benefit of king or queen—or even private property. It all seems such theoretical rubbish as not to warrant keeping awake.

When she eventually awakens, she wonders why everyone thinks this story is so important. The sermon reminds her of a Talmudic presentation she attended in Krakow; perhaps the text means this or that, perhaps something completely different, perhaps nothing, perhaps everything. A few times she feels certain that the writer of the work was merely jesting, but the sermoneer and his audience fail to appreciate—or even *see*—the jest.

At last, the sermoneer bows, receiving far more applause than he deserves. It's mostly polite, but enthusiastic in a few quarters.

As soon as Serjeant Ames rises from his seat, a scholarly looking man in black robes approaches him, followed at a respectful distance by an older man, obviously a well-heeled nobleman, with a handsome crest embroidered on the chest of his robe.

The scholar whispers in Serjeant Ames's ear, but Esther's hearing is sharp. "I beg you, Serjeant," say the scholar, "to act as one who's meeting me for the first time. Pray, speak of no meeting prior to this." His eyebrow arches questioningly.

Serjeant Ames, in his ingratiating way, assumes his most assuring expression. "Certainly, sir," he whispers, and then speaks loud enough to be heard by others, "And with whom have I the pleasure to speak, sir?"

The man's face relaxes as though much had depended upon the Serjeant's willingness to pretend never to have met him. "I am Sir Henry Cuffe, Serjeant, one of Lord Essex's secretaries. I welcome you to Essex House. You and your—" Cuffe nods toward Esther, as though not quite sure how to characterize her.

Serjeant Ames takes the cue. "Sir Henry Cuffe, this lovely young woman is Esther ... Ames, my distant cousin from the Continent who has only recently come to live with us at Holborn."

Though Cuffe beams at her, Esther has the distinct impression that his smile is born of courtesy alone, as though he finds nothing in her face or form that appeals to him in the slightest.

Esther offers him her hand. "Are you a member of the earl's family?" she asks.

Cuffe blushes, and he raises his hands in gentle protest. "Oh, no, no, no, no, Miss Ames," a familiar mannerism that causes Serjeant Ames to laugh into his sleeve. "I am not such a high-born personage as the earl." Esther finds something uneasy about Cuffe's gentle, professorial air.

There's something in this man that means trouble for someone close to her. She can feel it.

Cuffe turns about to the nobleman who's followed him to the Serjeant, and presents Noah to him. "Lord Sheffield, permit me to introduce Serjeant Noah Ames, one of Her Majesty's closest advisors outside of the Privy Council." He turns to Serjeant Ames for assurance. "Have I provided an accurate introduction, Serjeant?"

"Indeed, you have," says Serjeant Ames. "That's precisely where I spend most of my time … *outside* of the Privy Council."

Lord Sheffield laughs aloud. "That's what I like!" he says. "A fellow who doesn't take himself too seriously. Pleased to make your acquaintance, Serjeant, and that of your charming and beautiful young cousin."

Noah bows. "In fact, your lordship, you and I have met before, as we are neighbors."

"I'm sorry, Serjeant, that I seem to have forgot our earlier introduction. Might you remind me of the circumstances?"

"I expect you'll recall meeting my daughter, m'lord. She is Jessica, Lady Saint Ives, and her husband Jonathan, Lord Saint Ives. My wife and I accompanied them once to your home, only briefly."

Sheffield's eyebrows shoot up. "Why, of course! I remember them both. Delightful young people. And your daughter is most pleasing to the eye, much like her young cousin here. In fact, as I look upon your cousin, I see she resembles your daughter a great deal. I've heard that you are a Hebrew, Serjeant. Is this true?"

"'Tis, m'lord. I hope that it will not detract from your lordship's good will."

"Of course not," says Sheffield. "Serjeant, you are to be commended on your skills as a father and a father-in-law."

Noah bows again.

"So, Serjeant," says Sheffield, with Cuffe at his elbow, "how does our resident Hebrew feel about the coming advent of Utopia?" Despite the unnecessary reference to Noah's faith, his lordship is obviously of good cheer.

Serjeant Ames smiles fondly, as though he can barely credit the question. "*Are* we approaching Utopia, Lord Sheffield? For, if we are, I'd like to know how the land shall be peopled."

Several gentlemen gather 'round in hopes of hearing some of the clever words for which the Serjeant is renowned. Cuffe steps forward and answers for Lord Sheffield.

"Well," says Cuffe, stealing a conspicuous glance at Esther, "I should surmise pretty much the way *all* nations are peopled. Fathers beget children of their wives." This is met by general mirth, though Esther thinks it's not nearly clever enough to warrant such appreciation.

"Ah," says the Serjeant, "but where shall the fathers and mothers of these future angels hail from? Hmmm? I know of no *Englishman* who would suffer the Utopian impositions for a moment, let alone indefinitely. For example, I know of no Englishman—nary a one—who would allow the state to designate those of his relatives who *must* move to the colonies simply because the colonies need people. Nor do I see an Englishman abandoning his house in exchange for one chosen for him— by *lot*, no less. Yet, these impositions would be required of every resident of Utopia."

Lord Sheffield picks up the thread. "But, as for the exchanging of houses, where is the loss, all houses being mandated by law to be wholly alike?"

"M'lord," says Serjeant Ames, "as you certainly know, it's a tenet of English real property law that no two parcels of real estate are alike. Each is unique. The state of Utopia can *mandate* equality all it likes, but if we apply English law (with which, in this respect, nearly every civilized person agrees), then Utopia's mandate is unachievable and its policy a fraud. Besides, who do you suppose will end up residing in the *best* of these 'equal' houses? Perhaps those having a view of the town or the sea? Might it be those very persons who declare each dwelling 'equal' on behalf of the state? And, do you suppose those who make the designations will truly designate members of their own immediate families to be sent to distant colonies whose governance may be unstable indeed?"

"If not the English, perhaps you know of some *Hebrews* who would acquiesce?" suggests his lordship.

"Hardly, m'lord. Christian notions of privacy and equal justice were handed down to them by their Hebrew forebears. No self-respecting Hebrew would suffer the restrictions imposed by Utopia. According to this afternoon's thoughtful sermoneer, in Utopia one is forbidden to pass his leisure as he sees fit, but is rather instructed by the state what to do during such time. *No wine-houses permitted, no ale-houses nor brothels? All so there'd be no opportunities left for corruption?* Rubbish. Corruption breeds with men; it's inborn. *No privacy permitted? No locks on doors?* Nonsense. After a few weeks, every resident but those in power would have moved—nay, *escaped*—this Utopia."

While Serjeant Ames converses with Lord Sheffield, Esther can feel

Sheffield's gaze return to her repeatedly. As he's an older man, and married, his gaze makes her a bit uneasy.

"My word," says Sheffield, changing the subject of the conversation to the here-and-now, "Miss Ames, you are such a delightful creature, I simply must introduce you to my wife. *Perhaps this evening?*"

For some reason, Serjeant Ames and Cuffe exchange a look of utter bafflement.

CHAPTER 7

CHESTER SWINGS OPEN the stable doors and manhandles the two abductors inside, tying them tightly to separate posts. Lady Sheffield and her spicemaid perch on rustic stableman's chairs, and David paces before them, deciding how best to proceed.

Goodwife Nightwork, the innkeeper, leans against the stable's door jamb with one eye on the abductors and the other on the front door of the inn, lest traffic come by in search of food or lodging and find her gone.

Once the prisoners are tied off, Chester takes David aside.

"I know the way to examine, suh, if you'd like me to take the laboring oar."

"Do you know what to ask them?" asks David.

"Sure, sir. I've learned a few tricks in my years as Cambridge Castle jailer."

David silently runs through the disparaging descriptions he's heard of Chester's former charge, Cambridge Castle. "The jakes up on the hill," one man had called it; "a pisspot" was how the man's daughter had characterized it. Nevertheless, Chester is a good fellow, and seeking admission to the Tower Guard. A good report of his performance here might help him along with the organization's chief, Sir Walter Raleigh.

"Very well," David concedes. "Proceed."

Chester hitches up his breeches, affecting a swagger that David has not seen in him before, and places his face a half inch from that of the unarmed pistolier, who writhes in his restraints to escape the obtrusion.

"Who's yer master?" asks Chester.

"I've two," says the bound man sulkily. "God and meself."

Chester darts David a look of consternation but instantly returns to his quarry. "Was it *God* what instructed you to capture this noblewoman and carry her off against her will?"

"No," says the prisoner, "I never done that."

"Never done it? Well, *whodunit*, then? Your friend what's tied up next to ye?"

The pistolier shakes his head. "He never done it more than I."

Evidently finding this line of questioning unproductive, Chester takes another tack. "Well, what varlet were you takin' her to?" he asks.

"To no other varlet, suh, than Lord Swindon."

"Dare you to call Lord Swindon a varlet?" Chester demands indignantly.

"No, suh. It was *you* what done that."

"Me?" exclaims Chester. "Me? I never set eyes on the gentleman."

"Nor me!" says the prisoner.

"I got my eyes set on you *right now*, and that's sure!"

Chester looks to David in exasperation. While David is amused by the confusion, he suppresses a smile and twirls his index finger as though rolling a tiny barrel to tell Chester to move the interrogation along.

Chester leans into his quarry. "Lord Swindon's your master, then?"

"No, sir," says the prisoner. "As I said, it's a *free* man I am, and no lord's lackey."

"So, you were on a frolic, happened to set eyes on this distinguished lady, and just thought to take her back without any urging?"

"As I said, suh, I never set eyes on the gentleman."

"'Gentleman?' What, you varlet? Is this lady now a gentleman?" He turns about to look upon Lady Sheffield, blinks a few times to clear his vision, and turns indignantly back to the prisoner. "Even through the scales of age," he says, pointing to the mortified Lady Sheffield, "I can see this lovely lady is no gentleman."

"Nor are *you*!" says the other prisoner.

Chester turns sharply on him. "And *you*, swordsman! Are you the same as yaw friend here? Who *hired* the two o' you?"

The swordsman stands erect and proudly recites, "My partner and I are in the service of Lord Swindon!"

"What you *sayin'*?" says the pistolier.

"Just like we rehearsed!" replies the swordsman.

Lady Sheffield places her hands over her eyes and shakes her head.

David steps forward angrily. "Stop!" He turns courteously to Lady Sheffield and points to the prisoners with his chin. "Pardon, m'lady, but these men are fools."

Lady Sheffield sighs, drops her hand from her eyes, and rises slowly.

"*All* men are fools," she pronounces wearily. "If you wish to know what happened, you must ask me."

David bows perfunctorily, and escorts her out into the sunshine where they won't be heard. To his amazement, she makes no sign of protest when Constance follows them out of doors.

"You might as well know the truth," declares Lady Sheffield. "Before I tell you, however, kindly tell me who the two of you are, and who sent you."

"David Killigrew, at your service, madam. My companion is Chester, soon to be of the Tower Guard. We were sent after you by Lord Saint Ives."

"Lord Saint—the husband of Jessica, Lady Saint Ives?"

"Aye, madam."

"She's a charming woman."

"She is indeed, madam."

Lady Sheffield observes David warily. "You're sure you were *not* sent by my husband?"

David is surprised by the question. "We were not, madam. I assure you."

"For what *purpose* were you sent?" she asks.

"To save m'lady's life and ... virtue." David blushes.

She sighs. "My life was never in danger. And, as for my virtue, you're not *nearly* old enough to have saved it."

This last remark strikes David as ambiguous. Does she mean that it would take an older man to preserve her virtue now, or that she lost her virtue so long ago that David is not old enough to have been there to save it?

Before David can decide which is most likely, Constance places one hand on his shoulder and the other on his upper arm in a most proprietary manner.

"Oh, David," she sighs, almost inaudibly.

Lady Sheffield glowers at her. "Constance! Show me the respect of keeping your hands off this young man—at least while I'm *speaking* with him!" As Constance pouts and drops her hands, Lady Sheffield regards her with exasperation. "I apologize for Constance's behavior, Master Killigrew. The current crop of lady's maids seems to lack the least sense of decorum." She smiles at him. "Of course, you could make it easier for all womankind by being somewhat less ... pleasant-looking."

Constance gasps jealously at this bit of flirtation. David squirms. *All I came to do was rescue these women. How did I get onto the auction block?*

Lady Sheffield begins to pace. "Tell me, what was my husband's reaction to the scene we left behind?"

"*Scene*, madam?"

Apparently surprised by his confusion, Lady Sheffield's face falls in horror. "Did he not *see* the scene?"

"I—I don't know, madam. I've never had the pleasure of speaking with Lord Sheffield."

"Nor have I," she replies. "Nor has anyone else who's spoken with him, I assure you. Speaking with him is no pleasure." She turns her face away and mutters to herself, "Well, that would be *just* like him, wouldn't it? Never to bother seeing the scene for himself. The man pays me no heed whatever."

"I'm sure you exaggerate, madam, a woman as lovely as you are."

She raises an eyebrow in appreciation of the flattery, but then stamps her foot indignantly. "Not a whit. He hasn't paid me any attention in years. He barely knows I'm alive. All he does is visit Essex House every day and discuss impossible alternatives to the monarchy, which he finds more interesting than his own wife, if you can believe it. What's more, Her Majesty has grown to *loathe* Lord Essex, whatever the commons might believe. My husband, by fraternizing with him, stands to destroy what little remains of our tenuous standing at court."

While David has no objection to hearing her lament, for the moment he needs to bring her back to their present predicament. "If I may ask what 'scene' you left for him to see, m'lady?"

"Well," she replies, "it was a bit melodramatic: a ruffled bed with the linens tossed about, a few items of clothing strewn across the room (just some old frocks, naturally, nothing too costly), my looking glass laid on the floor—gently, of course. I couldn't bear to have it shattered. All *that* was done to show there'd been some coercion, mind you."

"When in fact there'd been *none*?" ventures David.

"You're a quick study," she sniffs. "I left no note or any such thing."

As David peers into the stables at the bound men forlornly awaiting their fate, he realizes that he was wrong to assume they're abductors. He turns back to Lady Sheffield.

"Then who, may I ask, are those two men?"

"Oh, they're ruffians," she replies with a dismissive wave.

"Ruffians? Have they mistreated you?"

She regards him skeptically. "Of course not."

"Of *course* not? How could you be certain they wouldn't?"

"Because, they knew that if they mistreated me, I wouldn't pay them what I owe."

David is astonished. "They're in your pay?"

"Well, nobody works for nothing, do they? Besides, I paid them only half."

"They work for you?"

"If not for me, then for whom?" she asks, glancing about. "For Constance?" She scoffs at her own suggestion.

David's mind is reeling. He needs to straighten this out right away. To his irritation, Constance's hands return to their former places on his shoulder and arm.

"Lady Sheffield, I must speak with you candidly." He glances at Constance. "Perhaps we should talk alone."

The lady shakes her head. "Constance has my full confidence," she assures him, then looks darkly at her maid. "Besides, she already knows everything. What's more, I doubt you could remove her hands from your person without the assistance of a surgeon. So, *speak*."

He tries to put this delicately.

"Some weeks ago, madam, it became the talk of Holborn that you and m'lord had been visited by Lord Swindon, and that"—he whispers—"he'd seduced m'lady."

"*Seduced?*" she asks incredulously, making no effort to keep her voice down. "The old man drinks so heavily, he needs assistance to rise from his chair! He has neither the inclination nor the vigor to seduce anyone, I assure you." Her tone softens, and she continues wistfully. "But he has a great deal of unentailed property ... and no living wife or other relations. It seems such a waste." She smirks. "In any event, I am unseduced."

"And unabducted as well, I take it?"

"Just so," she acknowledges.

"Then these men are not in the service of Lord Swindon?"

"They are not. I hired them to escort me to Lord Swindon's manor. If we were caught along the way—as we have been—they were to play my abductors and identify themselves as being in Swindon's service. You can see how that worked out. I promised to ransom them if they were arrested. I suppose there's no way to persuade you to pretend you couldn't find me, and leave me on my way to Swindon?"

He shakes his head adamantly. "I am in the service of Lord Saint Ives, madam, who evidently has some fondness for your husband and wishes to save him the public humiliation of reputedly having his wife seduced in his own house and then abducted from under his nose. I shall fulfill my service." He glances at the prisoners tied up in the stables. "Whose horses were these men riding?"

"Their own," Lady Sheffield replies.

"Then our parting will be simple. Your ladyship shall pay them the remainder of their … wages. I'll put them on their horses, extract their spoken promise to stay out of Holborn for a year, and send them on their way with a stern warning never again to meddle in the affairs of their betters. And I shall return your ladyship … and Constance … to Holborn and your husband's household."

"And what shall I tell my husband?"

"I urge you to tell him first that you were valiantly, nay, *heroically* rescued by Chester and myself, and that you'd been abducted … but not by Lord Swindon … rather, by some unknown admirer. You are, if I may say, m'lady, such a comely woman that your story should be met with great credulity." He eyes her warily until he's sure his compliment has turned the trick. "And we shall all keep our mouths shut about this affair until the Last Judgment. Have we a bargain?"

Lady Sheffield nods dourly.

Putting her diabolical (though admirably clever) plot to one side, David takes pity on her. "I expect your ladyship has been sorely missed and that you'll be greeted with open arms upon your return."

Lady Sheffield seems slightly mollified.

Constance coos, "Oh, David."

"Oh, shut up," he mutters and returns to the stables.

＊

LORD SHEFFIELD'S INGENUOUS invitation to introduce Esther to Lady Sheffield this evening has both Serjeant Ames and Sir Henry Cuffe squirming. Esther's interest is piqued.

"But, m'lord," says Serjeant Ames sheepishly, "is Lady Sheffield not away from home just now?" This is particularly interesting, as Esther cannot recall Serjeant Ames ever saying *anything* sheepishly.

Sheffield seems mystified. His face reddens. His mouth falls open, and hangs there. He looks quizzically first to Serjeant Ames, then to Cuffe. "Well, I'm sure I don't know," he says uncertainly. "Did she inform anyone that she was leaving?"

Serjeant Ames obviously knows something he's not saying, and evidently has no clue what to say. Instead, he poses a question to Lord Sheffield. "How recently has your lordship seen her ladyship?"

Sheffield looks to Cuffe as though Cuffe might have an answer. When none is forthcoming Sheffield says, "Well, of course, she was at home when Lord Swindon came to visit."

Cuffe clears his throat and mutters loud enough for Sheffield to hear. "Lord Swindon departed a fortnight ago, m'lord."

"Is it so long?" asks Sheffield. "Well, I'm dashed."

Esther is horrified that—whatever else may be going on here—this man is unable to remember the last time he saw his own wife: one who lives in the same house, no less. She wonders how large a house would need to be for such a thing to happen. She's seen the house numerous times, and it is a bit grand. Yet, it didn't seem so large that a significant personage could be misplaced in it.

Then she wonders with horror at the emotional distance that can evidently grow between a man and his wife. She desperately hopes that no such distance will ever grow between herself and David. A little two-room cottage would be preferable, one with a fireplace and a big bed—but not so big that someone might get lost in it.

"Now that I think on it," Sheffield blusters, "I haven't seen Constance for a few days."

"*Constance*, m'lord?" says Cuffe.

Though the Christian name is vaguely familiar to Esther, apparently it is not Lady Sheffield's.

Sheffield nods. "Yes, you know Constance, that pretty blonde spicemaid she takes with her everywhere, who always smells so enticing."

Esther is horrified to learn that the man only knows that his wife is in residence when he can sniff out her spicemaid. But Esther barely has time to realize that bit of foolishness before her mind flies off on a more personal tangent. She recalls overhearing Lady Jessica some weeks ago admonishing *David* for dallying with Lady Sheffield's spicemaid, and now David and that selfsame spicemaid have disappeared for several days—and *at the same time*! The blood drains from her face.

"Young lady," says Sheffield sympathetically, "are you quite well?"

"Yes, m'lord," she replies with as much composure as she can muster.

"You're perspiring, dear," says Serjeant Ames. "I'm afraid today's excitement may have been too much for you."

She smiles, though she aches inside. "Not at all, Serjeant Ames. I am not the retiring flower you imagine me to be." She looks into his eyes and, for the first time, wonders whether she can truly trust him, for she now recalls that a few short hours ago he suddenly went blank when she asked about David's whereabouts. Come to think on it, so did Lady Jessica … and Lord Jonathan. *So, are David and Constance an item? Am*

I the last to know? No, it cannot be, her heart protests. David has given his word.

Seemingly from nowhere, Serjeant Ames's associate Arthur Arden appears with a cup of cool water for Esther. She drinks a little, and thanks him. Arthur bows to the assembled.

"Arthur," says Serjeant Ames, "when did you arrive?"

"I've been here all the while," replies the strapping young blond fellow, "standing in the rear."

"Well, why didn't you join us right away?"

Arthur smiles uncomfortably. "I didn't wish to crowd you or … Miss Ames."

"Well, join us now. I expect Miss Ames will be pleased by your presence."

A merry glint forms in Lord Sheffield's eye, and he rumbles a laugh. "Her knight in shining armor."

"Won't you join us, Master Arden?" says Esther in her dusky voice, casting him a winning smile.

"If it please you, miss." Arthur bows politely.

Esther looks again to Serjeant Ames, and can sense his anxiety for her sake. He really is a dear. Whatever may be afoot with David, there can be no doubt Serjeant Ames loves her like a father.

"I'm quite alright, Serjeant Ames," says Esther. "I don't know what came over me. Pray, continue the discussion of Utopia." She tosses in a little white lie. "I find it enthralling."

Cuffe turns to Serjeant Ames. "And what say you of a *republic*, Serjeant? Or must any happy realm be governed by a king or queen?"

Serjeant Ames hesitates before replying. "History is littered equally with the ruins of republics and of the empires built upon their ashes. I'll admit there's something appealing about a republic, everyone being equal and all that, but I cannot imagine one sprouting up in England come springtime. History teaches that a republic can be maintained where men remain virtuous and civic-minded, but experience (that greatest of all teachers) shows that eventually a republic devolves once again into oligarchy or monarchy, and those formerly in charge of the republic become the new masters. As proof of this, we need look no further than Ancient Rome."

From behind the assembled notables comes a new voice, that of a tall man with dark red hair, attired in the gravest manner. "And so," he says, "it always comes down to Plato's warning, Serjeant Ames: *'Quis custodiet ipsos custodes'?*"

"Precisely, m'lord," says the Serjeant warily, and translates from the Latin for Esther's benefit. "'*Who watches the watchers themselves?*'"

The gentlemen all bow low to the tall newcomer, leaving Esther face-to-face with him. She blushes and curtseys low, as she's been taught by Mistress Ames.

"M'lord of Essex," says Serjeant Ames, noticing the tall man's fascination with Esther, "by your leave may I introduce my cousin Esther, who has lately joined our humble household from distant climes."

Essex smiles and extends his palm silently to Esther. As Esther has no idea what to do in response, the Serjeant mimes raising his right hand and placing it in his left. Hesitantly imitating his motion, she extends her right hand and places it gently into Essex's. When Essex bows to kiss it, though she feels an impulse to draw it away, yet she stolidly holds it there.

"*Enchanté, mademoiselle,*" says Essex in a breathy but manly voice.

"*O, merci, mon Seigneur!*" says Esther with equal breath. "*Je suis enchantée moi-même!*"

Essex smirks and turns to the Serjeant. "Beautiful *and* well-spoken, Ames. I might have expected. Tell me," he says with exasperation, "where do you find such exquisite creatures as this? And how do such creatures bring forth such plain folk as yourself?"

The Serjeant laughs quietly. "One of the eternal mysteries, m'lord. I've no idea, but am ever grateful."

"As well you should be," says Essex, his eyes pinned to Esther. "Well, please enjoy the remainder of your stay, my dear," he says. "Now if you will excuse me, I must speak with Serjeant Ames presently, as I leave for the country tomorrow and shan't return for a few weeks."

Esther is so unaccustomed to such attention that at first she stands mute, but then realizes a verbal response is called for. "Certainly, m'lord. Thank you so much for permitting me to attend." She carefully constructs and delivers a compliment. "Although we have only just met, I shall surely miss m'lord during your overlong absence." She curtseys again. In the corner of her eye, she can see Arthur beam at her with pride and good humor.

Essex turns and walks away, muttering in exasperation loud enough to be heard. "If only English noblewomen would learn such manners."

Serjeant Ames takes Arthur by the shoulder and escorts him to Esther. "Arthur, this may become unpleasant. Please escort Esther back to the house."

Arthur smiles. "It would be my privilege, sir."

As Noah watches them leave, a bulky man comes up behind and takes him by the elbow. It's Essex's steward, Sir Gelly Meyrick.

CHAPTER 8

MEYRICK FIRMLY GUIDES NOAH to the closed door of Lord Essex's study and stands beside him, facing the door. Noah knocks and waits nervously to be summoned inside.

Meyrick mutters quietly, "It's good to see you in good health, Serjeant Ames."

Noah nods, a little surprised by the courteous greeting. "And you, Sir Gelly."

"Come!" shouts Lord Essex through the solid doors, causing Noah's heart to race. Sir Gelly shoves open the door. Noah takes a hesitant step inside and glances about. Other than Sir Gelly, who lags somewhere behind, Noah is once again alone with the Earl of Essex.

Though the earl stands behind a dark wooden bureau in a well-appointed study, in Noah's heart every meeting alone with the earl takes place at the ends of the earth, surrounded by pits of fiery brimstone that bubble and smoke.

As his lordship seems preoccupied by a letter in his hands, Noah bows low and waits to be spoken to. The earl nods thoughtfully as he reaches the end of the letter, folds it, and tucks it away in a pocket in his doublet. He looks up at Noah.

"Ah, Ames! Thank you for coming, and bringing that delightful girl."

Noah bows deferentially. "Thank you for inviting me, m'lord. Though the invitation did not expressly contemplate my young cousin, I knew your lordship's courtesy to be expansive."

Essex chortles. "Your courtly compliments are always well-phrased, Serjeant, but your delivery has never been correspondingly obsequious."

Noah sighs. "I expect my lord would regard the least sign of my fawning to be false, and therefore insulting. It has never been my purpose either to deceive or insult your lordship."

Essex responds with a small noncommittal grunt. "I am told you are charged with investigating the two murders that took place on Bowyer's Row."

Noah can only wonder how Essex gets such information, invariably accurate and current. "That is correct, m'lord, but I am not the only one charged with such duty."

"So I've heard. You sound rather disappointed about that. Is the other investigator not to your liking?"

"He's a puritan, m'lord. I have heard that such persons are often mirthless."

Noah hears a snicker behind him and risks a momentary glance over his shoulder. It's Meyrick, who evidently intends to remain for the interview.

"Pardon me, m'lord," says Noah. "I thought we were alone."

"Naturally, you wish to be able to speak your mind, and I wouldn't have it any other way. Nevertheless, Sir Gelly has my complete trust. Close the door, would you, Meyrick?" The door clacks shut, and Essex looks to Noah expectantly.

"As I was saying," says Noah, "puritans are often believed to be quite mirthless. And this one seems preoccupied with ... every man's sexual practices." Although Essex tries to hide it, Noah can see that he suspects who it is. To his amazement, Essex drops the topic without further discussion.

"If I may be so impertinent as to ask your lordship a question?" Noah ventures.

Essex shrugs. "I suppose so."

"One of the murdered men was known to me when I resided at Gray's Inn. He was amongst the 'merry band,' I believe your lordship once called it, that spirited me out of London after the Lopez hearing in the Court of Oyer & Terminer."

"Identical twin, wasn't he?" asks Essex.

"Just so, m'lord. When your lordship left town a short while ago, I noticed that the twins had joined your retinue."

Essex shakes his head. "Despite appearances, Serjeant, they never joined our ... contingent. All I knew is that they supposedly had some urgent business to discuss with me, but never did. But, if you wish to know what they did while they were with us, I invite you to turn about and ask your old friend Sir Gelly. He spent more time with them than I."

Meyrick shrugs his shoulders, as well. "With us but a few days, the Bennetts. They kept whisperin' to each other, all urgent-like, barely passin' a word with anybuddy else. Because they was twin brothers, we took no note of it. Figured they'd tell us when they was ready. Then, the other mornin', we wake up and they're both gone like yesterday's rain.

Later that day, we heard one of 'em was murdered, and the other one missin'. I told me men to keep their ears pinned, but nobody's caught sight nor sound of 'em since then."

"Now that that's been covered," says the earl, "I understand that you've only now returned from an audience at Nonsuch Palace."

Noah nods.

"Has Her Majesty decided whether to extend my patent on sweet wines?"

Noah swallows hard and looks down. "I am expressly forbidden to disclose such information, m'lord. I hope you will understand."

Essex's ire is rising. "Understand? How can I understand? How can *anyone* understand that woman?"

"Her Majesty is not so complex a puzzle, when it comes to my lord."

"Enlighten me," says Essex. "How much longer must I remain in contrition before she summons me back to court? Tell me or, I swear by heaven, I shall return to court *without* her summons."

Noah wonders whether the earl recognizes that he's speaking treason.

"Which contrition, my lord?" says Noah, well aware that he's playing with fire.

Essex seems truly surprised by his question. "Do you think I have been less than contrite all these months?"

"To speak of storming Her Majesty's court? Does that not rather betray an unrepentant heart, m'lord?"

Essex's face reddens. "I spoke these words only between us, Serjeant. I thought we had an understanding."

Noah can hear Meyrick take a step toward him, but he dares not turn about. Instead, he says, "Your lordship's words shall remain between us, just as you expect. However, neither your words nor their sense need to be repeated for Her Majesty to know that your contrition these past few months consists mostly of show."

"How would she know that, Serjeant, but from you?"

"When I came here today, did not your lordship already know that I had gone to Nonsuch to speak with Her Majesty and been assigned to investigate the murders on Bowyer's Row, and that someone else had been appointed to conduct such investigation, as well?"

"Obviously."

"*How* did m'lord know those things?"

"Through private sources," says the earl, obviously intending to disclose no more.

"Indeed, m'lord, private sources … at the Queen's court. It's a busy place. People come and go for myriad reasons. A few are summoned by Her Majesty, but many are not; some seem to mill about aimlessly."

"Your point, Serjeant?"

"People come and go all day long at your lordship's court here at Essex House, as well. What assurance has your lordship that Her Majesty has no private sources here?"

Noah can see a chill pass through Essex's bones. Sir Gelly mutters under his breath and places a hand on Noah's shoulder. "Shall I remove him, m'lord?" he grunts.

Essex looks to Meyrick, then to Noah, arching a single eyebrow. Though Essex says not a word, Noah has no doubt that he's tacitly inquiring whether Meyrick is a spy for the Queen.

Noah looks pointedly at Meyrick's gruff hand resting on his shoulder. Meyrick, apparently understanding the silent dialog taking place between his master and Noah, drops his hand and takes a step backward to await the outcome.

Noah turns back to Essex and shakes his head almost imperceptibly. He can hear Meyrick's sigh of relief.

"M'lord," says Noah gravely, "by your leave I will answer your pending question and what I believe will be your lordship's remaining questions. Not out of impatience, but rather respect. First, as I have said, I've been forbidden to discuss Her Majesty's intentions concerning the possible renewal of your lordship's patent for sweet wines. I cannot nor will not betray that confidence."

The earl does not react.

Noah continues. "As for whether Her Majesty has any current intention to permit your return to court presently, she has not discussed it with me, but I will give you my best judgment: I doubt it."

Essex struggles to put his next thought into words. "But I … it's not as though I plan to cross the Rubicon …"

"Your lordship," says Noah, "your Rubicon was the Irish Sea, and you *did* cross it—in defiance of Her Majesty's most solemn edict. Moreover, it has long been well-known at court that, before returning to England (and invading Her Majesty's closet in most unfortunate manner), you openly discussed with your general officers your lordship's intention to return to England in command of an armed retinue. It took cooler heads to dissuade you from doing so, pointing out that it would have been precisely what Julius Caesar did when he crossed the real Rubicon in an act of open rebellion against the Roman council.

"To be blunt, m'lord, I have seen no change in Her Majesty's attitude toward your lordship since your return from Ireland, despite the best efforts of your remaining friends at court. Yes, you have friends at court still, but they are few in number and rarely heard in your interest."

Essex is too crestfallen to speak. At last, he musters enough energy to continue the conversation. "And so, now do you counsel despair?"

Noah shakes his head. "Never. I rather counsel *genuine* contrition. I counsel also that when your lordship returns from the country in a few weeks, you return without retinue of any kind."

"What? With no men *at all*?" asks Essex bitterly.

"From what I have now said, lordship, you must realize how seditious it appears when you encamp in London with your retinue and, worse, when you hire learned sermoneers to lecture them on alternatives to the monarchy. I need not remind your lordship that Her Majesty *is* a monarch—and our liege lord. This is neither Oxford nor Cambridge, m'lord, where discussions of a republic are mere philosophical exercises meant to expand the minds of young boys. The men of your lordship's retinue are of a quality permitting them to carry swords through the streets of London, and they are not young boys, but men. Some are grizzled veterans. To think that such men speaking openly of a republic will not alarm Her Majesty would be to define true madness."

Essex is so smitten by Noah's judgment that he makes no reply, except to signal Meyrick to lead Noah out the way he came.

MEYRICK'S KEYS AND WEAPONS jangle as he escorts Noah to the door that opens onto Chancery Lane. He smolders with unspent anger.

Before Noah steps through the door, he turns to Meyrick.

"Good day, Sir Gelly."

Meyrick's face turns dark red, and his voice is a strangled whisper. "Good day? And which 'good day' can follow your appearance here, Serjeant Ames?" With considerable force, Meyrick smacks the door jamb with his open hand, making a surprisingly loud boom. Still, he speaks no further.

Noah is careful to stand his ground without flinching. He senses the danger in either showing fear or leaving Sir Gelly in a fit of choler.

"Out with it, Sir Gelly," he whispers.

Meyrick seems on the edge of explosion, but to his credit he keeps his voice down to a whisper and speaks through clenched teeth.

"How can you *talk* to 'im that way?"

"I don't expect you to understand right away, Sir Gelly, but that is how he *needs* me to talk to him," says Noah. "It is how he *demands* I talk to him."

"Nobody *else* talks to him that way. He don't need *nobody* to talk to 'im like that!"

Noah wonders how he can lead Meyrick to understand the precariousness of Essex's position.

"To the contrary, Sir Gelly. He needs *you*— and as many of his other supporters as you can muster—to talk to him *just* like that. No matter how bad things seem to the earl, they can always get worse, and he needs to be reminded that there are things he *must ... not ... do*, such as attempting to return to the Queen's court without summons. His very head stands a-tickle on his shoulders, Sir Gelly. A worthy in such peril needs, nay, *deserves* your best advice. You are his steward. If *you* do not counsel patience—"

"Counsel?" says Meyrick. "He don't need no counsel from me. I'm not his bloody counselor. I'm his attendant. I obey his orders."

Noah pokes his finger into Meyrick's ample chest.

"Some orders are not fit to obey."

"Which orders?" asks Meyrick derisively. "The ones *you* don't like?"

"*Unlawful* orders," says Noah. "Orders that endanger Queen Elizabeth, for example."

"He ain't never given such an order," Meyrick protests.

"Nonsense," says Noah. "He's undoubtedly given many, but they've seemed simple little orders that could lead only incrementally to Her Majesty's detriment. So, you've obeyed them."

As Noah's still not getting through, he decides on another tack.

"Do you *love* the earl, Sir Gelly?"

Meyrick regards him sharply. "'Course I do. You *know* I do."

Noah can see that at last he's succeeded in piercing the brute's tough hide. "Then you owe him *more* than blind obedience. Can't you see he's a man at sea, sick at heart? He needs your encouragement to understand his position and come to terms with it, and to do only those things that will help him in future. He's a young man, after all. And he needs to be turned away from all forms of insolence and rebellion. Will you not do this ... for *him*?"

Meyrick is obviously confounded by the suggestion that it could be a disservice to his master to obey his orders. "I know lots of men who've lost their heads for disobeyin' orders like you say, Serjeant Ames."

"Oh, never fall back on *that*, Sir Gelly! I know you of old. You don't fear for your own life nearly so much as for his. Why, you'd sacrifice yourself in a moment for his sake—something you've no doubt come blessedly close to doing in the past." Noah carefully selects which words to leave in Sir Gelly's mind. He steps over the threshold and turns back before walking away.

"Prepare yourself, Sir Gelly, for there may come a time—and *soon*—when you'll need to choose between obeying his orders and saving his life—and his immortal soul to boot. Say your prayers that you may choose rightly."

———————∽οⅭ⅀∾οⅽ———————

JONATHAN SITS IN Noah's study by an open window, enjoying the clean autumnal scent wafting in from outdoors. To pass the time until Noah's expected return from Essex House, Jonathan reads portions of an old manuscript book about the expulsion of Jews from England more than three centuries ago.

The author, though skilled in the vagaries of the English language, occasionally abandons English entirely for what Jonathan conjectures to be German, though his German's not good enough to be certain. The manuscript is pleasantly scented but, when he moves his face closer to it, his eyes water and his nose begins to itch.

Lost in study a while, Jonathan overhears a man and woman engaged in leisurely conversation sauntering up Chancery Lane. As the two approach, he recognizes Esther's husky voice clearly. The man's voice is a bit less distinctive, but sounds like that of his old friend Arthur Arden. Arthur is evidently escorting Esther home, which means that Noah has remained at Essex House longer than expected. While Esther and Arthur chat amiably by the front door, Jonathan falls back into the study of the old book.

A short time later, his reverie is interrupted by a third voice, that of a second man. He hears Esther excuse herself, enter the house, and go upstairs, while the two men continue to converse by the front door. The discussion soon becomes heated.

Jonathan reluctantly places a marker in the book, puts it down, and goes to an open window by the front door to eavesdrop.

"Look," says Arthur in a whinging tone unbecoming an established barrister, "all I did was find the corpses and bring Serjeant Ames to see them. There's no cause for further inquiry into my personal affairs."

"Master Arden, it's a simple matter," says the other man. "Either you know Master Anthony Bacon or you do not."

Jonathan pulls back the curtain an inch to see the man's face and is surprised to see a puritan clad in customary black and white attire. There's something hurried about the puritan's posture, and he glances furtively over his shoulder as though he fears the appearance of ... someone. Probably Noah.

"I have met Master Bacon," confirms Arthur, "but his affairs are his own."

"You lived together with him at Gray's Inn, did you not?"

"He and I lived at Gray's Inn at the same time, but we hardly 'lived together.' We never shared rooms. He lives there no longer."

"Do you recall any signs of buggery on the man when you both resided at the inn?"

That decides Jonathan. This will proceed no further. He makes sure his coat of arms is prominently displayed on his robes and walks out the front door as though passing by. He comes between the two men and, with an air of nonchalance, walks directly into the puritan, knocking him back a few feet.

"Oh," says Jonathan as though he hadn't seen the man, "I beg your pardon." Jonathan makes a show of dusting off the puritan's robe. Seeing he tolerates that much (albeit with obvious annoyance), he proceeds to dust off the puritan's face gruffly.

"See here!" says the puritan at last, taking a step backward. Spying Jonathan's coat of arms, he bows and says, "Pardon my awkwardness, my lord."

"Not at all. Not at all," says Jonathan jovially. "Could have happened to anyone. Each of us plays the fool sometime."

Jonathan turns about and, smiling as though he's just noticed Arthur for the first time, grabs his hand and shakes it vigorously. "Master Arden! Why, how are you, sir? To what do I owe this visitation? Won't you come inside and tell me all about it?" He turns the amazed Arthur by the shoulder, shoves him into the house, and closes the door after him.

"Pardon me, m'lord," says the puritan, "but I was inquiring of that gentleman on ... official business."

Jonathan looks the puritan up and down skeptically. "Official ... *religious* business?"

"Not in the narrowest sense of the word, m'lord. I am cathedral constable at Saint Paul's."

"Oh!" says Jonathan. "Well, why didn't you say so, constable?" He points southeast. "Saint Paul's is about a half-mile that way. I was about to go out, but now that I see Master Arden has arrived unexpectedly, if you'll excuse me, I shall change my plans and visit with him." Jonathan winks at the constable. "He's a *very* busy man, you know. Very important."

"I'm afraid I haven't finished asking my official questions," says the puritan apologetically. "If I may have a moment of Master Arden's time before—"

"You may *not*, constable," says Jonathan, his show of bonhomie having evaporated in an instant.

"I'm afraid I must insist, my lord."

"We're half a mile away from your cathedral now. Bit outside your bailiwick to be insisting on things, wouldn't you say?" asks Jonathan with a wry smile.

"Yes, my lord, but—"

"Official questions, did you say?"

"Aye, m'lord."

Jonathan nods, as though weighing his thoughts. "Because, constable, Master Arden is a strapping young man. He's often importuned by both women and men with illicit proposals for the most outlandish indiscretions."

"Is that so, my lord?" asks the puritan with great professional interest.

"Oh, yes. He often has occasion to call the constable to lock up some mendicant or strumpet. Tell me. What was the subject matter of your 'official questions'?"

The puritan regards him suspiciously. "Why ... buggery, my lord," he replies apprehensively.

Jonathan straightens his back indignantly. "Why ... and you a *constable*, of all things! You should be ashamed of yourself, sir! Why, I shall call the constable on *you*, you dastardly man!" He looks the puritan keenly in the eye and places his hand awkwardly on the hilt of his sword. The puritan's eyes grow wide with fear, and he takes several steps backward.

Arthur, who's evidently been watching the whole time through the window, darts out of the door as in a panic and places his hand firmly over Jonathan's sword hand to stop him from drawing.

"Stop it, Arthur!" says Jonathan as he struggles vainly to free his hand. He glares threateningly at the puritan. "If you make me draw my sword, you varlet, you shan't feel the flat of it, I assure you!"

The puritan turns about and reaches a full run within a few steps. Jonathan shouts angrily after him.

"You'll want Southwark, you hypocrite! It's a mile southeast." He brings his hands up to his mouth to amplify his voice, lest it fail to reach his fast-vanishing victim. "Plenty of buggerers down there for your sort!"

The puritan quickly disappears in the direction of London Town.

Jonathan and Arthur, after collaborating in a momentary reprise of their school days together, collapse into fits of laughter that cease only when it occurs to each of them, as ever it must, that their carefree days of such camaraderie are never to return.

Serjeant Ames appears from his homeward walk up Chancery Lane wearing a heavy demeanor that lightens as soon as he spies Jonathan and Arthur. He bows to his son-in-law. "Good day, m'lord," he says.

Lord Jonathan bows in return. "Father," he says.

"I saw from some distance away that you and Master Arden have been enjoying yourselves. Care to share the jest? I could use one about now."

Lord Jonathan explains the puritan's unannounced appearance, his strange inquiry, and his sudden exit. Strangely, Serjeant Ames becomes more, not less, serious as the tale finishes.

Jonathan recognizes that expression all too well. "I sense we have transgressed in some way, Father."

"Well, I hadn't yet told you to expect that man nor explained to you who he is," says the Serjeant, "so I suppose nothing will come of your innocent jest. Any fault lies with me."

"Fault?" says Arthur. "Who was that man?"

"Did he not identify himself?"

Arthur equivocates. "Only to say that he's cathedral constable at Saint Paul's, and that he's investigating the murders on Bowyer's Row. As I knew *you'd* been charged with that responsibility, I'm afraid I didn't take him seriously. He just seemed a foolish busybody, preoccupied with Anthony Bacon and … buggery, of all things."

"And you could not imagine what buggery could have to do with the murders," says Serjeant Ames thoughtfully. "Nor can I. And yet we'll have to take him more seriously henceforth. Her Majesty has declined to remove him from the investigation. Besides," he says doubtfully, "I suppose there's always the possibility, however remote, that he's onto something. Come inside, gentlemen. I'd like to speak with you separately. Lord Jonathan, you first."

CHAPTER 9

NOAH ESCORTS HIS YOUNG FRIENDS into his house. Arthur takes a seat in the parlor while Noah and Jonathan move to Noah's study and shut the door.

Noah examines the spine of the book Jonathan left on the table and smiles fondly. "*The Jews of England.* I was wondering when your curiosity would get the better of you."

"I see Lady Jessica has informed you," says Jonathan, "that when my birth mother gave me up, she taught my adoptive mother the Hebrew Sabbath prayer."

Noah plops into his accustomed chair behind the bureau. "She told me some months ago, yes. It's a lovely tale. No doubt you wish to learn more of your origins."

"Yes," says Jonathan. "I can't help but wonder who I really am. Eight years ago, I became an orphan, having been raised by the Graves. the kindest couple in London. Yet, I have no idea who my real parents were. And now I've become a nobleman, married to a noble-woman, and yet ... somehow, I feel an impostor. If I'd been known to be a Jew by birth (if indeed that's what I am), I would never have been created a baron."

"True enough," says Noah, brandishing a paternal smile. "Your feelings of imposture are familiar to me. But *I* know who you are, and I needn't know the circumstances of your birth to know that. Let me ask you this, Jonathan: Who am *I*? Do you know me?"

"Sure."

"Would it make any difference to you if, instead of being born a Jew, I'd been baptized at birth into the Church of England?"

"I suppose not."

"So, we agree on that," says Noah. "Still, I recognize the feeling of imposture that comes of being thrust by circumstance into a position where others never expected to find us, and where we ourselves are not quite sure we belong. That raises another, even more profound question, which is whether you really *wish* to know where you come from."

"I do," replies Jonathan, doubtfully at first. He evidently gives it a second thought but arrives at the same conclusion. "Yes, I truly do. Can you help me?"

Noah nods. "Possibly, though there are few English Jews whose origins are as mine, and not Spanish or Portuguese. I see no more Spanish in you than in my own reflection. You are tall and light-skinned, as am I. Let me give it some thought. In the meantime, however, I need your help in the pending investigation into the murders on Bowyer's Row."

"Certainly," says Jonathan.

"You must keep this matter between us," says Noah. "There is no need for our wives or anyone else to know about such things."

Jonathan nods. "How can I help?"

"I need you to discover where I might find the surviving Bennett twin. He seems to have vanished from the face of the earth. Very likely he fears he's being hunted by the same person or persons who murdered his brother. I expect he's in quite as much danger as he thinks."

"I'll try to find him."

"Where will you begin?"

"Well, evidently, some years ago upon leaving Gray's Inn, he and his brother moved to Cheltenham. I suppose it would be a long shot to travel up there. Rather, I expect it's wiser to start locally. Perhaps some barrister resident at one of the Inns of Court kept in touch with one or both of the twins after they left Gray's Inn."

"Sounds logical. There's one other person to try if that fails. Unfortunately, he'd like to bash my head in about now. And, as for you, well ... he's *afraid* of you."

"Afraid ... of *me*?"

Noah nods. "He thinks you'd like to kill him though you have no just cause, and that ... you're quite mad."

"You're referring to Gelly Meyrick," says Jonathan with distaste.

"Well, you did threaten to blow his head off, albeit with an unloaded pistol."

"He had it coming to him," says Jonathan, "and you've quite a long scar on your chest to prove it."

"Yes," says Noah weighingly, "but then there was the time some years later when you heaved him through a window, nearly killing him. He still walks with a limp from that encounter."

"I did that only because he was about to say something derogatory about *your daughter*."

Noah chortles. "As we might say in court: 'Counselor, how do you know what he was *about* to say?'"

"He said her name."

Noah regards him sympathetically. "While I am ever grateful for your protecting my daughter's name from slander, even I would have encouraged you to wait for him to say something derogatory ... before taking corrective action." Noah shakes his head. "No, Jonathan, there's something about your fury at Meyrick that I've never completely understood, and it manifests in strange ways."

"Strange ways?" asks Jonathan incredulously.

"Yes. For example, I distinctly remember you blaming Meyrick for the death of dear old Graves regardless that he was nowhere near the place where Graves was poisoned—*if* he was poisoned, and Doctor Lopez was never able to confirm that he was. And, as I've told you, Lord Essex later confirmed to me that Meyrick had nothing to do with that entire incident. Yet, you and I know which of Essex's henchmen *were* there—namely, Skeres and Poley, but you've never harbored a grudge against either of them."

Jonathan seems hesitant to open up.

Noah sits up straight, as though ready to move on to other topics. "Of course, if it's too personal—"

"It's not that," says Jonathan. "It's that the event happened when I was so young. I'm not sure how much of what's in my mind is memory and how much imagination."

"A memory from young childhood, then?" says Noah. "I might have known."

"Sometime before Goodwife Graves passed," says Jonathan, "she was struck by a drunken horseman who'd ridden recklessly through the market district and knocked over many carts, including hers. I was in a house nearby for some reason I can't recall, probably sent to fetch something." His eyes tear up. "I heard the tumult and ran out of doors to find her sprawled unconscious in the dirt amongst some vegetables from a neighboring cart, as well as the inexpensive woven goods she some-times made and sold, to help feed us all. Very humble items, but serviceable, and she had her adherents." He rubs his forehead slowly. "She was hurt quite badly. I recall little of what happened next. I do remember that, a few moments later, I heard a man bellowing in a neighboring home about 'those bastards blocking the street,' who 'deserved what they got,' and so on. Evidently, one of our neighbors was tending to the man's scrapes and bruises resulting from the incident. When I asked another neighbor whose voice that was, he replied 'Gelly Meyrick.'"

"And you concluded that Meyrick was the drunken horseman?"

Jonathan shrugs. "I was a young child. I knew only that 'me mum' was hurt. She was bleeding from her hands and face, and her legs were badly bruised. It took many weeks for her to come right again. Anyway, some time later (I don't know how long), she died of plague ... which I always suspected she would have never done, but for the ... incident. Ever since then, I've felt a loathing for Gelly Meyrick."

"And that's why hearing his name rankles you," observes Noah. "Well, that's certainly understandable. Still, the impressions we receive at such a tender age can be unreliable." He sighs. "We'll try to keep you and Sir Gelly away from each other. Now I have one other thing to ask about."

Jonathan shifts in his chair, palpably relieved at the prospect of moving on from such a painful subject.

Noah continues. "That constable is preoccupied with the sexual habits of everyone he encounters," he says. "We may need to tangle with him eventually and, before that happens, I need to know what susceptibilities we have among us in regard to unnatural sexual improprieties."

Jonathan shakes his head. "I, for one, never dabbled in any such conduct."

"Very well," replies Noah. "You've known Andres Salazar since starting Eton?"

"I have."

"To your knowledge, has Andres—?"

"Not to my knowledge," replies Jonathan, "and, knowing Andres for as long as I have, I strongly doubt it. From an early age, Andres would rhapsodize about every pretty girl he met, till we all rolled our eyes."

Noah nods. "And Arthur?" he asks.

"I'd rather not say," says Jonathan, blushing.

Noah regards him impatiently. "Would you rather that ninnyhammer constable were to go to the authorities before I learn of it? You know the punishment Arthur could face."

"Death," confirms Jonathan. "If I tell you, what could you do to prevent that happening?"

Noah sighs. "I don't know, Jon. I will do everything in my power to avoid it. But I can't do anything unless I know what I'm facing."

Jonathan squirms uneasily in his chair. "When Arthur came to school, he was quite small, such as you'd never guess from the big, strong fellow he's become. During our first year there, he became the object of a notorious tormentor who was a couple of years older. 'Bellicose Billy,' we called him. It was generally believed that he was trying to force Arthur to perform unnatural acts with him. Arthur stopped eating for days, and couldn't sleep."

"What happened?"

"One evening, after lights out, we could hear Arthur resisting, and he was near tears. Another boy put a stop to it before it began, however, and Billy soon moved away, much to the relief of all of us, Arthur not least."

"Is that the only occasion that need concern us?"

"Perhaps not. Arthur was friendly with another boy who couldn't have been more different from his departed tormentor. The fellow was small like Arthur, and absolutely brilliant in languages. While the rest of us were struggling to learn the Greek alphabet well enough to sound out the ancient poems and plays we were responsible to know, this fellow would be walking alone in the woods every chance he got, reciting long passages aloud from memory.

"Once, during instruction, I can plainly recall the fellow bursting out into uncontrollable laughter. The instructor smacked him with a stick, as was common at the time, though it was infuriating to see done to such an attentive student, and demanded to know what he found so humorous. The fellow responded, 'Aristophanes.' He'd come across a jest, you see, in ancient Greek, and found it clever. After that, whenever it became obvious that he understood something the instructors had missed, they'd snarl at him, for here was an upstart who'd had no contact with Greek until coming to Eton and, within two years, was laughing aloud with the comedy and weeping with the poetry. The instructors—especially those who fancied themselves masters of the texts—found it all rather mortifying."

Noah nods. "What has this to do with Arthur?"

"Arthur was fascinated by the fellow," says Jonathan, "and they became fast friends. Sometimes, they would sneak about after 'lights out.' That was enough to get boys speculating and tongues a-wagging. Whether anything untoward actually happened between Arthur and this fellow, you'll have to ask Arthur. I never knew of anything other than rumor."

Noah nods thoughtfully. "Thank you, Jonathan, for your honesty. Where were you planning on going after your visit here?"

"I thought I'd have dinner with Jessica."

Noah smiles. "Please give her ladyship my compliments, m'lord. Oh, and send Arthur in on your way out."

Jonathan breathes a sigh of relief and shuts the door behind him.

The room is dark and a soft breeze wafts through it. Noah is so bone-weary after the ride home and his interviews with Essex and Meyrick (and now Jonathan) that he dozes off.

"I COULD COME BACK," says Arthur's soft voice.

The breeze through the darkened study is so pleasant that Noah has no sense where he is until he opens his eyes. He wipes them and clears his throat after what appears to have been an unintended nap. "No, please come in. How long was I—?" His mouth is dry.

"I saw you were asleep," says Arthur, "and decided to leave you for a while, so I spoke with Jonathan before he left. All in all, I expect you were out three-quarters of an hour."

"Thanks for the respite," says Noah. "Could you bring me a cup of water?"

Arthur's already thought of it, and hands Noah the cup he brought with him. Noah thanks him and sips it while he tries to recall what he wanted to ask. But Arthur begins without prompting.

"Jonathan mentioned to me that he'd told you of both boys who might have some bearing on this conversation. There's been no one else, and certainly not Anthony Bacon, whom I barely knew, so rarely did he leave his rooms at Gray's Inn. As Jonathan explained to you, first was Bellicose Billy, the cruelest caitiff at Eton. He did indeed force boys to perform on him, and he carried a knife. Nothing special, just a butter knife he'd pilfered from the dining room. When the headmaster learned a knife was missing (they were counted after every meal), he rousted the whole dormitory and made every threat he could imagine, but no one turned in Bellicose Billy, for fear of retribution. So Billy kept the knife as an implied threat against anyone who'd dare resist him.

"Well, one time he decided he wanted to be serviced by me, and I refused. This was after lights out, but there was plenty of moonlight in the room to illuminate what was happening. He made the mistake of drawing his knife. A moment later, he was kicked in the gut by a boy his own size, and collapsed to the floor.

"It was Jonathan, of course, who'd come to my rescue. The room came alive, and many others wanted to join in beating Billy, who was finally getting what he deserved, but Jonathan whispered them back to bed and told them to remain silent, so as to avoid alerting the proctor. Jonathan then proceeded in silence to pummel Billy mercilessly, though not in the face or anywhere else that could be seen. When Jonathan had completed his work and was red with fury, he picked up Billy's knife and held it in front of his face in a most threatening manner. I remember what he said as though it were yesterday. 'You'll take this knife right now to the proctor and tell him you found it on the floor by the door and that you'd like to return it.'

"Billy said, 'But then they'll know 'twas I who swiped it.' Jonathan replied, 'And you'll deny it, and nobody here will rat you out. But, if you do anything else, or anything more, I'll steal a knife of my own and feed you your own eyeballs before I cut your bloody throat. And from this moment on, you'll never bother anyone here again. You understand?'

"Billy nodded his head, and indeed he bothered no one during the brief time he remained at Eton, probably because he was so busy in the jakes. His belly'd been so roughed up, he could barely hold his shit. Or maybe that was just his fear of Jonathan in his guts. In any case, Billy's parents signed him out of school two weeks later, and he was never heard from again. Jonathan said he'd had to sleep with one eye open for that two weeks, but it was worth every sleepless hour.

"After that, Jonathan brought me along in every sport he was good at, which was all of them, and he and I became inseparable from each other and from Andres and the Bennett twins. Until then, we'd all been outcasts among the upper-crust boys we'd been thrown in with. Jonathan was known to come from poverty, Andres was Portuguese, the Bennett twins painfully shy, and I was quite small. But, after that incident, we were the envy of the school."

Noah nods with a smile. "No wonder you were thick as thieves when I first met you. Jesters, indeed."

Arthur takes a breath before continuing. "The other boy that Jon told you about was a different situation entirely." He sighs. "He was a prodigious scholar. Within two years of enrollment, he could read and write Latin like a Roman prelate, and Greek like Sophocles. You could tell that his pronunciation had been mangled by our instructors' (who'd probably never heard an Italian or a Greek speak in their lives), but his vocabulary and grammar were impeccable by the time he was *twelve years old*. And he understood the *sense* of the words, too. He knew without being told when something was funny or sad, and he could translate the written word from either of those languages faster and more accurately than his classmates could sound out their native *English*."

"Sounds like a remarkable mind," remarks Noah. "He reminds me of Sir Henry Neville in his younger days. So, what happened then?"

"Though he wasn't flamboyant," continues Arthur, "there was something undeniably effeminate about him. I probably would never have noticed but that I was continually reminded by others in the coarsest ways. Boys can be quite cruel, as I'm sure you know. Anyway, we became good friends. The other boys would conjecture and jeer, as though there was something physical about our relationship, but there never was."

"Never?" asks Noah diffidently, hating himself for prying so deeply into something that ought to be none of his business.

"Well—" Arthur starts, but brings himself up short.

Noah waits a respectful time for Arthur to gather his thoughts.

At last Arthur continues. "I'm going to tell you something I've never told anyone, not even Jon. One night, this prodigy and I sneaked out together for a forbidden walk in the woods. As he customarily took his walks alone, I felt flattered by the invitation. I thought, *perhaps he recognizes something special in me.*

"Anyway, there we were, gazing at the gibbous moon, speculating whether anyone lives up there ..." He smirks youthfully. "I don't know why I remember *that*." In an instant, his expression has changed to that of someone old enough to recognize the tragedy of everyday life. "Anyway he ... kissed me on the mouth. At first, I was taken aback. But my regard for him was so great ... I let him do it." Arthur shrugs. "I'll never know why. I suppose I was just so *surprised*. But there was no stirring in me, and he—bright as he was—sensed it right away."

"Did you love him?" ventures Noah.

"No *doubt* I loved him," Arthur sighs, "but as one brother loves another."

"What did he do when you refused him?" asks Noah.

"He drew away, looked at my face as though he wished to remember it always, and shook his head, as though disappointed in himself for misjudging me. Then he kissed me chastely on the forehead, as though with a parting blessing, and quickly strode off alone into the woods. I knew at once that I'd lost him as a friend, and wanted very much to tell him that he hadn't lost my regard in the least, but he was gone in an instant."

Arthur wipes his eyes with his hands, and draws a breath with a pained shudder. "I don't know whether it was from his sense of disappointment, embarrassment, or a groundless fear of betrayal, but ... he never spoke to me again."

"What happened to him?"

"That was March," says Arthur, as his eyes drop to the floor. "By June, he was dead. Consumption."

CHAPTER 10

THE NEXT MORNING, Esther is walking toward Lord Sheffield's town home to learn whether his wife has returned, when she sees the lady herself approaching on horseback, slowly rounding the corner onto High Holborn, conversing with some companion who's yet to come into view.

As this may be her only chance to discover whether David has indeed been away with Constance the spicemaid, Esther darts from the road and conceals herself behind a thick hedge along the boundary line of Lord Sheffield's property. Peering through a tiny break in the greenery, she sees to her dismay that Lady Sheffield's companion is David Killigrew.

David's long blond hair falls about his broad shoulders, streaming behind him in the breeze, and glistening in the autumn sunlight. Sometimes Esther wishes David was not so attractive to women ... to *other* women.

Behind Lady Sheffield and David, another man and woman ride abreast. She recognizes the man as David's middle-aged friend of recent acquaintance, Chester. Esther is unaware of precisely what role Chester played in Serjeant Ames's lately saving the Queen's life, but she's heard his skills and loyalty praised many times.

The woman riding beside Chester is (*ugh!*) the spicemaid Constance. She's a well-known flirt ... and possibly worse. Esther would not be surprised to see the girl swollen with child quite soon, which would serve her right—so long as it's not *David's* child, which would be catastrophic for David and for Esther's plans for their future together.

———————⟿∘⟸⟣⟿∘⟸———————

AFTER HELPING LADY SHEFFIELD to dismount, David begs her pardon and climbs the steps to Sheffield House. He lifts the heavy doorknocker and strikes it twice against the bronze family crest mounted on the door, an inverted chevron with two sheaves above it, and one below.

The door is opened immediately by a joyous Lord Sheffield. David bows but, before he can get a word out, Sheffield excitedly peers around him and clambers down the steps to his wife, whom he seizes in his arms.

"Oh, thank God, Anne!" shouts Lord Sheffield. "I *thought* I saw you from a window upstairs. Thank heaven for your safe return! I don't know *what* I'd do without you. I've missed you so awfully."

David cannot help but notice how different Sheffield seems from the aloof creature described by his wife. The fellow seems genuinely overjoyed by her return. Lady Sheffield, for her part, appears quite shocked by this effusive greeting and, after a moment's reticence, reciprocates her husband's strong embrace. They weep together.

While still atop the steps, David turns to gauge Chester's reaction to the unexpectedly joyous reunion. Chester shrugs and smiles, evidently as surprised as David. David then turns to Constance, who beams at him in her customary manner. She mouths two words to him, which he quickly makes out to be, "Oh, David." He rolls his eyes. She really must learn some new lines.

At last, Sheffield places his wife just far enough away to look into her eyes. "Did those wicked men harm you in any way, my dear?"

"Nay, m'lord," she says. "They wouldn't dare, for I told them you'd surely sent someone to find us."

"Good for you!" replies Sheffield. "You showed some pluck, eh? Hah! Those men were fools, weren't they?"

David chimes in. "Indeed, m'lord, I'm told that *all* men are fools."

Lady Sheffield regards David impatiently, obviously taking his point. "Evidently, all *women* are fools, as well, Master Killigrew." She wipes her eyes with a handkerchief.

"Killigrew!" shouts Sheffield. "Yes, that's the name I heard. David Killigrew!"

Sheffield approaches the steps and reaches a hand up to David, who descends and allows himself to be embraced. "Young man, thank you so much. You are the one sent by my friend Lord Saint Ives, are you not?"

"I am, m'lord, as is my friend Chester here, lent us by the Tower Guard."

Sheffield glances behind him toward Chester. "Yes, thanks to you, as well, Goodman Chester." He turns back to David. "You must tell me how you two managed m'lady's safe return. But first: Who sent those men to abduct Lady Sheffield?"

David waits for Lady Sheffield to begin, as was the plan.

"Those terrible abductors," begins Lady Sheffield, "never spoke a word to me the whole time they were spiriting me away. And when *these* two heroic gentlemen stormed into our room—"

David clears his throat noisily, and Lady Sheffield takes the point at once.

"—I speak of Master David Killigrew of Oxford University, and Goodman Chester, soon to be of the Tower Guard. Well, when they stormed into our room, they thrashed the abductors to within an inch of their lives and chased them off."

Sheffield nods, and turns inquiringly to David. "But did you chase them off before discovering who'd sent them?"

Lady Sheffield interrupts. "They were ... mute," she says hesitantly. "They couldn't speak ... at all."

David rolls his eyes. It was not the plan to pretend the abductors were mute. *And now our feet are planted firmly in the shifting sands of liars.*

Apparently confused, Sheffield turns to his wife. "But how could you be sure they were *mute*?"

David rolls his eyes. "Perhaps your ladyship so concluded on grounds that they did not speak *even between themselves*."

Lady Sheffield nods. "Precisely. They passed each other short little ... notes."

Sheffield scratches his head. "They could *write*? Well, then, couldn't you have forced them to write down the name of their master for you?"

"No, m'lord," replies Lady Sheffield feebly. "They were not *written* notes ... really. They rather gesticulated to each other with their hands, as one sees such people do ... from time to time. To ... note things."

Good Lord! She's as bad at lying as her abductors were. David searches for something to say. "M'lord," he says, "if you'd been there, you would surely have noted how uncommunicative they were."

Sheffield begins to pace. "Perhaps they were sent by Lord Swindon," he muses.

"No!" say David and Lady Sheffield at the same instant.

Sheffield looks to each of them. "But how can you be sure?"

Before the others can embarrass themselves, Chester clears his throat. "They was wearin' a coat of arms, m'lord, that was not Lord Swindon's. That's how we knew."

"Oh?" says Sheffield. "Whose coat of arms were they wearing?"

"I've no idea, suh," says Chester, evidently dismayed that he'd brought attention to himself.

David saves the day yet again. "I could tell the difference at a glance, m'lord. I'd got a brief look at Lord Swindon's coat of arms when he came to visit your lordship here in Holborn but a few weeks ago ... you see."

"But what did the *abductors'* coat of arms look like?" asks Sheffield.

David is stuck.

Chester chimes in. "I didn't know whose coat of arms the abductors was wearin', m'lord, but I got a good look at it." He points a finger at his own chest, as though to draw the coat of arms on it. "It was full blown ... uh ... it had an escutcheon, m'lord, with ... uh ... three red lions ... rampant in fields of vermillion and scarlet, suh. With a red dragon."

"A *red* dragon?" says Sheffield dubiously.

David is quite sure that Chester is simply piecing together words he once heard used to describe a coat of arms, and that he has no understanding of their meaning.

"Yes, m'lord," says Chester. "On the right-hand side. Three ... red dragons." He ventures as an afterthought, "And irises."

"You mean, the French *fleurs de lis*?"

"Yes, m'lord." Chester's voice trails off. "Also ... rampant, suh ... as I believe. Also red."

"My word," muses Lord Sheffield, "the whole *thing* was red. It's a wonder you could make out any of the charges."

While David understands a charge to be an image appearing on a coat of arms, he's momentarily lost in contemplating what a flower might look like "rampant." Fortunately, Sheffield appears not to have heard that part of Chester's response.

"Well, m'lord," says David, "it was a bit more detailed than that. As you can see, however, our Chester is no expert in English heraldry. Yet, it was clear to me that the preponderantly red coat of arms was not Lord Swindon's, and that's what's most important."

"It certainly is," says Lord Sheffield, rubbing his palms together, as though relieved to learn that there would be no means by which the abductor could be tracked down. "Won't you two gentlemen come inside and celebrate Lady Sheffield's return?"

Chester shuffles his feet. "I, for one, m'lord, am required at the Tower of London just now."

"M'lord," says David with a smile, "as my lady's rescue was put into effect by the dedication and quick thinking of Lord Saint Ives, perhaps I might relay your invitation to lord and lady alike. And I will be sure to come along, so long as my studies permit."

Sheffield looks to his wife for agreement. "That would be fine, m'lord," she assures him. "Lady Saint Ives is one of my favorites."

"Well, that's settled then," says Sheffield. "Please extend our invitation to tomorrow's dinner."

"Tomorrow's dinner. Yes, m'lord. Thank you." David bows again, and watches the apparently happy couple hand off the horses to the servants and repair into the house. When David turns about, he's surprised to see Chester is already gone.

———————— ⊸∘⟨⟩∘⊷ ————————

ESTHER HAS WAITED patiently behind the hedge to witness the coming moment.

Constance, who's the only one of the household still out of doors, takes David by the hand and leads him toward the hedge that Esther's hiding behind.

Is it her imagination, or did the spicemaid just glance directly at her? She suddenly feels very foolish, as though she's been visible all along, and might as well not have kept the hedge between her and the Sheffields' front door.

"Listen, Constance—" David begins to say but, before he can get the words out, Constance plants a deep, ardent kiss on his mouth.

Esther bristles, but closely studies David's reaction. At first he resists rather strenuously, and her heart soars. But his resistance only brings out the spicemaid's sluttishness, and she grinds her breasts into him like a common strumpet until he slowly yields, eventually kissing her in return with nearly equal ardor.

That whoring spicemaid!

Once the kiss is done, David steps back and excuses himself. "I'm pleased to have returned you to your accustomed home, Constance, but you really shouldn't have done that." He glances about. "It's a good thing no one was by to see." She smiles at him smugly.

Esther watches as David mounts his horse, passes the hedge without looking her way (*thank heavens!*), and trots away down High Holborn toward the Ames's residence.

When she looks back at Constance, the impudent spicemaid is staring straight back at her through the hedge, smiling triumphantly.

Furious, humiliated, and heartbroken, Esther marches back the way she came.

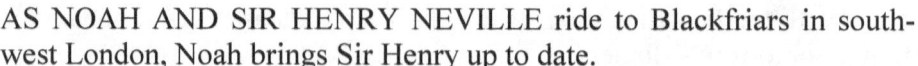

AS NOAH AND SIR HENRY NEVILLE ride to Blackfriars in south-west London, Noah brings Sir Henry up to date.

"What with the surviving Bennett twin in hiding," says Noah, "and Meyrick professing ignorance of his whereabouts, our investigation into the recent affairs of both victims came to a complete halt—until a letter arrived this morning from the Exchequer."

"What had he to say?" asks Sir Henry.

"He provided me with the name of someone who worked with the wardrobeman found murdered at Bowyers' Row. He should now be at the Queen's Wardrobe of Robes, which is right ... there!" he says, pointing to a stone building of several storeys.

Sir Henry chortles. "You needn't tell me where it is. When I was but a boy, I resided here in Blackfriars with my father, who was always penning some play or other. I spent many happy hours of study at the Wardrobe."

"Oh?" says Noah. "What skills did you learn there?"

"Disguise, for one. It's a skill I've used many times since."

Noah wonders how disguise might be used effectively by someone of such wide girth, but, before Sir Henry can elaborate, they arrive at the Wardrobe and hand off their horses to the stableman.

"Can I help you?" asks the gatekeeper as he's gently shoved aside from behind by an elderly man who squints as he bookishly strokes his beard. This must be Sir Buckley.

"Sir Henry Neville?" conjectures the nearsighted old man. "Is that Sir Henry?"

Sir Henry smiles at the man who must be an old friend. For once, Noah thinks, things will go smoothly.

"Sir Buckley," says Sir Henry. "It's wonderful to see you still in good health and still in charge of the King's Wardrobe."

"Ach!" the old man protests. "Not the whole Wardrobe, Sir Henry. I taught you when you were a small boy that the Crown's Wardrobe subsumes much more than clothing!"

"Such as all the weaponry and armor at the Tower of London!" recites Sir Henry proudly.

The old man laughs to see his pupil recall lessons learned so many years ago. "That's right. And it's the *Queen's* Wardrobe now. Come in."

Sir Henry points questioningly to Noah. "Oh, of course, Sir Henry. Your friend is also welcome."

Noah hands Sir Buckley the Exchequer's letter of introduction. "I'm very gratified you could accommodate us on such short notice, Sir Buckley," says Noah. "The Exchequer was kind enough to offer up your assistance in our investigation of the murders that took place at Bowyer's Row a few days ago."

"So you are Serjeant Ames, is that right?" asks Sir Buckley, as though this visit really should be about Sir Henry and not some barrister.

"Aye, Sir Buckley," says Noah. "I am much pleased to make your acquaintance."

"And I yours, Serjeant," says Sir Buckley, "especially as you have brought with you our old journeyman Sir Henry."

The old man turns at once to Sir Henry. "Let me look at you, Sir Henry," he says, as Henry takes a step forward.

The old man claps his hands in appreciation. "Sir Henry, you have grown stout and strong! Stout indeed!" Then he leans in and says, more softly, "We were all quite upset to hear of your father's passing. Please accept condolences from us, one and all."

"Of course," replies Sir Henry. "And your condolences are much appreciated, Sir Buckley. Permit me to reciprocate by assuring you that my father remembered his time at the Wardrobe as some of the most enjoyable of his long and happy life."

Evidently, the old man can barely contain his pride at hearing this, but instead of allowing himself to descend into fondness, he ushers his two visitors down the hall to a sizable dressing room at the rear of the structure.

In one corner sits a mechanical form in the shape of a woman's torso, presumably used to display a garment for its prospective wearer. The remainder of the room is occupied by storage trunks stacked four high, each trunk resembling a small coffin with a leather handle fastened to either end. Although they're filled with nothing heavier than clothing, Noah expects that each would need to be taken down, and eventually put back up, by two strong men.

"Now, where could Ralph have gone off to?" mutters Sir Buckley. "I told him this morning to meet me here a half hour ago." His eyes dart about impatiently. "I'm so sorry to waste your time, gentlemen. And I'm particularly disappointed in young Ralph, as Lady Thornbury is expected to arrive in less than an hour to try on a few gowns owned by Lord Thornbury's late mother."

"Which of these contains the lady's garments?" asks Sir Henry, finding a tag hanging from the topmost trunk on the nearest stack, and drawing it closer to read it. "Ah, it must be this one. 'Thornbury, Lady Agatha.' Was that m'lord's late mother?"

Sir Buckley smiles. "It was, Sir Henry."

"Well," says Sir Henry, "Serjeant Ames and I can easily take this down. Right, Ames?"

"Certainly, Sir Henry," says Noah.

"Oh, no!" says Sir Buckley. "I couldn't ask you gentlemen to take it down. It's much too heavy." But before he can finish protesting, Sir Henry and Noah firmly hoist the topmost trunk off the stack, and place it down on the wooden floor with a thump. Actually, it was far heavier than Noah expected, arousing his curiosity.

Sir Buckley, once again overcome with emotion to see his old pupil assisting him just as he had in the old days, draws Sir Henry away to exchange a private word.

Finding himself unattended, Noah's curiosity gets the better of him, and he lifts the latch on either side of the trunk, opening the lid just enough to let in a bit of light. He closes it gently.

"Very well, gentlemen," says Sir Buckley, "I'll summon Master Manager and tell him to bring Ralph along with him. Just a small caution, gentlemen: Master Manager has spent years reordering the storage system for all these many thousands of costumes and will not take kindly to any criticism on that ground ... or indeed any criticism at all. I'll return with him ... and Ralph ... in just a moment."

Noah clears his throat. "You shan't find Ralph with Master Manager, Sir Buckley."

The old man is brought up short, looking confused. "How could you possibly know that, Serjeant?"

"Because, unless I'm sorely mistaken, he's in this trunk."

CHAPTER 11

JONATHAN SETS OFF in search of someone who might know where the remaining Bennett is in hiding, or at least where the Bennetts went after leaving Gray's Inn some years before.

Though he left Gray's Inn a few months ago as a mere barrister and has returned this morning as a newly created baron, what he's found here has still made him feel rather insignificant in the scheme of things.

For one thing, his old room at Gray's looks quite small, compared to the way he remembered it. It's occupied by a snappish, rather sickly young barrister who appears to have taken up residence only recently. Among the few inanimate items in his room are Jonathan's old bed (which has somehow been rendered forlorn by his absence), an old and battered trunk, and a writing table too spindly to hold more than one book at a time. The books themselves are stacked on the floor in the form of a makeshift table, atop which sits a single candle in a base-metal candlestick covered with soot and hardened droplets of tallow. Evidently, this young man grew up even poorer than Jonathan and, thus far, has had considerably less success in persuading solicitors of his merit.

The young man professes to have no knowledge whatever that either the Bennett twins or Anthony Bacon ever resided at Gray's Inn, although he has vaguely heard of Anthony's brother Francis, though he can't place where.

After that mercifully short conversation, Jonathan cannot resist the urge to climb the stairs to Serjeant Ames's former rooms. The door is wide open, but there's no sign of anyone. Jonathan wonders what sort of barrister would be so careless of his things as to neglect to shut (let alone lock) his door. He gazes through the open doorway. Unfamiliar items of clothing are strewn across the bed. The chest has been moved across the room from its former place, and a large looking-glass in a wooden frame now rests upon it. It's as though the play's ended, the set's been struck, and all that remains is one bewildered player wondering whether the play he recalls was ever truly acted here, for not a sign of it remains.

He turns away and descends the stairs wondering whether he and Serjeant Ames could possibly be as important as now commonly believed, given that their former rooms (which were no doubt occupied by countless others before them) have rather coldly yielded themselves up to the next man in line without objection. He moves on to the building next door containing the rooms evidently once known as the "Inn of Glaucus."

Jonathan knocks on the door to Anthony Bacon's old room and an energetic young barrister opens the door. Before speaking, the man spies Jonathan's coat of arms and bows.

"Can I help you, m'lord?" he asks.

"Good morning. I'm Lord Saint Ives."

The man's eyes open wide. "Ah, yes, m'lord. Good morning. I've heard much about you. It is indeed a pleasure to make your acquaintance. I am Thomas Beadle, m'lord."

This fellow has a good bearing, which Jonathan finds a refreshing change from the taciturn fellow occupying his own former room.

"Beadle?" says Jonathan. "I've heard of you, I believe. I can't recall where, but good words came with your name."

Beadle beams with pride, but he speaks humbly. "I'm afraid you'll find no adventures in my past to compare with your own, m'lord. Yet am I pleased you've heard of me in a good vein. Won't your lordship come in and sit down?" He gestures for Jonathan to enter.

The fellow leads Jonathan to the best seat in the place, which is a comfortable upholstered chair. Though the other appointments are hardly sumptuous, they're of at least middling grade, with a few items showing an aspiration toward the better things in life. As Jonathan accepts the offer to sit, he nearly blushes to recall the creaky old thing he customarily offered visitors to his own room at the inn.

Jonathan gets right to business. "I am seeking anyone having knowledge of twin brothers, Cuthbert and Tobias Bennett, who were lodged here at Gray's some eight years ago and then left to establish practice in Cheltenham."

"Cheltenham?" says Beadle skeptically, as though it were located on the far side of the moon.

"A beautiful place," says Jonathan in its defense.

"Why, it's reputed to be one of the most beautiful places in Britain for a barrister to starve, m'lord. I've no idea how one could expect to build a practice out there." Beadle paces. "Let's see. M'lord suggests they left here eight years ago. I myself have no knowledge of anyone living here that long, though I've no doubt there are some still in residence from that time. Have you tried speaking with Master Treasurer? That is, if he can hear you."

"I suppose he's quite busy," says Jonathan. "If he hasn't time—"

"Oh, he has *time*," says Beadle, "and I'm sure he'd love to see you, m'lord. I meant only that he has trouble *hearing*."

"Oh, I see," says Jonathan. "Do you know if he's in his office today?"

"I expect he is," says Beadle fondly. "Master Treasurer rarely leaves the inn nowadays. He's advanced in years and cannot move about as freely as he once did. He's a good old man."

"Yes, he is that," says Jonathan, pleased to have a friend in common with this young barrister.

"Is there anything I can offer you, m'lord? I have some wine left from last night's dinner but, truth be told, it wasn't very good then and I doubt it's aged well overnight."

"I'll decline your offer of wine, Master Beadle, delectable though you make it sound. But, there's one more thing. I'm seeking out anyone with knowledge of Anthony Bacon's habits at the time he lived here at Gray's."

"Ah, yes!" says Beadle. "I've heard he occupied these very rooms some years ago, when he first returned from France. I don't know much about Master Anthony. I've heard far more about his younger brother Francis. Francis seems a rather brilliant fellow whom I would have expected to find greater welcome at the Queen's court than he evidently has."

"Oh?" asks Jonathan casually.

Beadle blushes and bows as though he's transgressed. "I regret deeply if I have spoken above my station, m'lord."

Jonathan breaks into honest laughter. "Thomas, my good man, please speak freely. I am myself of humble origins and encourage you to remember that not long ago I lived just downstairs."

Beadle's eyebrows shoot up. "In this building, m'lord?"

Jonathan shakes his head and tilts it toward his former rooms. "Next door."

"Indeed! Oh, not where that abstemious little miser lives now?"

"He looked rather poor and sickly to me," says Jonathan sympathetically.

"As for poverty, m'lord, he's known to have more money than anyone with equal experience at the inn, for all the good it does him. And if he's sick, it's because he's made himself that way by denying himself food, drink, pleasure … and friends."

"Sick at heart," muses Jonathan. "Perhaps the worst illness of all. Tell me whatever you know of Anthony Bacon."

Beadle shrugs. "Well, he's not returned here to the Inn of Glaucus since he moved out, m'lord, which is some eight years now."

Jonathan is surprised to hear such casual mention of the Inn of Glaucus, but suppresses his reaction. "What did you call it? 'The Inn of Glaucus'? What's *that*?"

"Well," says Beadle, searching his memory, "I don't rightly know. It's one of those old traditions everyone perpetuates even though nobody knows how it started. Denizens of the inn seem to believe that the name provides anyone who occupies these rooms with some sort of privilege to ignore his own mother. Honestly, I don't know why. I only wish my own mother were yet alive for me to cherish."

Jonathan nods. "Ignoring his mother is something Master Anthony has done all his life, and that rather fulsomely. And his mother is both wise and learned; in short, a mother most worthy of being heeded, evidently much like yours, may she rest in peace."

Beadle smiles. "And as is *yours*, m'lord, I'm sure."

Jonathan feels his smile wilt. "I'm afraid I know nothing of my mother."

Beadle's eyes flash at Jonathan's sad reply to what was intended as a cheerful comment. "I'm so sorry, m'lord. I just thought … well, you seem the kind of son who would naturally revere his mother."

Jonathan smiles wanly. "I suppose we'll never know." He changes the subject manfully. "Now, is that the only meaning you understand to the 'Inn of Glaucus'?"

"Aye," replies Beadle, "but now I know one thing more about Anthony Bacon for having met you, m'lord."

"And, for my sake, you'll forget it as soon as I leave. Do you know where Anthony Bacon is presently?" asks Jonathan.

Beadle shakes his head piteously. "I don't, I'm afraid. What little one hears of Anthony Bacon nowadays are mostly pathetic tales of ill health. But, as far as I know, no one knows where he's resided since Her Majesty ordered nearly everyone out of Essex House last winter, him included. If you have any connection with *Francis* Bacon, I expect he knows, but won't tell you. Otherwise, I'd seek out Master Treasurer."

A FEW MINUTES LATER, Master Treasurer admits Jonathan to his office at the inn. The curtains have been drawn snugly together, evidently long ago, as the place has not only a dim appearance but also a damp odor like a cave long undisturbed.

The old man dodders about, taking a long time to select a seat to offer Jonathan. He hovers ambiguously about a cushionless chair across from his desk, buried under stacks of loose, partially completed ledger sheets. He obviously wishes to offer Jonathan the chair, but lacks the vigor required to remove the papers. When Jonathan rises and places them on the desk, Master Treasurer appears greatly relieved and smiles at him through beclouded eyes before sitting at his own chair behind the desk.

"Lord Saint Ives," says the old man in an aged voice, "it is a privilege to have our humble inn graced with your lordship's presence, especially after your exploits and great success on the Queen's behalf."

Jonathan bows in his chair. "I count my days here as some of my most rewarding, Master Treasurer. And I see that the years between have treated you well. You're looking in the peak of health." This is a white lie, of course.

"Oh, no, m'lord," says Master Treasurer, "the years have been unkind to me. I seem to be suffering from all the tribulations of age at once. But tell me, m'lord, what is it that brings you to our humble dwelling?"

Jonathan shifts in his chair. When he resided at the inn, he would often tease Master Treasurer with some jest or other, but the old man's enfeeblement makes such commonplace banter seem impertinent, driving away all thought of levity.

"I'm seeking information about two gentlemen who resided here at the same time as I."

"Oh?" says the old man. "And who might they be?"

"Cuthbert and Tobias Bennett," says Jonathan.

A look of consternation comes over the old man's face, and he leans forward with his hand cupped by his ear. "Could you say the name once more, m'lord? Please pardon an old man's infirmity."

Jonathan leans forward and repeats the names.

The old man sits back in his chair and searches the ceiling above him. In a moment, he leans forward. "The last I heard of those two gentlemen—twins, weren't they?—they had moved on to Cheltenham. I recall that they left with a small remaining balance on their indebtedness to the inn. Nothing major. They were good lads, quiet. For a time, they wrote diligently, offering every assurance of their intention to pay, yet they never did, and their correspondence dwindled, first to a trickle then to nothing. Why do you seek them out, m'lord? I sincerely hope they do not owe your lordship money, for one might well despair of its being paid."

"Nothing like that," says Jonathan. *Where to begin?* "The Bennetts were among the residents of Gray's Inn who spirited Master Ames out of London after he made his argument in the Court of Oyer & Terminer in the Lopez case."

The old man smiles and claps his hands joyously. "The 'jesters,' they were called. And *you*, Lord Saint Ives, were chief among them. 'Robin Hood and his merry men,' I believe Lord Essex called you all." His mirthful expression drops away, replaced by grave contemplation. "I had a miserable few days after that, as Lord Essex demanded to review the inn's records of Master Ames's admission to practice, but I refused to yield."

"Admirable on your part, Master Treasurer. As you may recall, I was prepared to argue for clemency for Doctor Lopez when Lord Essex barged into the room, hauling you with him."

"Yes, that's true," says Master Treasurer. "I recall you and all your friends so beautifully attired, and the newly made *Serjeant* Ames in his silks up on the dais with Lord Burghley and Sir Robert. Serjeant Ames came down into the well and argued face-to-face with Lord Essex. I was never so proud of you all as that day. And who should then appear but the Queen of England! I was dashed. I'd never seen her before so close up. I thought I was about to be accused of something awful and my life would be over, but instead Her Majesty saved the day!" He raises his right fist and pumps it lightly in restrained imitation of a victorious soldier.

Jonathan smiles fondly on the old man. "For all but Doctor Lopez, yes, she did, sir. Your memory is perfectly intact, I see." He returns to the matter at hand. "But those two fellows I was asking you about—the Bennetts. Well, I'm afraid their story has a sad ending, at least for one of them. You see, one was murdered at Bowyer's Row recently."

Master Treasurer's eyes grow big, and he inhales in horror. "Oh, my word! I'm sorry to hear it. But one survives?"

"Aye," replies Jonathan.

"Where is he now?"

Jonathan smirks. "I was hoping *you* could tell me. We have no eye-witnesses to the murder, though there was another victim killed at the same time and place whose murder is being investigated at this very moment by Serjeant Ames and Sir Henry Neville."

There's an urgent pounding at the door. When Master Treasurer struggles to rise from his chair, Jonathan gestures for him to remain seated, and answers it himself.

It's Beadle, the young barrister inhabiting Anthony Bacon's old rooms. Plainly surprised to see Jonathan answering the door, his eyes open wide and he bows, extending his hand to Jonathan with a sealed note addressed to "Jonathan Hawking."

"Good afternoon, m'lord," says Beadle. "Someone—I don't know who—slipped this note under my door but a few moments ago. As you can see, it's addressed to your lordship. As you said you would be going to see Master Treasurer, I thought to find you here, and am pleased to see that you have not yet left the inn."

"Thank you, Master Beadle," says Jonathan.

Beadle bows and disappears down the hall.

Before returning to Master Treasurer, Jonathan opens the letter. In a neat hand is written today's date and:

Master Treasurer knows this handwriting. Meet me today at Drapers' Hall at one of the clock, sharp. Life or death.

Come alone.

That leaves Jonathan a little more than an hour to get there. *Why must the writer not be seen? Because he's in hiding and under threat of death? And, what's this? Master Treasurer knows his handwriting?*

Flustered, Jonathan returns to Master Treasurer, who now sits at his desk examining a file. "I was just rereading some of my old correspondence with Bennett," says the old man.

Jonathan surprises him by darting 'round the desk and gently taking the file from the old man's palsied hands. Master Treasurer's letters are atop the file, so he flips through a few pages until he finds another handwriting. Here he spies a letter begun with the greeting, "Dear Master Treasurer." He compares the writing to the words "Master Treasurer" on the note he was just handed. It's the same. He thrusts the note before the old man for confirmation.

"Are these in the same handwriting, do you suppose?" asks Jonathan.

The old man brings his eyes so close to each handwriting sample as almost to touch them with his nose. "They are the same," says the old man. Just to be sure, Jonathan runs his finger down to the signature, which belongs to one Cuthbert Bennett.

Cuthbert Bennett knows I'm here and wishes to see me.

Jonathan excuses himself and runs to horse.

CHAPTER 12

NOAH AND SIR HENRY briefly examine the fully clothed corpse while it's still in the trunk. Noah slides his hand around the back of the head and finds a single indentation in the skull, but no gouging. So, it was one hard blow, with a rounded bludgeon of some kind. The fatal wound is still moist with coagulate gore, and the body retains some of its natural heat, so the injury could not have been inflicted more than a couple of hours ago. Noah wipes his hands on a rag, and together he and Sir Henry put the body back as they found it and close the trunk.

Sir Buckley rushes back into the wardrobe chamber passing words with an irritated-looking fellow.

"I've told you nothing about why you've been summoned, Master Manager," says an exasperated Sir Buckley, "because these gentlemen *asked* me to tell you nothing."

Spying the trunk that's been taken down from its stack, the manager eyes Noah and Sir Henry suspiciously. "No doubt these gentlemen wish to take me to task for some perceived inconsistency or other defect in my storage system." He turns proudly to Noah, then Sir Henry, obviously unsure which of the two visitors he should be addressing. "Do you gentlemen have any *idea* how many costumes are stored in this one building? Thousands. And that's to say nothing of the plethora of additional items located at every one of the royal palaces. Well, gentlemen, do you wish to complain about some inconsistency in my storage technique?"

"Yes, we do," says Noah, "a rather grave one at that." Sir Buckley and Sir Henry both regard him curiously. "We saw several of your assistants walking freely about the building as we entered."

The manager seems suspicious. "That's where they're *supposed* to be," he sniffs.

Noah sternly beckons the manager with a crooked index finger. The manager approaches cautiously.

"Do you mean to say," asks Noah, "that your assistants are supposed to be free to roam the premises?"

"Why, of course, sir!" says the manager, regarding Noah dubiously.

Noah nods sagely. "I was under the impression that your system requires them all to be stored in trunks."

The manager's eyebrows rise, as though Noah's lost his mind.

Noah flips open the lid of the trunk at the manager's feet. "Like this one," he says.

The manager gasps and his eyes go agog. He crouches before the casket and turns the dead man's face towards him. "Why, this is Ralph! Poor sweet Ralph!" He rises. "What have you done to him?" demands the manager, the blood draining from his face.

"Precisely nothing," says Noah. "I am Serjeant Noah Ames. Sir Henry and I are here on Queen's business, so please answer our questions. Can you manage that?"

The manager nods, stricken by the death of his assistant and sufficiently admonished for his impertinence.

Noah begins questioning. "When did you last see Ralph alive?"

"Ten o'clock sharp."

"Are you aware that one of your assistants was recently murdered at Bowyer's Row?"

"Yes," says the manager apprehensively, as though the loss may somehow be blamed on him. "Goodman Teller," he confirms.

"Goodman Teller worked here at the Wardrobe?" asks Noah.

The manager gulps and nods. "He was a good friend of Ralph's there," he says, pointing to the dead man in the trunk. He brings his hand up to his forehead, and woefully sucks in a breath. "You don't suppose—"

"Master Manager, we're not prepared to suppose anything," replies Noah, "but perhaps you could tell us what *you* suppose." Noah offers him a seat.

The manager plops down with an air of resignation. "That's two now," he laments. "James Teller and Ralph. Death has taken them like a thief in the night."

Noah sits in a chair facing the manager's, and leans in sympathetically. "Did you know Teller well?"

The manager shrugs and sighs. "I knew him here at work. Same with Ralph. Very little otherwise. I think they lived together."

"Where?" asks Noah, noticing a startled glance from Sir Henry. Evidently, he's involuntarily thinking the same stupid thing. *Bugger, bugger, bugger.*

The manager searches his memory, but shrugs again. "I don't rightly know. We weren't friendly outside of the Wardrobe. They'd never been to my home, nor I to theirs."

"What do you know of Teller?"

The manager strains to recall. "Well, he mentioned that he was applying for an alternative situation—one paying a great deal more than he earned here."

"When did he mention that?" asks Noah.

"No more than a few months ago, I should think."

"Did he mention whom he'd be working *for*?"

"No, sir, although, truth be told, I doubt I was paying him much heed."

Noah regards him askance. "And why would that be?"

"It may seem unlikely to you, sir, but if you'd heard as many will-o'-the-wisps as I have, *you'd* stop listening, too. Sooner or later, it seems every one of them will tell me what he'll do as soon as his ship comes in—which is always imminent. It seems every one of them has a rich uncle (some an aunt) who's about to die and leave his dearest nephew a mattress full of coin. Either they're fooling themselves about their relatives' wealth or they're descended from the sturdiest misers ever made, as their rich aunts and uncles never seem to die. They just linger on and on, exhausting what little money they have on foolishness (such as rent and provisions, no doubt). And, when at last they go, they've already dispensed every farthing ever to pass through their grubby little fingers. If you look about, you'll see many assistants with gray hair still working for a living, a common symptom of poor men with rich relatives, if I may observe."

Noah finds the observation amusing. This fellow started off a bit rough, but he's come about. "But you mentioned that Master Teller was speaking of *alternative employment*, not rich relatives."

"Aye, sir," says the manager, "though I can't seem to recall ..." His voice trails off. He snaps his fingers. "Teller mentioned that he'd worked briefly for the Exchequer years ago." He shrugs. "Perhaps he was thinking of returning there."

Noah sits up. Now this is a spark! *But why would the Exchequer dispatch me to the Wardrobe when he'd formerly employed Teller himself? Why not just tell me what he knows?"*

"Did he say what he might be doing for the Exchequer?" Noah asks.

"No, sir, but Teller was good with numbers. Good with people, too. It's a shame he had to ... go the way he did." The manager risks another glance at the corpse in the trunk. "Ralph, as well. Good lads."

Noah rises, bows respectfully to the manager. "One last thing," he says. "Do you have any idea who could have done this?"

The manager purses his lips thoughtfully. "Just about anyone at the Wardrobe, I should imagine. These rooms are not locked during the day, nor are the trunks. Once someone makes it past the gate, I'm afraid he's pretty much got the run of the place."

"And the gatekeeper?" asks Noah. "Does he maintain a record of comings and goings?"

Though the manager is about to speak, instead he turns to Sir Buckley, who replies for him. "The gatekeeper knows on sight everyone who's supposed to have entry to the Wardrobe. There are too many comings and goings for him to record every one. But I've already asked him if there were any unusual visitors this morning."

"And?"

"No one unexpected … except the puritan constable."

———⇒∘⊂⊘∘⊂———

JONATHAN STABLES HIS HORSE, and finds the front door to Drapers' Hall wide open. He passes into a noisy common room that, although quite large, can barely contain the crowd of clothmakers and merchants bustling about. Many are attired in doublets, with the most important-looking bedecked in the unique livery of the drapers' trade.

Though Jonathan's attire has no obvious place among the assembled, his rich robes and coat of arms raise not a single eyebrow. The bustle about him continues unabated as he discreetly glances about for the surviving Bennett, or anyone who might have summoned him here on Bennett's behalf. Other than Bennett, Jonathan has no idea whom he's looking for or what to expect, so every miniature scene in the pandemonium demands his attention equally, leaving him both disoriented and exposed.

A young clerk arranging a stack of loose papers nearly runs into him, but veers off in time to avoid a collision. A momentary frisson of fear rides up Jonathan's back, as this *might* be the man who lured him to this place. *Am I in danger?* Jonathan asks himself. *Am I intended some harm?*

Two well-dressed men engage in an animated disagreement over the quality of a bolt of cloth, tugging at opposite ends of the selvage to make their points. Listening in on the conversation, Jonathan is unsurprised to learn their argument is centered around money.

Espying a notice board on a wall some distance away, Jonathan ambles toward it. Words are boldly lettered atop the board: "The Worshipful Company of Drapers." Below the lettering is an untidy accumulation of official notices announcing meetings and charitable events (some in the past) organized by the establishment. A few notices are partially hidden by later ones pinned over them.

Below the space reserved for official notices is a large area devoted to notes among members. Evidently, they're not particularly private, as many are legible in full to the casual passerby, while others are folded over—albeit only once—with the name of the intended recipient scrawled on the outside.

Jonathan vaguely recognizes an older gentleman standing by the notice board, although he cannot recall where he's seen him. At the same instant, the man sees Jonathan and a look of surprised recognition appears, followed by a discreet smile at the corners of his mouth. Noting Jonathan's noble raiment, the fellow bows, and Jonathan nods in return; neither makes any attempt to converse.

On the notice board, at roughly the height of Jonathan's eyes, he finds a folded note with his initials on its outward face, written so recently that the black ink still glistens. He removes it from the board and opens it. Its message is brief and alarming:

You were followed.

At that moment an uproar breaks out by the entrance.

"You have no business here, young man! You must go at once!" pronounces an official-sounding voice so loud it must have been intended to attract general attention.

"Remove his mask!" shouts another urgent voice.

There's a sudden surge in the voices and a sound of panic. "Get down! Grab him, sir! Take his pistol!"

At the center of the noise, what appears to be a deranged escapee from Bedlam Asylum aims a long pistol directly at Jonathan's head. Before Jonathan can react, he's tackled by the fellow he recognized mere moments ago.

A shot rings out, its *boom* intensified by the sheer walls and ceiling.

A missile thwacks into the wall a few feet above Jonathan. Tiny chinks of plaster explode from the point of impact, stinging his cheeks with tiny pebbles. The fellow who tackled him, similarly showered with white pebbles, leaps to his feet with a determination not often seen in someone his age.

"He's getting away!" shouts a voice near the entrance. "Grab him!"

Jonathan stands and brushes himself off, as his unknown savior draws a pistol and bolts off, lunging out the front doorway and quickly disappearing from view.

A man in Drapers' livery approaches Jonathan. "My word, that was a close call, m'lord!" he says, bowing respectfully. "I trust you are not hurt," he says hopefully.

Jonathan is chagrined. "No, sir, except in my pride. I seem to have been tricked into walking into an ambush." He surveys the many drapers gawping at him. "My only regret is that my coming here has unwittingly endangered your members and disturbed the peace of this fine establishment."

"Tut, tut, m'lord!" says the master, turning to his brethren. "What do you say, boys? Anyone hurt?" A roar of nays fills the hall. The master takes a step closer to Jonathan. "I am master of this place, m'lord." He glances about at the many excited conversations. "I'm afraid this violent business has distracted everyone from ordinary affairs. Would you care to join me upstairs in a spot of sherris, m'lord?"

Jonathan politely declines. "While I'm grateful for your hospitality, Master, I fear I haven't time. But, by your leave, I would like to remain here long enough to meet the fellow who saved my life upon his return ... if I may."

"Why, yes, of course!" says the master, looking a bit confused. "What fellow would that be, m'lord?"

Jonathan shrugs. "Well, I didn't get his name, but he was standing right by the notice board when the pistolier forced his way in."

The master obviously has no idea whom Jonathan means.

Jonathan feels a bit embarrassed. "The one who ran out the door in pursuit of the pistolier," he says.

Befuddled, the master turns to the assembled. "Did anyone see who ran after the gunman?"

"*I* saw, Master," says a young journeyman stepping forward, his voice ringing off the ceiling like the sound of a pipe. "It was the one they call Jacob."

"Jacob?" replies the master dubiously.

"Yes, Master. You know, the one who helps out ... with deliveries."

A momentary distaste runs across the master's face before he breaks into a smile. "Well, of course. Master Jacob."

As if summoned by name, that selfsame Jacob marches in through the front doorway, securing his pistol in the leather case strapped to his torso. He stops short, dismayed to see all eyes on him, and walks toward the master and Jonathan.

"M'lord," he says, bowing to Jonathan, then turns to the master. "He still 'ad the mask on when he disappeared from view, Master. Too much of a lead for me to catch up with 'im, sorry to say."

Jonathan smiles. "Thank you, Jacob," he says. "You appear to have saved my life. I am—"

"I know right well who y'are, m'lord." He turns about and announces in a loud voice: "Everybody! This is Lord Saint Ives, who saved the lives of thousands of our boys in Ireland by stoppin' a spy from deliverin' Mountjoy's battle map to the filthy rebels!"

Quite a tumult follows, with much applause and many huzzahs.

When the assembled quiet down, all eyes are on the master who, evidently seeing what's expected of him, bows deeply to Jonathan. "M'lord, welcome to our humble hall." He turns to Jacob. "Master Jacob, would you please go and see what deliveries need to be made today and report back to me?"

Though Jacob regards the master skeptically, he bows and leaves him alone with Jonathan.

"I expect you will wish to speak with Master Jacob before leaving," says the master, "but ... well," he continues hesitantly, "Master Jacob is a Jew, after all."

Jonathan skeptically arches an eyebrow. "He does not dress as a Jew," he muses aloud. "Still, I scarcely see—"

The master hastens to add, "Oh, please don't misunderstand me. *I* don't mind his being here at the Drapers', but there are those who do. It would be most embarrassing for me personally if your lordship were to be seen leaving the great hall with a Jew, rather than the master."

The faces of Jews Jonathan has grown to love pass before his eyes: his wife Jessica, her father Noah, Doctor Lopez. Though he refuses to be enlisted in denying them their due, he recognizes the need for a minimal concession. "Although I see your concern, sir, and shall of course be pleased to repair with you into the livery's offices, I obviously need to move without delay. I would be much obliged if you would dispatch someone to escort Master Jacob to the rear door, where I shall take my leave of you."

The master only half-smiles at Jonathan's half-concession to racial prejudice for, whatever escort he chooses, word is bound to circulate that his lordship left with the Jew.

AS JONATHAN STEPS OUT into the alleyway behind Drapers' Hall, Jacob greets him with an unfamiliar saddlebag, which Jacob opens to remove a modest cloak.

"I've taken the liberty," says Jacob, "of bringin' your lordship a partial disguise. As I was unable to catch your man, I thought it would help your lordship to avoid bein' recognized again in this part of town, at least for now. This cloak was lent me by one of the drapers for that purpose."

Jonathan doffs his rich cloak and hands to it Jacob, who neatly folds it and places it respectfully into the saddlebag.

"Now, if you'll follow me, lordship," says Jacob, leading him west through a few grassy fields and streets of packed dirt.

"Where are you taking me?" asks Jonathan.

"Why, to your lordship's mount! I assume you stabled your horse in Old Jewry, sir. Am I right?"

"Yes," says Jonathan, "but your route seems needlessly complex. After dismounting, I simply walked east on Lothbury Street to Drapers' Hall."

"And promptly got shot at!" says Jacob humorously. "Whoever took that shot at your lordship is unlikely to know the route I'm takin' ye."

"And what route is that?" asks Jonathan.

"Well, sir," says Jacob, "I dunno if I could recite it for ye step by step. These alleyways and fields don't all have names, leastways names known outside the ward."

"So, you're a local lad, eh?"

Jacob smiles at Jonathan with a twinkle in his eye. "Yes, m'lord, but not the only one." Without explaining, he points up ahead. "Right up there is Coleman Street. That leads south to Old Jewry. Coleman Street would be the place m'lord is in gravest peril from a gunman. So, if it's all right with you, we'll be cuttin' through some of these alleyways. Oh, don't fret, suh. I know 'em like the back o' my hand." They muffle their faces in their cloaks and dart south across the wide expanse of Lothbury Street.

As they dodge down a long, narrow alleyway west of Old Jewry lined by houses that seem neglected near the point of collapse, Jonathan stops.

"What's wrong, m'lord?" asks Jacob with the strangest expression on his face.

Jonathan glances about, and echoes of memories emanate from every window. A woman's voice, singing in a foreign tongue.

"I – I feel as though I've been here," says Jonathan.

Jacob solemnly casts his eyes down.

"I *have* been here," says Jonathan, "haven't I? Long ago." Unsure whether his legs can carry him any further until he solves the present mystery, he sits on a makeshift chair that seems to have been discarded in the alleyway.

"If I may ask your lordship a question or two ... beyond my station?"

"Of course, Jacob."

"Does your lordship come from humble beginnings about which ye know little?"

"Aye."

Jacob clears his throat, and his voice is dry when at last he ventures to speak. "Is your lordship's Christian name 'Jonathan'?"

"'Tis," replies Jonathan. "But how could you know?"

"And is your lordship's surname 'Hawkins'?"

"'*Hawking*,'" says Jonathan, correcting him gently as if speaking from a dream, as this old fellow seems to know more about him than he does about himself.

"Was your lordship reared by a clever fellow named 'Graves' and his goodwife—a sweet woman and an excellent cook?"

Despite himself, Jonathan feels his heart must break for all that once was—for all that is lost forever. "Aye," he croaks, barely getting the sound out.

Jacob sweeps his hand before him to indicate the alleyway and the humble buildings that surround it.

"This ... this *place* ... is where your lordship comes from," says Jacob.

Jonathan glances about the alleyway with new eyes. "This place?" he mutters with equal parts incredulity and certainty that Jacob is telling the truth.

"E'en this," replies Jacob, laughing gently at the humble surroundings. "This, and no other."

CHAPTER 13

THE WARDROBE'S GATEKEEPER runs his stubby finger down the list of this morning's visitors. Evidently, he's a better recordkeeper than his superior realized. "The puritan constable arrived at eight thirty, sharp," he says, holding his finger on the entry. He looks up at Noah and Sir Henry. "The Wardrobe don't get many puritan visitors. Stands to reason, I suppose. I've 'eard they don't like fancy dress, or theatrical costume. Is that true?"

Sir Henry exchanges a glance with Noah, and prepares to reply, but the gatekeeper holds his hand up as he catches sight of a deliveryman stepping up to the Wardrobe door with a portfolio of some kind under his arm. "Got yer pass, Edmund?" the gatekeeper asks.

The newcomer removes an official-looking document from a small pouch attached to his portfolio and exhibits it to the gatekeeper, who returns it and waves him in.

"You were sayin' somethin' about puritans, Sir Henry?" says the gatekeeper.

"Yes. I think they don't like much of *anything*."

Noah nods in agreement. "Do you have a precise record of when the constable departed?"

The gatekeeper moves his finger rightward. "Precisely ten after nine, suh. And he never left my sight."

Noah's surprised. "He never went inside?"

"No, suh. Leastways, never further inside than where yaw standin' right now."

Noah turns to Sir Henry and shakes his head. "Ralph was last seen alive at ten o'clock." He turns back to the gatekeeper. "When did he arrive this morning?"

"It was nine thirty, suh. He was an hour late to work."

"Was he often late?"

The gatekeeper shakes his head emphatically. "He'd have been discharged long ago, suh. Wardrobe won't put up with tardiness."

"Did Ralph seem upset or preoccupied when he arrived?"

The gatekeeper rubs his eyes, and thinks a moment before speaking. "Now you mention it, suh, he seemed—I don't know—a bit confused. I chalked it up to his gettin' no sleep, or maybe just bein' afeard to be reprimanded for his tardiness."

"Were you on duty without a break from eight to ten this morning?"

"Aye, suh. Got a break at eleven."

Sir Henry perks up at this. "Who took your place?"

"No one, suh. The gate's locked for that quarter hour."

"Was it still locked when you returned?"

"Aye, suh."

"Who else has a key to open it?"

"No one but Sir Buckley, suh. At least, that's what I been told. And, look here, gentlemen. If yaw thinkin' mebbe Sir Buckley would let somebody in while I'm on a break, best think again. I've seen 'im take a visitor to task—and no mistake—for raisin' a fuss when he couldn't get in while I was away on break. Sir Buckley's a real stickler for the rules. It'd be easier to break in through a window than to get through this gate while I'm on break."

"Has anyone *reported* a break-in?" asks Noah.

"None, suh."

"Thank you, Gatekeeper," says Noah, leading Sir Henry out to the street.

As they wait for the stableman to return with Bucklebury and Sir Henry's stout roan, they agree that they have no basis to suspect any particular person of the latest murder.

Sir Henry asks: "What individual wrote to you on the Exchequer's behalf to tell you where Ralph worked?"

Noah removes the letter from his pocket and shows it to Sir Henry. "It's from the Chancellor of the Exchequer himself: Sir John Fortescue."

"Hmmm," says Sir Henry, "a prickly old fellow, not to be approached unannounced. Still, we must ascertain what more he might know about these two dead fellows. I propose to write to him this afternoon for an appointment and beg for a prompt reply."

"Very well," says Noah. "Will you and Lady Anne be joining us for supper tonight at High Holborn?"

Sir Henry smirks. "Wouldn't miss it. Since I told Lady Anne that Jessica is with child, she's been clamoring to see her."

"Good. And it will give us a chance to confer with Lord Saint Ives. I wonder what he's learned."

AS JONATHAN WATCHES IMPATIENTLY, Jacob removes a long pipe from his cloak, stuffs the bowl with coarsely cut tobacco, and knocks at the door of a nearby house where he's evidently known to the occupant, an old woman wearing a coarse hairnet who shoots Jonathan a suspicious glance. Jacob and the woman enter the house briefly, and Jacob emerges alone, puffing his lit pipe, and holding in his hand a long, slowly burning length of hemp cord.

"What can you tell me of my parents?" asks Jonathan, at last.

"Old Graves and his wife never told you anything?"

Jonathan shakes his head forlornly. "They pretended not to know anything. I could see that they did, but I never pressed them. I knew they loved me, so I guessed they were withholding it for my own good."

Jacob smiles. "Yer a good lad, m'lord. I think ye got the nut of it there. But also, I think they wanted ye to think of *them* as yer real parents, and didn't want to complicate things in yer mind. Now, where to begin?"

Jacob ponders, savoring the smoke.

"Names are always a good start," suggests Jonathan. "What was my mother's name?"

"Well, you've gone and asked about the parent I knew less well, m'lord. She was introduced to me as 'Emily,' short for 'Emeline,' which she said was the name given her by the nuns."

"*Nuns?*" asks Jonathan.

Jacob nods. "At the orphanage in"—he lets go a puff of smoke—"*Flanders*, as I remember."

"So, she was reared by nuns," muses Jonathan. "And her family name?"

Jacob shrugs. "I know only the one she got by marryin' yer father, and that was 'Hawkins'."

"Where did they meet?" asks Jonathan.

"Right here in London, if you care to know."

Jonathan is surprised. "What a strange expression! If I care to know? Of *course* I care to know. I wish to know everything."

Jacob regards Jonathan skeptically and takes a long draught on his pipe, blowing out a long puff of grey smoke. "Maybe old Graves was right not to tell ye *some* things. I'm not sure it's meet ye know everythin' *I* know about yer parents. It might change the way ye think of the world ... of yer noble *self*, even."

"I barely know *what* to think of myself," protests Jonathan, "as I know so little about my origins. Please, hold nothing back."

"You're sure, suh? I'd hate to be taken to task for tellin' ye things that make ye … uncomfortable."

"How did my mother and father meet?"

"They were introduced by a woman who goes by the name Yetta."

The name hits Jonathan like a thunderbolt. "Yetta?" he asks incredulously. "That same Yetta who brought Noah Ames to England?"

"*Serjeant* Noah Ames, the Queen's own barrister!" Jacob's hearty laugh quickly turns into a chesty cough.

Though Jonathan fails to see the humor, Jacob apparently regards it as something of an imposture for someone of humble origins to achieve greatness in England. Or perhaps Jacob is laughing because Noah was known by a humble Hebrew name before the Queen gave him the famous English name by which he's now known.

"Aye," says Jonathan, "that is the same Noah Ames of whom I speak."

"Then, m'lord," replies Jacob, "I'm also speaking o' the very same Yetta, though she woulda brought yer mum here some years after Menachem, er … Noah Ames." He turns his face askew, as though doubting that Jonathan understands the significance of this information. "You know Yetta? I think she's still about."

"I'm sorry to inform you," says Jonathan hesitantly, "that Yetta has passed, though I never had occasion to meet her. But she was known for transporting to England young Jewish people suffering difficult circumstances abroad." He kicks a small stick on the ground, momentarily lost in thought. At last, his gaze returns to Jacob. "So … I'm a Jew?"

"Well, I suppose that depends on who y'ask. If you ask *me*, then, yes, you're a Jew—because your mother was—but most Gentiles would say no."

"Because my father was not," Jonathan says with certitude.

"That's correct, m'lord. Oh, but you need never worry about *my* tellin' anybuddy, as I've no intention to. More'n happy to keep it to meself. Your lordship's got some well-earned advancement in this kingdom, and I hope ye thrive in it."

"And my father?" asks Jonathan.

As the fire in Jacob's pipe dies down, he chokes, and spits a small black ember onto the pavement. He empties the pipe onto a bare patch of ground, stamps out any remaining embers, stuffs the bowl with fresh weed, and relights it with the burning hemp. "Now you're askin' about yer dad, who's somebuddy I knew well. Your father was *Peter* Hawkins. You recognize the name 'Hawkins'?"

"No," says Jonathan.

Jacob's eyebrows rise in surprise. "Well, I guess ye *have* heard the name 'Francis Drake'?"

Jonathan snorts. "Of course. Everyone knows *that* name."

"A lotta people know the name 'Hawkins,' as well. There was a time not long ago when the Hawkinses owned just about every important ship at Plymouth, 'cept those belongin' to the Crown. Francis Drake was related to the head of the family, whose name just happened to be 'John Hawkins.' Sound familiar? Your lordship's one of 'is name-sakes, 'course. So, you're related to John Hawkins and to Drake, as well."

Jonathan's interest is piqued. "Did you know John Hawkins?"

"I met 'im a couple times in his younger years. 'Course, he became quite an important person later on, knighted after the Spanish Armada and all. By then, he'd naught to do with me. Died only a few years back." Jacob takes another long draught on his pipe.

"Did you know Sir Francis Drake?" asks Jonathan.

Jacob laughs so hard he gags, and smoke belches out of his mouth like a furball from a cat.

Jonathan smiles. "Did I say something droll?"

"No," says Jacob, regaining his breath. "Just never get used to hearin' Drake called '*Sir* Francis'." He cocks his head as though granting a concession. "'Course, he *earned* it. Never was a seaman did more to save Queen and country. But I knew 'im from when he was called a 'pirate' (though Her Majesty called him a 'privateer'), even 'slaver' (though no one ever dared call 'im that to 'is face). To yer dad and me, he was just 'Cap'n Drake.' But to get back to yer dad *Pete*—"

"Yes," says Jonathan. "What was he like?"

Jacob smiles warmly. "He was a good man. *Too* good to become a 'great person,' as he used to call the social climbers in his family—though he did put in for a commission after he met yer mum. Unfortunately, he passed on before he could get it. Before that, he was just a sailor's sailor. Never cared for his family's money or property. And his religion was *seafarin'*, so he managed to stay out of the religious fights the English were havin' with each other. Yer dad and me were close mates. We'd sign on for the same voyages, always for Drake. Well, *almost* always; a seaman's gotta pay the rent when he's on land, same as everybody, so sometimes we'd just take whatever job come up.

"Yer dad was known for bein' the best weapons handler there was—in or out of Her Majesty's service. He could use any weapon like it was made for him. Cannon, bow and arrow, cross-bow, long sword, short sword, musket, pistol, spear ... brickbat, if that's all he had." He chortles. "And, if he had nothin', he'd bash in a man's head with his bare hands. I seen him do it more than once. He'd only one weakness."

"What was that?" asks Jonathan.

Jacob lowers his voice, as though to avoid being heard speaking ill of his friend. "Ill temper, sometimes. Once he got goin', there was no stoppin' 'im. Messed up his better judgment from time to time. But *I* could always calm 'im down, make 'im see reason. Graves could, too. After a few voyages, Graves'd join yer dad and me, and we'd watch out for each other." He takes his pipe from his mouth and resumes his former affability. "See any of yer dad in ye?"

"More than I dare to admit," replies Jonathan.

"Good with weapons, are ye?"

Jonathan nods. "Not as good as Peter Hawkins, evidently, but fairly good. I must confess that I also share his occasional ill temper. Fortunately, I've been educated as a barrister, so now my anger is expressed more in words than blows."

Jacob regards him sagely. "Careful about the urge to deliver *real* blows, m'lord. It'll sneak up on ye. Well, to get to the point, in—1577, I'd guess—Peter met yer mum. She was a beautiful woman, very ... honest and plainspoken ... and she brought out the very best in old Pete. She told him about bein' mistreated at the orphanage, and his heart went out to her. He'd always been kind and generous to his friends but, for her," Jacob rolls his eyes, "he just couldn't do *enough*. He soon realized he couldn't live without 'er." He chortles. "You shoulda seen Graves's jaw drop when I told him Pete was gettin' hitched. But yer mum loved him so much. We was all happy for 'im. He'd never had anyone like 'er in his life.

"One day, word reached us that Drake was preparin' to raid the Spanish gold trade *west* o' South America, on the Pacific side. Till then, nobody'd bothered the Spanish galleons till they reached the Atlantic, so this voyage promised a good chance of catchin' 'em unawares, and we knew there'd be plenty of boot for the crew at the end of the sail. The three of us signed up for Drake's flagship, *Pelican*. It was durin' the voyage, o' course, that Drake gave it the name it's become famous by: *The Golden Hind*.

"Before Pete left for Plymouth, he collected every debt owed to 'im.

He scraped together every bit o' gold and silver he could, and taught Emily to hide it so's only she could find it. He even changed Emily's family name (and *yours)* just enough so no creditors could claim it. It wasn't so much; mebbe enough to keep body and soul together for a couple o' years, but he figured she could take in sewin' and add enough to make it last till he come back. Unfortunately, he never did."

"Did he succumb to illness?" asks Jonathan.

"Nope," replies Jacob, "though I seen lotsa good men go that way on the voyage. But not Pete. He went down fightin'. The thing Pete loved most in the whole world was stealin' gold from the Spanish, and whenever he got his chance, he took it. We captured the Spanish galleon *Concepcion* after a long pursuit. Pete was in the boardin' party, and got shot by one of the Spanish crew who'd been ordered by his own officers to stand down. Pete died on the spot. It was a dirty shot and a dirty shame. Drake ordered the man who shot 'im to be arrested, tried, and keel-hauled. After that, the *British* crew started callin' the ship what the *Spanish* crew'd called it all along: *Cacafuego*, Spanish for *Fireshitter*. Drake docked to let off passengers, officers, and crew, somethin' the Spanish would never 'ave done if the tables had been turned.

"After that, we came back to England by the *long* way. We were the first ever to go 'round the world under one commander. Magellan's crew woulda done it fifty years earlier, but he died *en route* in the Philippines. Anyway, when we got back to Plymouth, there were only sixty of the *Hind's* original crew left alive, including Drake himself, Graves, and me. We'd been lucky to survive, though the boot wasn't quite what we'd hoped. The Crown took most of it. I suppose that was only fittin', as the Queen footed the bill for most of the expedition. Graves and I collected Pete's share and turned it over to Emily.

"Little did we suspect when we left that yer mum was with child, namely *you*, m'lord. By the time we got back, m'lord was two years old. Graves wept when he saw ye the first time—he loved yer dad so much— and felt awful that yer dad didn't live to see ye, nor for you to see him. And I suppose mine own tears weren't far behind."

Jonathan poses the question he's contemplated most often all these years. "Did my mother give me away because she ran out of money?"

"No, she would never do that," says Jacob, sighing. "She got the consumption. She was just too weak to care for ye any more. She died a few months later, but not until she turned you and 'er remainin' money over to Graves and his wife. You mentioned that you were called to the bar, so I expect you went to university."

Jonathan nods. "Oxford."

"Well, Pete's share of the expedition is where the money come from. Graves would never spend a farthin' of it on 'imself or 'is wife, even if they was starvin'." Jacob empties his pipe with a nail and puts it away. "You wait here, m'lord. I'll go fetch yer horse. I was nearby much o' the time you was growin' up. So, if y'ever wish to know more about yer beginnin's, I'll be pleased to tell y'all I can remember."

"I shall take you up on that kind offer, Jacob. Thank you for saving my life today, and for the personal history lesson. How may I reach you?"

"Just pin up a note in the Drapers' Hall," says Jacob, "or ask for old Jacob. If ye can't find me, m'lord, I'll find *you*."

CHAPTER 14

AFTER MISSING HIS ONLY SHOT at Lord Saint Ives, the masked pistolier bolts out of Drapers' Hall and sprints west down Lothbury Street.

Though there was much gun smoke and shouting at the Drapers', no one but a single old man interfered with either the attempted shooting or the gunman's escape. Now the same old man who knocked Lord Saint Ives out of the line of fire is in hot pursuit of the pistolier, keeping pace with him—even *gaining* on him slightly. Just as the pistolier nears panic, the old man runs short of breath and stops, watches after him a short while, and reluctantly turns back.

The gunman, himself winded, slows to a trot. As he passes the high-walled graveyard behind an old church, Cuthbert Bennett thrusts his leg out and trips him. The gunman tumbles forward, striking his head hard on the pavement, bloodying his mask and leaving him motionless.

Cuthbert glances around. As there's no one about to see, he drags the insensate pistolier behind the high wall of the graveyard, where a grave gapes wide in anticipation of a burial the following morning. He drags the unconscious man behind an unkempt hedgerow, drops him face-down onto a patch of dirt next to a well, and tosses the spent pistol out of reach.

He turns the gunman face-up, binds his hands firmly together with segments of rope, and then does the same with his feet. Now that the gunman can't move, Cuthbert takes a good look at his face and recognizes him to be Meriton, one of the conspirators responsible for his brother's death.

Cuthbert raises a bucket of water from the well, immerses a cloth he often uses to wipe his mount, and brings the sopping cloth back to the prostrate Meriton. He seats himself securely on the man's chest, knees planted heavily on his shoulders, and wrings out the cloth, raining rivulets of water onto Meriton's face.

At first, Meriton's eyes open woozily. Then, alarmed to see Cuthbert, he strains to sit up, but soon realizes he's bound and immobile.

Cuthbert brings his face down toward his victim's.

"Why did you try to shoot Lord Saint Ives?"

"Let me up or I'll tell ye nothin'," Meriton snarls.

Cuthbert slaps his face. "Oh, you'll answer me," he says confidently, drawing a long, dangerous-looking knife from his scabbard, "because, if you don't, I'll kill you right now. Don't make me repeat my question."

"Why not?" says Meriton with open disgust.

Cuthbert flicks the knifepoint quickly across Meriton's cheek, and the blood begins to trickle. "Ask me 'why not' again. I dare you."

Meriton whimpers, evidently realizing that he's misjudged his assailant. "No need for bloodshed," says Meriton sulkily.

Cuthbert flicks his knife across the other cheek with the same result. Now there are two rivulets of blood, one flowing gently down either side of Meriton's face, all the messier for mixing with the copious water. "Don't say anything other than to answer my questions. I know you've been looking for me and following Lord Saint Ives. I also know you killed my brother and that fellow from the Wardrobe outside the church, so believe me when I say I won't hesitate to kill you. *Now, why did you try to shoot Lord Saint Ives?*"

Horror finally comes over Meriton's face. "I took a shot at him because he's helpin' *you*."

"Oh? And how would you know that?"

"Because you sent him a note today askin' 'im for help."

"And how would you know *that*?" demands Cuthbert sternly.

"I was watchin' 'im when he got the note at Gray's Inn, and I followed him to Drapers' Hall."

"So, you were spying on Lord Saint Ives to begin with," Cuthbert declares.

Meriton makes no reply.

"How did you know the note was from me, and that it asked him to meet me at Drapers'?"

"I'd rather not say," says Meriton.

Cuthbert twirls the knife and smiles darkly. "I see I haven't yet made my point."

But before he can bring the knifepoint to bear again, Meriton blurts out, "I forced that barrister to show me the message." His breathing is fast now, on the point of blubbering.

"The barrister upstairs?"

"Aye."

"So, you followed the messenger up to his rooms?"

"Aye. I went up there just after Lord Saint Ives left for the treasurer's office."

"Why did you kill my brother Tobias?"

With his cheeks bloodied, Meriton's contemptuous smile is especially hideous. "Because he was a *buggerer*!" He practically spits the words into Cuthbert's face. "The law woulda got 'im, anyway."

Cuthbert drags the knifepoint lightly across Meriton's forehead, whose face is now a bloody mess, forcing him to squint to see through the blood seeping into his eyes. Unless Cuthbert's mistaken, sweat has begun mixing in with the water and blood. "That's *not* why you killed him. Is it?"

"Good enough reason," Meriton pouts, offering no further motive.

"Whom else are you following?" demands Cuthbert.

"Me? No one."

"And your friends, whom else are *they* following?"

"I dunno," Meriton says dully.

"I don't believe you," says Cuthbert after a moment's thought, and twirls the knife in the air.

"If I tell ye any more, they'll kill me," Meriton protests in near panic.

"And if you don't, *I'll* kill you," says Cuthbert. "Tough situation for you."

Suddenly, an unexpected, infuriating sneer of superiority returns to Meriton's face. "Just what d'ye think you're playin' at?" he asks. "As soon as you let me up, I'll tell 'em where you are, and they'll kill ye."

"That's precisely what *I* was thinking," answers Cuthbert regretfully.

He deftly places the knifepoint a couple of inches behind Meriton's chin, and jams the blade up through his tongue and palate hard into his brain. Meriton stiffens, twitches once, and moves no longer, his eyes wide open but sightless.

Cuthbert wipes his blade on the grass. He drags the corpse to the open grave and tosses it in, grabs a shovel, jumps down into the pit, and carefully conceals the body under an even layer of soil. Climbing out of the grave, he returns to the well, where it takes several bucketfuls of water to clean the blood and soil from his face, hands, and boots.

He conceals Meriton's long pistol on his person as well as he can. Once he's satisfied he can pass unnoticed on the street, he prepares to slip out of the cemetery and lose himself in the foot traffic.

Just as he's about to step off, however, he realizes that he left the mask on the ground where he first tossed his quarry. He picks it up and examines it. It's a hideous affair, the mouth twisted into a lunatic snarl revealing rotted yellow teeth. One eye is white, the other bloodshot. Both are wide open, ringed in a bruised black, and sunk into an imitation of rotting skin. He flings the mask toward the hedgerow in disgust, hard enough to lodge it deep in the greenery.

But he unknowingly misses his mark and, as he steps out into the street, the bloody mask falls to earth, where it lazily wafts wherever the breeze takes it.

———————◦◦◦———————

IN THE UPSTAIRS PARLOR, Lady Jessica gazes out the window at the gnarled fields of late autumn. While Esther looks on patiently, Marie begins the urgent repair of a split seam in Esther's evening frock.

Marie, with a moue of irritation, decides to reply to Esther's earlier remark. She removes the sewing needle from between her lips, stabs it into the pin pillow, and turns to Esther indignantly. "You most certainly *shall* meet with him, young miss! He'll be arriving shortly, and you shall be awaiting him at the door."

Esther rises in protest. She pouts, and in her huskiest voice she pronounces, "But, Mistress Ames, David doesn't *love* me! At least, not *only* me!"

Marie looks to Jessica for assistance in persuading this silly young thing of the importance of being seen by the right men under the right circumstances, but Jessica seems lost in a world all her own. She stands blankly at the window, overlooking the leafless trees behind the house, her hands folded over her swollen belly. Marie cannot tell whether she's holding her belly protectively or out of some other preoccupation. Either way, it's easy to see what's on the girl's mind. But that will have to be addressed later.

For now, Marie says to her, "M'lady, have you anything to add that might put Esther's mind at ease about Master Killigrew's intentions?"

Jessica turns toward her, glassy-eyed, as though previously unaware that her stepmother and cousin were even in the room.

Marie raises an eyebrow expectantly.

"Master Killigrew's intentions?" asks Jessica as if in a dream. "I assume they're the same as every other man's." She smiles absentmindedly and pats her belly. "'Women grow by men,' they say."

Esther gasps.

Marie rolls her eyes. That was about the most unhelpful thing Jessica could say, and she's alarmed by her unaccustomed thoughtlessness. "*M'lady*," Marie says sternly, "please go to my room, dear, where I may attend your ladyship more closely."

Without so much as a glance at Marie or Esther, Lady Jessica floats off impassively in the direction of Marie's room.

Marie sighs sympathetically, and places Esther's dress on the settee. "Esther, dear. I simply don't have time to do this just now. I've brought the needle and thread to stitch the seam. Do you suppose you can manage it without me?" She rises to go, as she's confident of Esther's skill with a needle.

"Certainly," says Esther. "But—Mother?"

Marie stops in her tracks, dreading the next question.

Esther asks, "What's wrong with dear Lady Jessica?"

Marie sighs loudly. "Nothing I haven't seen many times, my dear, and nothing that need concern *you*. At least, not now."

"But—"

Marie cuts her off. "It's all to do with having a child, my dear. We'll speak of it when the time comes. Now, attend to your sewing and get dressed … And *please* try to open your heart to Master Cheerful. He's everyone's favorite, you know." With that, she disappears after Jessica.

Esther turns the frock over in her lap to find the broken seam. She scoffs to herself, remembering the spicemaid ardently kissing David.

"*Everyone's* favorite, indeed."

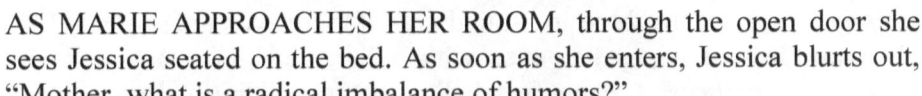

AS MARIE APPROACHES HER ROOM, through the open door she sees Jessica seated on the bed. As soon as she enters, Jessica blurts out, "Mother, what is a radical imbalance of humors?"

"Imbalance of humors?" Marie echoes. "It's something the physicians say when someone is ill."

"But what does it mean?"

Marie looks about to be sure she's not overheard. "Between us, I think it means, 'we have no idea what's wrong with this patient.'" As Jessica remains obviously unsatisfied, Marie elaborates. "According to the physicians, there are four humors in the body: black bile, yellow bile, phlegm, and blood. A patient's attitude supposedly depends upon which is predominant in her body."

"And a *radical* imbalance of humors?"

"Well, I suppose that would mean someone's quite ill," she replies, then scoffs. "But I don't believe it. This 'humor' business is a lot of rot with a pedigree. It's been about for a thousand years, but that doesn't mean it's true."

"Still," Jessica urges hesitantly, "the physicians believe it."

"Perhaps because they know no better." Marie regards her step-daughter skeptically. "What's all this rubbish about humors?" she asks, though she strongly suspects where all this is leading.

Jessica is close to tears. "Lady Sheffield says that three women in ten die in childbirth." She runs to Marie and buries her head in her shoulder. "O, Mother, I do not wish to die! What good is a child to me if I cannot live to nurse it and help it grow?"

"There, there, dear," Marie coos. She shakes her head mournfully. "No one's dying. My goodness! You should be dreaming of first steps, little shoes, and Christmases, and instead your mind goes straight to dying. *Pish!* It was *irresponsible* for Lady Sheffield to say such things. As she's borne no children of her own, she's merely repeating what she's heard from others."

Jessica pleads. "Oh, please don't fault dear Lady Sheffield, Mother. She told me only because I asked her repeatedly, and she *warned* me that she was just saying what she'd heard."

Marie plops Jessica back onto the bed, and kneels before her. "Jess," Marie says in her most reassuring voice, "it's not three in *ten*. I suppose it's more like three in a *hundred*. Oh, and *those* three …" Her voice trails off and she shakes her head with pity. "Why, there are women in this realm who give birth while having nothing to eat, who live in barns with pigs. Filth everywhere. And rats! I should think that accounts for a *preponderance* of the three-in-a-hundred—if there even are so many."

Lady Jessica wipes her eyes with a handkerchief. "But … some-times … *sometimes* … even fine ladies die in childbirth. Even *queens* have been known to do so."

Marie regards her skeptically. "Sometimes, a fine lady will die when a statue falls on her. Yet, do we live in fear of statues? People die crossing the street all the time, yet we don't cower on the roadside for fear of being squashed, do we?" She tries to bring some cheer. "Why, we'll get the finest midwife in London. I know her personally. She's scrupulously clean. She helped to deliver all my children … except Stephen"—her voice drops to bare audibility—"who arrived like a thief in the night."

Jessica bursts into childlike laughter despite her fear, and replies with a runny nose. "It's so comical to think of Baby Stephen as a thief!"

Marie is pleased to have hit at last on something that works, even if inadvertently. She strokes Jessica's hair. "Indeed, he was the most welcome of tiny thieves! Just as the future Baron Saint Ives or his lovely sister shall be. And we'll even make sure to have Aunt Beth preside over the proceedings. What do you think of that, dear?"

But instead of smiling at the mention of Beth, Jessica falls to weeping again. Marie sits beside her on the bed and holds her tightly, every heaving sob shaking her to the core.

When Jessica calms down at last, she says, "Aunt Beth was unable to save my mother—her own cousin. I do not wish to die at Aunt Beth's hands, too!"

Marie was dreading this. "You mustn't think that way, Jessica," she says. "Aunt Beth loved your mother as a *sister* more than a cousin. I've heard she tended your mother day and night for two months. If she couldn't save her, then no one could have." But she can see that her plea on Beth's behalf has failed, and Jessica's supplicating expression nearly breaks her heart. Marie sighs. "I don't know *how* I'll tell Beth, but if you still don't want her there when the time comes, then she shan't attend—and there an end."

Jessica hugs Marie as though she's been reprieved from a death sentence.

But Marie is dismayed. Except for her favored midwife, there's no one she wants to have in attendance more than Beth, who has an exceptional reputation for caring for the sick, especially new mothers.

"Now," says Marie, "go and wash your face." But before Jessica can go, she adds sternly, "And one more thing." Jessica turns to her. "Kindly assure your cousin Esther that it is *not* David's sole intention to get her with child—which is practically what you told her!"

Jessica nods with a smile before running off.

Marie resolves to discuss all this with Noah as soon as the occasion presents itself.

CHAPTER 15

AS ESTHER SENSES that David Killigrew will be arriving early for supper, and as she's been instructed to greet him, she quickly finishes mending the seam of her frock and returns to her room to wash and dress.

Her reflection in the glass is well groomed, but there's something severe in her expression that Mistress Ames will not wish to see, so she practices smiling pleasantly, as she's had enough experience in polite company to know that a false smile will often pass as the real thing, or will at least be more favorably received than an honest pout.

She calls a familiar kitchen maid into her room to check her appearance before preparing to greet visitors.

"Why, Miss Esther," says the maid, as though responding to an absurdly easy question, "you look *lovely*! Any man who's not a fool would fall in love with you straightaway. 'Course, with that comely face, you could hardly look otherwise." Catching a glimpse of her own rather plain face in the glass, the maid smiles wistfully. "Women like me have to put in a lot more effort."

"Don't be silly, dear," says Esther reassuringly. "You have a very pleasing aspect."

"You think so?" asks the maid hopefully.

"Certainly. And you cook like every man's dream."

Before the maid can reply, Esther hears rapidly approaching hoof-beats, and knows in her bones it's David. She goes to the front door where, through the small side window, she sees that the sun will soon complete the sweep of its arc. The visitor takes a surprisingly long time to appear, considering how fast his horse was approaching. When at last the knock comes, Esther puts on her best smile and opens the door.

It's David, as she expected. He hesitates outside, a chill breeze blowing his long blond hair about his face, rustling through his clothing. Though he's come down from Oxford, he's dressed more like a wayfaring soldier than a student. With a strange hesitancy, he looks Esther up and down, as though—despite her smile—he's unsure how he'll be greeted.

"Master Killigrew," she says with feigned equanimity, "won't you come in?"

David takes two modest steps into the hallway and Esther closes the door behind him.

"Good e'en, Miss Ames," he ventures, handing her his scarf and cloak. "How have you fared these past weeks?"

"Oh, very well, master," she says, accepting his things, "and thank you so much for coming down from Oxford to sup with us this evening." She climbs the stairs to hang them in the upstairs closet. Turning the corner, she peeks down at him and finds his blue eyes following her like forlorn puppies. Descending once again, she asks, "Would you care to rest until supper, master? You've come such a long way."

He poses a question of his own. "Is Serjeant Ames at home, Miss Ames ... Esther?"

"The Serjeant is yet away, Master Killigrew," she replies reservedly. "He is expected within the hour. Is there something I may do for you in his absence?"

He looks longingly into her eyes. "You could repair privately with me to Serjeant Ames's study to discuss ... matters between us ... if you would."

She arches an eyebrow innocently. "And what matters might those be, Master Killigrew?"

Glancing about, David seems confident he won't be overheard here in the hallway, but he lowers his voice nonetheless. "Why, matters of *love*, Esther. Have your feelings for me spoiled so soon after seeming so fresh but a month ago?"

"'But a month ago'?" echoes Esther. "'But a month ago' you hadn't disappeared for two days without explanation, only to return with Lady Sheffield and her trull of a spicemaid."

"Trull?" he says skeptically. "'But a month ago' you wouldn't have known the word. Pray, who taught it you?"

"Thank you for noticing the improvement in my English," she replies in genteel manner, then snaps back, "But what difference does it make where I learned the word? Her reputation is well known. She's a harlot."

David's eyebrow shoots up. "A harlot? Yet another new word in your lexicon. Please, Esther, that is insulting."

"To whom?" she asks. "To you or to her?"

"To her, me, and *you*, if you must know, but most unbecoming to you, as it comes from your mouth."

"So, you will *defend* your lady fair?" she says pugnaciously.

"Just whom are you characterizing as my lady fair?"

"Your spicemaid!"

"*My* spicemaid? For your information, young miss, I *have* no spicemaid, nor have I a harlot nor a—" Esther's earlier word escapes him.

She supplies it. "A trull."

"Yes … whatever that may be. I told you that I will explain all, as soon as I'm released from my oath of secrecy."

"And to whom did you swear this oath?" demands Esther suspiciously.

David sighs. "I told you in my letter: I cannot say."

"Well, when *can* you hold forth on the topic, Master Killigrew?"

He stares despondently at his feet. "As soon as I'm released from my blasted oath."

Beside herself with frustration, Esther decides to test his honesty. "Well, perhaps you can tell me *this* without breaking your oath: Did you—or did you not—kiss the spicemaid *on the mouth* upon your return to Holborn?"

He looks at her, confused.

Gad! she thinks. *He doesn't even remember! Do his kisses mean so little to him, that mean so much to me?*

At last it dawns upon David's face that he recalls the spicemaid's kiss. He looks to Esther so imploringly that it nearly breaks her heart. But she's hardened it, having sworn to herself never to relent unless the matter is resolved.

David does not reply, but droops miserably.

"Go to your room *at once*, Esther!" pronounces Mistress Ames. The lady of the house has appeared out of nowhere, having made no sound of approach. Yet, somehow, there she stands, not three feet behind Esther. "This is not how we treat guests in this house."

———————— ⟶∘◖⟿∘◗⟵ ————————

ESTHER RELUCTANTLY PREPARES to obey her mistress, her face a study in mixed feelings. David finds embarrassment in her expression, to be sure, and anger, but mostly … just plain hurt. He desperately wants to take her in his arms and explain where he was for those unaccounted days. But he can do so only if he's released from his oath.

And what of the spicemaid's kiss? How can he ever explain *that* away? He'd neither initiated it nor sought it. It had been Constance's idea alone. But he *had* kissed her back. Not at first, perhaps, but eventually. Perhaps Esther is right to be hurt; perhaps he doesn't deserve her love.

As Esther turns to go, David feels the heat rise in his face. Red-faced, he now must face the mature Marie Ames, whose expression is inscrutable. She's angry, to be sure, but seems somehow touched with sympathy for him. Mostly, she just seems weary. She sighs. "Cheerful, you're not resembling your nickname," she observes.

"No, madam. How could I be cheerful? I know not how to tell Esther I love her without having Lady Sheffield's stupid spicemaid thrown in my face. I fear—I fear Esther will never be persuaded of my love."

"You give her—and yourself—insufficient credit, David. She *already* loves you, or she would not be so hurt." She regards him askance. "Did you *really* kiss that girl so recently?"

"I do not mean to pardon the unpardonable, Mistress Ames, but the girl seized me and planted a kiss so ardent that it could not be denied without my shoving her violently away, which would have been ungallant on my part. It happened in broad daylight by Sheffield House. As I thought no one would be the wiser, I *stupidly* thought it simpler to kiss her back—so it would *end*. It went no further than that, madam, and Esther must have been spying to see it."

"Spying? From where?"

He shrugs. "The opposite side of the road, perhaps." An alternative hiding place occurs to him. "Perhaps the same side of the road, but the opposite side of the *hedge*."

"David, I do not ask you to break your oath, but I need you to tell me if it was imposed upon you by Lord Saint Ives. I have *some* sway with his lordship."

She's right, of course, it *was* Jonathan, and David weighs whether it would be so horrible to tell her by *whom* he was sworn. Would telling only *that* truly cost him his immortal soul? Could he possibly regret it longer than he would losing Esther?

"Mistress Ames," he replies at last. "There are but three things I may tell you, and I swear to you on my soul they are true. First, I love Esther with all my heart and would gladly forsake all other women forever for her sake. Second, I did not dally with the spicemaid in that instance, nor barely spoke with her during my absence. Finally, I will do my best to prevail upon the person who demanded my oath to release me so that I may explain to Esther the true reason for my absence. I ask only one thing from you."

Marie cocks her head inquiringly.

"I ask," he says, "that you tell Esther nothing of what I have just told you." He frowns. "This is *my* problem, and only I can mend it."

She regards David thoughtfully, and accedes with a nod. "Very well," she assures him. "But you'd better do it soon, before Esther's doubts give rise to a settled disappointment."

NOAH RETURNS TO THE HOUSE to find its large supper table crowded with his nearest and dearest. Before the corpulent Sir Henry Neville is a bottle of sack and a large cup. Seated next to her husband, Lady Anne seems to have found a bottle of white wine nearly as much to her liking. Indeed, she seems pleasantly in her cups even before soup is served.

Mistress Ames is flanked by the young ladies of the house. Lady Jessica is unaccompanied. (Jonathan appears to have been delayed in appearing, and Noah wonders what that might signify.) Beside Esther sits David Killigrew, fresh from Oxford. And next to David is Arthur Arden.

The din of large pots and spoons emanating from the kitchen suggests that five servants at least are bustling about supper.

"Sir Henry, would you be so kind as to recite the prayer?"

"Certainly. But before doing so, I must tell you that Lady Anne and I are required up in Billingbear for a few days."

"All is well, I hope," says Noah with concern.

"Oh, yes, yes," replies Sir Henry. "We have some guests coming who are only to be in Oxfordshire for a short while, and we must keep up traditions, mustn't we?"

"Naturally," says Noah. "But what of our appointment with the Chancellor of the Exchequer?"

Sir Henry nods emphatically. "Yes, I've thought of that. He's granted permission for you to call upon him at any time during the next three days. He'll be working at the Pell Office at Westminster the whole time. If I were you, I'd take along the heroic Lord Saint Ives. Sir John is much enthralled by tales of derring-do."

Noah smiles. "Well, in that case, we'll just have to muddle through during your brief absence. Now about that prayer ..."

Sir Henry leans forward and places his hands together. "Bless, O Father, Thy gifts to our use and us to Thy service; for Christ's sake. Amen."

"Amen," say all the assembled.

Sir Henry draws a robust swig from his cup, and muses aloud. "Ames, I don't see how an unreformed Hebrew such as yourself can say 'amen' to a prayer to Jesus Christ."

It's become a ritual for Sir Henry to bring this up when dining with Noah, perhaps because he so enjoys Noah's stock answer. "Why, Sir Henry, we were through all that years ago. Although you've just recited the prayer, you've failed to notice that it's addressed to our mutual God 'for Christ's sake.' I think we owe God a great debt of gratitude for Jesus and the message he preached whilst he lived. If only more Christians would live by his words than die by them, we'd all live in a better world."

"Amen to that," says Lady Anne, noticeably slurring her words.

"Easy on the wine, dear," mutters Sir Henry.

"You can tell me to stop drinking," she says under her breath, "when I can tell you to stop *eating*."

Noah suppresses a laugh, and turns to Jessica. "What's detaining Lord Saint Ives, m'lady?"

"I'm sure I don't know, Father. I was about to ask you the same thing." There's something unsettled in her voice, though Noah cannot fathom what it is.

The soup is taken away, and the main dish served, a roasted beef. As they complete the course, hoofbeats are heard slowly approaching down High Holborn.

David, as though recognizing the horse's gait, rises from the table and bows, politely asking pardon to go out of doors to greet Lord Saint Ives. Noah surmises that he needs to ask Jonathan something private that cannot wait.

———————⊸₀⊂⟐⊃₀⊂———————

AS DAVID STEPS OUT of the back door, he's surprised to see that darkness has already entirely overshadowed the autumn evening. Though a biting breeze has blown away most of the clouds, there's no moon as yet, and the stars alone are too weak to illuminate Jonathan on horse- back, who appears to David as a slowly approaching silhouette outlined by a few points of light on the horizon behind him.

"Permit me to assist, m'lord," says David, extending his hand for the horse's reins.

"David," says Jonathan as he dismounts, "it's good to see you, old man."

There's something in Jonathan's voice that suggests he deliberately took the long way home—to contemplate something of importance, no doubt.

"Did you learn much about the murders today?" asks David, leading the horse to the stables.

Jonathan replies as though nothing could have been further from his mind. "I learned quite a bit about *myself* today, although I also learned that Cuthbert Bennett is trying to contact me, and that, at least today, I was being followed."

"Followed?" says David. The idea puts him on his guard, and suddenly the peaceful night seems full of threat. "By Cuthbert himself or someone else?"

"Not sure."

As they approach the stables, the Ames's stableboy emerges and takes the reins from David's hand.

"Before you go inside, m'lord," says David, "would you please come away from the house a moment. I've something urgent to ask of you."

"Of course," replies Jonathan, accompanying David back toward the road.

"Well," says David, squinting across the way toward the unfinished foundation of Jonathan's new town home, "Esther won't so much as talk with me unless I tell her what I was doing when I disappeared a few weeks ago."

"Disappeared?" says Jonathan. "Oh. You mean the whole Sheffield business?"

David's eyes, having adjusted to the dark, catch furtive movement among the new foundation. Probably a fox.

"Aye. After Chester and I delivered Lady Sheffield and her spicemaid to her town home, Chester rode off. Once I was alone with Constance, she seized upon me."

"*Seized* upon you?" snorts Jonathan. "You mean, she fell to the ground in a fit of *grand mal*?"

"What? Of course not. She—kissed me." David takes a half step to the side, so he can see past Jonathan and keep an eye on the … fox, or whatever that is.

"How awful for you," Jonathan says sardonically.

"And Esther saw it," adds David.

"*Oh*," says Jonathan, beginning to see the problem. "Esther? What was she doing there? Visiting Lady Sheffield?"

"I've no idea how she saw it, but she did."

"Is that all?" asks Jonathan skeptically. "Well, Esther ought to know that *any* woman is privileged to kiss a fellow on the cheek without his being called to answer for it."

"I ... kissed Constance back," David confesses, "on the mouth."

Jonathan's eyebrows rise. "The plot thickens," he says, a bit annoyed. "But what has this to do with me? I'm tired and I'd like to—"

"I need to assure Esther that I wasn't off on some overnight tryst with Constance."

"And you want me to release you from your vow of secrecy so that you may assure Esther that you've never had more than—what—a *daytime* tryst with the girl?"

Now it's David who's annoyed. "This is serious, Jonathan. It was *you* who sent me off to retrieve Lord Sheffield's wife because she'd been abducted. As it turned out, she hadn't been abducted at all but—in a good turn for *you*—I brought her back nonetheless. Now I need a good turn from you. I need you to relieve me of my oath of secrecy."

"David," Jonathan says, shaking his head in amusement. "Women are too easy for you to get. I had to *earn* my lady's love, and it very nearly cost me my life. All you need to do is walk by women, and they swoon."

"What are you talking about?" says David. "They don't."

"Oh, but they do! And your eventual wife, whichever unfortunate she turns out to be, will just have to understand that. Her rivals will be after you as long as you live."

"What has this to do with relieving me of my oath?"

"Precisely my point. It has *nothing* to do with it. I sent you off to fetch Lady Sheffield—"

"And her spicemaid," David interjects.

"And her spicemaid," Jonathan concedes with some irritation. "But here's where my reasoning becomes subtle, so kindly pay close attention. *I never asked you to smooch her spicemaid. In public, no less.* Esther's not cross with you for disappearing for a few days. She suspects you've been tupping the maid! And you can't lay that carcass at my doorstep."

David pouts. "Well, I've *not* been tupping the maid."

"Look, David," says Jonathan calmly, though exasperated, "Lord Sheffield's marriage and future happiness depend upon his never learning that his wife was in the process of abandoning him. If you tell Esther—well, you know how women are. They tell each other *everything!* If you tell Esther, they'll all know in a day's time, if it even takes that long."

"But it's only important that it never be learned by Lord Sheffield!" David protests.

Jonathan shakes his head dismissively. "I won't have him play the fool in that fashion, with everyone knowing but him. Why don't you just tell Esther the same lie you told Sheffield? That you saved Lady Sheffield from her abductors."

"And make a fool of Esther, rather than Sheffield?" shouts David.

"Keep your voice down," growls Jonathan. "That could be heard in the house, David, and you'll embarrass Serjeant Ames." He regards David skeptically. "It's hardly a sin to repeat a white lie if telling it wasn't a sin to begin with. And you told it to Sheffield with only the best of motives. But, you're right, I can't let you say even that, as it's sure to get the whole pot boiling."

That makes no sense to David, and he's approaching wit's end in this argument. Even if he weren't, he's too distracted to continue, as the dark figure across the way just dodged from one hiding place to another behind a completed section of the foundation. And it's no fox. It's a man—and a fit one, by his movements.

David leans into Jonathan and whispers. "Don't turn 'round, Jon. It appears you're *still* being tailed."

Jonathan opens his eyes wide, but makes no sound.

David continues. "He's hiding behind a section of your new house. Stay here a moment, and I'll roust him for you. Better draw a dagger, but keep it out of the light so he can't see it glisten. I'll drive him toward you."

David slips behind the Ames's house, circles around the other side, and steals across the way to approach the intruder from behind, if he hasn't already slipped away. He hasn't. David slowly eases up behind the intruder with his dagger drawn. When he's reached a spot perhaps six feet behind the intruder, he says in a conversational tone, "Inspecting the masonry?"

Before he's got even the first word out, the intruder gasps and leaps like a surprised rabbit over the wall in Jonathan's direction. Though Jonathan momentarily gets a hand on him, he was evidently mistaken in assuming himself the intruder's target, as the intruder quickly shakes off Jonathan's grasp and bolts for the Ames's rear door.

AS THE PLATES ARE CLEARED AWAY, Noah hears what appears to be an angry shout from David outside, which quickly recedes. Waiting only for his guests' cups to be refilled, he resolves to offer a toast or two to distract their attention from the angry discussion between Jonathan and David.

Noah rises with a cup of wine in his hand. Though Marie tries to catch his attention, Noah is far too full of bonhomie this evening to be discouraged from toasting his ladies.

"I would like to offer a toast to the happy progress of Lady Jessica's future family." Before he can finish, Jessica rises from the table, begins openly weeping, and runs upstairs.

Marie glares at Noah as though this is somehow his fault. To distract the company from Jessica's unexpected departure, Noah raises his glass again, this time in Esther's direction. "Let us toast the steady progress of a newfound friendship between two of our most precious young people, even though one is outdoors. To David and Esther."

"*Cheerful* and Esther!" shouts Sir Henry, and downs a cup of sack in their honor.

Trembling, Esther bursts into tears. She staggers to her feet and follows her cousin up the stairs.

Marie looks at Noah with daggers. "Pardon me, Serjeant Ames," she says impatiently, and follows her weeping charges up the stairs, their sobs still audible to all.

Despite herself, Lady Anne bursts into besotted laughter. "I'm sorry," she says, barely able to breathe. "Noah, you should see the look on your face!" Sir Henry and Arthur politely cover their own faces to conceal their laughter. "Perhaps you should spend more time at home. A few domestic events appear to have escaped your notice."

Noah downs the full cup in his hand and takes a deep breath. "Well," he says to his dwindling company, "it appears as though I've been playing the jester. What shall be our next form of entertainment?"

Lady Anne sits up with a smile. "*Wrestlers!*" she shouts like a king in his banquet hall, waving her cup with abandon.

Just then, the back door springs violently open, nearly knocked off its hinges. Jonathan and David fall in through the open doorway. To Noah's horror, at first they seem to be tussling desperately with each other—until he spies a *third* man in the crush.

CHAPTER 16

THE TUSSLE ENDS with the third man being stood bolt upright from behind by David, who holds the man's throat firmly in the crook of his arm and presses a knife to his back. The kitchen staff looks on in amazement, while Sir Henry and Lady Anne peek around the doorway with great interest.

It takes a moment for Noah to recognize the intruder despite the ample candlelight in the kitchen. The man's face has become ashen and emaciated since it was last seen several weeks ago, and his thin beard is unkempt. But there can be no doubt he's the surviving Bennett twin.

Before Noah succumbs to the temptation to address him by the name "Bennett," he notices all eyes watching him, and it occurs to him that it might be vital to keep the man's identity secret.

Noah turns to the staff. "As the meal is complete, the ladies will retire to the upstairs parlor."

"Oh!" whines Lady Anne, stamping her foot. "Not fair!"

Sir Henry mumbles something in her ear.

"Oh, I know that, Henry," she replies impatiently and wobbles off in a huff to the front staircase.

Noah asks Cook to stay, who curtsies in reply. He thanks and dismisses the remainder of the kitchen staff with an assurance that they'll be paid in full promptly on the morrow, and a stern command to repeat nothing of what they've seen or heard this evening on pain of imprisonment at the Tower.

Once they've taken their cloaks and gone from the house, Noah dispatches Arthur to guard the ladies and ensure that they hear nothing of what will be said. Arthur seems disappointed to be excluded from the interview of Master Bennett, but he accedes in good humor, as always.

Jonathan, seeing that their captive is well in hand, lights a lantern he finds by the door and takes it out to the stables, returning in a moment with his saddlebag. "Winter's coming," he observes, as he's thrust in through the doorway by a chill gust and closes the door firmly behind him.

"Serjeant Ames?" says Bennett in ingratiating tones, drawing suspicious looks from Jonathan and David.

"Master Bennett?" says Noah.

"Sir, I see that you have supped. I've not eaten in three days and drunk naught but small beer. Might I perhaps—?" The poor man looks as though he might keel over from hunger.

"Do you mean us harm, Master Bennett?" asks Noah.

Bennett sighs and shakes his head. "None, sir. I swear on my soul."

David laughs darkly. "Well, you meant *me* plenty of harm at Burghley House. That's sure."

Bennett seems sincerely apologetic. "I did not recognize you, Master Killigrew. If I'd remembered you as the lad who'd delivered messages for Sir Henry years earlier, I would have greeted you quite differently."

David greets this with a skeptical snort.

Noah turns to Cook. "Please clear the table and put out a well-laden plate for Lord Saint Ives, and another for our new guest. Small beer. I want no wine or other spirits at the table." He glances past Sir Henry into the dining room and sees Lady Anne's bottle still on the table. "Bring Lady Anne her wine upstairs."

David leans into Cuthbert. "One false move, and I'll take you outside and slit your throat."

"And you'll have my blessing to do it," says Noah dourly. "But I rather expect Master Bennett will acquit himself well."

———————⟶∘◅▱▻∘◅———————

THE WINDOWS RATTLE in the mournful wind as Noah, Sir Henry, Jonathan, and David sit at table, watching Cuthbert warily while he awaits some supper. When his plate arrives, he dives into it like a man who hasn't seen food in weeks and expects never to see it again.

"Slow down, Master Bennett," chides Noah. "What goes down fast, comes up faster."

"Quite right," says Cuthbert, making an evident effort to resume some level of decorum. "I've just been ... so hungry. Thank you so much, sir. You're a blessing to us all."

"You've had a very hard time of it lately," says Noah sympathetically. "Tell me, sir. Which Bennett are you?"

Master Bennett sighs. "I'm the *only* Bennett now," he says sadly. "I'm Cuthbert, though it didn't seem to matter much until Tobias ... until

Tobias died."

Noah says, "I've been charged with investigating Tobias's murder, Cuthbert, so I wish very much to learn whatever you know about the circumstances leading to his death. But first tell us why you came here this evening."

"To murder *me*, no doubt," says Jonathan under his breath.

Cuthbert seems saddened by Jonathan's suspicion. "No, my lord, although I was aware that someone else had taken a shot at you at Drapers' Hall."

"A shot?" says Noah in astonishment. "And what on earth was m'lord doing at the Drapers'?"

Cuthbert replies. "Lord Saint Ives had kindly gone there at my request," he says. "When I realized m'lord was at Gray's Inn, I sent him a note asking him to meet me at the Drapers' and to ensure that he not be followed. Permit me to assure you all that I neither took the shot nor wished it to be taken."

"How comforting," says David sardonically.

"Why the Drapers'?" asks Noah.

"I knew it to be a very busy, very *public* place at that hour of the day," says Cuthbert, "and I never dreamed that anyone would be so brazen as to take a shot there, at either Lord Saint Ives or myself. But these men are ruthless. They'll kill me or anyone they think is trying to help me, which is why I came here under cover of darkness—so as not to endanger you, Serjeant Ames, nor any of your household. Anyway, I reached the Drapers' first. When his lordship arrived, I saw at once that he'd been followed, so I straightaway pinned a note to the notice board alerting him to the danger."

Noah looks for confirmation to Jonathan, who takes a sip of small beer and nods. He reaches down into his saddlebag, withdraws a note, and tosses it onto the table. It says, *You were followed.*

"You might have stayed to tell me in person, Cuthbert," says Jonathan.

"I intended to do so, m'lord. I posted the note there only as a last resort … in case I were to be attacked first," says Cuthbert. "But when I saw the pistolier spot me and put on his horrid mask to conceal his identity, I knew he wouldn't be dissuaded from violence merely by the public character of the place. I ran out, expecting him to give chase. After all, 'tis *I* they want dead, not your lordship. I was escaping west on Lothbury Street when I heard the shot behind me. I turned and saw the pistolier running my way, nearly blinded by his mask and not so very far behind, so I took cover in an old graveyard and lay in wait for him."

Jonathan reaches into his saddlebag and tosses a blood-stained mask on the table. "Is this his mask?"

"Good heavens," says Noah. "What a ghastly thing!"

Cuthbert gasps to see it. "That's *it*, my lord. May I ask where you found it?"

Jonathan nods. "On Lothbury, just outside the old walled cemetery. It was drifting freely about the street. Whose blood is on there?"

"Well, not mine. It's the pistolier's, I should imagine."

"Who was the pistolier?" asks Jonathan.

Cuthbert is reluctant to answer.

"Out with it," says Jonathan.

Cuthbert nods. "I hesitate only because such knowledge could place you all in danger."

"You've already accomplished that much by coming here," says Jonathan impatiently.

Cuthbert seems defensive. "Please believe me when I say I tried to avoid coming here, m'lord. It's why I arrived on foot and in the dark of night. It was either that or starvation. I can't be seen in any inn or tavern in London, you see. They're everywhere. Everywhere." He shivers, and glances about as though someone might leap through the window at him at any moment. But the howl of the wind is all that comes in from outside. "I didn't expect to find your lordship here. Nor you, Master Killigrew. To the contrary, as you both had good grounds to suspect me, I hoped to avoid you both. I came to seek succor from Serjeant Ames, who has kindly provided it."

"For the final time, Cuthbert: *Who shot at me?*" demands Jonathan.

Cuthbert lowers his voice. "Meriton. He was one of Essex's men."

Noah sits up. "*Was?*"

Jonathan and David exchange a pointed glance.

Cuthbert stares absently at a random point on the table, well aware that Noah could arrest him on the spot if he were to confess to murder. "I expect Meriton shan't be bothering your lordship again. As far as I can tell, he was not stalking me at Essex's request, but rather on behalf of someone in Essex's *household*. There's quite a bit of faction there, just as at the Queen's court, with each party trying to pull Essex this way or that."

"Which faction was Meriton working for?" asks Noah.

"I don't know. As soon as I saw the deep divisions in Essex's household, I refused to get involved. Tobias felt the same way, but—"

"Tobias *joined* one such faction?" asks Noah.

Cuthbert's face turns red. "Oh, I doubt Tobias felt strongly enough about any faction to join it, but he became fast friends with someone who evidently had."

"Was his name 'Teller'?" asks Noah, curious to learn whether the two men killed together were friends.

The redness in Cuthbert's face deepens, and he rubs his ragged beard with the back of his knuckles. "Yes."

The wind sings outside the dining room windows and rises to a peak. As it falls, it rattles the windows for good measure. Noah exchanges a knowing glance with Jonathan, who's all too willing to let Noah take the lead in delving into the uncomfortable topic of Tobias' sexual preferences.

"Was Tobias inclined toward ... *men*?" asks Noah gingerly.

Cuthbert covers his eyes with his hands and silently weeps for some time. All the while the room is silent, except for the sound of women chattering upstairs, their voices emanating from some feminine realm far, far away.

Finally, Cuthbert nods.

Noah follows with a question he's sure the puritan constable will ask, given the chance. "Did Tobias belong to a conspiracy of men engaging in such ... acts?"

Cuthbert wipes his eyes on his sleeve. "I'm not sure what you mean, Serjeant Ames. Do you mean a conspiracy of men formed for the purpose of engaging in ... buggery?"

That's Noah's question, of course, but it suddenly seems so foolish that he's ashamed to have asked it. Still, the question must be posed. "Yes," says Noah, "that's what I mean."

And then Cuthbert does something none of them would have thought possible so soon after weeping. He laughs. Seeing Noah's embarrassment, he says, "Pardon me, Serjeant Ames, but I—I can't imagine why such activities would require a conspiracy of any sort. I suppose men of such stripe congregate with one another, just as men of any other stripe do. But to constitute a conspiracy, they'd need to have assembled for an unlawful purpose. It requires no great assemblage of men to carry off the crime of buggery, does it? I should think the commonest number would be ... two?" he conjectures.

Noah looks to the unusually quiet Sir Henry, who returns his gaze enigmatically, as though to say, *Well, Ames, there you have it. In response to the world's most foolish question, you've been properly schooled by someone having half your learning.*

"So, it was Teller who'd joined the faction," proposes Noah, "and Tobias who just went along?"

"And paid with his life," says Cuthbert sadly.

"But it was Teller's own faction who killed him, was it not?"

"That's certain," says Cuthbert, "and now they're trying to kill me."

"But, why?" asks Noah.

"I'm unsure, but I've narrowed the probabilities to two. It's probably because they suspect that Tobias told me about their plan, which he didn't, though he did tell me who some of them are."

"And their alternative grounds?" asks Noah.

"They're trying to kill me before I can revenge my brother's death upon them."

"But surely revenge is not your plan," suggests Noah.

Cuthbert ignores the comment. "Tell me, Serjeant Ames. Why the interest in Tobias's sexual proclivities? Are they pertinent to your case?"

"I doubt it, but there's a constable looking into the matter who seems to think it's central to the killer's motive. He's cathedral constable at Saint Paul's ... a puritan."

For a moment, Cuthbert seems lost in thought. "What's his name?"

"What-God-Will Knott."

"I beg your pardon?"

"It's one of those facetious puritan names. His surname's Knott, so his father named him What-God-Will. And here we thought puritans had no sense of levity."

"His father was a typical puritan," observes Cuthbert bitterly. "The only time in a man's life when he really ought to be sober ... and he makes a joke of the name his son will be called by the rest of his life. That's not levity. It's cruelty. Permit me to look into this fellow Knott. I suspect his activities go beyond the constabulary."

Cook knocks on the door from the kitchen and enters with a loaf of bread. She hands it to Cuthbert. "Here ye go, suh. May it do ye much good."

Cuthbert rises and bows in gratitude. "Thank you, Cook."

As Cook returns to the kitchen, Noah beckons Cuthbert with a crooked finger and hands him a small bag of coins.

"Thank you, Serjeant Ames," says Cuthbert, tears of gratitude welling up in his eyes. "Should you permit me to return in three days' time, I shall strive mightily to have useful information for you by then."

Noah nods. "Only stay safe and warm until then, Cuthbert, and be certain you are not followed here."

Cuthbert bows and turns to the back door. When he opens it, he's hit with a blast of icy air that presses its way into the dining room. He forces himself to take a step into the bitter night, and shuts the door behind him.

"Poor sod," says Jonathan. "He has nothing, no one, and no decent place to rest his head on this wild night."

"Perhaps he'll yet prevail against his enemies," says Sir Henry. "One never knows."

David, who's been watching Noah quietly, says, "And what do *you* think, Serjeant Ames?"

Noah starts as if roused from a sound sleep. He runs his finger along his lips and shakes his head sadly.

"I fear he is far gone," he says, barely above a whisper. "Far gone."

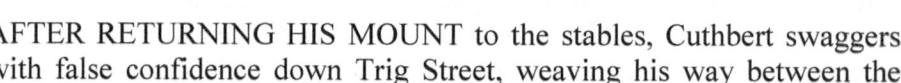

AFTER RETURNING HIS MOUNT to the stables, Cuthbert swaggers with false confidence down Trig Street, weaving his way between the houses of ill repute in Queenhythe, a rough part of town named for a busy dock that juts out into the Thames.

Lest Cuthbert be recognized by one of his brother's killers, he draws his hood tight about his face, though the greatest danger at this moment does not arise from them. Nor does it arise from the many drunken sailors found on the street at all hours of the night, but rather from the ruffians and whores who prey on them. For that eventuality, he keeps a dagger in his hand … and his hand in a shallow pocket.

Though it's a short walk from the stables to his lodgings, it's fraught with peril. One fortunate enough to escape being rolled must yet avoid being struck by any of the sundry objects thrown out of the brothels' higher storeys, such as empty wine bottles, full pisspots, and the occasional whore.

He breathes a sigh of relief as he turns off the street into Nancy's place, an inn housing two separate businesses. Occupying the street level is Nancy's discreet three-bedroom brothel, which holds no interest for him. On the top floor is a row of small rooms let to sailors and other transients interested primarily in privacy and a night's sleep, a part of the trade that's badly neglected in this part of town.

Nancy is an older woman who must have been a pleasing sight in her heyday, as she still has ready takers of old (mostly toothless salts nowadays) whom she swats away with both hands and a hearty jeer.

Cuthbert takes one of the tapers, lights it on an adjacent wick, and nods respectfully as he passes her on the way to the staircase up to his room.

"Hope ye don't mind," she says, causing him to stop on his way. "I moved yer bag to the far end of the hallway. Much quieter there. Just how ye like it. Did I do right?"

"Ye done good, Nancy," he says, and winks at her. "Thanks."

As he awaits her pithy response, a young man he recognizes descends the stairs quickly and walks straight past him out the door without so much as a glance in any direction. Once he's gone, Nancy says, "Don't like that one. Dunno why he keeps a room here, as he barely uses it. Just goes up there a few minutes and walks out the same time every night without sayin' a word."

"Well," says Cuthbert, "does he return for the night?"

"Pshaw! Don't see 'im again till next night the same hour."

"But I suppose he pays, right?"

She smirks and nods. "Every Friday on his way out, he plunks a few shillin's on the counter. At least the count's right, though not an extra farthin' for the help."

"That hardly sounds sporting," says Cuthbert. "Do *you* do up his room?"

She shakes her head. "He don't allow nobuddy in there."

"Odd."

"You know 'im?"

"No," lies Cuthbert pleasantly. "Have a good night, dear."

Once upstairs, he tramps down the narrow hallway to the room at the end and opens the door. As his bag is there as promised, he shuts the door behind him. He places the taper down on the small table, takes a spindly chair from the corner and quietly jams it under the doorknob to prevent anyone from entering unheard.

That done, he blows out the taper and sits in the dark at the corner of his bed contemplating what to do next, for the man who walked past him unawares was Caim, who's Essex's footman and one of his brother's murderers.

———⋙○⟐○⋘———

IN HER BED AT THE AMES'S, Esther has tossed and turned on the edge of sleep since overhearing David departing for Lothbury with Sir Henry and Lady Anne. Evidently, David prefers the comfort of his

London family to Esther's tantrums.

And who can blame him?

Her thoughts return to the day when she peered through the hedge to see David kissing Constance. But he didn't really kiss her. Rather, it was *she* who kissed *him*.

Well, and so what? David kissed her *back*, the blackguard.

But Constance obviously did it only to taunt Esther and instill doubt over David's faithfulness. *And now I've given her precisely what she wants. I've enabled that stupid girl to drive a wedge between David and me. I've alienated David so he might run back to her!*

Oh, it's maddening!

She begins perspiring under her blanket and kicks it off despite the howling of the autumn wind outdoors. As she cools down and drifts off, her recurring dream returns. She's back at Bowyer's Row just before the murders. She can hear the voice of the chief conspirator. And she's certain she's heard it again since the murders took place, but she can't recall where. And, try though she might, she cannot catch a glimpse of his face.

She drifts into a deeper slumber, and her ears are filled, as they have been each night of late, with the sound of the Thames splashing against the dock ... at Queenhythe.

CHAPTER 17

"IT'S A GREAT PRIVILEGE to meet you, Lord Saint Ives," says the Chancellor of the Exchequer, Sir John Fortescue. "Our boys in Ireland would be in a rough spot indeed if you hadn't stopped that map getting out of the country."

"Oh, I couldn't say about that," says Jonathan humbly. "Once I grabbed the map, Sir John ... well, I was in a rough spot myself and never learned the details."

Noah is delighted by the results of Sir Henry's advice to bring Jonathan with him to Westminster. Fortescue is indeed an avid patriot, and fascinated with Jonathan's exploits. Noah resolves to wait quietly through a bit more banter before bringing Sir John to the point of the meeting. At last, he finds an opening.

"Thank you so much," says Noah, "for giving us the name of the fellow at the Wardrobe, Sir John."

As though just noticing Noah for the first time, Sir John says, "Oh, certainly. What was the fellow's name? I seem to have forgotten."

"Ralph," says Noah.

"Ah, yes," replies Sir John. "And how did that work out?"

"*Work out,* Sir John?"

"Yes, did he tell you what you needed to know?"

This is embarrassing. Evidently, Sir Henry passed along no information whatever when scheduling the present appointment.

"Well, to be frank, it didn't work out at all well, Sir John. Ralph had been murdered by the time Sir Henry and I arrived at the Wardrobe."

Sir John's mouth falls open in horror and he collapses into his chair. "Good Lord!" he says. "What has happened to young people today? First *this* one's murdered, then *that* one. Can't they learn to live and let live? *Tsk, tsk.*"

"So you see," says Noah, "we come to you in a profound predicament. We have no one to ask about the first murdered man Teller because the only man to come to our attention who knew him well, namely Ralph, was himself murdered, evidently to silence him."

"Yes, I see," says Sir John.

"May we ask," says Jonathan in his most ingratiating manner, "how Ralph's name came to your attention?"

Without a moment's hesitation, Sir John replies. "Billingsley."

"Sir Henry Billingsley?" asks Jonathan.

"The very same," replies Sir John. "He mentioned to me that he'd heard of Teller's murder, and then he mentioned that one of Teller's friends had applied to him for a position collecting—not taxes—oh, what *was* it?" He snaps his fingers. "Patent royalties."

Jonathan is about to speak again, but Noah places his hand over Jonathan's to silence him for a question of his own.

"Any *particular* patent royalties, Sir John?"

"Oh, yes. It was a new monopoly patent … for sweet wines. *What am I saying? New?* Why, the first patent granting a monopoly over sweet wines was issued by Edward the Third in 1373 and invalidated by Parliament four years later. So such a patent could hardly be called a new thing under the sun. But to get back to the patent of which you inquired. It was a reissue of an expired patent formerly belonging to—"

"The Earl of Essex," says Noah grimly, without a hint of doubt.

Sir John's eyebrows shoot up. "Why, yes! My word, Serjeant. How did you know this?"

"Everyone at Her Majesty's court knows of the earl's expired patent, Sir John," replies Noah. "I'm interested to learn how Billingsley came to know Ralph, and what he knew of Ralph's connection with Teller."

"Oh," says Sir John, shaking his head. "I wouldn't know any of that. You'll have to ask Billingsley. He was here this morning."

"So recently?" asks Jonathan.

"He's here quite often, as you might imagine. Nearly all the money he collects on behalf of the Crown ends up here at the Exchequer."

"Nearly?" says Jonathan with surprise.

"Well, he's allowed a commission on such monies as he collects, of course, which in turn depends upon how much his collectors will admit to taking in."

"*Admit* to?" Jonathan echoes him again.

Sir John sighs, and addresses Jonathan as though he were a student who'd arrived for the first day of class. "Billingsley is a scrupulous collection master. However, he has no choice but to rely on collectors who personally visit those owing money to the Crown. As you can imagine, some may be"—he equivocates—"unscrupulous."

"They report less than they collect, so they can keep the difference for themselves?" asks Jonathan.

"That's called 'filching,'" says Sir John, "and there's scarce chance of it continuing for long."

"Why?" asks Jonathan.

"Because, when the collector is dispatched to collect royalties, he brings with him his master's calculation of the royalty amount due, and presents it to the sweet-wine dealer. (I'm using 'dealer' instead of 'stockist,' because the patent owner could impose the obligation to pay royalties upon those selling goods *to trade*, as well as to those consuming the goods.) If the collector returns with less than the full amount, the master need only pay a call to the dealer to find out whether he paid more than remitted by the collector. Even if he never visits the dealer, eventually the debt will grow to the point where legal action against the dealer becomes necessary, and then the collector's scheme will out. That's why only a dunderhead would try filching, and he'd soon be discharged and prosecuted."

"But I assume there are more subtle collectors who abuse their office for unlawful profit. How do *they* do it?" asks Jonathan.

"Well," says Sir John, "let's assume that the new patent owner decides to charge each sweet-wine dealer a royalty based upon each case of sweet wine sold by that dealer. Under such circumstances, we must begin with the universally recognized premise that dealers in sweet wines (or indeed any items subject to patent royalties) declare fewer sales than they actually make, in order to pay less in royalties to the patent owner.

"The first thing the dishonest royalty collector must do is to *gain the trust* of the sweet-wine merchant." Sir John juts his index finger into the air, as though making a grand philosophical point. "Trust is the key." He smiles devilishly. "*Misplaced* trust, that is.

"Let's take an example using round numbers. Let's say the amount of the royalty due, based upon the dealer's declared sales, is ... ten pounds, and that that's the amount written on the collection master's calculation. The collector lets slip to the dealer, however, that *additional* sales by the dealer have been discovered, and that the master *should* have charged the dealer *twelve* pounds, and that he would have done so but for the efforts of the collector, who heroically persuaded the master that it would be unfair to ask the dealer for twelve pounds. The underreporting dealer will believe that he's saved two pounds through the illicit cooperation of the collector and his master.

"The collector will caution the dealer, however, that he can assure continuation of such savings only if the dealer gives the collector one-half of the dealer's savings. In our example, that's *one* of the two pounds apparently saved. Hearing this, the credulous dealer will be inclined to give the collector the extra pound he requests and will feel he's saved one pound on the transaction, when in fact he's *lost* one pound. The dealer's expectation is, of course, that the one pound he pays in excess of the master's calculation will be remitted to the master."

"But it won't be," suggests Jonathan.

"Of course not," says Sir John. "In fact, the extra pound will be kept by the collector. Now, the collection *master* has no clue that this subterfuge is even going on, for what is there to tip him off? He's not receiving a farthing less (or more) than the amount of his calculation. And there's the beauty of it: A master who's been paid in full has no reason to doubt his collector's honesty, nor has he any reason to send someone to investigate the dealer's shortfall in payment."

Jonathan laughs. "Because there *is* no shortfall!"

"Correct, m'lord."

"In fact," says Jonathan, "the collector's not filching from the Crown at all, is he? He's rather cheating the *dealer* out of money he suspects the dealer has cheated from the Crown."

Sir John nods with a smile.

Jonathan is skeptical. "But what if the cheated dealer catches on?"

Sir John regards him skeptically. "How might he do that, m'lord?"

"Well," says Jonathan, "I suppose he could talk to some other dealer who pays royalties on the same patent."

"That would be the dealer's *competitor*, m'lord. What incentive would one competitor have to tell another that he's paying less than required in royalties? Even if the competitor were to be so inclined (and he wouldn't), the royalty amounts paid by each dealer would vary in accordance with how many sales of sweet wine each is reporting, so comparison might not be so simple."

Lord Jonathan nods. "Suppose our dealer were simply to go to the collection master personally and *ask* whether he's been receiving half the bribe."

Sir John smiles. "The dealer would wish to avoid that at all costs, m'lord. If he *had* been receiving a savings, it would surely cease. No, the master would inevitably deny participating in any such scheme, and the dealer would have no way of knowing if he's telling the truth. Moreover, the *dealer* would be confessing to bribery of either the collector alone or *both* the collector and the master, either of which is a serious crime.

"Note, m'lord, that the scheme doesn't work *if the prospective dealer has been honestly reporting his sales.* Successful execution of such a scheme requires that the *victim* has something to hide—to ensure that he can't run to the authorities for fear his own wrongdoing will be discovered. Crooked collectors even have a saying for it: 'Never trust an honest man.'" Sir John smirks. "The honest man is the only one who can call the constable."

Jonathan claps his hands in amusement, and lets go a hearty laugh. "You've seen it all, haven't you, Sir John?" Sir John joins in the laughter.

Noah cannot help but smile at Jonathan's mirth in grasping the fraud. It reminds him of the youthful, curious Jonathan who resided at Gray's Inn years before.

"It must be lucrative business to be a collector of patent royalties," ventures Noah.

Sir John agrees. "Yes, even for an honest one. For an unscrupulous one, it's a veritable gold mine. You should see the cutthroat competition for a vacant position."

The remark triggers a suspicion in Noah's mind, but he reserves it for private discussion with Jonathan. "Sir John," says Noah, "where do you suppose we might find Master Billingsley?"

"Well," says Sir John, "he mentioned that he'd be here at Westminster all day." Sir John turns toward the open door and shouts. "Cantwell!"

Sir John's harried-looking chief assistant appears. "Sir?"

"Where's Billingsley?"

The assistant looks up at the ceiling, exhales loudly, and returns his gaze to Sir John. "Don't know, Sir John. I last saw him when he was here with you this morning."

"Very well," says Sir John as he rises. His two guests follow suit. "Please escort these two gentlemen to his office. Gentlemen," he says, "I doubt you'll wish to await him all day, but you might leave him a note requesting an appointment."

"Thank you, Sir John," says Noah.

Sir John bows low to Jonathan, and nods perfunctorily to Noah.

———————⊃∘⊂⊘∘⊂———————

AFTER LEAVING A NOTE for Sir Henry Billingsley, Noah and Jonathan ride back to Holborn at a leisurely pace with a cold breeze from the Thames at their back.

"So," begins Jonathan, "have we learned anything of value in our investigation?"

"A great deal, I should imagine," replies Noah.

Jonathan regards him with surprise.

"For one thing," says Noah, "it seems far more likely now that Teller's dream of obtaining wealth was not completely without foundation—assuming Billingsley confirms he was in the running for a job collecting patent royalties."

"You suppose someone killed Teller to eliminate a rival for the position, and then killed Ralph to ensure we'd never learn why?"

"Entirely plausible, don't you think? It doesn't answer all our questions, but it gives us a way forward."

Jonathan equivocates. "Sure, but why would a whole conspiracy of daggers be needed to kill just two men? And why would they also murder Tobias Bennett?"

"To throw us off the trail," conjectures Noah. "Until now, we've only been interested in finding a motive that applies to both victims, which might be that they were being punished for betraying the conspiracy. But that may be an illusion. Tobias's murder might have been committed solely to conceal the conspirators' motive for murdering Teller."

Jonathan shrugs. "I suppose it's at least possible that Tobias himself was seeking a job as patent collector. Seems a bit unlikely, though."

"Especially in light of Sir John's assurance that competition for the position is 'cutthroat,' one important question for Billingsley is: Who were the other candidates for the position?"

"I suppose," says Jonathan, "we'll find out when we meet with him."

A moment passes without conversation.

"I wonder how Cuthbert is faring," muses Jonathan.

Noah shakes his head, and shifts to an alternative topic.

"Jonathan, do you know why my daughter wept and ran upstairs when I toasted the coming addition to our family?"

"She has some notion in her head that she may die as a result of childbirth and never get to know her child," says Jonathan. "I suppose it's a common worry for women in her condition."

"If there's anything Marie or I can do to assuage her fears," says Noah, "please let me know. Lady Jessica should be happy at this time of her life, and it pains me to see her so anxious."

"I've been turning myself inside out to find a way to ease her fears. If

I come up with one, you'll be the first to know."

"And there's one thing more," says Noah. "Mistress Ames has told me that Esther is decided against any union with David because he refuses to tell her where he went during his recent absence. Evidently, she suspects him of being unfaithful … with a local spicemaid, no less."

Jonathan rolls his eyes. "He wasn't unfaithful," he says with exasperation. "But he was a little indiscreet in kissing the spicemaid goodbye."

"I know where he was during his absence, Jonathan," says Noah.

"How did you learn it?"

"While you were away, Esther and I attended a sermon at Essex House, where Lord Sheffield inadvertently made it obvious that he had no idea that his lady was absent from the house. As I know you're fond of Sheffield, I expect you sent David to retrieve the lady … and her spicemaid, who had disappeared along with her." He glances at Jonathan to see his reaction; he's shocked. "In any event, the burden is upon you to think of a way to extricate David from his painful position. I assume you do not wish Esther and David to remain apart because David helped you recover Lady Sheffield."

Jonathan says solemnly, "I shall think of something, Father. It is much on my mind."

As the Ames residence comes into view, Jonathan cannot help but to ask, "Why would you assume it was David I sent?"

Noah laughs. "Because that's whom *I* would have sent. He's a good lad, honest and virtuous, and women find him most persuasive."

"That's his curse," mutters Jonathan under his breath.

CHAPTER 18

DURING HIS RIDE to Ewelme Manor in South Oxfordshire, Sir Helvius Cinna is favored by crisp autumn weather, making it a pleasant jaunt through fallen leaves of shiny red and gold, and crumbly brown. Careful not to upset his wig or makeup, he flicks away any leaf that wafts down onto him.

Sir Helvius rides up to the wooded rear entrance to the manor house, dismounts, and ties off his sturdy roan to a post. As he heaves his considerable bulk up the rear steps, a burst of cold wind strikes him from behind. Though it would take a veritable gale to disturb the footing of anyone so stout as Sir Helvius, he nevertheless finds the cold blast an unwelcome reminder that winter is not far off.

Before knocking at the door, he glances about the rustic grounds. Although he visited this place years earlier and was once invited inside, it amazes him that the manor is classified in the national books as a "palace." True, it was occupied once or twice by Henry the Seventh and later Henry the Eighth, but it lacks the stony permanence that customarily goes with the designation "palace." He knocks.

The door opens, and Henry Cuffe greets him with a smile and a bow. "Good evening, Sir Helvius," he says. "Won't you come in? The Earl of Essex awaits."

Sir Helvius steps inside. "Are we otherwise alone?" he asks.

"Aye, sir," replies Cuffe. "'Tis just we three."

"A present-day triumvirate," says Sir Helvius, disappointed to find that his allusion to Ancient Rome has escaped the learned Cuffe, "but I was expecting Sir Gelly Meyrick to make us four."

Cuffe shrugs. "Sir Gelly is at home with his wife in Herefordshire, sir. His lordship allows him time to spend with his family."

"How kind of the earl, and how very like him."

"Please follow me, sir."

The library doors swing open and the earl steps through as if on cue. "Please come in, Master … Cinna, if you would. We have so very much to discuss."

"I was hoping to stay but a moment, your lordship. Master Cuffe has been entreating me since my return from abroad to come and speak with you on an important—but unspecified—matter, and I do not wish to slight your lordship. However, my wife and I have guests at our home, and I wish to avoid slighting *them*, as well. They're my wife's family, and I'd never hear the end of it. I hope your lordship will understand my predicament."

"Well, it shall take a bit more than a moment, Sir—"

"Helvius, m'lord."

"Yes, Sir *Helvius*," says Essex. "Um, please come in, and let's close the doors for a bit of privacy." Sir Helvius follows him into the library. As Cuffe enters last, he closes the doors behind him.

Essex plops himself down in a chair. "Enough of this 'Sir Helvius' business. I doubt your theatrical disguise would accomplish much if you were to be seen by anyone who already knows you to be Sir Henry Neville. Surely we can speak freely here in the library."

Sir Henry takes a proffered seat and shakes his head dourly. "It was my understanding, m'lord, that I would remain 'Sir Helvius' during the present business at all times and for all purposes."

Essex looks to Cuffe, who nods, confirming that this was indeed the agreement.

"Very cautious," sighs Essex. "Very well. Here is the gist of it. Master Cuffe here has persuaded me that if we press this matter of demanding an audience with Her Majesty, it's likely to cause a great rift at court, and I may well be called upon to act as regent for the remainder of Her Majesty's reign. I have corresponded with Her Majesty's heir presumptive, King James of Scotland, and he has expressed no objection."

Sir Henry suspected that Cuffe's continual prodding was in furtherance of some such wild scheme. "And how might *I* be of service to your lordship in such event?"

"You're highly esteemed in Parliament," observes the earl. "It's generally acknowledged that you would be Secretary of State by now, if the office were not already occupied by the dwarf Lord Robert."

"Is that the position your lordship would have me fill in the event of a regency?"

Essex nods. "What do you have to say to the invitation?"

Sir Henry suspects that his mettle is being tested in anticipation of a scheme of which he would roundly disapprove if he knew the whole truth. "I would say only this: I would be pleased and grateful to achieve the office, but I would discourage his lordship from taking any action to seek it for me, or to seek for himself either a regency ... or a crown."

Cuffe throws his hands up in exasperation. "Well, how will it happen, Sir Helvius, without *action*?"

Sir Henry fires back, "And what action would you propose, Master Cuffe?"

"I would urge his lordship to place the Queen in a position where she has no real choice but to accede to the appointment of his lordship as regent ... or abdicate the Throne."

The air in the room has suddenly thickened.

Sir Henry shifts in his chair and speaks quietly. "You're talking high treason, Master Cuffe. I strongly urge his lordship to abandon thought of any strategy that would do violence to Her Majesty's person, or so much as threaten to do so."

Essex protests casually. "I would no more harm the Queen than you would, Sir Helvius. She's my cousin, after all. But suppose the Queen were persuaded to make such a choice without danger—or fear of danger—to her person."

Sir Henry considers the case in the abstract, and begins to soften. "In that case, your lordship, I would sooner fill the office myself than see it filled by someone of less experience and dedication."

"You would?" asks Cuffe, seeming mollified.

"I cannot imagine," says Sir Henry, "how Her Majesty could be persuaded of such a thing. But if she were to do so freely—by fair means and argument—then I would be pleased to fill the position."

Essex rises. "Well said, Sir Helvius. Do you suppose your ... Hebrew friend could be persuaded to come along? I ask only because Her Majesty looks to him for his honest advice."

Sir Henry weighs the question. "Your lordship describes Serjeant Ames as a Hebrew. And so he is—in worship. But in his daily life he comes perilously close to idolatry. And his idol is Elizabeth Tudor. Your lordship would do well to impart to him *nothing* of these thoughts. Indeed, your efforts at keeping him in the dark will need to be superlative, for he will catch you out from the least chink of daylight, and he's not wont to equivocate in matters of Her Majesty's safety."

Essex nods sagely. "Thank you for coming. Out of an abundance of caution, we will limit our communications with you to a bare minimum. When the time approaches, we'll let you know. In the meantime and forever after"—his eyes flash—"*you were never here*. You may go."

Sir Henry bows and follows Cuffe to the rear door.

"Thank you again for coming, Sir Helvius," says Cuffe with a faintly patronizing smile. He sees Sir Henry to the door and shuts it behind him, but Sir Henry can hear him turning on his heel and tramping back toward the library, as though only one of many items on a long checklist has now been completed, and many more remain.

Sir Henry hoists himself into the saddle. Before prodding his mount forward, he gazes in the direction of his destination of Billingbear. The path ahead has darkened, the sky gone gray, and the fallen leaves that were so bright and uplifting in the sunshine now seem so much colorless litter strewn in his way. At the edge of sight, dark clouds threaten a nasty soaking before he reaches home.

Essex and Cuffe seemed well pleased by his words, artfully framed as they were, but as he prods his mount forward into the coming storm, he shudders—and wonders whether this is what it feels like to sell one's soul.

CHAPTER 19

IT'S NOT THE HOWLING of the biting wind out of doors that causes Noah to toss and turn in his bed, but rather a growing fear that events are beginning to fall together in a terrible, inexorable way just beyond his understanding—and the years have taught him that events beyond his ken are likewise beyond his control.

Though the Essex affair weighs most heavily on his mind, for some reason tonight his thoughts are fixed on his dearest friend, Sir Henry Neville. Each perplexing detail of Sir Henry's life surfaces momentarily in the moonlight like a shiny corpse bobbing to the surface of the Thames, then quickly subsides into the depths below, only to be replaced by another, equally disturbing.

Sir Henry's always been a dear friend to Noah, yet he's maintained steady relations with Noah's adversaries, the Earls of Essex and Southampton. While Sir Henry has always assured Noah that, in this dukeless kingdom, maintaining good relations with earls is simply good business, it has always struck Noah that Sir Henry's professed regard for the earls was more sincere than feigned.

A few weeks ago, upon Sir Henry's temporary return to London from his French embassage, he placed some papers on the table, with a few still-sealed letters that recently arrived during his absence. One of the letters was addressed to Sir Henry by Cuffe, one of Essex's secretaries. As soon as Esther saw it, with her second sight, she pronounced it "wicked" and urged Noah to destroy it before it could be opened.

It occurs to Noah that one of the papers Sir Henry tossed onto his table was a receipt from the Stationer's Register, dated a few days earlier, for the deposit of three playscripts: *As You Like It, Henry the Fifth,* and *Much Ado About Nothing*, which raises another point of mystery about Sir Henry.

Sir Henry's always denied writing for amusement, insisting he has no talent for it. Whenever the topic of writing has come up, he's shifted attention to his father, reciting how his *father* was the one who wrote plays and masques. But over the years, evidence has mounted that Sir Henry's protestations are false.

Eight years ago, Noah accompanied Sir Henry to the debut of *The Jew of Malta*. When the play ended, Sir Henry escorted Noah backstage to meet Christopher Marlowe, and praised the playwright's invention of a wicked character who gleefully explains his every scheme to the audience. That was a memorable moment for Noah, and he could not but admire Sir Henry's familiarity with playwrights and theaters. When Marlowe was murdered some months later, Sir Henry grieved his death for a long time.

But Noah never thought to inquire how Sir Henry had come by such familiarity, shrugging it off as yet another of the many privileges enjoyed by members of the noble houses.

Later that day, Sir Henry's footman mentioned that, whenever the playwright Shakespeare would visit the Nevilles, he'd bring along a bag of coins. *But why?*

Some years later, in company with Sir Henry, Noah viewed Shakespeare's *Merchant of Venice*. Following the performance, Noah berated Shakespeare backstage for dubbing a young Jewish character "Jessica" and her Christian suitor "Lorenzo," evidently after Noah's daughter Jessica and her Christian husband Lorenzo.

Yet, on that singular occasion, who was it that assuaged Noah with a respectful explanation and apology? Was it Shakespeare (who, truth be told, did nothing more than don a penitent expression)? No, it was rather *Sir Henry*, whose connection with the play seemed rather attenuated.

Just a few days ago Sir Henry revealed that, as a child, he'd spent a great deal of time at the Wardrobe, where he learned the arts of costume and disguise.

And then there are Shakespeare's plays themselves. The name "Neville" was extolled several times by characters in Shakespeare's *First Part of the Contention*, the second play to be based upon the life of the feckless Henry the Sixth. But it's a memory of the *third* play of that cycle that occupies Noah's half-waking mind, an event that took place during the early tribulations of Doctor Roderigo Lopez.

SIR HENRY HAD TAKEN up temporary residence at Gray's Inn, to keep an eye on his young relative Arthur Arden. During one of Henry's worst fits of gout, Doctor Lopez had prescribed for him the medication "colchicum."

A day or two later, when Sir Henry suffered a flare-up at Parliament, he found he'd inadvertently left his medication in his quarters, so he sent a somewhat ambiguous note asking Noah to fetch it for him: "Forgot my gout medicine," it said. "Please bring it to me at Westminster. You'll find it in my study—Thanks, Neville."

Noah can remember every detail of the incident:

The note reached Noah at Neville's Lothbury house, where he showed it to the Nevilles' footman, Walker. (Literacy had always been one of Walker's most valued features, a rare skill without which no one could survive in a household full of verbal Nevilles and Killigrews.)

Walker seemed worried by the note. "Sir Henry won't die if he doesn't get his medicine, will he?" he asked.

"No, no," replied Noah, "although I've heard that a bad case of gout feels like getting one's foot caught in a trap." Walker winced at Noah's description. "All this medicine does is to relieve pain. Is Mistress Anne at home?"

"Honestly, sir, I don't know. She may be gardening in the back. Come to think on it, she mentioned something about going to the bootmaker with her lady's maid this morning. She's probably out. Why don't you go right up to the study? Master Henry's note doesn't say exactly where he left his medicine, but I've no doubt you'll find it."

"I shan't be long," Noah had assured him, "and you needn't wait. Sorry for the abrupt visit."

Noah'd stridden up the walkway into the house. Finding no one at home, he'd gone upstairs to Henry's study, where he found the door closed, but not locked. He opened it, and scanned the room. Everything seemed in order, but no gout medicine leapt out at him. He struggled to recall the container that Doctor Lopez had placed it in before handing it to Henry. Try though he might, he could not envision it.

There were only a few places in the study for medicine to hide. There was a bureau containing three drawers, and two small side tables with one drawer apiece.

Noah thought the bureau most likely. The center drawer was made shallow to provide ample room for one's knees below. While it looked capable of holding a portfolio, pen, and ink, it seemed an unlikely candidate to serve as Henry's makeshift apothecary. The right and left drawers were much deeper. Only the one on the left had a lock, and a key protruded from it.

With some trepidation, Noah turned the key and opened the drawer.

Inside sat a small burlap sack atop a stack of handwritten papers. Thinking the sack might contain the medicine, Noah picked it up, but a sheet of paper stuck to the bottom. Evidently the ink on the top paper had still been wet when the sack was placed upon it and had formed a viscid bond between the two.

Noah firmly plucked the sack from the paper, which wafted to the floor, landing face up.

At the top of the page was a curious heading: "*The True Tragedie of Richard Duke of Yorke:* Gloucester's Final Lines. Page 3."

This was apparently to be the third play in the Henry the Sixth cycle, as Noah had already seen the first two. Although the third play had not yet appeared upon the public stage, it was already widely anticipated. If this was a script of that play, he could see that it would end with the hunchback Richard of Gloucester assuring the audience that he would win the Crown by playing the ruthless Machiavel. (This was obviously intended to indulge the staunch view of many an Englishman that Richard, who would later become the infamous Richard the Third, had usurped the Crown by murdering his brother's two young sons, to be forever known as the Princes in the Tower.)

Here on the floor of Henry Neville's study lay an apparent emendation to the playscript. In wonderment, Noah picked it up and placed it on the bureau. Below the heading, the following lines had been penned in iambic pentameter, which helped Noah commit them to memory on the spot:

> *I can add colors to the chameleon,*
> *Change shapes with Proteus for advantages,*
> *And set the murd'rous Machiavel to school*
> *Can I do this, and cannot get a crown?*
> *Tut! were it further off, I'll pluck it down.*

Something was deeply wrong here. Noah plopped onto the floor, bewildered. He'd never seen Shakespeare's handwriting, but the handwriting on this page was nearly as familiar to Noah as his own. It belonged to *Henry Neville.* At first, Noah had assumed that Shakespeare left this paper with Henry for safekeeping, but why would it be written in Henry's hand?

Had not Henry praised Marlowe for inventing an openly wicked character for the *Jew of Malta*? Then, is not this emendation to Shakespeare's playscript one that Henry Neville *himself* would have made to render Richard more like the delightfully wicked Jew in Marlowe's recent play?

Suddenly apprehensive that he might be discovered at any moment, Noah rushed to replace the paper and check the sack for the medicine. No medicine was there. He searched every remaining drawer in the room, but there was no medicine to be found. Then he realized what had happened.

When Henry handed the message to Cheerful, he must have instructed Cheerful to seek Noah first at Gray's Inn. When Noah was not there, Cheerful had galloped to the Neville home in Lothbury, where Henry had undoubtedly told him to look for Noah next.

Noah's face reddened, and he smacked himself in the forehead. Henry had meant Noah to locate the medicine in Henry's study at *Gray's Inn*, not here at Lothbury.

He felt humiliated, disoriented, and horribly guilty, having completely misinterpreted Henry's instructions, and having (without permission) entered Henry's private study at Lothbury, opened his locked drawer, and examined his private papers. Noah berated himself for being not only stupid, but untrustworthy.

Making sure that everything was restored to its original place, Noah closed the study door stealthily behind him, and stepped as lightly as possible down the stairs. Opening the front door of the vacant house, he was relieved to find that Walker had faithfully tied off his horse and gone on to other business.

Noah remounted and trotted back toward Gray's Inn, expelling all thought of the private paper his friend had never meant him to see. Feeling quite foolish, he readily found Henry's vial of colchicum in the study at Gray's Inn and brought it to Westminster.

Two months later, Noah attended *The True Tragedie of Richard Duke of Yorke* with Henry Neville. As Gloucester recited the last five lines of his closing speech, Noah whispered the lines he'd memorized that day at Lothbury.

The emendation penned by Henry Neville had been incorporated verbatim into the playscript.

—◦⋐⫸◦⊂—

NOAH BREAKS INTO a cold sweat, as the likeliest explanation for what he saw and heard those many years ago has at last penetrated his brain. The plays popularly attributed to William Shakespeare were apparently written at least in part by his good friend, Sir Henry. And

Marie's eldest son was partly right all along. The plays *had* been written by a genius.

But the genius wasn't William Shakespeare. It was Henry Neville.

Noah comforts himself with the pointlessness of his fevered speculation. Logically, neither Sir Henry nor his plays (if they truly are his plays) can have much to do with an incipient rebellion.

Can they?

———————————

AT THAT MOMENT, in the darkest corner of a smoke-filled tavern across the Thames in Bankside, Sir Charles and Sir Josceline Percy (whom Lord Grey was about to draw his sword on in the Saracen's Head, until Noah and Sir Walter Raleigh came to their rescue) await the arrival of their quarry.

"That's he," mutters the impetuous Sir Josceline, pointing discreetly to a senior fellow who's entered, removed his hat and cloak, and taken a seat alone at a small table with a single taper.

"Let's go and speak with him," says Sir Charles, "and—for heaven's sake—will you let your elder brother do the talking for once?"

Without invitation, the two young knights take seats flanking the newly arrived Augustine Phillips, business manager of the Chamberlain's Men. The tapster pours Phillips a half-pint and walks away, wiping his hands on his apron.

"Master Augustine Phillips?" asks Sir Charles.

The old fellow turns cautiously toward Sir Charles, then toward Sir Josceline, sizing each of them up. He seems less than impressed.

"Who wants to know?" he mutters impassively, taking a sip.

"We're the Percy brothers. I'm Sir Charles. This is my younger brother, Sir Josceline."

Phillips nods, his right eye twitching from the smoke. "Then I'm Augustine Phillips," he says.

"We have business for the Chamberlain's Men, Master Phillips," says Josceline, drawing a dirty look from his elder brother.

Phillips shakes his head. "I'm not … That is, this is not where the Chamberlain's Men do business, gentlemen. I can be found at the Globe most weekdays."

"It's better we don't meet you there," says Sir Charles. "Our business is … unusual. In fact, it's best we not be seen with you at all."

Phillips eyes him defensively. "Because actors are little better than vagrants?"

"Not at all," says Sir Charles. "We're quite fond of actors."

"Well, gentlemen," says Phillips, somewhat mollified, "what is your proposition?"

"We wish to have a play performed."

"Ah. Where?"

"The Globe, I should think," says Sir Charles.

"That'll cost you," says Phillips, tapping his empty cup. The tapster refills it and goes away again. "And we can do it only if the play's in our recent repertory."

"'Tis," Sir Charles assures him, and his brother echoes, "'Tis."

Phillips nods wearily. "We'll need at least a fortnight's notice ... and money—a *lot* of money, as we'll have to close the Globe for the day and lose the whole day's receipts. When would this be?"

"It could be as early as late January," says Sir Charles.

"Plenty of time," says Phillips with a shrug, and finishes his ale. "I'll contact you to let you know how much the players demand. Now if you'll excuse me ..." He rises to go.

"But you don't even know where to *find* us," Sir Josceline protests.

Phillips chuckles. "I do if I've guessed the play correctly."

"Which play, do you think?" asks Sir Charles with amusement.

Phillips glances about to be sure he's not heard.

"Richard the Second?"

The Percy brothers exchange a shocked glance.

"Don't think yourselves so opaque, gentlemen," says Phillips with a smirk. "It's an old play, and it's the only one in our repertory about the lawful deposing of an English monarch." He drops a generous coin on the table and dons his coat. As he walks out, he says, "I'll find you at Essex House—or Drury. And please pass my best regards to the earls."

CHAPTER 20

THE FOLLOWING NIGHT is unusually warm, but a wind high in the air, pushing the clouds along, threatens a return of the deep freeze. At the very hour when Caim habitually leaves Nancy's place, Cuthbert chafes his sides in the shadows of the alleyway across the street, secretly awaiting his appearance.

The noisy street is sporadically illuminated by the torchlight of drunken traffic. Cuthbert is all in black, disguised with a false mustache and blacking makeup. He carries a bag packed with a face mask and a small assortment of carefully selected weapons, including a dagger, a cudgel made of hardwood tightly wrapped in a sheath of thick leather, and a short-barreled snaphaunce pistol.

A few minutes late, Caim comes into view through the open doorway and unexpectedly stops at Nancy's counter. The two pass a few brief words, their expressions businesslike all the while. Perhaps he's extending his stay. Or cutting it short. Cuthbert can't tell from here. Whatever the topic of their brief encounter, it won't deter Cuthbert from his task of getting Serjeant Ames the information he needs.

Caim emerges through the doorway, bounds heedlessly down the stairs to the street, and turns sharply to his right, away from the river. Cuthbert follows, keeping to the shadows, although his stealth seems superfluous, for Caim strides on like a man with perfect confidence in both his path and his personal safety. He never so much as glances sideways, let alone behind. In a few minutes, he turns down a narrow street and Cuthbert follows at a safe distance.

At the dead end of the street sits a boisterous tavern annexed to an inn that Cuthbert knows all too well, as it fell to him several times to visit the place for the sake of his late brother Tobias, whether to extricate him from an ill-fated romantic entanglement or to settle his accounts with the innkeeper, for this has long been known as a place of assignation to sinners of every stripe. And Tobias excelled at sins of the flesh.

It's a good thing Cuthbert's left a safe distance between him and his quarry, because at the next corner Caim stops suddenly and backs into the shadows. Cuthbert slips into a doorway.

His wait is not overlong, for in a few minutes two men approach on the opposite side of the street, walking arm in arm toward the forbidden inn, turning repeatedly to gaze into each other's eyes. One is small and delicately built, the other somewhat stauncher and wearing puritan garb, of all things.

At first Cuthbert is dubious that a puritan could be a catamite, but then upbraids himself for having doubted it. Indeed, if there were no puritan catamites, puritans would seem the only group having no such men among them.

But could this be *Serjeant Ames's* puritan? The one who accuses everyone *else* of buggery? Wouldn't that be the height of irony? He shakes his head and sighs, realizing quite to the contrary, that it would make a great deal of sense for a puritan with a weakness for men to accuse everyone else of that same weakness in the hope of placing himself above suspicion.

But to march others to the *gallows* for sharing one's own predilection? Cuthbert shivers. *What cold betrayal!* He can't help but wonder whether Tobias might have fallen victim to just such a pretender as this. Perhaps even this very one.

Cuthbert continues to observe from the shadows. As the two men enter the inn, Caim emerges from the darkness to follow them as far as the open front door, stopping outside their view. Inside, the recent arrivals nod to the innkeeper as they pass, and follow the street-level hallway to the last room on the right—which they've evidently hired for the night, for they appear to enter with a key.

On a count of perhaps twenty, Caim enters the inn and stops before the innkeeper long enough to palm him a coin, clearly by pre-arrangement. Caim pads down the hallway, and knocks on the very door the puritan and his friend just passed through.

As Cuthbert recalls, though most guests at the inn have the good sense to keep the curtains closed, some are indiscreet enough to leave a window open, as though mere cries of pleasure and pain could suggest nothing of their illicit activities. He needs to know what's going on. Are Caim and the puritan in league with each other? Who is the small man?

To find out, he reluctantly resolves to do something so distasteful that he's done it only once before—and that in aid of Tobias—which is to sneak around back. As he recalls, the inn backs onto an alleyway abutting the windowless brick wall of a building he's never bothered to identify. He quickly counts the windows on the front of the inn, and proceeds on the vague memory that each has a corresponding window at the rear.

Keeping a respectful distance from the rear of the inn, in the darkness he begins counting off each window he passes so he'll end up near the room entered by the puritan and his small friend … and Caim.

Before reaching his destination, to his surprise he passes a large open casement off the hallway, big enough for a man to pass through with only modest discomfort. Come to think on it, it was open last time he was here, as well. Evidently, it's left ajar as an escape hatch for guests to use when the night watch makes one of its infrequent raids on the local sinners. Alternatively, he supposes it could be used by a visitor wishing to avoid being seen entering or leaving. Perhaps it's both.

Cuthbert finishes his window count, and finds he's in luck. There's a small open casement off the puritan's room. He presses his back up against the building and inches toward the open window to eavesdrop.

"You're hurting him!" says a hefty voice. "Let him go. Just tell us what you want."

This must be the puritan speaking, for the small man couldn't possibly have a voice so deep. Nor could the voice belong to Caim, whose lower-class style of speech is all too familiar to Cuthbert.

"Tell you what I want?" says Caim with a cruel edge. "What I want is to cut this one's lips off. That'd make him even uglier, if that's possible. You'd have to find some other bunghole to fill then. Wouldn't ye?" A fearful whimper follows, apparently from the captive.

Cuthbert wonders what the scene looks like inside the room. Is the small man tied to a bedpost while Caim tickles his face with a knife-point? Very likely. Perhaps the puritan is tied to a chair some distance away.

"You're enjoyin' this, aren't ye, puritan?" says Caim. "You want me to make him squeal?"

"No!" says the puritan. "Of course not! I'm fond of him. Please. Let him go and I'll do whatever you want."

"Well, first, let's find out sumthin' o' this little bugger. What's yer name, boy?"

The captive's response is muffled, as though he's gagged.

"What d'ye say?" says Caim. "Hmmm? Tell me, or I'll cut y'again. Much worse this time."

"Starr," comes the meek reply. Evidently, the gag has been removed.

"Not yer *catamite* name. Yer *real* name!"

"Starr is my real name, sir," the high voice supplicates. "Myles Starr. It's my real name. I have no catamite name."

"And how d'ye earn yer daily bread, hah? What'd ye *do,* ye little imp, besides rent out yer pitiful body to all comers?"

"I'm a tax collector," pleads the captive. "I collect money for the Crown."

A rumble begins low in Caim's gut, erupting into a laugh. "What kind o' king would hire the likes o' *you* to collect money for 'im? What d'ye do if they say no? Bite 'em on the ankles? *Ach,* it's a sorry state of affairs that comes from havin' a queen so many years."

The puritan interjects. "Now that you know his name and what he does, why don't you take our money and leave us alone?"

"I don't want yer bleedin' money," says Caim, as though wounded to the quick. "I just don't want either o' you two collectin' royalties on Essex's patent."

For a moment, there's silence, punctuated by a quiet whimpering. Cuthbert wonders how badly Starr's been cut.

"Is *that* what this is about?" asks the puritan in surprise.

"'Tis," replies Caim.

"For your information," says the puritan, "the earl no longer owns a patent. His expired some months ago."

There's a scraping sound, and Starr emits a barely suppressed shriek.

"'Zat so?" asks Caim matter-of-factly.

"Stop hurting him," says the puritan.

"Ye'd rather I hurt *you*?" says Caim.

Silence.

"Didn't think so," says Caim with contempt. "Now, you was tellin' me about Lord Essex's patent. What was it you said—that it was *expired?*"

"Well, there's a patent in existence, but—"

"Oh," says Caim, feigning surprise, "then you *know* which patent I'm talkin' about."

"The Queen issued a new patent in her own name," says the puritan, "and appointed Billingsley to collect royalties on it. So, you see, it has nothing to do with Essex."

"Nothin' to do with *Essex,* eh?" echoes Caim in angry tones. "What do ye take me for? A fool? Mebbe I'll just slice this blighter's throat right now. Then I'll have only *one* o' you buggers to worry about. Yeh," he says contemplatively, "mebbe then I'd have yer full attention."

Images flash through Cuthbert's mind of his brother being knifed to death by Caim and his henchmen. Unable to tolerate Caim's cruelty any longer, he pulls on his mask, takes his pistol in hand, deftly leaps through the open casement into the hallway, and rushes to the door which, to his amazement, he finds unlocked. He enters and snaps the door shut behind him, holding his pistol to the fore.

The scene that greets him is indeed bloody, but not nearly as grisly as it might have been if he'd delayed another moment.

Starr, naked from the waist up, is in the clutches of Caim, who brandishes a knifepoint against his chest. Starr bleeds from a long horizontal cut across the chest, and another across the belly. Neither looks deep, but the victim is terribly pale and torpid, as though he's about to pass out from loss of blood. The puritan is tied to a bedpost in one corner, pretty much as Cuthbert imagined.

"If this blighter don't want yer money," says Cuthbert in an accent well beneath his former station, "I'll be pleased to take all of it. Drop yer purses to the floor."

Caim is still recovering from the shock of his sudden appearance, so Cuthbert addresses him before things get out of hand. "And you, yer bloodthirsty bastard, don't think I wouldn't take pleasure in blowin' yer brains out."

"You ... *dabbler*," retorts Caim with disgust. "Do you have any idea who yaw dealin' with?"

Cuthbert turns his full attention to Caim. "I have some idea ... *pig*."

"*Pig?*" says Caim, and takes two quick steps toward him.

But Cuthbert was anticipating this and sidesteps him, so that in an instant he's actually *behind* him. With all his strength, Cuthbert brings his bludgeon down onto Caim's head, sending him insensate to the floor where he lands face-down with a thud.

Cuthbert instinctively takes a step toward the prostrate man who killed his brother, aims the pistol at his head and cocks it.

"Stop!" the puritan protests. "Can't you see he's unconscious? He's no threat to you now, so you've no right to shoot him."

Though Cuthbert is secretly grateful that his hand has been stayed, he's infuriated by the puritan's pompous tone. "What are you," he asks, "a barrister?"

"A constable," says the puritan demurely.

"Fer Saint Paul's?" asks Cuthbert.

The puritan regards him with shock, evidently realizing that Cuthbert knows who he is and can expose him as a catamite whenever he so wishes.

"Is yaw name Knott?" asks Cuthbert.

Even in the dim light of a few tapers, Cuthbert can see the puritan's countenance redden, and fall in defeat. Sweat, which for some reason had not appeared before Cuthbert entered, now glistens on his forehead.

"Yes," admits Knott.

Cuthbert points the pistol toward the bloody, half-naked catamite squirming on the floor in agony, and asks Knott: "Were you really gonna let him *kill* that man?"

"I was trying to persuade him *not* to do so," says the puritan. "Are you going to see me prosecuted?"

"What," says Cuthbert, "fer buggery?" He shakes his head with contempt. "I wouldn't even *threaten* to do that. But *you* would, wouldn't ye?"

Knott evidently musters within himself a last tattered vestige of pride, though it's barely enough to raise his chin. "What are you talking about?" he demands defensively.

Cuthbert walks over to Knott, and leans into his face. "You threaten men with that bilge all the time, don't ye? You put 'em in fear for their very lives for bein' catamites ... when you're no better."

"What do you mean, 'no better'?" says Knott.

Cuthbert points his pistol at Starr, who's still writhing in pain. "You think yaw better than him?"

Knott looks at Starr with disgust and turns his nose up. "I should hope so," he mutters.

Cuthbert returns both pistol and bludgeon to his pocket and, with an empty hand, slaps Knott in the face so hard his palm stings. He spits out the words: "Filthy hypocrite!"

Cuthbert steps over Caim's unconscious form, finds the knife that was used to cut Starr, and places the handle in the small man's quaking hand. "This bugger'll probably cut ye loose," he says, "though for the life o' me I'll never understand why."

Cuthbert departs the way he came in, quite forgetting to steal anyone's money, thereby giving Caim cause to ponder who he really was.

CHAPTER 21

THE COLD MOONLIGHT is no brighter than it was on Cuthbert's previous visit to Serjeant Ames's house, but the welcome warmth of early evening has departed abruptly, and the free wind howls once more. At least this time there's no one conversing outside who could discover him prematurely.

The house is dark, but for a single taper burning in each of two windows at the rear. If he squints, he can make out the faintest red glow of smoke escaping the chimney. So there's *someone* at home, which is a relief, as this is the night he promised to return with such information as he could gather.

In the quiet of the stables, the boy warms his hands at the fireplace. Cuthbert can discern three horses in the dim orange light. The large black one is Bucklebury, who belongs to Serjeant Ames. The other two appear nearly equal to Bucklebury in size and strength, if not beauty; these surely belong to Lord Saint Ives and Cheerful Killigrew. Evidently, Sir Henry Neville is absent, as is Arthur Arden.

Cuthbert darts from shadow to shadow, at last reaching the back door of the house. He strains to hear any noises from inside, a task made more difficult by the strong wind whipping around from the north. After a few moments, he makes out the murmur of male voices in subdued conversation. There's no sign of women, children, or servants.

Cuthbert is dismayed by the heightened level of his own fear. Even before tonight, there was plenty to worry about. Caim had no doubt issued orders to his many henchmen to slay him on sight, with only secondary concern for secrecy. But now that Caim's been knocked cold by a stranger roughly the same size as Tobias, Cuthbert has little doubt there are numerous men searching for him right now at any place he might frequent. From now on, he must avoid all eyes whenever possible, as well as any suggestion of a connection with Serjeant Ames, as that would no doubt place at risk not only the good Serjeant, but everyone in his ken ... his wife, his daughter, his friends, and all.

Repressing his fear with great effort, he takes a deep breath and knocks almost inaudibly. Inside, a chair scrapes along the floor. Footsteps approach. His heart pounds and he shrinks from the door, hoping to glimpse whoever answers it before he himself is seen.

The door is opened by David Killigrew, his face and form silhouetted in the firelight. As his face juts out the door, his blond mane and sharply defined jaw lend him the appearance of a young Viking of old. He's long had the nickname "Cheerful," but his stolid countenance this evening provides no hint of why.

Cuthbert's heartbeat returns to a normal rhythm.

"Are you sure you've not been followed?" whispers David, his eyes darting from left to right, though he can surely see little way in the darkness.

"As sure as I can be, Master David."

Cuthbert's stomach chooses just that moment to speak up, which reminds him that he's eaten nothing all day.

At the kitchen table sit Lord Jonathan and Serjeant Ames, their faces illuminated by a single taper. At the setting laid for Cuthbert waits a generous plate of hot stew beside a loaf of rough bread.

"Welcome, Cuthbert," says Serjeant Ames. "Please enjoy your meal, and speak with us a while. You must be freezing in that thin cloak."

Cuthbert sits before the plate and immediately dives into the food. "Thank you, sir," he replies, adding, "My cloak's been thick enough up to now, in light of all my activity this evening. I've been following Caim."

"Lord Essex's footman?" asks Serjeant Ames. "Why him, particularly?"

"Quite by chance, he'd taken a room in the same inn as I at Queenhythe."

"But why would he be of interest?" asks Lord Jonathan.

Cuthbert wipes his mouth on a serviette. "He's of interest to me, m'lord, as I expect he killed my brother. I would provide you with the basis for my suspicion, but I think it best for now that I share no such knowledge." He takes a sip of wine. "In just a moment, I expect Caim will be of interest to *you* gentlemen, as well, for I discreetly followed him to an inn known as a place of assignation for illicit lovers and catamites."

"Go on," urges Serjeant Ames. "I assume it's not your news that Caim is a catamite."

"He's not," replies Cuthbert, "though I agree that it would be of little interest if he were. No, he himself was lying in wait for someone. I didn't know for whom, until his quarry appeared."

Lord Jonathan bangs a closed fist on the table anticipating Cuthbert's answer. "Don't tell me it was the puritan!"

Cuthbert is taken aback by the sudden noise in an otherwise quiet room. He looks up, and is relieved to find that Lord Jonathan is not angry with him, but rather eagerly awaiting his answer.

"Please, son," says Serjeant Ames patting Lord Jonathan's hand, "allow Cuthbert to tell the tale his own way."

Cuthbert nods to Jonathan. "I *must* tell you it was the puritan, m'lord. Or I shall have but half a tale to tell."

"I knew it," says Lord Jonathan, rising and beginning to pace, "that officious little *bastard*."

Cuthbert continues. "Caim lay in wait for the puritan, who arrived in company with another man, a catamite, as it soon turned out, quite compact and neat in appearance, though by the time I got a closer look, he was a wreck. Anyway, the puritan and his friend entered the inn and went straight to a room at the back, opening it with a key already in their possession. Caim then went inside, handed something to the innkeeper which I took to be coin of the realm, and followed them close behind.

"Having been there some years earlier, I knew something of the place. I sneaked 'round back and was reminded that they leave open a casement back there, large enough for someone to pass through. Nearby, I found that the puritan had left open another, smaller casement through which I could hear Caim threaten to murder the catamite unless he and the puritan agreed never to collect payments on Lord Essex's patent."

Serjeant Ames exchanges an astonished glance with both Lord Jonathan and Cheerful, and Cuthbert takes advantage of the pause to finish his cup of wine and pour another.

"Lord Essex's patent? Why, this information is of great use to us," says Serjeant Ames at last. "What happened next, Cuthbert?"

Cuthbert shrugs. "Well, when it started to get rough in there—I *heard* Caim cut the small man twice, hurting him rather badly—I leapt in through the large casement and entered the room in the guise of a thief— fully masked, of course. I found the puritan tied to a bedpost, with Caim across the room threatening to cut the small man further. I commanded them all to drop their purses to the floor, which was evidently too much of an affront for Caim. He called me an amateur or some such thing, and I called him a pig. He came at me, and I used the occasion to knock him cold with my friend here." Cuthbert removes the bludgeon from his pocket and places it at the center of the table. "After that, I established that the puritan is indeed Constable Knott of Saint Paul's constabulary."

Noah nods. "So, Knott himself is a catamite?"

Cuthbert nods confidently. "No doubt, sir. Given what happened when Knott arrived with the small man, I don't think he expected to meet with Caim. So, they must have gone there for illicit purposes."

Cheerful chimes in. "I suppose it's possible the puritan and the small man went there merely to divide money between them."

Cuthbert shakes his head. "That seems very unlikely. If they needed to exchange money, it would have been cheaper and safer to do so furtively on the street than to risk being seen together at that ... infamous place. Besides, Caim addressed the small man as a catamite several times without objection by either the puritan or the man himself."

"Very likely," says Serjeant Ames, removing a small piece of paper from his pocket and holding it between himself and the candle so that it can be read by only himself. But Cuthbert can make out that it's a list of some kind.

"Tell me, Cuthbert," says the Serjeant. "Did you learn the small man's name?"

"Yes," replies Cuthbert, straining to recall. "Caim tortured it out of him. Starr. Starr was his name."

Serjeant Ames's eyes move down the paper, searching for a particular item and pausing at one with a start.

"First name 'Anthony'?" asks Serjeant Ames.

It sounds wrong to Cuthbert. "No, sir." He pats his forehead with the palm of his hand as though to dislodge a stuck item of information. To his amazement, it comes to him. "Myles. Yes. Myles Starr. May I ask, Serjeant Ames, what that paper is?"

"I don't suppose there's any harm in your knowing now. It's Master Billingsley's list of men who've applied to collect royalties on the patent formerly belonging to Lord Essex." He sighs. "One of the names is 'Anthony Myles Starr.'"

"Any other names that might be of interest to me?" asks Cuthbert, dreading to hear his brother's name.

"Yes," says Serjeant Ames as he looks grimly at Cuthbert. "*Teller*. I expect I needn't mention to you that Goodman Teller's body was found alongside Tobias's on Bowyer's Row."

The wind howls out of doors. Indoors, the tapers gutter in a chill breeze that somehow seeps in through the cracks.

At the sound of Tobias's name, Cuthbert suddenly loses his appetite.

He puts down the crust in his hand, and stares at the taper in a trance. At last he mutters, "So, Tobias was merely an innocent bystander, then."

Noah replies. "There's no reason to suspect that *either* Teller or Tobias had planned anything unlawful or dishonest. They were likely *both* innocent victims of someone else's avarice."

Cuthbert nods almost imperceptibly, still staring at the taper. "And the avarice was Caim's." He looks up at Noah. "Wasn't it?"

"Perhaps," Noah says, sighing. "But Tobias may have introduced Teller to whatever conspiracy they'd joined, and there's no telling for certain what he had in mind." Noah recalls Essex's momentary look of recognition at the mention of the puritan constable. "What's more, the avarice may go up the chain of command beyond Essex's footman. And that brings me to my next point.

"Cuthbert, you are a marked man. No one must learn you've spoken with any of us, and you can no longer remain in London. Lord Jonathan, please tell our companion of your plans for him, if you would."

Jonathan sits up straight and observes Cuthbert as though unsure he's doing the best thing. "I came upon a fellow at the Drapers' by the name of Jacob."

"A Jew?" asks Cuthbert innocently.

"Yes," says Jonathan with some irritation. "Why? Do you know him?"

"No, m'lord. I merely surmised based upon the Old Testament name."

Noah snickers. "You'll be taking a lot of puritans for Jews, if you continue such surmises."

Lord Jonathan resumes his explanation. "Jacob is a good, honest companion. I'll bring you to him when we've finished here. Jacob and his wife, an invalid, live in a small house in Surrey, and they've assented to my request to take you in and keep you safely out of sight."

"Until when?" asks Cuthbert.

Noah interjects. "Until I direct otherwise. If you're captured or even seen by Caim's men, you'll present an immediate danger to my family, and I won't have that. Is that understood?"

"Aye," replies Cuthbert, "I meant ... no impudence, Serjeant. I understand fully."

"I'm not sure you do," says Noah.

Cuthbert's surprised by Noah's sudden change in mood.

Noah settles back in his chair. "Do you know the First Commandment ... from the Bible, Cuthbert?"

Cuthbert's more than a bit unnerved by the topic's sudden shift to theology. "I believe I do," is all that comes to mind.

"Ah, then, what does it say?"

"'Thou shalt have no other gods before Me.'"

Noah says wistfully, "I've often *heard* it recited that way by my Christian friends." He shakes his head disapprovingly. "But that omits the all-important *first* part, which in our Hebraic tradition rather expresses the whole point. The part you've recited—indeed all *ten* of the Commandments—are little more than an elaboration on the one line you've omitted."

Cuthbert waits patiently.

"The First Commandment begins," says Noah, '*I am the Lord thy God.*'"

Cuthbert ventures a respectful correction. "But ... that's a mere declaration. It's hardly prescriptive, which would seem to be an essential attribute of a *commandment*."

Noah shakes his head as though speaking to a pupil. "No. It's an *exhortation* to remember always that *He* is God, and *you* are not. Just as *I* am not. And who in the Bible declares, 'Vengeance is Mine'?"

Cuthbert delves into a sparse and musty recollection of these long-neglected passages. Then he remembers. "'Vengeance is Mine,' saieth *the Lord*,'" he recites with some self-satisfaction. "Oh, but that's in Saint Paul's *Epistle to the Romans* somewhere. Have you become a student of the *New* Testament, as well, Serjeant Ames?"

Noah smiles and shakes his head indulgently. "It appears first in *Deuteronomy*, which is *Old* Testament."

"I yield as always to the gentleman's superior learning," says Cuthbert with a respectful nod. "But what has this to do with matters at hand?"

Noah's scholarly expression changes to one of sorrow. "It's come to our attention," he says, "that a local gravedigger recently spied a bloody corpse in a grave he'd dug the day before. He spotted it just as a coffin was about to be lowered onto it, and managed—with a great deal of effort and soiled clothing—to exhume it before laying the coffin in, much to the waiting family's horror, as you might imagine." Watching Cuthbert closely, he continues. "The corpse fit the general description of your old friend Meriton."

Cuthbert's face falls as he realizes that Noah has invoked Scripture to tell him—circuitously, and therefore deniably—that he *knows* Cuthbert murdered Meriton to avenge Tobias's murder—and all without so much as alluding to the Commandment that says, "Thou shalt not kill."

Studying Cuthbert's reactions, Noah's certain his point has been duly noted. "I don't know that there's proof enough there to convict a killer," he says quietly, "but if any more of Essex's men turn up as corpses, *our* alliance is done, and you'll have to answer to the Crown as best you may. Is that clear?"

Cuthbert inhales and exhales despondently.

"Pellucid, sir."

CHAPTER 22

NOAH NERVOUSLY APPROACHES the Westminster map room where he joined Lord Robert Cecil, Francis Bacon, and Sir Walter Raleigh last year to hear Lord Mountjoy's plans for subduing Ireland. That meeting had been convened by Her Majesty, but she fell ill and was unable to attend.

Today's meeting has been convened at the request of Noah himself, who sent letters to Robert Cecil and Francis Bacon only this morning asking them to join him here at noon "should their other affairs permit." There was insufficient time for them to reply, so he'll have no idea until he enters whether they'll attend.

The door to the map room is closed and, as he turns the knob, his heart flutters, half hoping there's no one inside; for if either Cecil or Bacon attends, he has little hope of getting through the meeting without revealing more than he cares to. He swings the door open, where he's patiently awaited by both Cecil and Bacon.

He shuts the door firmly behind him, glances about to ensure that there's no one else present to overhear the meeting, and gazes a moment at his powerful friends, for that is how he thinks of them. Other than Jon Hawking, there's not a man in the world whose friendship he values more than theirs ... save Sir Henry Neville.

"Serjeant Ames," says Lord Robert. "To what do we owe this singular summons? I must confess to being more than a bit surprised to be invited to a 'secret meeting.'"

Noah clears his throat. "I'm afraid I had no choice, m'lord," he says, taking a seat close enough to permit him to be heard without speaking loudly.

Francis Bacon wears a worried expression. "Has this aught to do with your investigation of the murders at ... at ..."

"Bowyer's Row," says Noah, completing the thought. "Yes, it has, and there have been at least two related murders since then. But we're getting ahead of ourselves. I must start by informing you that I've discovered a foul conspiracy afoot at Essex House."

"Conspiracy?" says Lord Robert sternly. "You mean against Her Majesty's reign?"

Noah wishes they'd allow him to explain things in his own way, but that's a rare luxury he learned to forego during the practice of law.

"Well," replies Noah equivocally, "while there may be such a conspiracy, m'lord, that of which I speak today does *not* appear to extend so far, as its immediate object seems to be obtaining monies by illicit means. Now, whether the conspirators intend to use such monies in furtherance of a rebellion against Her Majesty is uncertain, but I doubt that the sums involved would be sufficient to arm such a cause to any great degree.

"To get to my point, as I know you're both busy with other matters: One man was murdered at Bowyer's Row to eliminate him as a candidate for employment by Henry Billingsley in collecting royalties on the reissued patent in sweet wines. Another man was murdered at Bowyer's Row simply to silence him or to conceal the killers' motive for murdering the other man. Since that time, yet another man has been murdered to shut his mouth."

Lord Robert frowns skeptically. "So the motive for murder was a rivalry for a position collecting money for the Crown?" he asks. "I would have thought the compensation for such a position would be insufficient to scrap over, let alone to commit multiple murders."

Noah was ready for this. "Well," he says, "if a collector is dishonest, there's at least one proven method by which he might enrich himself at the expense of those paying the royalties." To his companions' astonishment, he adds: "Such was explained to us at length by the Chancellor of the Exchequer, who has evidently had occasion to detect and confront such practices."

"Fortescue explained it to you?" asks Bacon with surprise.

"Aye," confirms Noah, "Sir John, personally."

Lord Robert leans forward. "Noah, you said 'us.' Who was there besides you when Sir John explained this to you?"

"Oh, I'm sorry," says Noah. "I neglected to mention that Lord Saint Ives has been assisting me in the investigation. Before the meeting, Sir John had evidently learned of his lordship's service to the realm and took quite a fancy to him. As a result, he took great pains to explain the technique. It's a bit elaborate, but one can readily see how it works. I'll explain if you wish—"

"Spare us," says Lord Robert holding up the palm of his left hand.

"Over the years, we've discovered so many ways for a thief to aggrandize himself at the expense of the Crown, I've come to believe such techniques are *innumerable*."

Francis's face takes on a bitterness that Noah has never before seen there. "This intrigue has the smack of Henry Cuffe about it," he declares.

"Cuffe?" says Lord Robert. "The name is familiar, but—Oh, that's right. He's one of Essex's secretaries."

"Why, Master Bacon," says Noah with surprise, "I was unaware that you're acquainted with Master Cuffe."

Francis sneers in most uncharacteristic fashion. "That foul republican is behind every effort to aggrandize Essex at Her Majesty's expense. Have you traced the conspiracy to him yet?"

"Not to him personally," replies Noah, "I must admit."

"I'm unsurprised," says Bacon. "He delegates every distasteful task to his underlings, and so maintains his own sham reputation at their expense."

"Indeed?" says Noah. "When I've spoken with him, Master Cuffe hasn't seemed particularly militant in any respect, but rather … professorial."

Francis grimaces and shakes his head emphatically. "Don't be taken in by his scholarly disguise. Beneath it, he's horn-mad."

Noah furrows his brow. "But surely you overstate, Francis."

"If but once you move him on a point of contention," says Bacon gravely, "you'll see him rave."

Lord Robert clears his throat a bit impatiently and brings them back to the matter at hand. "Noah, how can we assist you in detection and apprehension of the murderer? I assume that's what you wanted to talk about."

Noah sighs. "At this point, I would ask two things, and both need be handled with the utmost discretion and kept secret ever after. First, I would ask one of you to instruct Billingsley (without mentioning either me or Lord Saint Ives) to send a written notice to those obliged to pay royalties on sweet wines that, until further instruction, they must personally bring the amount of their indebtedness to Billingsley's clerk at Westminster, there to await a sealed receipt. If I'm correct in my belief that the murders arose out of a rivalry for an itinerant collector's job, Billingsley's notice should have the effect of removing any motive for further murders."

"Simple enough," says Lord Robert, writing. "What else?"

Noah purses his lips a moment. "My other request is a bit more sensitive, I'm afraid."

Sir Robert peers up at him questioningly from his notes and says nothing, just as was his father's custom long ago.

Noah shifts uneasily. "The problem is that I've already asked Her Majesty's indulgence on this, and she declined it rather peremptorily."

Bacon says, "If circumstances have changed, I don't suppose Her Majesty would flatly resist our request that she reconsider. What do you need?"

"Well," replies Noah hesitantly, "the cathedral constable at Saint Paul's has taken an interest in the case, and Her Majesty has once declined to remove him at my request."

Lord Robert nods. "I was there when you asked her. Oh, but you provided her no basis whatever for your request. Am I misremembering?"

"No, Lord Robert. Your memory is impeccable, as ever. I—hesitated to mention to her a certain offensive curiosity that completely overwhelms the man. Indeed, the reports of witnesses who've met him are embarrassing and highly distracting. He's a puritan, you see ... and ... preoccupied, nay, *consumed* with the possibility of other men's buggery. He sees it everywhere, even where it's not."

"What's his name?" asks Lord Robert.

Noah shakes his head, reluctant to say it. He forces himself.

"His name is What-God-Will Knott."

After a moment of realization, Lord Robert bellows a laugh. "What do you say, Francis?" he says, recovering his breath. "We should bar him for his *name*, if for no other reason." He places his pen down and enjoys another hearty laugh at the puritan's expense. "I'm shocked to learn the cathedral constabulary would suffer a puritan in its service. Those people are held in such contempt by church *and* state."

Noah is certain Lord Robert's sense of levity has prevented him from noticing the glint of fearful recognition in Francis Bacon's eyes.

"Worse still," says Noah, "—and this I could not know when I first brought the question to Her Majesty—Knott appears to be compromised in the case, as he favors a candidate of his own for the itinerant collector's position."

"I met Knott some years ago," says Bacon. "He is odious. I have no objection to recommending Her Majesty remove him, especially in light of his conflict of interest and the good Serjeant's progress in the matter."

Although Noah's somewhat relieved, he yet needs one more concession. "On this point also, I respectfully request that both of you—and indeed Her Majesty—give not the least hint to anyone that Knott's been removed from the case at my urging, as it could place both myself and my family in the path of the murderer or murderers in question." Having unburdened himself of his requests, he sits back. "And there's the end of the agenda for my urgent meeting. I heartily thank you both for coming and for your cooperation."

Lord Robert and Francis Bacon nod to each other. Lord Robert rises and gathers his papers together.

"I'll tell Billingsley myself," Lord Robert tells Noah. "On the question of the cathedral constable, I'll raise it with Her Majesty tomorrow, and let you know discreetly whether she'll go along."

Noah bows. "Many thanks to you both," he says.

⟩∘⟨⟨∘⟩

LATER THAT AFTERNOON Noah and Jonathan meet by arrangement outside Westminster Hall for the ride back to Holborn. Bucklebury sets a leisurely pace, and Noah feels no need to rush him.

A cold breeze nips at their faces. The deciduous trees have lost all their red and gold leaves, and now appear no more than gnarled sticks in the garish light of the setting sun.

"Christmas cannot be far off," says Noah impassively.

Jonathan looks at him askance. "My, but you're cheerful," he says. "Bad day at court?"

Noah gives Jonathan a full report of this morning's meeting with Lord Robert and Francis Bacon.

Jonathan asks, "Don't you have enough yet to arrest Caim on a charge of murdering Master Teller and Tobias Bennett?"

"Not by a long shot," says Noah despondently. "There was little evidence at the murder scene on Bowyer's Row. And no eyewitnesses have come forward, nor are they likely to, as they're no doubt familiar with Caim's technique for dealing with adversaries."

"What about the murder of the other one?" asks Jonathan. "Teller's lover at the Wardrobe?"

"Ralph? The evidence that Caim was the culprit is circumstantial only, and the probative value of any such evidence would depend on our first proving Caim guilty of the original crime on Bowyer's Row. Otherwise, the murders could be made to seem coincidental."

"You told Lord Robert and Francis Bacon nothing of your suspicion of Caim?" asks Jonathan.

"Not a word. What they don't know, they can't repeat. Not that I expect they would if they knew what was at stake, but I can't afford to fully inform them of that, either. If Caim were to learn 'twas *I* who urged Billingsley to withdraw his search for an itinerant money collector, he'd be furious at me. Caim no doubt has a horse in that race—although we don't yet know who it is—and Caim's not someone I would care to have angry with me. He's positively ruthless."

Jonathan nods. "And why did you request secrecy concerning Knott's involvement in the 'race,' as you call it, through his 'horse' Starr?"

Noah shakes his head gravely. "For that to become generally known would bring about the worst result. First, Knott and Starr would be exposed as catamites, which would ruin them both. Though that might happen anyway, I'd just as soon not be the one to destroy them. On a more personal level, however, Caim would come after me—after *us*."

"Why us?" asks Jonathan.

"Remember," says Noah, "Caim believes that the only person beside himself who knows of Knott's association with Starr (besides Knott and Starr themselves, of course, both of whom have strong reason to maintain secrecy) is the thief who broke into their trysting room while Caim was there. The 'thief' was Cuthbert, of course, and Caim may already suspect that, though he's yet been unable to find him."

"Aha!" says Jonathan. "And if Caim *were* to hear you're the one who identified Knott's conflict of interest in the murder case, he'd conclude that you learned of it from Cuthbert."

"From whom else *could* I have learned of it?" asks Noah with a shrug.

Jonathan continues reasoning aloud. "And, since Caim can't find Cuthbert, his only way to get at him would be … through you." He turns up his collar against the blustery wind. "Suddenly, Christmas doesn't promise much of a respite from either court politics or your murder investigation, does it?"

"Indeed, it does not," confirms Noah, "which is a shame. Would you consider the precaution of taking your lovely bride on a journey somewhere outside London for the yuletide?"

Jonathan sighs. "She seems to be prone to severe headaches at the moment, and won't travel in her present condition. No, she's made it clear that we're permanent lodgers at your home in Holborn until she brings forth your grandchild."

"What a blessing and a *relief* that will be!" says Noah.

"I'd wager a penniless Jewish orphan from Poland never expected to live to be a grandfather."

Noah smiles. "And you'd win your wager—if only you could find someone to take it."

<hr />

MARIE WAS FIRST TO RETIRE, and left a single taper burning for Noah, as he often retires later than she. As he changes into his bed clothing and prepares to join her, he gazes on her comely face and form, and wonders why the world never leaves him alone long enough to enjoy the blessed warmth of her bed and body without distraction and worry.

Ah, well, he tells himself, *if I were lazy I'd be less in demand at court, but then I'd be unworthy of Marie. And what good would that do me?* He wonders in passing whether he would appreciate his gifts more if he had a clearer mind to enjoy them, and then dismisses the whole question, as it presupposes that he had a choice in the direction of his life, when he never did.

As he lies in the dark, he tries to concentrate on the gentle sound of Marie's breathing, but the wailing wind eventually drowns her out and he drifts off to its plaintive moan.

Noah's in a vacant theater at night, sitting among the favored seats alongside the stage. A quiet scene is being performed with but one actor, playing an aging woman. She faces away from him, fussing with something in a pot in the fireplace, perhaps a porridge. He's never seen such a realistic fireplace on stage before. In fact, this doesn't seem to be a stage any longer.

The theater is gone, but the scene unchanged. The fireplace is vaguely familiar, then he recognizes it as the one in the kitchen cottage at the Tower of London where he first met the Queen on an autumn night many years ago. He's in that very kitchen now. The woman taps a wooden spoon against the inside of the pot, covers it, and rests the spoon on the cover.

As she begins to turn toward him in the red glow of the fire, at first he dreads seeing her face, for he now realizes this is no actor in a threepenny costume, nor is it a man. It's Queen Elizabeth, not as she was then, but as she is now. Her expression is one of impatience, and she regards him silently with a sore disappointment that makes his heart ache.

He's suddenly aware that there's someone standing beside him, a companion whose face he cannot see. But she can see it. She gazes at his companion's face in evident disgust, and points Noah toward the back door tacitly inviting him to leave. She shakes her head dourly at Noah, and speaks some words that echo as though they've been uttered into an iron pot, her lips unsynchronized with the words emerging from them:
    "Amicus inimici mei amicus meus nequit."

He awakens with a start. *The friend of mine enemy cannot be my friend,* she said. There's a hollow in the pit of his stomach. Something is wrong.
    Something is *very* wrong.
    Is there a traitor among us?

CHAPTER 23

WITH THE SUFFERANCE of Her Majesty, Lord Robert, and Francis Bacon, the Ames's Christmas season passes surprisingly free of further intrigue. True, each week more knights and other men of "quality" seem to crowd into both Essex and Drury House. But their singing foolish songs, drinking heavily, and entertaining puritan sermons appear to pose no immediate threat to their neighbors ... or to the established order.

Every year, without telling anyone but Noah, Marie prepares a unique New Year's gift for Her Majesty's wardrobe. While Noah is not much of a gift enthusiast, he's come to enjoy sharing the thrill that Marie garners from it all.

So skilled is Marie at designing items to the Queen's taste that Her Majesty makes sure to wear one (or even two) on state occasions and when appearing in public. This arouses great jealousy in the nobility, who annually gift the Queen with an item of gold or jewelry worth a king's ransom, which is politely accepted but somehow never seen again. Fortunately for Noah and Marie, the jealousy is never directed their way, as no one else knows who confers the mysterious items upon the Queen, so they're commonly assumed to be handiwork of the Wardrobe.

As midwinter approaches, Marie receives from Italy an item she's been awaiting a long time. Following tradition, she waits for one of those rare occasions on which she and Noah are alone in the house, then has him cover his eyes in a corner of his study while she lays out the gift for his perusal before wrapping it for Her Majesty.

Following a tradition of his own, Noah peeks at Marie through a crack between his fingers, as he's simply unable to forego the pleasure of watching her fuss about preparing the gift for presentation. Watching her is *his* New Year's present. Nor does he feel any real regret about cheating in this way, as he's only watching *her*, avoiding so much as a glance at the gift itself.

"Very well, Serjeant Ames," says Marie proudly. "You may open your eyes." She spreads her arms in presentation. "Voilà!"

He drops his hands from his eyes, and says with enthusiasm, "Why, Marie, that's *magnificent*!"

She smiles from ear to ear, then regards him with suspicion. "You really like it?"

"Absolutely! What's more, Her Majesty will be thrilled. I'm certain."

"*Certain,* are you?" she asks dubiously.

"Why, of course!"

She pouts and points to the items on the tabletop. "Then ... what is it?"

He adopts the dramatic posture of one falsely accused of duplicity. "Why ... it's *three* things, isn't it?"

"Very good, Noah. You can count. What are the three things?"

He takes a step toward the items as though to get a better look, but he's really playing for time. "Well," he says at last, "this one is a mask to cover the upper part of one's face, isn't it?"

"Yes, it is," says Marie, as though to a willing pupil. "When would Her Majesty wear such a mask?"

"When she doesn't wish to be recognized?" he ventures.

"Such as ... at a masquerade ball?" asks Marie.

"Certainly," he says. "And it's truly beautiful, especially with that little"—he points to things he cannot name—"those little blue things on the edges. And the gold ... um—"

"Gold *leaf,*" she says. "I'm glad you spotted those. I was afraid they were too small to be noticed, but I didn't want it to be gaudy. Her Majesty *detests* gaudy."

"It's not the least bit gaudy," he says reassuringly.

"And what are the other two pieces, pray tell?" she asks suspiciously.

"Why, they're—" He takes a step closer and bends to look at them.

"Don't touch!" she says. "No touching!"

"I wouldn't *think* of touching them," he says defensively. The two items are a matching set of ... something the size of earrings. "Well, each is gorgeously painted with Her Majesty's crest, of course." He looks up at her. "How do you suppose the craftsman painted them so sm—"

She interrupts him. "What *are* they?" she repeats impatiently.

"Well," he says, "they're items for ... wearing." It's weak, but almost certainly accurate.

She shakes her head, obviously disappointed that he's learned nothing over the years about the finer aspects of clothing accessories.

He suddenly notices a place on either side of the visor that would snugly hold a decorative pin. "Well, they're pins, aren't they? Of course they are. They go *here* .... and *there*. Oh," he says, a bit confused, "but if they're mounted on the mask—and they bear Her Majesty's crest—won't people know it's *she* behind the mask?"

"Not necessarily," replies Marie. "Someone else might wear Her Majesty's mask, if she were to let them."

"Marie, such a person could be subject to arrest on grounds of impersonating the Sovereign."

Marie nods smugly. "That's why I had the pins fashioned so they could be used elsewhere."

"But they fit the mask *perfectly*," he observes, a bit baffled. "You just suggested that she'd wear the mask when she does *not* wish to be recognized. Did you not?"

"Of course," Marie replies as though addressing a dunce. "But she'll *always* wish to be recognized. She's the *Queen of England,* for God's sake!" She rolls her eyes. "Honestly, Noah," she says with exasperation, "you are *hopeless*."

He takes her in his arms. "And you are ... *wonderful*!" he says. She looks down demurely in that way of hers, and he kisses her long and deeply.

⟶∘⟁∘⟵

LORD JONATHAN'S NEVER BEEN so happy having so little to do. With the blowing snow kept safely out of doors and a beautiful young wife growing his first child in her belly, life is just so wonderfully cozy. Noah and Marie have stocked in a plentiful larder, and there's enough firewood to get them through even the harshest of winters.

But even in the most enchanted times, nature takes her course. Lady Jessica grows more plump by the week. Though Jonathan greets the prospect of the blessed event with nearly unalloyed joy, each advancing week seems to cause Jessica greater concern. Her headaches, though occasional only, have grown worse. Although she's made it a practice to avoid speaking morbidly, Jonathan can see that morbidity is still very much on her mind and growing in tandem with their coming child.

One morning while he and Jessica are still abed, Jonathan decides the time has come for him to broach the topic of Aunt Beth's assistance in the delivery. When he does, Jessica presses her face so hard into her pillow that it muffles her words.

"I don't wish to discuss it," she says with a break in her voice.

He strokes her long hair. "I don't suppose there's much to discuss, is there? No one can make up your mind for you, but I, for one, want what's best for my lady fair and the precious little baby she'll soon hold in her arms."

Muffled weeping escapes her pillow, and a pit of despair grows in Jonathan's gut. The most frustrating thing about demonstrating affection is that it often seems to deepen—rather than relieve—the loved one's despondency.

"Have you heard any news of Lord Essex lately?" he asks, abandoning what seems a hopeless topic.

Almost instantly, Jessica turns toward him. Though her eyes are still teary, her mind has visibly moved on. Nothing titillates like the prospect of gossip. She wipes her eyes and says, "I've heard that Lord Essex said something awful about Her Majesty when she didn't answer the letter he wrote for her birthday."

"Really?" he asks.

"Oh, yes," she says, sitting up fully engaged.

Jonathan's love for his wife wells up in his chest until it's near overflowing. "What awful thing did he say?"

"Well," she says with intimate excitement, "you know how vain Her Majesty can be about her appearance, especially now that she's more advanced in years."

"I suppose that's a trait she has in common with her subjects," he observes.

"I suppose," she confirms. "But Lord Essex said something terrible about her posture."

"No!" says Jonathan with just that patronizing incredulity she seems so to enjoy.

"Yes!" she says wide-eyed. "Lord Essex said she's an old woman whose mind is as twisted as her carcass."

Jonathan can feel his face drop. *That stupid, self-defeating man.* He sighs. "I'm afraid he wasn't just insulting Her Majesty's posture, my dear, though he *was* doing that—and rather crassly. Though a carcass may be a living thing, the word clearly connotes an animal that's already dead. But *principally* he was saying that her thinking is embittered and clouded by age, which is far worse."

"*Is* that worse?"

"*Much* worse," he replies.

"Why?"

"Well, the Queen reigns only so long as she maintains her mental sanity. Anyone calling into question the soundness of her mind is flirting with a charge of sedition and a sentence of death."

"Can she really have someone put to death for that?"

He nods gravely. "Such is the breath of kings."

Jessica seems lost in thought and then, as she's wont to do, asks a profound question in the most childlike manner. "What if Her Majesty's mind *were* succumbing to old age?"

He's a little surprised by the question.

"It's not," he assures her.

"But what if it were?" she insists. "I mean, the monarchy goes back so far, there must have been *some* Sovereign who lost his mind. Mustn't there?"

"Well," he shrugs, "I suppose there must have been one or two. The law of monarchy was not my specialty while practicing law, but my recollection is that a suggestion of madness would properly be made privately to the royal family by a peer of the Crown, who would no doubt be taking his life in his hands. Then, if all agree, a bill of regency could be adopted in Parliament appointing the king's heir apparent to act in the king's place during his incapacity."

"And if not all agree?" she asks.

"Then England faces a major problem and the possibility of civil war. A very delicate topic, both politically and legally. Not one I'd care to dwell on."

While Jessica seems lost in thought, Jonathan revives his first concern. "I suppose you've decided on the midwife recommended by Mistress Ames?"

His question brings back her sense of reality, but fortunately not her weeping. Instead she speaks seriously. "Oh, Jonathan, how I wish my mother were here to watch over me."

He places his feet on the floor and sits crestfallen at the edge of the bed.

What can one say to that?

———————————⊰⊱———————————

THE TWELFTH NIGHT revels at Gray's Inn are especially raucous in this new year of 1601—*memorably* so to the Ameses, their Holborn neighbors, and all within earshot.

A few days later on January 9, as the sun sets and supper is cleared away, there's an alarmingly strident knock at the Ames's front door.

Esther runs to open it and is surprised to see the windblown form of David Killigrew, as he hasn't been to the Ames's residence since visiting along with Sir Henry and Lady Anne on Christmas Day. Blood pounding in Esther's ears, she does her best to curtsey impassively.

"Won't you come in, Master Killigrew?" she says, avoiding eye contact.

He hesitates outside a moment, wishing that his heart would forget to flutter as it does whenever he sees her. That hope is dashed instantly. He wants her so badly, he cannot help but resent her power over him.

Playing the perfect hostess, she takes his elbow and draws him into the house as best she can, being so much smaller than he. "I would have thought you'd already be off to Oxford for examinations."

Keeping his boots and cloak on, he removes his cap and gloves but gently declines to yield them up. "I was about to leave Uncle Henry's at Lothbury when I heard a bit of disturbing news."

"Oh?" she says sympathetically, "I hope there's been no illness or death in the family."

"Which family?" he asks pointedly. Before it's even out of his mouth, his heart leaps, wishing that their families were one and the same.

"Why, the Killigrews and the Nevilles, master," she says. "But I meant to include any family you might care for."

That sounds to David like a hopeful expression that she might become a member of a family he cares for. But, of course, she already is, for he cares deeply for the Ameses.

"There's no illness or death in any family I care for," he protests, "at least to my knowledge. Lord Sheffield knocked on Sir Henry's door as I was about to leave. He was alarmed, so I thought I'd deliver the news in person."

"I do hope that Lady Sheffield has not disappeared yet again," she says.

"To put your mind at ease, Esther, I can tell you that Lady Sheffield has *not* disappeared again." It takes every bit of determination for him to refrain from adding that she was never abducted.

Esther pauses as though she's forgot his reason for knocking.

While David would love to gaze upon Esther's face all night long, she's convinced him he'd get nowhere. "Are Lord Jonathan and Serjeant Ames at home?" he asks at last.

"Oh, yes … of course," she says awkwardly. "I shall summon them at once. How silly of me!"

She disappears, and a moment later Serjeant Ames appears with Lord

Jonathan and Arthur Arden in tow. None is dressed for outdoors. Only Arthur is wearing boots.

"What is it, David?" asks Serjeant Ames with concern.

"It's Lord Grey, sir. Lord Sheffield called at Sir Henry's a few minutes ago as I was about to head out for Oxford. He asked if I could stop here and tell you what's been happening. Evidently, he learned that Lord Grey has organized a few of his attendants to aid in confronting Lord Southampton on horseback shortly."

"Where?" asks Noah glumly.

"The Strand, not far from Essex House."

Noah considers the situation. "That's not far from Raleigh's home at Durham House, either," he says. "He's Grey's former shipmate. How I would dearly *love* to leave this to him! But—who knows?—he may be unable to get there in time. He may not even be at home. Besides, if Lord Grey is bringing attendants (assuming he can sober them up sufficiently), any fight could become a general mélée, and those are too often taken as license for the settling of private griefs. The constable could be finding bodies for days, especially in this snow."

"Serjeant Ames," says David, "if I may: What ever is the *reason* for this long-running grudge between Lord Grey and Lord Southampton?"

Noah sighs and shakes his head in dismay. "Lord Grey, while serving in Ireland under Lord Southampton, led a charge against the Irish without first obtaining permission from his superior officer. Southampton then had Grey imprisoned *one day* for his insubordination."

David is waiting for more, but nothing comes. "That's all?" he asks.

"That's all *either* of them will let on. The Privy Council and the Queen have enjoined them to stop this feuding, but Lord Grey simply will not let it go."

Noah turns to Jonathan and Arthur, and claps his hands loudly. "Well, boys, we've overstayed the yuletide. To horse!" Scratching his head, he looks about. "Blast," he mutters, "where are my boots?"

"They're up here, sir," comes Esther's voice from upstairs, "with your cloak and your guests' items." Arthur charges upstairs to help Esther bring down their heavy things.

Noah turns to Cheerful. "It will take us a few minutes to ready ourselves, David. Though I don't wish to delay your return to Oxford a moment longer, might I prevail upon you to stop at Durham House to tell Sir Walter what you've heard, and tell him we'll be along?" He brings himself up short. "Come to think on it, why are you traveling at night in such weather as this?"

"Just thought I'd get an early start, sir. I was planning on staying at an inn a short way out of town." He leans into Noah and mutters, "With Esther rejecting me, sir, there's no reason for me to stay a moment longer. I couldn't take another night of solitary study by the same lonely fire."

Noah glances upstairs to make sure he can't be heard. "Jonathan never addressed this problem for you?"

"Not yet, sir," says David, turning to the door. "I'll go and notify Sir Walter."

CHAPTER 24

BY THE TIME they leave Noah's house, the sun has gone down. The snow has stopped falling, the sky has cleared, and the snowy street reflects the moonlight brightly enough for them to ride with little hazard. But a blustery wind fitfully blows sharp crystals of snow into their horses' eyes, forcing them to stop every few houses.

Noah rides slightly ahead of Lord Jonathan and Arthur. He leads them off Holborn, and south onto Fetter Lane to Fleet Street, which becomes the Strand.

After a short but halting ride, Noah peers west down the Strand, which is deserted but for a distant, lone rider on a white horse near Arundel House, who's slowly approaching. Alongside the rider walks a young torchbearer of perhaps ten or eleven years. Hoping that Lord Sheffield's alarum was based upon naught but empty rumor, Noah brings Bucklebury to a halt and awaits a peaceful conclusion to the quiet scene.

Suddenly, three galloping horsemen—two bearing torches—come up behind the lone horseman and his boy, and swiftly bear down on them. For a brief moment, the hapless victims seem unaware of the threat.

"Come on," says Noah, shaking Bucklebury's reins, "we may be in time to stop this." But the blowing snow slows them down again, and the fight unfolds too fast for Noah and his friends to intercede immediately.

The three threatening riders come to a sudden halt as soon as they reach their quarry. The two torchbearers stop their mounts a few feet off, lifting their torches high to light the area.

The third rider draws his sword. "Hah!" he shouts. "The bugger-boy Southampton needs assistance from his *own* little bugger-boy. Draw your sword, m'lord, and put off meeting your Maker for a moment or two."

Bucklebury's hoofbeats are muffled by the snow, permitting Noah to recognize the swordbearer's voice as belonging to Lord Grey. Noah assumes that Arthur recognizes Grey's voice from the shouting match between them at the Saracen's Head.

Lord Grey repeatedly swings his sword in Southampton's direction, his swinging becoming more and more reckless as Southampton steadfastly refuses to draw.

"*Draw*, you bastard," Grey shouts. "If you won't fight like a man, perhaps I'll cleave your bugger-boy's head in twain."

Grey steers his mount menacingly toward the boy, who's frightened out of his wits, and repeatedly swings his sword in a level arc over the boy's head.

"Let the lad be," shouts Southampton. "He's a stranger to our quarrel."

But Grey continues the provocation until the boy begins to whimper. In a moment's distraction, the boy instinctively brings his hand up into the path of the sword's arc and, with a *chunk*, his hand flies off, coming to rest in the snow at the foot of one of the torchbearers' horses.

The boy's eyes go wide and his breath comes in short gasps, as the realization begins to sink in that he's lost his hand forever, for no good reason and through no quarrel of his own.

"M'lord," says the foremost torchman with a touch of panic, "this is mayhem. Let's go now, before we're apprehended."

The boy lifts his truncated wrist up to his face and begins to wail miserably.

Lord Grey, obviously humiliated by the hideous result of his own stupidity, sheathes his sword, grabs Southampton by the lapels, and begins pounding him mercilessly about the head and shoulders. Southampton falls to the ground, and Grey leaps from his horse and continues to pummel him.

As Noah at last draws close enough to intervene, he draws his pistol and aims it at the blustery sky. "I am Serjeant Noah Ames," he shouts in his most official voice. "I command you to cease this flagrant violation of orders of the Queen and the Privy Council!"

Grey is about to ignore the order, lifting his right fist as though to deliver a decisive blow to Southampton's face.

Noah's fires his pistol. Though it contains no ball or shot, Lord Grey doesn't know that.

Its report seizes Grey's attention at last. He drops Southampton's bloody face onto the snow and leans forward near exhaustion, each breath steaming in the frigid night air.

Southampton writhes in pain, while his boy kneels in the snow, watching in horror as his wrist pulses blood onto the once-white snow.

Two new figures approach, running full tilt from the direction of Durham House. As they reach the perimeter of the torchlight, the faces of Sir Walter Raleigh and Cheerful Killigrew come into view.

Noah's pistol shot has drawn the curiosity of neighbors indoors, as well, who light tapers and jut their heads out of windows to gape at the fray.

Sir Walter calmly takes control.

"You!" he shouts to the torchbearer who counseled Lord Grey to abscond, and then points to Cheerful. "Hand this young man your torch and dismount at once."

But the torch carrier looks to Lord Grey and awaits guidance, which infuriates Sir Walter.

"Don't you *dare* look to your master," says Sir Walter with open disgust. "He's already led you sorely astray once this evening. You're in the *Queen's* custody now, and you'll do as I say *when I say it!*"

To Noah's amazement, Sir Walter leaps up from the ground with what seems no effort at all, grabs the torchman by the lapels, drags him from his horse, and lays him out on the ground, heedless of the torch tumbling into the snow.

Without a moment's hesitation, the other torchbearer dismounts and hands his lit torch to Cheerful with a bow. Cheerful accepts it silently, and tenderly picks up the boy's severed hand in a pocket kerchief.

Sir Walter points to Arthur. "Master Arden! With Serjeant Ames's permission, I ask you to bring this boy and his severed hand to the Warder's surgeon at the Tower at once. Speak to Warder Gardner or Francis only, both of whom I believe you've met, identify yourself as Serjeant Ames's assistant, and show them the boy's wound ... and hand." Arthur accepts the bloody kerchief from Cheerful, hoists up the whimpering boy behind him on the saddle, and rides east as quickly as he can over the unsure footing of a snow-covered street.

Raleigh unceremoniously hauls Lord Grey up and away from Southampton's prostrate form, brings him to his feet, and shoves him rudely into his horse. "I'll be with *you* in just a moment, m'lord," he says, as Grey's horse snorts indignantly.

It's the earl's turn. Sir Walter lifts the wobbly Southampton off the street and gently stands him up as squarely as possible, dabbing his facial wounds with a fresh kerchief.

"Would you care to go home, m'lord?" he asks respectfully.

Southampton nods. "Thank you, Sir Walter," he mumbles through his wounded mouth. Even in pain, he has the breeding to turn most of the way toward Noah before grunting out, "And you, as well, Serjeant Ames."

Sir Walter and Noah bow lightly.

"M'Lord Saint Ives," says Sir Walter, "I would be much obliged if you would escort Lord Southampton and his mount to his residence at Drury House. I'll see that his boy is returned to him after the surgeon has attended to his wound."

Jonathan helps Southampton to remount, remounts himself, and (as Wych Street has been removed for the widening of the Strand) leads horse and rider off in the direction of Little Drury Lane.

With his hand, Sir Walter commands Lord Grey's two henchmen to hand off their mounts to him and stand next to their master, who looks as thoroughly abashed as if he'd been caught with his breeches down worrying the sheep.

Sir Walter catches sight of neighbors still gaping out of their windows. "Back to sleep," he shouts angrily, "every last one of you. Or I'll bring *you* along to the Tower." Tapers are extinguished and casements creak shut with such speed that Noah would have laughed had he not just seen such a grievous wound inflicted on Southampton's boy.

Sir Walter addresses his prisoners. "Thomas Lord Grey of Wilton and your two servants: I hereby arrest you each and all in the name of Queen Elizabeth and her Privy Council."

"Sir Walter," says Lord Grey equably, "I have something to say, if I may."

"I'm not *sentencing* you, Lord Thomas," Sir Walter mutters with irritation. "Just *arresting* you."

"I know," says Lord Grey, "but I feel I owe you and the good Serjeant an explanation."

Sir Walter looks questioningly to Noah, who reluctantly nods.

"All right," says Sir Walter to Grey, "have your say."

"Southampton and Essex," says Lord Grey, "are planning an armed insurrection against Her Majesty to take place only a few weeks hence. When I learned of this, I quite lost my temper. For which I'm truly sorry. That's all I wish to say."

"Have you a response, Serjeant?" asks Sir Walter.

"Lord Grey," says Noah, "are you suggesting that a threatened insurrection by the master in some way justifies your lopping off his innocent servant's hand? The hand of a wee lad, I might add?"

Lord Grey is prudently silent.

Noah shakes his head. "There are *innumerable* ways of demonstrating one's displeasure more effectively and less cruelly than that. Tell me something. I have heard that this grudge you bear Lord Southampton

184 | NEAL ROBERTS

arises out of his jailing you for a single day for attacking the Irish rebels without first obtaining his permission. Is that the cause of your grudge?"

Lord Grey clears his throat. "It was at one time, sir, but this attack was for more recent outrages."

"Cutting off the servant's hand is a wildly inappropriate response to any wrong committed by the master. Wouldn't you say? Or have we left the world of reason for the one behind the looking glass?"

Lord Grey purses his lips and makes no response.

Sir Walter shakes his head in dismay. "M'lord, I could lock the three of you in the Tower to await arraignment. However, given your lordship's barony and the invaluable assistance you've provided the Crown concerning the present threat to Her Majesty's reign, I'll give you the choice of the Tower or the Fleet Prison, where Her Majesty has already said she would commit you if you broke the peace with Lord Southampton."

"How's the Fleet better?" asks Grey distantly.

"Either way, you're imprisoned at Her Majesty's pleasure, but once you're in the Fleet, you've already begun serving your sentence, however long Her Majesty may make it."

Grey sighs. "Take us to the Fleet, Sir Walter. Thank you. And, once again, I regret the disturbance."

"Tell that to the poor child," says Sir Walter. "Now, the three of you: Mount your horses and prepare to follow me to the Fleet. I expect you shall behave on your honor." He looks dubiously at Grey's attendants. "I'm confident Lord Grey will not violate such a trust, but what of the two of *you*? 'I place you on your honor.' Do you know what it means?" The two servants nod, but Sir Walter explains anyway. "It means if you try to escape, I'll blow your bloody brains out all over the nice white snow. *That's* what it means. Now, on your life, wait here with your master."

With Noah still in the saddle, Sir Walter takes Bucklebury's reins and leads him a few feet away to avoid being heard by his prisoners. He looks up at Noah and speaks in a lowered voice. "It's a sad state of affairs when Her Majesty needs to rely on such rash men as this to retain her Crown."

Noah nods mournfully. "We take our allies as we find them, Sir Walter."

Sir Walter shrugs. "Go home, Noah. I've persuaded Cheerful to stay at Durham House tonight. Your newest 'daughter' has nearly crushed him. Is there anything you can do?"

Noah shrugs. "Don't know, but I hope so."

Sir Walter returns to his prisoners, grabs the reins of their horses and leads them toward the Durham House stables, so he can get his own mount for the ride to the Fleet.

As the Fleet-bound party disappears from view and the wind picks up, Noah glances at the fresh puddle of blood being slowly obscured by blowing snow.

"Bloody madness," he mutters to himself. "Where will it end?"

———————⇒○⊂⁓○⊂———————

LATER THAT JANUARY, Sir Ferdinando Gorges takes a temporary leave from his post at Plymouth to travel to London in response to an urgent summons from the Earl of Essex. Sir Ferdinando sailed with Essex during the Islands Voyage and, like every other statesman in Britain, he's heard of Essex's troubles. But he has no idea how his presence in London could help Essex bring matters to a successful conclusion.

A few days later, in the chilly morning of the first of February, Sir Ferdinando rides his favorite horse through Westminster. Up King Street he canters, then trots east where he soon comes upon Essex House on the river side of the Strand.

Curiously, Essex's stableman meets him outside the gate. One glance at the stables tells why. It's full to overflowing. Sir Ferdinando dismounts.

"I was told you'd be arrivin' this mawnin', Master Gorges," says the stableman as he takes the reins, "and was told to give yaw horse the very best o' care. As ye can see, though, the stables is full, so we've been givin' every horse four hours in the stables and keepin' 'em outside the rest o' the day. If that's a problem, suh, and you won't need yaw horse at a moment's notice, I'll be pleased to stable 'im on the earl's account at one of the commercial establishments not far from here."

Sir Ferdinando looks up at the clear blue sky, and notices a patch of high wispy clouds approaching from the west. "What if it rains ... or snows?" he asks.

"Then we'll move 'em all to comfort and safety, suh. But it don't look like snow nor rain now, does it?"

"No, but all the same," says Sir Ferdinando, "please bring my horse to a commercial place and let me know where he's stabled."

"Very well, suh."

Sir Ferdinando palms the stableman a coin, probably larger than he should, and steps up to the gate. As he no longer has a horse, there's no need to open the full gate. Essex's footman admits him through the wicket.

"Welcome to Essex House, suh," says the footman. "I'm Caim. The earl's waitin' for ye in the back library. There's some other gentlemen back there, too. Just go straight down the main hall, and it's at the end on yer right. Can't miss it."

As soon as he enters the house, Sir Ferdinando finds himself amidst an impressively loud bustle of gentlemen, many military in bearing, though he recognizes none from his time in service. Some of the gentlemen appear to be down in their cups, even so early in the morning, and a few are wedged in the corners of couches, sound asleep with their chins on their chests.

Coming to the end of the hallway, he knocks on the door to his right.

"Come," says Lord Essex's voice.

At first, Sir Ferdinando opens the door a crack, so as to avoid being seen as barging in. His eye falls first on a lone, burly fellow at the far end of the room suspiciously eyeing another man of about forty years, in the garb of a scholar, who stands proudly behind the earl. Some bad blood between those two, or so it would seem.

Pushing the door open far enough to admit himself, Sir Ferdinando is warmly greeted by the earl, who's surrounded by perhaps twenty men and seems in a fine mood.

"Come in, Sir Ferdinando. Come in," says Essex. "I don't believe you've been introduced to these gentlemen." He turns to a middle-aged fellow who gives Sir Ferdinando a kindly smile. "This is my stepfather, Sir Christopher Blount," says the earl. "Sir Christopher, permit me to introduce Sir Ferdinando Gorges, an old shipmate of mine who's been elevated to Governor of the Fort at Plymouth."

"It's a pleasure to meet you, young Sir Ferdinando. I've heard much about you. Welcome, welcome. Have you meet Danvers?" He turns to a man of about thirty with his back turned and taps him on the shoulder. "Danvers, it's Sir Ferdinando Gorges!"

Danvers turns toward Ferdinando. "It's so good to see you, Sir Ferdinando. I expect you and I met in Ireland while we were both fighting for Lord Essex."

"Very likely," says Sir Ferdinando. Evidently, neither remembers the other.

"We'll be going to see Lord Southampton on the morrow," says

Danvers. "Do you recall him?"

Sir Ferdinando smiles. "Of course I recall him," he says. "The more pertinent question is whether *he* recalls *me.*"

Danvers laughs and waves off the concern. "He's sure to remember you. He's a prince among men. Southampton helped my family in so many ways when he was the only one who *could* have. Quite an important person to know."

"I look forward to meeting him," says Sir Ferdinando politely.

Danvers darts a glance toward the professorial fellow he saw upon entering. "That scholar is Cuffe," says Danvers, "a real firebrand who was excluded from Lord Essex's presence for some time by Gelly Meyrick, his lordship's steward. It was Lord Southampton who eventually overruled Meyrick." His eyes search the room, and he points with his chin to the burly fellow Sir Ferdinando spied in the back of the room. "That's Meyrick the steward," he says.

"Gentlemen," says Cuffe loudly to all present, "if you'd be so kind as to give your full attention to Lord Essex." He sits, and Essex rises.

"Gentlemen," says Essex, holding forth. "I have called you all here because there's something in common we lack, something desperately important to each of us in his own way. And that is ... a place in the court of our beloved Queen. Now, you have all suffered long absence from court, largely owing to your association with me when we all strove on Her Majesty's behalf in Ireland—"

The assembled shake their heads in disapproval.

"For *other* reasons entirely, m'lord," says one.

"Nothing to *do* with your lordship," mutters another.

"You are too kind, gentlemen," says Essex insistently. "But I can say of my own knowledge that you have long been excluded solely on account of your association with your humble servant." He looks at them with determination. "Now, at last, it is time we *do* something about it."

"But what can be done, m'lord," asks Sir Ferdinando, "when the monarch has turned her face against us?"

Essex does his best to seem surprised by the question. "Why, you can look to your own defense, and stand fast with me. With me by your side, you can stand on your *own* merit ... assert your *own* strength ... and place *yourselves* back in the court." Essex begins to pace. "For years— since a time prior to our joint service in Ireland—there have been ... elements at the court who've taken every opportunity to turn the Queen against me, to worm their way into her ear and arouse her suspicion—or even outright condemnation of my every move .... my every *syllable.*"

A questioning mutter arises among the assembled.

"But who are these varlets of which my lord speaks?" asks one bearded fellow. "Let's call them out and have done with them," he says to general approval.

Essex raises his chin proudly. "Stout hearts!" he says with delight. "Would you have me speak their names aloud?"

The bearded questioner looks about him and finds general assent. "Aye, we *would*, sir."

To Sir Ferdinando, Essex's argument has a theatrical quality to it. It seems heartfelt, to be sure, but well planned nonetheless.

"Very well," says Essex as though his arm's been twisted and he cannot refuse. "I'll say their names. But gentlemen," he says, "our discussions must stay among those in this room for, should they become known at court, they will surely be met with the most *severe* disapproval." He looks out on the assembled. "Lord Cobham is one such varlet, as you would have him called," says Essex, carefully watching for his friends' reactions. There's little reaction to Cobham's name, though most of these men know him and some served under him.

"Another will be no surprise to you, I expect," says Essex. "Robert Cecil, lately dubbed 'Lord Robert.'"

A joker in the crowd shouts. "That's one and a *half* so far, m'lord."

An angry one adds, "I propose we feed the dwarf to the birds on London Bridge."

"That would be cruel," the joker retorts. "To the *birds*, as he'd nary make a meal." This is followed by general merriment.

"Who else, m'lord?" asks another.

Essex is evidently considering how much further to push his luck. Having experienced no resistance to this point, he firms up his resolve and raises his chin again.

"Sir Walter Raleigh," he pronounces. It's immediately obvious he should have stopped earlier, as the reaction to Raleigh's name is subdued, if not downright puzzled.

Sir Ferdinando rises. "But surely, my lord," he pleads, "Sir Walter cannot be mentioned in the same breath as the two sycophants you've named."

Essex seems puzzled, but forbearing. "Master Gorges, I can produce any number of witnesses who will swear upon a book that Sir Walter is the worst offender. Evidently, he regards his success as requiring my absolute exclusion from court. And, what's more, Sir Walter was involved in a serious, unprovoked attack on Lord Southampton not a fortnight ago."

Sir Ferdinando takes a moment to allow these accusations to sink into his mind. He bows. "Then I beg pardon, m'lord," he says. "Though I knew Sir Walter of old, I know naught of his conduct at court nor in any street brawl, and therefore bend to the general will."

"No need to seek pardon, Sir Ferdinando," says Essex magnanimously. "Free speech has ever been, and *remains* yours wherever I shall hold sway. We are proud to have you among us." He turns to the general assemblage. "At Lord Southampton's invitation, I shall send word to a select few of you to meet with m'lord at Drury House at noon tomorrow, where the topic for discussion shall be our mutually desired course. But those of you not summoned may rest assured that you are so beloved and *needed* by the rest of us that you have been omitted solely for your own protection. Until noon tomorrow, then, please enjoy my hospitality as best you may."

Essex bows to general approval, and allows himself to be escorted by Cuffe to the family's private quarters upstairs.

Meyrick bolts out a side door without speaking to anyone.

Sir Ferdinando accepts a cup of wine and does his best to focus on his conversations with the others present. But in the back of his mind, he dwells upon his high regard for Sir Walter. Though Essex nearly hanged Sir Walter on the Islands Voyage, yet Sir Ferdinando has never once known Sir Walter either to criticize Essex or to suffer others to do so.

Sir Walter is a good man.

And, no matter how distant ... he's a kinsman.

CHAPTER 25

THE FOLLOWING DAY is the Feast of Candlemas.

Drury House, like the overcast day outside, is cold and damp. At the head of the room is the Earl of Southampton, a thin gentleman of angular face and light complexion, with reddish hair and a wispy beard.

Sir Ferdinando is surprised to find that Southampton, instead of comporting himself like an experienced general and announcing his decisions, rather resembles a courtier patiently inviting discussion and argument on each question till a consensus is reached.

"As some of you may know," says Southampton, "Lord Essex has been engaged for some time in correspondence with King James of Scotland. Although King James has not been *officially* designated by Her Majesty as heir to the English throne, he has wisely ingratiated himself with her, and she has—not in so many words, mind you—informed her intimates that she wishes him to succeed her.

"The authorities assure us that we need not be concerned with the competing claim of the Infanta of Spain, which would descend through a daughter of the ancient John of Gaunt. While the authorities are unanimous that—the male line having died out—we must seek our new sovereign through a line of descent through the female (or 'cognatic') lines, yet we need peer no further into the past than King Henry the Seventh, who had two daughters (in addition to a son, namely, our sainted King Henry the Eighth). The true claim has descended through Henry the Seventh's eldest daughter, and shall land squarely on King James of Scotland.

"All this is merely to say that the measures we are about to discuss have been disclosed to the Queen's intended successor, who has made no objection to them."

The rear door creaks open and a pair of heavy boots enters. Several heads turn about to catch a glimpse of a stout gentleman of singular appearance.

Southampton smiles at the new arrival with a hint of levity. "So pleased to have you in our midst, Sir Helvius," he says.

The new arrival, who clearly would have preferred to go unnoticed, bows to his lordship and silently takes a seat at the rear.

"Who's that?" Francisco whispers to Danvers, who's seated beside him.

Danvers tenses, then shrugs. "Never saw him before in my life."

Southampton clears his throat. "To continue," he says, "it remains open for consideration whether our plans shall be restricted to Whitehall or should be augmented to add the Tower of London."

A baron rises to speak, resplendent in a cloak emblazoned with his barony's colorful coat of arms. "I think we shall be fortunate to take *either*, my lord. In light of the difficulty in taking even one, it makes most sense to concentrate our forces on whichever such stronghold houses Her Majesty, as it is her capitulation that will determine whether we win the day or no."

Southampton nods indulgently. "Well spoken, baron. That appears to be the emerging consensus. The difficulty with the proposal arises out of Her Majesty's mobility. That is, we can't be certain *where* she'll be when we get started, or whether she might even be moved during our advance. But let us leave that for discussion later in today's session, for I doubt that all those in attendance have yet heard even our most basic intention." He speaks up to ensure that he's gained everyone's attention. "Our plan is to populate the court—all at once and without warning— with those friendly to our cause, thereby placing the Queen in a position where she has little choice but to suffer the return of Lord Essex to her court long enough for him to obtain redress against those vicious courtiers who have schemed so long to destroy him."

A momentary silence hangs over the room.

"But that's the trick, isn't it?" observes a skeptical gentleman. "How are we to 'populate' the court all at once, when none of us will be admitted even singly?"

Southampton nods indulgently. "A fair question. It is our hope that a simple show of force will be sufficient."

This leads to a murmur of doubt.

"A show of force?" comes the questioner again. "Do you mean to say that we expect to *intimidate* the guard at Whitehall into offering no resistance?"

Southampton equivocates. "Though many of the guard are admirers of Lord Essex, we suppose some *token* resistance is to be anticipated, but nothing in earnest."

Another gentleman rises, from the north of England by his speech. "M'lord, any show of force in the precinct of Her Majesty will be met rather with outrage than submission, especially taking into account Her Majesty's own pugnacious temperament. I know of mine own experience that the guard has been instructed *to presume* that anyone bearing arms in the Royal Presence is a traitor to be arrested at once or, should he resist ... to be slain on the spot."

Southampton attempts to shrug off the remark. "Oh, we're over-anticipating at this point."

The rotund Sir Helvius rises in the rear.

"Not a whit, m'lord," he says in the practiced tones of an experienced public speaker. "If you'll think back but a few years, Lord Essex himself very nearly lost his right hand for carrying a sword into the Presence, in fact *would* have lost it, were it not for the Queen's Jew."

The earlier questioner stands and barks a laugh. "Perhaps we should each bring a Jew as protection!" Emboldened by the laughter, he adds, "Better not give them swords or, before you know it, England will be a *Hebrew republic*!" This is met with general mirth—a welcome relief in light of the gravity of the question on the floor.

Sir Helvius, who has not partaken in the laughter, says: "Any plan involving violence—or even the implied threat of violence—to Her Majesty's person ... is sheer madness." And, with that, he sits.

Danvers rises to revive Southampton's proposal. "In case we are met with resistance, m'lord, what forces shall we have at hand?"

Southampton assures him, "Lord Essex counts one hundred and twenty nobles, knights, and gentlemen who will rise to our support."

Sir Helvius rises again. "Do you mean they've sworn to support us in the Queen's court with swords, m'lord, or merely to cheer us on from the safety of King Street? There's quite a difference."

Southampton is chagrined. "What would you counsel, Sir Helvius? A continuation of what we've done until now ... which is *nothing*?"

Sir Helvius shakes his head dourly. "I shall neither counsel nor consent to any action involving injury or restraint to Her Majesty's person, nor any action likely to be *perceived* as a threat of such injury or restraint, for it is sure to be met with the penalties of treason. And which of us has not had occasion to see those awful penalties extracted at Tyburn?"

Sir Ferdinando finds great wisdom in this portly knight.

A young man rises. "M'lord, if I may. For those who've never met me, I am Sir Charles Percy, and I rise to propose that we multiply our support among both the nobility and the commons by providing them with theatrical *example* of the lawful deposing of a King of England." This is met with puzzlement. "The Chamberlain's Men will be playing the tragedy of *King Richard the Second* at the Globe this coming week. As you'll recall, King Richard bogged England down in interminable Irish wars. The play depicts the peaceful transfer of power from King Richard to the humble and near-silent Bolingbroke, son to John of Gaunt. I urge you all to attend with me this coming Friday and Saturday, and to bring with you all those you can from every station of life. I know that Lord Monteagle, my brother Sir Josceline, and Sir Gelly Meyrick are with me in this." When his suggestion is met with lukewarm assent, he adds, "I hasten to add that m'Lord Essex is much moved by the play, a prose version of which was even *dedicated* to his lordship."

Southampton nods. "Lord Essex is indeed much moved by it. That I know. By God, it's worth a try, Sir Charles. But rest assured that m'Lord of Essex has at hand many other ways to rouse the citizenry."

Sir Helvius rises once more. "M'lord, I'm vaguely familiar with the play and, marvelous though it may be in certain respects, we must remember that the usurper Bolingbroke asserted a claim to the throne that was, in merit, very near to King Richard's. While Lord Essex is of unquestionable birth, he is hardly heir apparent."

Southampton appears to be much less pleased with this fat knight than when he first waddled in. "It is at least debatable," says Southampton, "whether Bolingbroke was King Richard's heir apparent, Sir He— Helvius, for an heir of Mortimer, Richard's designated successor, yet lived at the time of Richard's death. But leaving that aside: We, far more justly than Bolingbroke, urge no deposing of a prince of England. We rather seek to preserve the interest of King James, who *is* rightful heir. Unlike Bolingbroke, we propose *at most* a regency—and that only with Her Majesty's consent. By contrast, the traitors at Her Majesty's court that were mentioned by Lord Essex to some few of us yesterday urge *usurpation* of the Throne by the Infanta."

Sir Helvius looks askance at Southampton. "Which 'traitors' are these, my lord?"

"Why, Lord Cobham, Robert Cecil, and Sir Walter Raleigh, to be sure!"

Sir Helvius is thunderstruck by the naming of this triumvirate. While he sets his shoulders in preparation to reply, he evidently thinks better of it, and resumes his seat in evident dismay.

An earlier questioner again rises. "How many guards protect the court from incursion?"

"We're unsure," says Southampton, "but we expect approximately the same as our number, that is, one hundred and twenty, give or take."

"And if they resist in earnest?"

"Then," says Southampton, "we shall overcome them."

"By dint of *persuasion*?" asks another doubter.

"Well," says Southampton, "first we shall assure one and all that no harm is intended Her Majesty."

"What of the three ministers m'lord just mentioned?" asks another. "If they're present, they'll surely urge Her Majesty to resist. Are they to be taken?"

Southampton glances at the fat knight, obviously hoping for his continued silence. "They *are* to be taken, and dealt with by Lord Essex ... according to their individual treasons."

The words hang like a shroud over the assembled. Each in his own way knows what Southampton means: Lord Cobham, Robert Cecil, and Sir Walter Raleigh are to be put to death without further ado.

To the extent some in attendance may have been nurturing hope that their participation in this affair would consist of nothing more than polishing their medals and showering oak leaves upon Lord Essex in the Royal Presence, their illusions have now been dispelled.

Heads will roll.

Quite possibly their own.

Sir Ferdinando rises. "Gentlemen, I have been contacted indirectly by Sir Walter Raleigh, who has asked me to confer with him at Durham House."

"About what?" asks Southampton.

"The message was somewhat vague, but it mentioned the risks I have undertaken by taking leave of my captaincy of the fort at Plymouth without royal warrant."

Those assembled shout or mumble their objections. "He'll take you, and never allow you to return to us," says one, to general agreement.

Southampton calls a halt to general discussion on the topic, but adds his final note. "Under no circumstances should you meet or confer with him now, Sir Ferdinando, for your own sake as well as the sake of this venture. If you feel some familial obligation to meet with him, do it later, and somewhere he cannot overpower you." He points south to the river. "Tell him you'll meet him at a time of your own choosing in a wherry out on the Thames within sight of Essex House. We'll see how bravely he comports himself then."

Sir Ferdinando bows and resumes his seat. To him, the notion of storming the Queen's court, especially when one of the objects is the execution of Sir Walter without trial, is not merely foolhardy, but repugnant. He begins to formulate a plan of his own to remain among the conspirators and hinder their cause.

AT NOAH'S HOUSE a few blocks away, the bedchamber where Lady Jessica has begun "lying in" for the birth of her first child is one of only two rooms kept warm all the time.

The other is Noah's study, where Noah now stirs the coals in the fireplace in preparation for another piece of wood he's about to place on top. The coals hiss angrily at him, as though resentful of the disturbance.

"What makes you think there's a supporter of Lord Essex among us?" asks Lord Jonathan, who's looking more than a bit frazzled this morning.

"A few things," Noah replies, "but I must admit that foremost among them is ... a dream of Her Majesty that I had recently." He studies Jonathan's reaction out of the corner of his eye.

"Dreams and portents?" says Jonathan skeptically. "What *other* things?"

"Well, for one thing," says Noah, "there seems to be precious little secrecy about *Lord Essex's* situation. Why should ours be any better guarded?"

Jonathan shrugs. "Because there are fewer of us. How can Essex have *any* expectation of secrecy with seventy or eighty people jammed into Essex House and another twenty or so in Drury House? I'll wager Essex doesn't even know who some of them are. Why do you suppose they've become more active of late?"

"I can well surmise," says Noah. "Ever since we rendered it impossible for Essex's henchmen to recapture the proceeds of the sweet wine monopoly, I expect Essex's credit has run out. Knights are reputed to eat like horses and drink like fish. Provender and ale cost money." He jostles the grate back into place after tossing in the fresh wood. "How is Jessica?" he asks gingerly.

Jonathan's eyes well up with unspent tears. "I confess I am deeply concerned for her welfare."

Noah is alarmed, but determined not to seem so. "Why?" he asks. "What's happened?"

Jonathan sighs. "As you know, I see her only a few minutes each day and have to fight my way past her maids to reach her. This morning I held her in my arms for only a few moments. She was awake, but barely so, and she told me she had an awful headache that began days ago. When I kissed her below the ear, I could … I could *feel* her heartbeat on my lips. It was very strong. *Too* strong."

"Do you wish to summon a physician?" asks Noah calmly.

"I don't know," says Jonathan. "That's a perplexing question. I'm afraid they may do more harm than good."

"The midwife, perhaps?"

"Perhaps," says Jonathan, nodding. "I suppose there's little she could do to make things worse."

"And you can instruct her not to make any incision or administer any nostrum unless you've approved it in advance."

"That I will certainly do," says Jonathan, somewhat mollified. "Tell me, did Jessica's mother have a throbbing pulse late in her term?"

Noah can feel his face being studied by Jonathan. "Not that I recall," says Noah blithely, in the hope that his white lie will go undetected. "However, you might call on Beth. She knows much better than I."

<hr />

AT ESSEX HOUSE THAT EVENING, in the footman's private chamber adjacent to the servant's quarters, Caim seethes silently as he listens to three of his most trusted henchmen. Every one of them has failed him, and each one finishing his tale casts his eyes to the floor.

Caim begins asking questions.

"Not one o' you has seen hide nor hair of Meriton?"

When no one else replies, Tadson speaks. "Not since the attempt on Lord Saint Ives at the Draper's, suh."

"And you're still not *sure* the shooter was Meriton, are you?" asks Caim.

"Well, suh … only by process o' debilitation."

Caim regards him with disgust. "It's 'elimination,' you idiot!"

"Meriton's the only one of us what's missin'," says Tadson. "Who else would take a shot at Lord Saint Ives, suh?"

"Why did *Meriton*? Why would *any* of you take a shot at him? Those were not your orders, which was to kill Bennett's brother on sight. No more, no less. And none of ye did *that,* neither!"

All three shake their heads.

"It's like they fell off the earth together," says Tadson.

Caim's ire is getting the best of him. "Not one person in this bleedin' city's seen *either* of them in all this time?" No reply. "Well, I'll tell ye what *I* think. *I* think the three of ye's gone soft. How many people d'ja put in fear of the knife? Roughed anybuddy up? Nah. It's just not *worth* it to ye."

"We couldn't find any reason one person would know maw than another, suh," offers Tadson. "We can't just pick up some stranger from the street and put him under the knife. Ye want us to rough somebuddy up, tell us who. Nay, just *point* us at 'im!" The other two grunt in agreement.

This redirects Caim's anger at himself. Truly, the problem is that *he* hasn't identified anyone likely to know the whereabouts of either Cuthbert Bennett or Meriton.

"Well, let's see," he says. "You boys told me that, near as you could tell, before the gunman could get off a shot, Lord Saint Ives was tackled by some old cadger who works at the Drapers', right?"

"Right, suh," says Tadson.

"And he chased the gunman a ways before turnin' back?"

"That's what they said at Drapers'."

"What's he do there?" asks Caim. "Sweep up the place?"

Tadson equivocates. "Well, he might, suh. But that's not why they keep the Jew there. Turns out he's a pretty trusted figure. If there's money or goods of real worth goin' in or out, he's put in charge of it."

Caim rolls these ideas about in his devious mind. "Did you say he's a Jew?"

"Aye, suh," replies Tadson. "Everybuddy knows they're trusted with all sorts o' money ... and jools, suh. Never seen one get picked up for stealin', neither."

"Nah," grunts Caim deep in thought, "if they steal from a Christian they know they'll get punished good. If they steal from another Jew, they settle it amongst the tribe. They all talk the same made-up language. They all know each other. Thick as thieves, they are." In a moment, he snaps his fingers. "I wonder if he knows the *Queen's* Jew."

Tadson shrugs. "Dunno, suh, but Lord Southampton's told us never to lay hands on Serjeant Ames—He's *untouchable*."

"I wonder what his lordship meant by that," mutters Caim aloud. "I mean, did Southampton mean the Jew's too high up to be touched, or that Southampton tried to turn 'im to our side but couldn't."

Tadson shrugs. "Such questions are for men what get higher wages than us, suh. We just know'd it meant to keep our hands off 'im. And that's all we *needed* to know."

Caim ignores the remark, lost in his own thoughts. "What else did his lordship tell you?"

"Well," says Tadson, scratching his head. "Southampton said that the Jew Serjeant's wife ain't no Jewess. Said she was raised up in Southampton's own manor house, but that she's ungrateful and holds no love for Lord Southampton. Oh but, suh, he was clear we shouldn't lay a hand on *her*, neither."

"Of course not," mutters Caim. "That's Southampton's way. If a man's untouchable, so's his wife. What else did he tell you about the Jew's wife?"

"Said she used to be married to a little Spaniard who made her rich."

Caim nods absentmindedly. "Is that all you know about her?"

Tadson looks to his two fellows, who snicker. "That, suh, and that she's about the prettiest woman anybuddy's ever seen. In fact, the Jew's surrounded by beautiful women. His daughter's married into nobility."

"Twice," offers one of the other dolts.

Caim turns to his three assistants. "Turns out you three aren't as useless as I suspected." He hands each of them a coin. "Now go and get drunk, and forget all about this. I'll take care of it."

The three bow their way out with surprised smiles.

"Thank ye, suh," says Tadson. "And God bless ye."

But Caim's mind has already moved on. He's fairly certain that Meriton's dead. But he still needs to know where Cuthbert Bennett is, which is information that Serjeant Ames may—or may not—have. Even if he has it, he won't willingly give it up. *I need to get hold of something he values.*

What does Serjeant Ames value? A man surrounds himself with what he values most, which in the Serjeant's case is quite obviously beautiful women. The Serjeant and his wife are untouchable. His son-in-law and daughter are nobles, which makes *them* untouchable even without a specific instruction from Essex or Southampton.

Perhaps there's another beauty the Serjeant treasures who's a mere commoner, or a visitor even. Perhaps such a girl could be abducted without specific permission. If something were to go wrong, and Caim had to kill her, would it mean his head?

Possibly, but against this fear he must weigh the golden enticement of slitting Cuthbert Bennett's throat.

CHAPTER 26

TWO DAYS LATER, Sir Henry Neville disguises himself as Sir Helvius once again, this time to meet with Cuffe in a private room at Drury House.

As Sir Henry approaches the private room, he decides to enter talking. "I assume you deemed this meeting essential, Master Cuffe, as I'm taking a great risk in appearing here again."

Cuffe nods reassuringly. "I wished to speak with you about the coming papist upheaval, Sir Helvius. Before moving on to that topic, however, Lord Southampton wished me to tell you how terribly perplexed he was by your remarks at Drury House the other day."

"Perplexed?" asks Sir Henry. "How so?"

"Well," replies Cuffe, "it was on account of your reservations that no consensus was reached. Now Lord Southampton is unsure whether he can rely upon you to accept the office of Secretary of State, should it ... become vacant."

Sir Henry sighs. "Please assure the earl that I remain available to serve the nation in that capacity, provided that Lord Essex's plan is carried out lawfully with Her Majesty's consent, and that she neither suffers nor is threatened with harm."

Now Cuffe is perplexed. "But how are we to extract her consent if she feels no jeopardy?"

"That's precisely the point," says Sir Henry. "You cannot coerce her to consent. Consent given under coercion is a nullity."

Cuffe adopts his professorial air. "Permit me to put to you a contrary case, Sir Helvius."

Sir Henry sits back and nods indulgently.

"Suppose the barons of this realm were to oppose certain laws and extractions imposed by the King. For the sake of discussion, let us refer to him as King John. And further suppose that they surround him on the field at Runnymede and coerce his withdrawal of such hated laws and extractions."

Sir Henry completes Cuffe's presentation of the case. "... and what if the barons were then to compel the King to sign a document, which we may call ... oh, for argument's sake ... Magna Carta?"

"Just so," says Cuffe with evident satisfaction.

"Do you know what 'Runnymede' means in the ancient tongue, Master Cuffe?"

Cuffe is abashed. "No, Sir Helvius."

"It means," says Sir Henry, "'meeting place,' which implies that Magna Carta was agreed to in a regular meeting between the King and his rebellious barons. So there is no reason to suspect coercion."

"But," says Cuffe, "you will admit that King John signed Magna Carta only to remove the threat to his crown?"

"I admit no such thing, Master Cuffe. Any act of ordinary prudence can be made to seem the result of coercion. It's all a matter of degree. But, if you like, I shall take the case as you've presented it, and say that if the barons placed the King in immediate fear of his life should he refuse to sign, then it could fairly be said that Magna Carta had been signed under coercion, and that it should therefore be regarded as having no legal effect."

Cuffe smiles smugly.

"However," continues Sir Henry, "Magna Carta's history did not end there. Several times in the years that followed, the Crown abrogated—then *reinstated*—Magna Carta with modification. As it cannot be earnestly proposed that the Crown's *every* such reinstatement was made under immediate threat of coercion, at best your case is ... muddled."

Cuffe, who prides himself on his scholarship, is crestfallen at being bested. Sir Henry quickly urges a return to the main topic. "Now, Master Cuffe, we could bandy cases back and forth all day long and get nowhere, or you can tell me how I can help stop these bloody papists from gaining sway."

"Why, you can assist Lord Essex in every possible way," says the subdued Cuffe, apparently a bit surprised by the question.

"I truly wish to help Lord Essex," says Sir Henry with a sigh. "But if I were to assure him that he has a chance of success in invading the Queen's court, I would be assisting him to naught but the gallows, for the endeavor would be foolhardy. That I cannot, nor *will* not do. Her Majesty will refuse to relinquish a jot of her authority, and will prick down his name—and those of many others—for execution."

"But how can you know this?"

"Master Cuffe, I have known Her Majesty since she was a young woman, tender enough to shy away from killing a deer. Yet, over these many years, I have seen her change and grow. Though she is still genteel in her manners, she has a steely toughness now, not far below the surface. After all, at need, she put her near cousin Mary Queen of Scots *to the axe*, even though Mary was mother to King James. And Her Majesty now favors King James as her own successor. Think of the cold calculation in that, Master Cuffe. Believe me, Her Majesty will over-come her womanly softness to defend her claim to the Crown without mercy—and without *favor*."

Suddenly Southampton's voice comes, seemingly from nowhere. "But Her Majesty is often *wrong* about many important matters, especially Lord Essex. Wouldn't you agree, Sir Helvius?"

Though Sir Henry is tempted to remark on the earl's sudden appear-ance or respond to his question, instead he keeps his remark on point. "It's no less true for having oft been said, m'lord: 'The Queen may sometimes be wrong, but she's always the Queen.'"

Southampton smiles upon Sir Henry. "You are a man of great learn-ing and honor, Sir Helvius. We ask only two things of you: first, of course, that you share with no one any jot of what you have heard or said in our discussions. Second, notwithstanding that you have at last received from the Exchequer the money needed to resume your embas-sage, we request that you place yourself in some accustomed place at Whitehall this Sunday morning and delay your departure for France until the outcome of Lord Essex's plan is known."

Sir Henry rises and bows deeply to the earl. "It will be this coming Sunday, then?" he asks nervously.

"Aye," replies Southampton.

"*Ergo, alea iacta est?*" Sir Henry asks. *So, the die is cast?*

His listeners' faces fall in tandem, as though a petard has just blown down the door, for they recognize Sir Henry's Latin phrase as containing the fateful words spoken by Julius Caesar as he crossed the Rubicon on his march toward Rome in violation of the Senate's edict, thus ensuring a bloody civil war.

Southampton nods somberly and replies:

"*Alea iacta est.*" *The die is cast.*

"Then this business concerning the papists can await the outcome," says Sir Henry, as he rises and turns to go. Reaching the door, he bids a good day to the two who remain, and shuts the door firmly behind him.

Cuffe remarks, "Sir Helvius has quite a flair for the dramatic."

Southampton mutters, "If you only knew the half of it." He assumes the seat formerly occupied by Sir Henry and asks matter-of-factly, "Why was I not informed, Master Cuffe, that you were present when m'Lord Essex met with Sir Helvius at Windsor?"

"No reason, m'lord," Cuffe assures him. "Lord Essex thought it advisable to forego making firm plans for our common venture until we were assured that some weighty person was prepared to take the place of Lord Robert, should his place become vacant. Lord Essex supposed— and I could not disagree—that Sir Helvius was a person of such heft (if m'lord will pardon my foolish figures of speech). As we knew Sir Helvius would soon be receiving guests at his Windsor residence, we thought it advisable to feel him out without delay. We didn't expect your lordship to dislike our decision."

Southampton nods weighingly. "As you know, I have been exceedingly fond of Sir Helvius as long as I've known him. Still, I cannot help but wonder: Did he speak in the same tenor at your earlier meeting as he did the other day at Drury House?"

"Well, then as now, he insisted there be no mistreatment or threats directed toward the Queen."

"And," continues Southampton, "what were his initial views on our chance of success?"

Cuffe makes a show of thinking back. "He expressed his view then, as now, that our plans are foolhardy and suicidal."

"Well, if you knew Sir Helvius's innermost thoughts, then—Good *God*, Cuffe!—why did you and Lord Essex invite him to meet with men ready to put their lives and fortunes on the line in this endeavor?"

Cuffe looks despondently toward the floor, and answers the question contemplatively, as though he himself posed it. "Because both Lord Essex and I thought he'd keep his mouth shut."

Southampton supposes it was a natural enough assumption that someone who's joined a conspiracy would have the good sense to avoid spreading dissension among the conspirators. *But as I could have told them, Sir Henry would never believe himself a conspirator, but rather a fellow traveler preparing to lend a hand should the endeavor succeed, but having nothing to lose if it failed.* Remembering why he came over from Essex House, he draws a fragment of paper from his pocket.

"Here are the plans for taking Whitehall this Sunday, to be shared only with those having an absolute need to know," he says, and begins reading his tiny scrawl. "Sir Christopher Blount and his detachment to guard the outer gate, Sir John Davies the hall, and Danvers the Presence Chamber. Unless Lord Essex orders otherwise, the only men to enter the

Privy Chamber and come face-to-face with the Queen shall be Lord Essex and myself."

"And what shall happen at Essex House?" asks Cuffe.

Southampton replies, "All those not going to Whitehall shall remain indoors at Essex House, arming themselves with sword, dagger, and whatever firearms they may have at hand. The moment Lord Essex departs Essex House to speak with the town fathers, every book in the library shall be moved to block the windows against intruders or anyone tempted to take a shot at us. The ladies shall remain upstairs in the residence. The fireplace on the top storey shall be kept ablaze at all times, should it become necessary to burn our papers ... but, God willing, it will never come to that."

They sit in stoic silence for a few minutes, each struggling in vain to imagine a scenario where the plan meets with success.

Southampton silently rises and departs, Cuffe a few minutes later.

"HOW LONG HAS YOUR HEAD ached in this way, my dear?" Jonathan asks Jessica early that afternoon. She mumbles something that sounds like "forever," and turns away from the light of the single candle as though it were a blazing sun.

He loves her so, her pain is palpable to him, and he can bear it no longer. "My dear, something is very wrong. I know of no other case where a woman with child has suffered such agony for days, and so near to term. I shall write to Aunt Beth at once."

When for the first time Jessica makes no sign of protest against his proposal, he's unsure she's heard him. But no matter, for he's determined to write Beth regardless of Jessica's preference. He goes to the desk and pens a note to Beth describing his wife's condition and seeking advice. He runs down the stairs and hands the letter to the stable boy with instructions for immediate delivery.

WHEN ESTHER VISITS the mother-to-be a few minutes later, she's alarmed to find her in such pain. Truth be told, she's as anxious as Lord Jonathan for the welfare of Lady Jessica and the child in her womb. Esther kisses her on the hand and retreats to her own room.

Early that Friday evening, Esther is briefly visited by David. Though he pledges his undying love for her as always, he declines to pester the frantic Lord Jonathan for leave to tell her where he was during those few bothersome days. Though Esther admires David's devotion to his friend, doubts remain about his devotion to *her*. She goes to bed.

As she sleeps, she and all of London are overtaken by the coldest, darkest hours of the morning of Saturday, February 7, 1601—the day before the rebellion.

Esther tosses and turns while recalling her old dream of Bowyer's Row. She's bedeviled by images of bloody black-robed conspirators murdering two young men, and haunted by the later image of an unidentified blond man being run through from the rear while trying to avoid violence.

Again she finds herself troubled by the sense that she's heard the voice of the chief conspirator in waking life. But she's simply been unable to recall his face.

On the edge of waking, she turns to lie on her back, and then somehow recalls that the conspirator's voice belonged to Lord Essex's footman, Caim, who admitted her and Serjeant Ames to that boring sermon.

Now at last she can see his face staring at her impassively.

But he's not in her dream.

He's in her room.

CHAPTER 27

WHEN THE PINK GLOW of day at last breaks in the eastern sky, Beth
Fernandez is fully dressed and ready to be picked up from her home in
Southwark. She watches impatiently through her front window as the
cart arrives, its driver sleepy and rumpled. She opens the door with her
purse in one hand and a small leather bag in the other, steps into the
sheltered vestibule where the air feels fresh and inviting, and locks the
front door behind her.

The driver dismounts.

"Top o' the mornin', madam," he says with the faintest Irish brogue.
"Is that your only bag?"

She nods. "'Tis."

The driver places the lone bag carefully in the cart behind his seat,
still wiping his eyes from a sound sleep. He takes a footstool from the
cart and places it on the ground to enable Beth to climb into the seat next
to his.

"Don't mean to be presumptuous, Miss Fernandez," he says deferentially, "but I thought, this bein' a pleasant winter's mornin', you might
wish to sit up front with yer 'umble servant." When she doesn't respond
immediately, he says, "'Course, if you'd rather—"

"That will be *fine*, Goodman Driscoll," she assures him. Stepping
around a snowdrift, she places one foot onto the stepstool, and Driscoll
gingerly hoists her into position. He assumes the driver's seat next to her,
takes the reins in hand, and steers the cart gently away from the house,
avoiding as many snow drifts as possible.

The cool breeze that felt so inviting in the shelter of the vestibule
now nips at Beth's checks. She lifts her scarf up to cover her mouth.

They ride a while in silence.

As they're about to come down from the bridge into London, Driscoll decides it's time to confirm their destination. "The missus told me
you was headin' to Holborn. Is 'at right, Miss Fernandez?"

"Yes. I'm visiting my niece. Lady Saint Ives," she says with barely suppressed pride.

"That the same young lady what lived with you in Southwark after 'er husband died?"

"The same," she says with surprise. "I'd quite forgot that you and I
have been neighbors so long, Goodman Driscoll. Please forgive me. I see
you haven't forgot Lady Jessica."

He wags his chin, as though she's suggested something that could
never happen. "Oh, there's no forgettin' a lady like that, miss, so refined
and so comely. Goodwife Driscoll would tell me about 'er every time
she'd see 'er: what she was wearin', how she wore 'er hair. Y'know, that
sorta thing."

Beth smiles with pride. "Lady Jessica *is* a lovely person." She pulls
Lord Jonathan's note from her pocket. "Know what this is?" she asks,
waving it at Driscoll.

"No, ma'am, I don't," he says indulgently. "I'm hopin' you'll tell
me, though."

"It's a note from Lady Jessica's new husband, Lord Saint Ives, asking me—"

"Not *the* Lord Saint Ives, madam," he says with astonishment. "Not
the gentleman what saved so many of our boys in Ireland?"

She bristles at the interruption. "There's only *one* Lord Saint Ives,
sir," she assures him, "and that is he you speak of. And he's asked me to
lend a hand in m'lady's hour of need."

Driscoll's expression changes to one of concern. "Oh, I hope nothin'
bad's befallen Lady Jessica, miss."

"Not at all. In fact ... if you can keep a secret," she brings her voice
down to a stage whisper, "she's with child."

His eyebrows shoot up. "And yaw to help in deliverin' a lord ... or a
lady!"

She nods proudly. "Just so."

"And not just *any* lord nor lady, neither," Driscoll remarks as they
pass Saint Paul's, "but the eldest child of the heroic Lord Saint Ives. Ye
got a right to be most proud!"

She glowers as though he's forgotten something quite important. "I
expect," she says indignantly, "that Lady Jessica also had *something* to
do with the child."

Just as Driscoll nods and laughs quietly at his own oversight, the
peace of the predawn hour is shattered.

A cart moving at reckless speed careens around a corner right in
front of them, threatening to tumble over onto them or collide with them

head-on. To their amazement, it manages to right itself quickly enough to avoid catastrophe and slips past them in the opposite direction at breathtaking speed.

Shocked, Driscoll nearly drops the reins. Quickly regaining his composure, he draws his horse to a halt. But before he can so much as turn his head to confront the driver of the offending cart, it veers recklessly around the next corner and disappears southward toward the river.

Beth lowers the scarf from her face and takes a moment to compose herself. Tiny beads of perspiration have formed on her scalp and the back of her neck; they feel like icy pinpricks in the cold breeze. A glance over at Driscoll shows him to be even more dismayed than she, for he stares forlornly into space as though having narrowly escaped the Reaper.

He urges the horse onward.

"Sorry for that ... incident, miss," says Driscoll. "Seems that bloke was up to no good. Musta been runnin' from somethin'."

"I quite agree, Goodman Driscoll," replies Beth. "Such people ought to be tossed in the Clink, and the key dropped in the Thames."

"Oh, but not up here in London Town," Driscoll says.

"No?" she says curiously.

"Naw. Up here they'd be thrown in the *Fleet*." He smiles. "Key'd be tossed in the same river, though."

Though his little jest touches just the right note to cast out their residual fear, conversation remains scarce for the rest of their ride.

"Here we are on High Holborn," says Driscoll. "If you'd just point out the right house, miss."

She points to the Ames's residence. "It's that one, across the way from the partly laid foundation."

"Who's gonna live in the new house when it's done, I wonder," he says.

"That will be the new town home of Lord and Lady Saint Ives," she declares, proud of her advance knowledge.

"Won't that be nice?" he says as they pull up in the path to the Ames's house. "It's a rare thing nowadays, keepin' a family together more than a generation."

Beth nods wholeheartedly, finding Driscoll a bit more feeling than she gave him credit for. "Stop the cart here and accompany me to the rear door, if you would," she says, a little embarrassed. "No need to disturb the house at such an early hour."

Driscoll helps her down with her bag and through the rear door. Standing in the kitchen, she pays him his fee plus a bit more. He thanks her heartily, high-steps back into the driver's seat, and begins his return trip.

As no one in the house seems to be stirring yet, Beth shuts the door behind her and hangs her hat and outer cloak on a peg near the door.

She finds it a little disconcerting that, although she arrived before the help, the door opened without a key. *Anybody* could have entered with no resistance whatever.

She carries her little bag up the stairs to Jessica's room, knocks lightly at the door, and steps inside without waiting to be admitted. Jessica lies asleep atop the blankets in her maternity gown, her swollen belly quite prominent.

Nearly eight months along, Beth guesses. The girl's come a long way toward motherhood, yet she looks anything but peaceful. Her face is drawn and taut, much as her mother's was at the same point in her pregnancy. Blankets and pillows are strewn every which way—a reliable indicator that she's been wrestling with angels all night.

Across the room, Jonathan has obviously fallen asleep while reading, as he's leaning forward in his chair with his face resting on a writing table and his eyes closed. A book lies askew at his feet. Beth picks it up and holds it in her hand.

"Lord Jonathan," she whispers.

The poor man stirs, but only faintly. He must be exhausted with worry.

"Lord Jonathan," she repeats.

Jonathan sits up straight, blinks his eyes a few times to focus on her face in the pale morning light, and rubs a crick in his shoulder.

"Beth," he whispers in surprise. "Oh, thank God you're here." He glances past her at his wife, his face contorted with worry. "She's been tossing all night. Talking to herself. Last night, when I allowed her to stand, I was sure she'd fall. She was speaking nonsense to me, and then ... all of a sudden ... she went blank. I was prepared to break her fall but, instead of falling, she lay quietly back on her bed, thank God."

"I've come to help, Jonathan," says Beth. "How long has she been in distress?"

"More than a fortnight now," he confesses.

"More than—Why didn't you write me sooner?" she asks.

He regards her with the sorriest expression. "I wanted to, but Jessica ... she ... she's afraid you can't save her, because—" He pauses, unwilling to finish the thought.

"Because I couldn't save her mother," says Beth, completing a thought that cuts her like a knife. Near tears herself, she firms up her will. "Her mother's affliction was much the same as you've described, m'lord. Tell me, has she seized or convulsed?"

"How do you mean?" he asks.

"Well, Jonathan," she says, searching her mind for a seizure he may have observed, "have you ever seen someone with the grand mal?"

"Yes," he says with horror. "Oh, God! Does Jessica have the grand mal now?"

"No, she doesn't, m'lord, and you must not overreact to what I'm saying. Now, has she suffered a seizure that looks like grand mal?"

He becalms himself. "No, she hasn't ... at least, that *I* know of. You can ask her maidservants."

She looks about. "Speaking of maidservants, where *are* they?"

He rolls his eyes. "They refuse to come in while *I'm* here. They say, as madam is lying in, it's improper for me to be here."

Beth purses her lips dourly. "I shall set them straight on that right quick. But first things first. I need to explain to Jessica what happened to her mother. Oh, I can't *believe* I've let it go this long without telling her. That's my fault, not yours." She points to her leather bag. "I know of something that should stop the progress of her symptoms. If we use it and things go as expected, the threat will subside within a few hours, then end entirely as soon as she delivers. But I need to gain her confidence first, and her consent to administer the remedy."

Jonathan nods gravely and nudges Jessica. "Jessica, darling," he says. She begins to stir. "There's someone here to see you, dear. Please sit up and speak with her."

Jessica opens her eyes, full of doubt. "Who is it?"

"It's me, dear," says Beth.

Jonathan gathers up a few of the pillows that Jessica scattered about during the restless night, and props her up on two of them. A tiny ray of sunlight touches her face, and she cringes as though it burns. Jonathan blocks the ray with his person, and she opens her eyes fully, although they're still less than fully focused.

"I heard you were feeling unwell," says Beth, "and thought I would stop by to see for myself."

Even in his fatigued state, Jonathan admires how Beth has sidestepped the question of how she learned of Jessica's plight.

"Auntie Beth," says Jessica tearfully, "I am in so much pain. I feel short of breath all the time, and my head ... feels as though it will *explode*."

"I expected you might be having those problems, dear. Rest assured that your head shan't explode, and things will turn out fine if you receive the proper care."

Jessica looks at her a bit confused. "Why would you ... have suspected ... I was having ... headaches?" asks Jessica.

By Jessica's pained expression and disjointed speech, Beth can see she's suffering from an awful headache as they speak. "Because I've seen it before, dear. I've worked with midwives for years, remember. I thought you knew that."

"No," says Jessica. "You never mentioned it, because ... Mother died after giving birth to ... me. I suppose that's why."

Beth sighs. "Jessica, your father has explained to me that you doubt my midwifing skills because your mother Rachel was in my care when she ... passed."

Jessica sucks in a breath, and grimaces as one betrayed. "Father should *not* have—"

"Doubt not your father, dear," says Beth. "He cares for you more than himself. There is no loving father in the world who would defer to his daughter's preference if he thought that doing so might ruin her health. And as for his hurting *my* feelings, well, he knows me well enough to realize that I would be furious with him if he *didn't* tell me." Beth sits at the edge of the bed and takes Jessica's hand in her own. "If you would permit me, my dear, I would like to explain to you what happened to your mother at the time of your birth."

Jessica's tears begin to flow, but she nods in agreement.

"Your mother and father were secretly wed in 1568."

"Why was their marriage a secret?"

Beth smiles, as Jessica's impetuous questioning brings to mind the pretty little girl who wanted to know so much about her mother that she would never let Beth complete a thought without interruption.

"They were wed secretly, dear, because she was Hebrew, as were all the other members of your father's family. If your father were known to be a Hebrew, he could not be admitted to the bar, so Uncle Avram purchased a small house in my name where your father and mother could secretly meet and, at least for a few days at a time, live some semblance of a married life. Well, of course, because they loved each other so much, they couldn't help but give life to the sweetest, most beautiful lass."

Jessica's tears now flow freely, and she makes no attempt to conceal them.

Jonathan marvels at how quickly Jessica has succumbed to the enchantment of Beth's tale of her mother. Her expression is that of a little girl hearing a particularly touching folk tale.

"Yetta—remember Yetta?" asks Beth.

Jessica nods.

"Yetta had asked me to escort a young Jew from Southwark to a remote place in Scotland in order to escape an uprising in his home country on the Continent. In those days, when Yetta asked any Jew to do something for a child in danger, we simply did it. She'd sacrificed so much for us all—and had so seldom asked a favor—that it would have been unconscionably selfish to decline.

"Unfortunately, it took me months to identify and then *locate* the person into whose custody I was to deliver the child." She shakes her head in remembered frustration. "The Scots of the north are a backward and secretive lot. But that's a story for another winter.

"When I left on this mission, none of us knew that Rachel was with child. As it turned out, she was nearly six months along when I left, but she'd carried the child so slenderly that no one suspected.

"By the time I returned, I found Rachel near to term, and she'd been suffering for well over a month with severe headaches that eventually became seizures. Now, any midwife with half a mind knows that a bout of severe headaches during pregnancy is a dangerous turn of events and that something needs to be done, for once the seizures begin, nothing seems to stop the progression of the illness, and the patient often dies.

"I asked the midwife what she was doing about it. She replied that she was well aware of the danger, so she'd been administering 'salts.' When I asked *which* salts, she produced an earthen jar containing a white salt she'd got from the local rabbi, who said the salts were 'special' to the Jewish people (as though their effect was religious or magical). He'd given her the jar with the assurance that the salts were from the Dead Sea, but never asked what use was to be made of them.

"The midwife had been administering small quantities to Rachel all the while, but they'd accomplished nothing. At that point, I could have strangled the girl."

"Why?" asks Jessica.

"Because they were the *wrong* salts. There are many different salts in the world, dear, but only one can prevent a pregnant woman from having these awful headaches and suffering convulsions. And *that* salt does not come from the Holy Land."

"Where can it be found?" asks Jessica quaveringly, wide-eyed with hope.

"In a much more accessible place," says Beth. "*So* accessible that you shall laugh to hear its name."

Jessica absentmindedly reaches for her husband's hand, and Jonathan's heavy heart leaps with relief at this sign that hope has returned to her and that he's been readmitted to her world.

"Dear Beth," Jonathan says dramatically, "is this miraculous salt guarded by dragons? I shall take to horse at once! Just say where it may be found."

Beth laughs. "To find it, one must travel to deepest … Surrey."

"*Surrey?*" exclaim Jessica and Jonathan together.

Beth nods. "Epsom, to be precise. There's a bitter salt spring there, where the chalk of the North Downs meets the London clay. When one boils out the water, it leaves a salt which, to my knowledge, is the *only* one that will do the trick."

"Shall I send for it?" asks Jonathan.

"You already have," says Beth, forgetting herself. "That is to say, *Noah* has. You see, I brought an ample quantity with me in that leather case on the floor."

"How does one administer it?" asks Jonathan.

"To speed things along, a small quantity is administered by mouth. It can be mixed with just about any drink—containing no oil—such as weak beer or water. If you're going to use water, you should boil it in a vessel first, cover it, and set it out of doors to cool, then add the amount of Epsom salt I shall prescribe, and Jessica shall drink it up. After that, it's customary to pat down the patient with a watery solution of the salt every few hours. If the headaches return, it may need to be administered orally again."

"That is all?" asks Jessica.

"Yes, dear," replies Beth. "These headaches are not the only thing that can go wrong before, during, or after birth, mind you. But it's one thing we should soon be able to strike off the worry list."

While Jonathan and Jessica breathe a quiet sigh of relief for the first time in weeks, Beth steps out of the room and closes the door behind her.

There's a sudden commotion downstairs.

"Noah! Noah!" comes Marie's shout. It sounds desperate. "Come at once!"

Beth runs to the staircase and looks down at Marie, who's in a panic at the foot of the stairs. "What's happened, dear?" asks Beth.

Marie places a hand on each of her cheeks, and cries out.

"Oh, Beth! *Esther's been taken!*"

CHAPTER 28

NOAH FRETS OUTSIDE the closed door to Esther's room. His heart pounds as he struggles to maintain a stoic face. If anything bad happens to that girl, he has no idea what he'll do.

"I haven't touched a thing," Marie assures him through her tears, while Beth tries to calm her down. "Everything is exactly as I found it."

"Is—" Noah begins to speak, but his throat is so tight his voice croaks. He forces himself to swallow. "Is Stephen here?"

As though beckoned, Marie's adult son Stephen appears, still rumpled from bed. "I was asleep in the back servant's room when I heard the commotion," he says, rubbing his eyes. "What's happened?"

"Oh, Stephen!" says Marie excitedly. "Esther's been *taken!*"

"Taken?" says Stephen. "Mother, what do you mean, *taken*?"

"I mean *taken*!" she growls, showing a side her son has rarely seen. Beth tugs at Marie's arm. As Marie allows herself to be led away, she glowers angrily at Noah. In that single look she lays blame for this disaster squarely on his shoulders.

"We'll find her, Marie," he says. "And we'll bring her back. And whoever did this—"

She turns on him. "I don't give a whit what happens to whoever did this. Just bring Esther back to me!"

"I shall," Noah assures her as she's led away. "Stephen," he says, "David is staying at Durham House—"

"I thought he was back at Oxford for several days now," replies Stephen, scratching his head.

Noah shakes his head sadly. "He should have been, but he ... he was trying to work things out with Esther, and he just couldn't bring himself to go." He sighs. "I'm going into Esther's room now to see what I can find. In the meantime, don't bother to dress properly, just put on a heavy cloak, grab a horse—Bucklebury, if none else is ready—and fetch David at once. Tell him what's happened."

As Stephen turns to run for his heaviest cloak, Noah takes him by the shoulder and draws him in close. "I'm keeping my voice down because I don't want your mother to hear. Put on a long sword and a dagger, and tell Cheerful to do the same. And *by God* keep your eyes open! We don't know who's out there or how many there are. They've already been here once this morning, and they could be watching us right now."

Stephen nods grimly and runs for his cloak.

Noah opens the door to Esther's room. Although it's upsetting to contemplate what happened here, it could look much worse. The blankets are amiss. Her shoes are gone. But there's no sign of real violence. No blood, thank God. The poor girl must have done as she was told. The casements are unopened, but that's unsurprising, as they would have been too small for a man to fit through alone, let alone one encumbered by a hostage, however slight in stature.

Carefully placed on the chest is what appears to be a throwing-sized stone wrapped in a single sheet of paper. On the outside is written, "Sjt. Ames." He picks it up and gauges its weight. It's hefty, and he cannot help but imagine smashing it into the face of the man who took Esther.

But there's something to be learned here: The perpetrator chose not to announce his departure by throwing the wrapped stone through one of the windows in the house, as had clearly been his plan—Why else the stone?—That shows the perpetrator exercised some level of prudence, for slipping away quietly enhanced the likelihood that Esther's absence would go undiscovered for a while, thus improving his chances of getting away clean. It also implies that the note was not written here, but rather in advance of the breaking and entering. So, whatever else the perpetrator may be, he's not mad. He's devious. Evil, certainly. But not mad.

Noah turns over the stone and unfolds the paper. Inside is a note written in a deliberately sloppy hand—probably applied by the perpetrator's left. The spelling is phonetic and the grammar makeshift, to say the least, but the sequence of thoughts is coherent, and, after studying the note for a minute or two, Noah translates it into comprehensible language:

> If you follow the instructions in this note strictly, your precious niece will be returned to you in good condition. You must tell me where to find Cuthbert Bennett. He murdered my friend, and that's a crime for which he shall pay at once. When you've at last got it through your Jew head that you've got no choice, write a note containing the information I've requested, fold it, and (you personally) nail it to the fence on the east side of the Bear Garden at Bankside by noon today, then return at

once to Holborn.

There's more than one of us, so don't leave anyone to discover, or interfere with, whoever fetches the note. If the note's not there, or if you try to snatch up my man or have him followed, your dear young cousin will be DEAD within minutes. And you'll be to blame.

Noah ponders what he may learn from the note. Why the mention of his Jewishness? It could reflect nothing more than ordinary Jew-hatred, of which there's no shortage in London. But it could also mean that the perpetrator believed it could in some way be relevant to his knowing Cuthbert's hiding place. Strangely, Cuthbert is indeed residing outside of town with another Jew. But if the perpetrator knew that, of course, he wouldn't need to hear it from Noah.

The note asks for no money whatever, so avenging the death of the man Cuthbert killed may well be the perpetrator's true motive. Otherwise, what would the perpetrator have to gain?

And why demand that Noah post the note in *Bankside*, of all places? The perpetrator's convenience, most likely. Regardless whether the perpetrator is working alone or in league with others, one or more of them expects to be in Bankside about that time. What's in Bankside to bring them there? Bear baiting, obviously ... the food market, the church ... and several theaters.

Curiously, it seems the perpetrator gave not a moment's thought to the possibility that Noah might have no idea where Cuthbert is hiding. Why would he be so confident in Noah's knowledge? Noah's fairly certain Cuthbert was not seen coming or going from the house. But what if he were seen *inside* the house? Who might have informed the perpetrator?

Who was present when Cuthbert appeared? Sir Henry and Lady Anne were here when Cuthbert first appeared, as were Arthur, Jonathan, Jessica, and David ... and *Esther.* His stomach turns just to think of what she might already be suffering.

True, a few servants were also present on Cuthbert's arrival, but Noah's known them all for many years, and they would never have carelessly bruited any such thing about, especially after being admonished not to do so. Nor does it seem possible any of them could be the actual perpetrator of such a dastardly act as this. Might one of the servants have been threatened? Might one be in someone's pay?

But who would have enough interest in Cuthbert to bribe or threaten a servant? Not Essex, certainly. Besides, having women manhandled has never been his style. He's always been absurdly courtly to women, especially pretty young ones like Esther. It seems unlikely anyone would have one of Noah's servants on salary, although Sir Walter is constantly telling Noah he's more important than he thinks.

Perhaps the perpetrator assumed that Noah's elevated stature at court would enable him to invoke any means necessary to find out Cuthbert's whereabouts, if the stakes were high enough. And they couldn't be much higher than they are now.

He turns back to the note, specifically, to four words that required no emendation. "He murdered my friend." But whom did Cuthbert murder? Although Cuthbert didn't admit to killing anyone, he did recognize the bloody mask. It had been worn by the man who shot at Jonathan. *Oh, who was it?* Try though Noah might, he can't remember the name, but … then it comes to him. *Meriton.* Meriton was one of *Caim's* men. Could the perpetrator be Caim? Surely Meriton had had friends besides Caim, so it might yet be someone else.

But then Noah remembers the scene described by Cuthbert on his second visit. He'd followed Caim to an inn of ill repute to which Knott and another fellow repaired together, and then broke into their room wearing a mask, announcing that he was there to rob everyone, Caim included. So, Cuthbert interrupted Caim in his attempt to dissuade Knott and his friend from applying to collect royalties on Essex's expired patent. Cuthbert also knocked him cold, which would be quite an insult to someone as self-important as Caim.

On that occasion, Cuthbert had been disguised, true. But Caim had heard Cuthbert's voice and it might have resembled Tobias's closely enough for him to suspect the robber was Cuthbert. And his suspicions would have been further aroused by Cuthbert's foolishly neglecting to rob anyone, which had been his announced purpose in breaking in.

Caim is shaping up as the prime suspect. Where would he hide Esther once he abducted her? And where is he now?

Then, a question takes root in Noah's mind that could be fundamentally important and provide a solution to the whole abduction:

Why would Caim, other than to fetch Noah's note from the bear baiter's fence, expect to be in Bankside at noon today?

While Noah's mind is all a muddle in Esther's room, Beth appears at the door.

"I'd recommend," she says quietly, "that we withhold any knowledge of Esther's plight from Lady Jessica."

Noah looks at her inquiringly.

Beth nods. "Excessive worry will do her no good in her present condition."

"Are you able to help her?" asks Noah.

"I've just given her the only remedy expected to work in a case such as this. She's resting quietly."

"So, you feel optimistic?"

Beth sighs. "I expect it will work."

"Thank heaven for some *good* news," he says.

"A bit of prayer couldn't hurt," she replies. "The remedy does have one possible unintended effect, however."

"What's that?" asks Noah.

"It can cause early delivery. I'm confident, however, that we could save at least the mother in that eventuality. And quite possibly the child, as the pregnancy is nearly to term."

He looks up at her imploringly. "But I need both."

"You do indeed," she says, "though we have to accept what God gives us." She sighs. "Your wife wants Esther back. You take care of that, and I'll take care of Jessica."

"Thank you, dear Beth," he says and kisses her on the forehead. She pats his shoulder reassuringly and plods up the stairs.

After a few moments alone—agonizing, when all Noah can think of is Esther—the front door bursts open.

David enters. Noah is taken aback by his fierce expression.

"It was Caim, wasn't it?" asks David.

Before Noah can respond or ask David for his reasoning, Stephen tramps in. "We rode past Essex House on the way back here," says Stephen with disgust, "and Caim was standing outside looking so cold-blooded that butter wouldn't melt in his mouth. He had the nerve to doff his cap in our direction."

Noah knits his brow. "If, as David suggests, it was Caim who abducted Esther, how could he have returned to Essex House so quickly?"

"That *does* limit the places where he could have taken her," says David darkly, "although we're not precisely sure when the abduction took place, and he might have handed her off to a confederate." He says with exasperation, "I'd like to just go over there and kill him."

"Stephen," says Noah, "thank you for your efforts. Meanwhile, go and dress properly. You may have more to do before this is over with." Stephen nods and goes off to the servant's room currently serving as his own.

"David," says Noah angrily, "has it occurred to you that if you *were* to kill Caim now, you might thereby be killing Esther?"

David shakes his head. "I spoke carelessly."

"Well," says Noah with exasperation, "I can't afford to have you say or do *anything* careless right now. And, if you need me to state the obvious, you are no more privileged to kill anyone than Cuthbert was. Regardless whether it was Caim who did this, the perpetrator will face the *Queen's* justice, not yours."

David glowers. "The Queen didn't do bloody much to protect Esther," he mutters sullenly.

Noah glowers at him. "David, *you've* been a Queen's man. Could *you* be everywhere at once?" He rolls his eyes in exasperation. "Essex House looks about to blow apart at any moment—"

"It's happening tomorrow morning," mumbles David.

Noah's stunned. "What?" he says incredulously. "*What's* happening tomorrow morning?"

"The incursion into the Queen's court," says David impatiently, as though his remark was so clear it could not have been misunderstood.

"My God, when … how did you learn this?" asks Noah.

"One need only spend a little time in any tavern near the Strand, as I did last night. It's like every one of those buffoons has run mad at the mouth. They don't even make a respectable *show* of keeping quiet."

"My God!" Noah says in amazement. "What *else* have you learned?" he demands.

"Not much. This afternoon, they're going *en masse* to the Globe Theater to see a play. *Richard the Second.*"

So *that's* why Caim will be in Bankside.

David's attention returns to Esther. "Where could he have taken her?"

The door to Jessica's room opens and closes upstairs, and Beth's unmistakable footsteps approach the top of the stairs. Noah goes to the foot of the stairs and looks up at her.

She shakes her head in disbelief. "Noah, I think you should come to Jessica's room for a moment."

"Has she taken a turn for the worse?" he asks, his stomach turning at the prospect.

Beth shakes her head. "Not at all. But, well—you'd better come up."

"Good lord, Beth!" says Noah. "Now?"

She nods.

Noah turns to David. "Follow me," he says.

When they reach the top of the stairs, Beth observes, "You wish to know where Esther can be found." She opens the door and admits Noah and David, holding her finger to her mouth to ensure their silence.

Jessica is in bed. Jonathan's absent. All is quiet.

Noah turns to Beth. "Is this some sort of jest?"

"Wait for it," she says and points to his sleeping daughter with supreme confidence.

Jessica turns in her sleep and, with her face at peace and her eyes closed, speaks one word slowly and clearly:

"Queenhythe."

She makes no move toward waking as Noah and David watch her, slack-jawed. Instead, she repeats the same word in precisely the same tone.

"Queenhythe."

Beth leads the two men out by the hand, closes the door quietly behind her, and says, "Let me tell you one more thing that came to mind when Jessica first spoke this word a few minutes ago. As my neighbor and I were riding here before dawn this morning, the streets were empty. Yet, as we passed Saint Paul's, we were nearly struck by a cart speeding from this vicinity like a bat from hell. When it passed us, it veered south."

"Toward Queenhythe," ventures David. "My God, she's a witch," he mutters in wonder and looks to Noah. "Esther's a witch?"

"Don't talk nonsense, David," says Noah without explanation. "Beth, were there passengers in the other cart?"

"None that I could see," she replies.

"Did you catch a glimpse of the driver?" asks David.

"Unfortunately, no. Before we thought to look, the cart was *upon* us—then *past* us."

"If it took you a half hour to get here, Beth, then when would Esther have been abducted?"

"Just before first light," she says.

Noah turns to David. "And when did you see Caim at Essex House?"

David estimates. "Perhaps a quarter-hour ago."

"That's enough time," say Noah and David at once.

"The gods are on our side in one additional respect," observes Noah. "On Cuthbert's second visit here, he told us he'd got a room at a boarding house in Queenhythe, and that Caim kept a room there."

"Did he say precisely where it was?" asks David.

"No."

"I'll go and fetch Cuthbert," says David, turning to go.

"No!" says Noah. "Not all blunderbuss like this. Someone could be watching as you leave the house, although I doubt it, as I expect Caim is working alone. We'll have to do this cleverly."

Stephen appears, properly dressed, which reminds Noah of something.

"David, is Sir Walter still at Durham House?" asks Noah.

"He was when I left, and made no move toward leaving."

"Stephen," says Noah. "Take a brief message to Sir Walter at Durham House. If he's not there, find him at the Tower of London. Avoid being seen from Essex House or Drury House, if you can."

"Aye, sir," says Stephen. "Where's the message?"

"It's a *parol* message," says Noah. "You must commit it to memory and forget not a jot. Ready?"

Stephen nods curtly.

Noah observes the gravity of young Stephen's face, and wonders how men so young could be capable of understanding the importance of what they're asked to do.

"Here it is," he says. "'Double the guard at once. Take agreed measures for tomorrow morning, Sunday.'"

Stephen repeats it verbatim. Noah nods, and Stephen runs out the door.

Noah turns to David. "I think I have a way to assure Caim's absence from the boarding house when you arrive there."

CHAPTER 29

AFTER AN EARLY DINNER, Essex's supporters divide themselves into two groups, all heading to Bankside and the Globe Theater to see *Richard the Second*.

While some choose wherries to row them across the Thames, that mode of transport poses a possible problem for the theatergoer; it means there will be no horse awaiting him at whichever stairs he chooses to disembark upon in Bankside (unless he's made arrangements in advance, which is something few do). That means he'll have to walk a bit, which presents no problem as long as he's ambulatory and the weather holds up. To go on horseback, on the other hand, poses the converse problem; that is, when one arrives at the theater, he needs to stable his horse.

Most of those who haven't adequately exercised their horses (or themselves) for a few days, take to their mounts and proceed double-file along Thames Street to London Bridge. As they reach the Southwark end of the bridge, church bells clang out their noon call, and many in the procession murmur the Lord's Prayer.

Caim rides at the head of the cavalcade, ostensibly to chase rabble from its path but, overtaken by fatigue and the soporific hum of praying men, he nearly falls from his horse.

"*Hoy*, Master Caim!" says an old baron, jarring him awake. "What wench had *you* up all night … or did she have ye up early this morning?"

"The important thing is, she had him *up!*" replies another bawdy baron, waggling an index finger at the sky to demonstrate his all-too-obvious point.

Caim smiles at the general merriment, even though it's at his expense, but inside he's deeply uneasy that the old baron came so close to guessing the true reason for his fatigue. There's a woman, to be sure, but not that sort, and if things don't turn out just right, she might just cost him his head.

Caim asks Sir Gelly to lead the procession the rest of the way to the Globe, and veers off toward the bear-baiting pits.

A few minutes later, Caim clops slowly around the perimeter fence at the Bear Garden looking for Serjeant Ames's note, berating himself for failing to realize that the theater bills slapped haphazardly all over the fence would render it difficult for him to spot it.

At last he spies what appears to be a fresh note nailed to the east side of the fence. Before approaching, he glances about to see if he's being watched. The Bear Garden must be between shows, as there are few people in the immediate area. In the distance to the south, a few men mill about, one or two with horses, but no one appears to be watching him. In one quick motion, he rips the note from its nail and opens it.

Bearing the Serjeant's signature and seal, the note consists of one line:

You're looking at Bennett. Now release my niece.

Caim casually folds the note and shoves it quickly into his pocket.

Now he gazes with greater interest at those milling about in the distance. There's one man standing apart from the rest, languidly holding the reins of a big black steed far too noble for the likes of Cuthbert Bennett. Caim focuses on the man and, for a brief moment, gets a good look at his face. It *must* be Bennett, as he's the spit and image of his dead brother; a bit thinner, perhaps, but that's no doubt the natural result of running and hiding, which he's done a lot of lately. He seems to be in no rush and, for the whole time Caim's been gazing at him, he hasn't so much as glanced this way.

Caim ponders what the devil Ames was thinking when he arranged this. To Caim's devious mind, the likeliest answer is that Ames has arranged to sacrifice Bennett to get his niece back. Not a bad exchange, really; one he might make himself. But there's one thing Ames doesn't know: His niece has seen Caim's face, and he can't afford to let her go ... ever. She's been allowed to continue breathing even until this moment only because Caim might need to prove she's alive, depending upon Ames's possible demands.

At the back of Caim's mind, he realizes Bennett's appearance here *could* be a trap, but that seems unlikely, for Ames would realize that the writer of the ransom note could have left a confederate with his niece, with instructions to slit her throat if the writer fails to return by a designated time. Ames is simply too clever to have Bennett lead him off on a "wild-goose chase," as Shakespeare might say.

While Caim's been wool-gathering, Bennett has mounted his impressive steed and begun to canter south.

Though reluctant to miss the special performance at the Globe, Caim follows him with blood in his eyes.

IN THE BACK LIBRARY at Essex House, Essex and Southampton review and improve their plans for tomorrow's venture.

"But how can we be certain that the men in the guard chamber will be separated from their halberds?" asks Southampton.

Essex rubs his eyes and takes a moment to regain focus. "I've been to the guard chamber countless times. The men keep their halberds in a fixed array on the rear wall." Irritated, he squints at Southampton through bloodshot eyes. "Haven't we been through these details enough times?"

Southampton can see an explanation is needed. "I just thought—"

Essex interrupts him. "I do apologize for my tone, Wriothesley. I haven't been sleeping much lately. No sooner does my soul find a dry little island than Lady Essex drenches it with a storm of tears and a *hurlecan* of woe. She keeps me up half the night, beside herself with worry."

Southampton nods. "My home life is as badly disturbed. Even with all the unease among the men here, I sleep better on a couch at Essex House than at home in my own bed."

Essex smirks. "Perhaps you can arrange a couch for me at Southampton House."

There's a knock at the library door.

"What now?" says Southampton.

"Come," shouts Essex.

The stableman opens the door a crack. "There's a gentleman at the gate to see you, m'lord. An official-looking one. I caught him asking everyone's name."

Essex awaits further information, but the stableman just stands at the door looking uncomfortable.

"Has the *gentleman* a name?" asks Essex.

"I'll go and see, suh," says the stableman.

"Please do," says Essex.

The stableman closes the door and tramps away toward the gate.

While they wait, Essex turns to Southampton. "Where's Caim? Oh, that's right! He's at the Globe with all the others." He shakes his head wearily. "A stableman to keep the door. Makes you wonder who's tending the horses."

Another knock, and the stableman juts his head in. "Says he's Robert Sackville, m'lord."

Essex looks to Southampton for further identification.

"Eldest son of Dorset, Lord Treasurer," says Southampton.

"Show him in," says Essex.

In announcing the visitor, the stableman does his best impersonation of Caim, who customarily announces visitors stiffly in a voice easily twice as loud as necessary. "Robert Sackville, m'lord," he says, admitting the man, bowing out, and closing the door behind.

Sackville bows to both earls, looking ill at ease, searching his memory.

Southampton sizes him up. About forty years of age. Not the brightest candle in the chandelier. Creature of indolence.

"The Lord Treasurer," pronounces Sackville deliberately, "has asked me to convey to you his highest salutations and friendliest regards."

Essex nods indulgently. "Sure it wasn't his highest *regards* and friendliest *salutations?*"

Sackville sucks in a short breath and corrects himself. "Quite right, m'lord. That is what my father said to say. I do apologize."

"No apology necessary," replies Essex. "In fact, if *I* may impose upon your good offices, Master Robert, I would ask that you convey to your esteemed father both m'Lord Southampton's and mine own highest regards and friendliest salutations."

Sackville nods with interest. "I certainly shall do so," he says.

A painfully long silence ensues.

"Well," says Sackville, "I suppose that I have completed my business here, so I shall bid my lords both adieu." He turns on his heel.

"There is one thing further I'd ask of you, sir," says Essex.

Sackville turns back. "What is that, m'lord?"

"I ask your assurance as a gentleman," says Essex, "that you shall not repeat the name, number, or description of those you've seen here at Essex House this afternoon."

Sackville hesitates, chagrined. "Most certainly, m'lord. Not a whit of it."

"Thank you for your assurance, Master Sackville. Good day."

Sackville bows again, a little uncertainly, and departs.

After a respectful wait, Southampton bursts into laughter. "Well, that's a few minutes we'll never have back."

"Wouldn't you like to see him when he gets back to his father?" says Essex. "'Yes, I could, Father. I could name many gentlemen at Essex

House, but I am not at liberty to say. Pardon me, m'lord, but I am duty bound.'"

Southampton snickers. "Somehow," he says, "I think he'll tell all."

"No doubt," replies Essex.

They resume their intimate discussion of how to achieve the delicate balance of forcing their way into the court while not appearing to do so, when there's another knock at the door. The same stableman opens it, but this time he looks a bit more severe.

"M'lord," he says, "Sir John Herbert of the Privy Council is at the gate. He says he's Second Secretary of State."

Southampton sits up stiffly and turns to Essex. "Pardon, m'lord," he says, turning back to the stableman. "Is he alone?"

The stableman nods. "Looks to be, m'lord."

"First, usher everyone in the house into this library—"

"Everybody, suh? There's quite a few out there."

"How many?" asks Southampton.

The stableman shrugs. "Perhaps a dozen."

"Bring them all in if they care to come, and leave that door open so they may come and go as they please. Then, ask Herbert if he's come alone or accompanied," orders Southampton. "If alone, admit him at once. If he's accompanied, come and fetch me, and I'll speak with him at the gate."

The stableman looks to Essex, who nods in confirmation, and goes to carry out Southampton's orders.

Essex looks admiringly at his friend. "Setting the stage, eh?"

Southampton shakes his head. "I just don't want our friends having any doubts about our commitment to this affair. If they see us alone with Herbert, they may grow suspicious that we're selling them out and, if that happens, by this evening there'll be no one in this house but you and I."

Barons and knights begin meandering into the library by ones and twos.

The stableman appears with a gentleman in tow whose age Southampton estimates at fifty. Though he's of sober temperament, he seems to have injected a spring in his step for the occasion.

Herbert has no apparent trouble recognizing the seated gentlemen as Essex and Southampton, but his eyes dart anxiously at the others milling about the library.

"Good e'en, m'lords," he says in a seasoned voice.

"And good e'en to you, Master Secretary," says Southampton.

"I have a written message here for Lord Essex by orders of Her Majesty." Herbert hands Essex a folded note.

"Sherris?" asks Southampton, who pours a small cup and proffers it to Herbert.

As Essex accepts the folded note, a much smaller note falls from it into his lap. With no change of expression, he deftly scoops it up, puts it in his pocket, and looks about discreetly to see if anyone else saw it. Fortunately, they all seem to be attending to Southampton's proffer of sherris.

Herbert politely declines the sherris, though his eyes light up at it. "I'm afraid I couldn't, though I very much wish to," he says. "I must return to a meeting of the Council taking place nearby."

"Oh?" says Essex. "What draws the Council out of its usual haunt at Westminster?"

"It's the Lord Treasurer, m'lord," replies Herbert. "He's not feeling well, and we thought it a good idea—this once—to 'ride circuit,' if you will, on his account."

"How very thoughtful of you," says Southampton.

Essex unfolds the large note and reads it silently.

"Ah, Master Herbert," says Essex when he finishes. "Is it not possible the Council is riding circuit for *my* benefit, as well?" He points to the writing on the note. "Evidently, I'm ... summoned there." He makes a show of equivocating. "I must confess there were times when I was pleased to join the Council for discussion. What is the topic today, m'lord?"

"Don't go!" says a grumpy old baron, evidently not caring what Herbert thinks. "It's a trick, m'lord! They'll snatch you up!"

Herbert arches an eyebrow at the scurrilous (though possibly correct) imputation. "I expect your lordship's conduct at Essex House would be on the agenda, among other things. But no one's going to snatch you up, m'lord."

"And if I were to go," says Essex, "might not the Lord Treasurer communicate his present malady to those in attendance, thereby compounding my already abundant ailments? As you can probably see— and as Lord Southampton and I were discussing shortly before you appeared—I haven't been sleeping at all well ... for a number of reasons."

"Detain him, m'lord!" shouts another rabble-rouser.

Essex turns to address his vocal supporter. "We shan't detain Master Herbert, my friend. He has many cares to attend to that have nought to do with the various plots laid on my life." He turns to Herbert. "Please pass along my regrets, Sir John."

Sir John pauses, but then looks about at the angry barons who'd no doubt contest anything he says. He settles on something conciliatory. "Along with others on the Council, m'lord, I wish you well, and so take my leave." He bows silently to both Essex and Southampton, turns, and exits the way he came.

As the library door is shut behind him, an uproar commences, everyone congratulating everyone else for their stellar performance in turning away a member of the wicked Privy Council.

Essex rises, holding up the small paper that fell from the larger one.

"What's that, m'lord?" asks one.

"It's a note that was hidden within the one from the Privy Council."

"What does it say?" asks a near-sighted baron near the rear.

Essex prepares to read it once he has everyone's full attention. "It reads, 'Essex, you are led astray by pretending supporters. Look to yourself!'"

The room is silent, everyone realizing that the Privy Council has just called every man in the house a liar.

Essex looks his men in the face and says with a catch in his voice, "Would that the Privy Council were as faithful to Her Majesty as you, blessèd brothers, are to me." Slowly, they come to life and begin to applaud. "But … however much Her Majesty might hold her councillors in high esteem, never—*never!*—could she love them … as I do you!"

The room erupts once more in celebration of its leader.

CHAPTER 30

AT BANKSIDE, Stephen Rodriguez watches Caim disappear over the horizon in pursuit of Cuthbert. He reaches into his saddlebag, removes a bound assembly of three sizeable torches, and leads his horse to the riverside, where three beggars warm their hands at an open fire.

"Good morning, gentlemen," he says to them as he approaches. Their eyes flash suspiciously.

"What would you plan on doin' with *that*, suh?" says a surly one.

"By your leave, I propose to light it in your fire there," replies Stephen.

"You look like you got plenty t'eat," says the surly one. "What's in it fer *us*?"

"My proposition," says Stephen, having given it no prior thought, "is that I pay you each tuppence, and we call it even. Is that acceptable?"

"Tuppence apiece?" says the vagrant. "Must be a pretty important ... what *is* that thing anyway?"

"It's a *beacon*, sir," replies Stephen. "And you're correct. It's fairly urgent." He glances about at several other groups of vagrants warming their hands at other fires nearby. "On the other hand, yours is not the only fire in Bankside. I suppose I *could*—"

"A shillin' for the lot of us," says the surly one, doubling the demand to fourpence apiece. "Take it or leave it." Behind his back, his friends make an unwitting dumbshow of their conviction that their friend has badly overplayed his hand. One hides his face in his hands. The other raises his hands heavenward in supplication, as though to cry "ye gods!"

Stephen takes a better look at them. They're a ragged lot stuck out here in the cold with no reliable lodgings or meals.

"Done," he says to their great surprise, tossing a shilling to the one who sought divine intervention. As they whoop and dance with their newfound riches, Stephen shoves the assembled torches in the fire.

The beacon catches fire almost instantly. Even in the full sun of day, its flame is blindingly bright. Stephen walks his horse the few feet to the edge of the Thames and waves it from side to side for those awaiting the signal across the river at Queenhythe.

He continues waving while he awaits the return beacon.

"WELL, THAT'S IT, THEN," David says to Chester. "You can wave the return beacon."

Chester's eyes go wide as though he's forgot something.

David shakes his head impatiently. "Don't tell me you've lost it."

"No, no, suh," replies Chester, opening his saddlebag and removing the single torch that will serve amply as a confirmatory beacon. He shows it to David. "It's right here, suh."

"Don't show it to *me*," says David. "Light it, for heaven's sake, and show it to *Stephen*!"

"*Stephen*, suh?" says Chester.

"Yes, Stephen ... *across the river!*" says David, pointing to the triple beacon still being waved at them from the opposite bank.

"I haven't a flame, suh," says Chester.

David points to two old women chafing their hands by a smoky fire of twigs that still have moist leaves attached. "Use theirs!"

As Chester races toward the fire, he clumsily drops the torch, and watches in horror as it bumps and clatters its way down the embankment and into the Thames, where it sinks out of sight.

Even if they were to retrieve it now, it certainly wouldn't burn.

Not to be deterred, Chester grabs the unlit end of one of the larger twigs comprising the old women's fire and lifts it over his head, inadvertently flinging burning leaves and cinders in every direction.

"Hey, cadger!" says one of the women. "Are you *mad*?"

But Chester ignores her and continues waving the burning twig until the beacon across the river is extinguished, sure confirmation that his flimsy fire has been seen. Relieved, he flings the burning twig into the Thames, which hisses to receive it.

David walks over to the two old paupers and hands them sixpence apiece. "Sorry about my mad friend, ladies," he says. "Please accept these for your troubles."

The old paupers bow respectfully and back away. "Bless you, suh," says one.

But the other points to Chester. "Better see to your friend, kind suh," she croaks.

David turns to see Chester smiling triumphantly while his cloak smolders and smokes. Evidently, a live ember is stuck to it somewhere.

"Chester!" shouts David. "Remove your cloak at once and give it to me!"

Chester looks at him without understanding, but complies nonetheless. As he hands over the cloak, he shivers in the cold and is about to say something when he realizes it's burning. "Well, for the love of God, would ye look at that!" he exclaims.

David draws his dagger, locates the ember at the back of the cloak just below the collar, and cuts it out as neatly as he can, leaving a ragged hole about six inches in diameter. He hands it to Chester, who puts it back on and chafes himself mightily.

David shakes his head in exasperation. "We'll get it mended later," he says. "In the meantime, there's a change of plans."

"How, suh?"

"Give me your Tower identification. I'll enter Nancy's place first and pretend to be you."

Chester looks hurt. "Why, suh?" he pleads. "My cloak's not smokin' no more."

David shakes his head. "I think I'll be a more believable member of the Tower Guard."

"How so, suh?"

"Chester," says David impatiently, "your cloak has a six-inch hole in it … and you smell as though you've been sweeping chimneys."

Chester's face falls. "Very well, suh. What shall I do instead?"

"Wait outside the inn with Esther's cloak—I doubt Caim has taken care to see to her warmth—and make sure nobody enters who could try to stop me from rescuing her."

———◦◦◦———

CONFIDENT THAT CAIM is engaged somewhere far away, yet unsure whether anyone's upstairs with Esther, David enters Nancy's place, steps up to the counter, and smiles at her, catching her eye.

Nancy turns to him with a girlish leer. "Well, with those baby blue eyes, you must be sellin' *sumthin'*!" she says. Although it sounds inappropriately flirtatious from a woman of her years, there's something about her that makes it rather pleasant.

"No, not selling a thing," he says. "In fact, I'm here on official business." He flashes Chester's identification papers.

Her face falls. "Oh, drat! Whatcha lookin' faw now? Besides a few shillin's."

"I need to go upstairs and search one of the rooms," he says.

"Can't let ye do that, suh. Them's private dwellin's. They got right o' key on me. And I can't let anyone in ... 'cept in an emergency."

"Ahh," says David calmly, "but this *is* an emergency. You see, I'm not looking for something. I'm looking for some*one*, and *not* one of your tenants, I assure you, but rather someone who's been abducted and is being held against her will in one of your rooms."

She's obviously surprised by the accusation, but hardly shocked.

"You wouldn't know anything about that, would you, Miss Nancy? Because, that would make you an accessory to a very serious crime."

"'Course not," she says at once, though David can see in her eyes the knowledge that many crimes have taken place in her inn, leaving her the richer for it.

"I thought not," he replies, and slides a sovereign toward her on the counter. "And there's *another* for you on my way out the door."

"Now, what 'ave I gotta do for that?" she asks suspiciously.

"Three things: Lend me the key to Room 22, keep your mouth shut about my being here, and don't allow anyone upstairs till I'm gone. I should be only a few minutes."

"All right, then," she says, depositing the coin in her apron. "Best get to it." She takes the key from a pigeonhole and slides it to him discreetly. "Now don't forget you took that while I wasn't lookin'."

David palms the key and climbs the stairs. He sneaks down the hall to the room Cuthbert described, and listens through the door. Hearing nothing, he takes the pistol from his pocket and turns the key.

As he opens the door, his heart aches to see his beloved Esther gagged and blindfolded, tied tightly to the bedframe and seated on the floor. As she hears someone enter, she whimpers. He closes the door behind him.

"It's all right, Esther," he says in a quiet voice. "It's me, David. I've come for you."

For a moment, she freezes as though stunned, then begins to sob quietly.

He removes the blindfold first, so she can see that it's truly he, and also that he's holding a finger to his lips. Quiet is essential. Next, he removes the gag and cuts her restraints. He picks her up off the floor and seats her gently on the bed.

"It was Caim, wasn't it?" he asks.

She nods tearfully.

"Did he hurt you in any way, or ... touch you inappropriately?"

"Yes, David. It hurt to be tied up, carried in a woolen sack, and tossed into a bouncing cart. In doing those awful things, he touched me inappropriately."

He looks at her with concern.

"But not the way you mean," she adds.

There's a surreptitious knock at the door, followed by a man's voice.

"Caim?" says the voice. "Caim, is that you?"

Damn! It's one of the few hazards David didn't anticipate—a confederate in an adjacent room.

David holds the pistol in front of him as he opens the door, doing his best to look as though he belongs there.

"Who are you?" asks the man at the door, as though he expects he's accidentally happened upon an unfamiliar co-conspirator.

"I'm Chester," says David. "Who are *you*?"

"Tadson," replies the man, eyeing the pistol in David's hand. "What's that for?"

David looks down at the pistol with chagrin, shakes his head as though it was an unnecessary precaution. He turns it about, and holds it by the barrel. He smiles at Tadson apologetically. "Sorry about this, Tadson," he says, "but I've got only two hands." He smashes the gunstock into the man's face, breaking his nose and knocking him cold.

Tadson collapses to the floor in a heap.

David fishes in his pocket for a sovereign and hands it to Esther. "Let us go together, dear. I'm afraid I'll be encumbered as we leave, so I'll ask you to pass the coin to the woman at the counter downstairs."

Esther stands, a bit woozily at first, and walks out the door a few steps ahead of David, who drags Tadson by the front of his collar and follows a few steps behind.

When they reach the stairs, Esther descends with her customary mincing steps, while David lifts Tadson's head carefully off the floor and drags him down headfirst, his heels striking every wooden step with a thump.

Esther approaches the counter and plunks down the sovereign David gave her. In a flourish of her own, she curtseys to Nancy, who stands slack-jawed in amazement that this beauty has been held hostage in her inn for an unknown time. Esther raises her chin and continues proudly out of the front door.

As Nancy's insensate tenant is dragged past the counter, she regards David skeptically. "You're ... *sure* you're from the Tower Guard?"

David nods reassuringly. "No doubt," he replies. "And the Tower's where this fellow's headed."

—⟶○◁▱▷○⟵—

SIR GELLY ENTERS THE GLOBE with the bulk of Southampton's party but tramps off to the upper tier in search of privacy. Though that tier's often reserved for nobility, for some reason all of Essex's noble companions have chosen seats in the foremost rows behind the groundlings, and Sir Gelly has assured himself that his knighthood renders him worthy of admission to the third tier—at least for a performance, such as this, that he helped to arrange.

He would have invited either Caim or Tadson to join him; he's comfortable enough with them. But Caim wandered off by the Bear Garden, and Tadson hasn't been heard of since yesterday. So much for companionship.

As Sir Gelly steps onto the upper landing, he pauses a moment to admire the ornate painting of celestial bodies on the ceiling. He's never seen it so close-up before. Very colorful. So full of fancy.

Psssssst!

He cringes to hear the sound, for it means someone's vying for his attention just as he's looking to be left alone. He searches about for the source of the hiss. There's no one on this tier yet but one stout fellow seated at dead center. He looks vaguely familiar. Sir Gelly quickly identifies the face and figure as belonging to Sir Helvius, one of the outspoken knights who attended this past weekend's meeting at Drury House.

Sir Helvius beckons Sir Gelly with a smile and a friendly wave. Sir Gelly bites his tongue, but reciprocates in as friendly a manner as he can.

"Won't you sit down, Sir Gelly?" says Sir Helvius. "How've you been this week?"

As Sir Gelly takes a seat on the common pew next to Sir Helvius, he notices how hard the bench is, and wonders whether he'll be able to endure it for a full two hours.

"I rented an extra pillow," says Sir Helvius, handing it to him. "It costs but a penny, so I always take an extra in case I run into another worthy theatergoer, such as yourself."

"I'll take it, Sir Helvius," Sir Gelly jests, "and give you tuppence for it."

"Hah!" says Sir Helvius. "I'd have doubled my money, too! Believe it or not, there are avid theatergoers so poor that they forego the pillow as an extravagance. But you needn't. Have you seen the play?"

Sir Gelly shakes his head. "Nah, but I know the history all right."

"A play's not a simple depiction of events, as I expect you know," says Sir Helvius. "It's poetic. A kind of fictionalization."

"It'd have to be, I suppose," says Sir Gelly.

The play opens and they watch a good deal of it in companionable silence. But, when the scene comes where the banished Bolingbroke returns to England, Sir Gelly looks around to ensure no one's nearby to hear a remark he means for Sir Helvius alone. "Bolingbroke comes back to England while King Richard is abroad in Ireland," says Sir Gelly. "Bolingbroke—by strength of his character *alone*, mind ye—is greeted by enough friends to form an army big enough to surround King Richard upon his return to England." He turns to Sir Helvius skeptically. "And Shakespeare expects us to believe that all these noblemen committed high treason against the King—puttin' their lives, their families, and their lands at risk—just to ensure Bolingbroke gets *his* ancestral lands back? Truly? Ye think Bolingbroke's promised *nothin'* to these 'friends'?"

"His friends are virtuous," whispers Sir Helvius with a shrug.

Sir Gelly waves off the remark. "I've met lotsa noblemen—even a few virtuous ones—but never one who'd stake his fortune to save somebody else's—*unless* he had a solid prospect of gainin' somethin' fer '*imself* that only a king could deliver." He points to the players acting the parts of noblemen. "These lot knew full well Bolingbroke was goin' for King Richard's crown." He smirks. "They were bettin' the *peerage* on it!" He shakes his head sadly. "And Lord Essex thinks his loyal friends'll act like this imaginary lot onstage."

Sir Helvius smiles weighingly.

A bit later in the play, Bolingbroke kneels before King Richard.

KING RICHARD:
Fair cousin, you debase your princely knee
To make the base earth proud with kissing it:
Me rather had my heart might feel your love
Than my unpleased eye see your courtesy.
Up, cousin, up; your heart is up, I know,
(*He points to his crown.*)
Thus high at least, although your knee be low.

BOLINGBROKE:
My gracious lord, I come but for mine own.

KING RICHARD:
Your own is yours, and I am yours, and all.

So incensed is Sir Gelly by these lines that he rises to go. "Stupid rubbish," he mutters. "Kings and queens don't give away their crowns."

"Are you not enjoying the play?" whispers Sir Helvius.

"If you would know my mind on that score, suh," says Sir Gelly, "I'll be pleased to discuss it with you out o' doors. But I ain't stayin' for the rest of this."

Sir Helvius shrugs and rises. "I'll come with you, sir. I know this play too well already, and would fain know your mind."

As the two knights walk together outside the Globe, Sir Gelly remarks, "I like the play well enough, but I don't *believe* it."

"Of course not," says Sir Helvius. "Only a child believes a play once he's left the playhouse. You do not believe it because you're not a child."

"Do you really think no adult believes a play?" asks Sir Gelly.

Sir Helvius shrugs. "A willing adult may permit himself to believe it, but only while the play proceeds. Once it ends, so must its spell."

"That's where you and I part ways, Sir Helvius," says Sir Gelly. "I know an adult who continues to believe this play like it's Gospel."

"Who?" asks Sir Helvius.

"Lord Essex," says Sir Gelly. "He's so taken with the play that he's followin' it like a roadmap."

Sir Helvius' expression changes slowly from realization to horror. "That cannot be," he says hopefully.

"Aye, *'tis,*" Sir Gelly assures him. "Lord Essex is mad with desperation. I can't explain his actions any other way."

"Then the playwright should be right shamed of himself," says Sir Helvius sadly, "for forgetting that the purpose of playing is to hold the mirror up to nature, not to cajole life into imitating art."

"Lives will be lost on account of this play," says Sir Gelly wistfully. "But you've got a clear conscience, Sir Helvius. You spoke out against the madness when it mighta mattered. It took some courage to do that." Shielding his eyes, Sir Gelly glances at the icy sun sinking toward the western horizon, his heart now fixed in despair. Almost blithely, he realizes that this is one of the last sunsets he'll ever see. And all because another man was driven by desperation to believe that hope alone could breathe life into a stage play.

"Besides, Sir Helvius," says Sir Gelly with a sigh, "it's not like you wrote the play."

CHAPTER 31

LATE THAT AFTERNOON, when David, Chester, and Esther arrive at the Tower of London with their captive Tadson, they're brought to the office of Sir Walter Raleigh, where they find him conferring with Serjeant Ames.

Esther is so relieved to be in Serjeant Ames's company again that she hugs him tightly and weeps on his shoulder for quite a while. Serjeant Ames, though plainly harrowed for the past few hours by Esther's abduction, is much relieved by her rescue.

David assists the venerable Yeoman Gardner in shackling Tadson and escorting him to a small, secure cell. Though David has been to the Tower of London only a few times before, it seems to him that the guard is quite thin, especially considering the trouble expected tomorrow. He supposes the missing portion of the Tower Guard has been relocated to Whitehall in defense of the Queen.

By the time David and Gardner return to Sir Walter's office, Esther's had ample opportunity to recount how she was abducted by Caim and placed into storage at Nancy's place. She's somewhat calmer, though still quite ill at ease.

Sir Walter starts giving orders. "Yeoman Gardner, I want you, Francis, and Chester to go to Serjeant Ames's residence in Holborn at once. Yeoman Gardner, you will transport to Sheffield House such members of Serjeant Ames's household as he shall designate, and remain there to guard them. Francis and Chester, you'll remain behind at Serjeant Ames's residence to protect against any interference with Lady Jessica, who is presently lying in, and if the midwives are reading the signs properly may already have commenced labor. Chester, as I recall, you have wartime experience, so I may call you away tomorrow. But Francis is there for the duration."

Sir Walter turns to Noah. "If I know Lord Saint Ives, he's distracted beyond reason and getting in everyone's way. Please persuade him to get some sleep, as his lordship shall no doubt be required. I'll send for him at some point early tomorrow, if only to get him out of the house. Do you suppose this abduction had aught to do with the present trouble at Essex House?"

Noah gives it some thought and equivocates. "Only tangentially. It's a long story. I suggest, however, that this Tadson fellow in your keep may know more than he lets on about it and, given the gravity of the charge, may be willing to give information immediately in exchange for leniency."

———————⇒∘⟨⟨⟩⟩∘⊂———————

NOAH, GARDNER, AND FRANCIS canter ahead and disappear from sight in a moment.

David and Esther lag behind, sharing a saddle. Chester follows them at some distance to respect their privacy. In fact, however, there's little conversation between David and Esther, and what there is seems trivial to both of them in light of the frightening and potentially deadly events of the past few hours.

As they arrive at the Ames residence, David helps Esther down from his horse, and Chester brings both horses to the stableboy.

"I do not *wish* to go to Lady Sheffield's," says Esther.

"That's strange," says David coolly, "because I don't recall Serjeant Ames asking your preference. And it's *his* decision that you shall go there."

"Am I the only one to go?" she asks, as David opens the front door, revealing quite a bustle inside.

"Look around, Esther," he says. "Mistress Ames and her three children are going, too. Frankly, you should be very grateful that Lord and Lady Sheffield have consented to take you in."

Esther folds her arms and plants her foot. "I shan't go."

Treating her as he would a petulant child, David leads her gently by the elbow to Serjeant Ames's study for a private talk. Though they find the study already occupied by Gardner, Chester, and Francis, those burly fellows silently slip away the moment they spy the feuding couple's approach.

"What are they even doing here?" demands Esther.

Assuming the question is not merely rhetorical, David replies. "They're here to protect Serjeant Ames's family," he explains. "In case you've forgot—although I don't see why you would, as you seem to forget nothing else—you're a member of the Ames family who was abducted this morning, and your abductor is still at large—as far as we know."

"Why hasn't Caim been arrested?" she asks.

"Esther," he says impatiently, "we expect a great deal of trouble from Caim's *employer* presently. Caim will surely show up soon. At some point tomorrow, the Queen's men are bound to see him and, when they do, they'll arrest him."

"Will they?"

"Yes," he says, and then mutters, "unless I see him first."

"What are you saying, David?" she asks.

"I'm saying I have a score to settle with Caim."

"If you see him first, will you arrest him?"

"Possibly," he says.

She whispers to him, "Please assure me that you won't fight him."

His face hardens. "I don't see why that's any concern of yours. Besides, what difference would my assurances make?" he asks. "You don't believe them anyway."

Marie walks into the study, all bundled in cloak and gloves. At the front door wait her three children dressed much the same, as well as a traveling chest that's tied shut. "We're all ready, dear," she says to Esther. "Have you packed your things?"

Esther curtseys to Marie. "No, madam. I arrived just a moment ago."

"Well," says Marie, "this chest contains most of your clothing. As we're only going as far as Sheffield House, we can send tomorrow for anything we've forgot. Come, put on your warmest cloak and let's get started."

"Yes, madam," says Esther. She turns back to David. "Thank you for rescuing me, David, and please stay far away from Bowyer's Row." She stands on tiptoe to kiss him on the cheek. To her amazement, he blushes, and there's a tragic look in his eyes.

Outside, Francis loads the chest onto the cart while the passengers bundle in together. Marie smiles reservedly at her two younger children, who seem excited and frightened in roughly equal parts. Stephen, wearing a warlike face, sits in the driver's seat with the reins in one hand and a pistol in the other. Yeoman Gardner climbs into the cart almost as though he's one of the family, except that he's facing backward and holding a loaded musket.

Esther wonders what kind of violence is expected in London tomorrow, and how Lady Jessica will fare here if she needs help. She takes some comfort in knowing that there are several strong men present to ensure Jessica's safety, but she's concerned that the only women in the house with Lady Jessica will be the maids and Aunt Beth.

Esther climbs into the cart last, facing the Ames's residence. It's the first real home she's had in years, and she feels much in danger of losing it. As the cart moves off to Sheffield House, she watches both the house and David's handsome figure fade into the darkness together.

Except for the Ameses and David, she's alone in the world.

———————————— >o꘏꘏o< ————————————

CAIM TAKES HIS EYES OFF Cuthbert Bennett's receding horse long enough to check the sun, which is getting low in the sky.

He's been following Bennett southwest for well over an hour, and thinks it strange he's got no closer to catching up in all that time. True, that's a big horse Bennett's got there, but ... wait ... doesn't the Jew Serjeant have a big black steed like that? Could that be his?

Related questions pop up in his mind. Caim's seen an occasional glint of light reflecting off some item of metal on the horse's neck. Or could it have been a handheld looking glass? Has the rider been looking back at him all the while through the glass? That would explain why the rider's never got much further ahead, nor dropped back in all this time.

A humiliating question arises: Could it be that the rider up ahead is *not* Cuthbert Bennett? The rider hasn't turned his head about once in all the time he's been followed. Perhaps he's been watching Caim through a looking glass so he cannot be identified as someone other than Bennett.

And then another possibility hits him right in the gut. *They've drawn me out of London so they could rescue the girl. She saw my face, and surely realized she's seen it before, at Essex House's gate. But, wait, until they find and speak with her they have no idea I'm the one who abducted her! Nor do they know of my foothold in Queenhythe, so they haven't the least idea that she's holed up at Nancy's place! And at the very least, Tadson would slit her throat at the first sign of trouble; those were his instructions.*

But wait. What if it was Bennett who robbed Knott and his buttboy at that sleazy inn? (He couldn't have come away with much. Caim had had only two sovereigns on his person when he was knocked cold, and they were missing when he came to, along with Knott and his catamite friend. The thief probably got away with a few more pounds from Knott and his friend, but what of it?) Even if the robber *was* Bennett, that doesn't mean he'd learned of Caim's hideout at Nancy's. No, that *can't* be it.

He thinks of the playgoers at the Globe. By now, the theater has let out and Essex's supporters are returning to Essex House to eat supper and make final plans for tomorrow's venture. And here am I, two hours south of the Thames. If I don't turn back now, I'll miss the meeting. But the Serjeant couldn't have known of any such meeting, could he? *No.* So, why has he taken the trouble to draw me so far out of London?

With a sinking feeling in the pit of his stomach, Caim realizes two things. First, he has no idea *why* the Jew bothered to lead him so far astray, which means the Jew knows more than Caim's given him credit for. Second, Caim realizes that he's *not* going to catch the rider he's been chasing all this while. Still, he can't bear to tear himself away without first confirming that the rider is Cuthbert Bennett. At this point, the rider is a half-mile ahead, and just about to go over a grassy rise.

Caim stops his horse and waits in the saddle watching the rider go over the rise and disappear on the other side.

Caim waits. And waits. And waits some more.

At last, the rider on the big black horse reappears, stopping atop the rise. Raising his left hand to block the setting sun, the rider obviously catches sight of Caim waiting a half-mile off. He certainly *looks* like Cuthbert Bennett. For a moment, the rider just sits there, watching. Then, evidently realizing the jig is up, he waves broadly at Caim to ensure he's got his attention, then makes an exaggerated gesture designed to make Caim's blood boil; he ostentatiously bites his thumb. And it *does* make Caim's blood boil, but not enough to draw him further from London.

Caim shakes his fist at the rider, turns about, and gallops north toward London. Every few miles, he forces himself to glance behind. Though he couldn't catch the rider, the rider *could* catch him, if he were of a mind to. Caim almost wishes he would, so he'd have the pleasure of strangling the bastard without further ado.

He contemplates the few available methods of transport back into London. A wherry is out of the question; he'd have to stable his horse at Bankside at least overnight, which he cannot do as he'll undoubtedly need his horse for tomorrow's duties (perhaps even tonight's, as Essex has taken to using him as a high-level messenger). That leaves nought but London Bridge. Once he's left that, he'll be going west to Essex House, and will pass by Queenhythe where, if time permits, he can check on the girl tied up in his room at Nancy's place.

Less than halfway back to London, he firmly decides he can't return to Essex House until he confirms there's nothing amiss with the girl at Nancy's. While he could kill the girl if she's not already dead, disposing of the body immediately might pose a problem, as both he and Tadson will be required at Essex House all evening and well into morning. Besides, best keep the girl alive for the present. He could use her as a chip for bargaining with the good Serjeant, just in case things go wrong during the planned incursion into the Queen's court. The best he can hope for is that nothing at Nancy's has changed.

———————————— ⟶∘⟸⬤⟹∘⟵ ————————————

THE SUN HAS NEARLY TOUCHED the western horizon as Caim clops his way nonchalantly down Trig Street in Queenhythe. In the unlikely event that the girl's been rescued, a lookout may have been left there to spot him.

As he approaches Nancy's, he's alarmed to see an armed guard posted outside her door and precious little traffic moving in or out.

"Hey, you!" shouts the guard, and Caim's heart leaps into his throat. "You got business in this establishment?"

The question implies that the guard has no idea who he is, but he'll need to be wary. Caim replies as calmly as he can. "I was just in the market for a pint."

The guard beckons him over.

With a gulp, Caim dismounts, ties off his horse, and approaches the guard with a forced smile.

"The place ain't closed," says the guard. "I'm just here to catch the fella what's been up to no good. Caim's 'is name. Ye know 'im?"

"Never 'eard of 'im," says Caim, "but if I do I'll be sure to let ye know." He nods to the guard and walks past. To his surprise, Nancy is at the counter. He's unsurprised to see she's shocked to see him.

"Got a dining room on this floor with a little privacy, Nan?" he says with a wink.

She points to a closed door. "Will it be just you, suh? Or will you be havin' company?"

"Just me," he says. "I'd just like to be left to me own thoughts."

"Go ahead in, then. I'll 'ave the girl bring in yer pint."

He enters the little room and closes the door. He sits with his hands folded on the table, ever conscious that the guard could decide at any moment that he fits the suspect's general description. After what seems an eternity, Nancy herself comes through the rear door to the room, commonly used by her whores. She's got a pint in her hand.

"Yaw mad comin' down here, with what you've done," she says.

"What 'ave I done?" he asks.

"Everythin'," she whispers. "A guard from the Tower o' London came in here, went upstairs, and fetched the girl you tied up there. *When the devil did you sneak 'er in 'ere? Turns out she's a niece of the Queen's Jew lawyer. What the devil were you thinkin'?*"

"Not my cleverest move, was it?" he says apologetically.

She shrugs. "To answer that, I'd have to know more about ye than I care to."

"Is that all that 'appened? He just took the girl and left?" asks Caim hopefully.

"No, and yaw gonna love this," says Nan. "He knocked yer friend out cold, and dragged 'im out of 'ere by the scruff."

"My friend?" he asks.

"Tadson," she says.

A wave of nausea rolls over Caim. If Tadson's at the Tower on charges of abduction, he'll tell the authorities *anything* to escape the hangman, and he knows a great deal about Caim's extensive and serious misdeeds. Even more immediately, Caim will have no choice but to inform Essex and Southampton that Tadson's in Crown custody. By tomorrow morning, Tadson could spill everything he knows, which is everything. He takes another swig. He'd dearly love to kill Tadson before he can talk.

"Was Tadson dead?" he asks hopefully.

Nan looks at him as though he's mad. "Didn't look that way, but I s'pose he *mighta* been. He was out to the world."

Caim takes a long draught on the pint. "Woulda made things a lot simpler. Did they say where they were takin' 'im?"

She nods. "Tower o' London."

This bit of news nearly makes him choke on his ale. There's no way he can break into the Tower. He has neither knowledge nor strength of numbers.

"The Tower?" he asks. "Yer certain?"

"That's what the man said."

"How long ago was this?" he asks.

"Couple hours."

Fast workers, he thinks. Who did it? It couldn't have been Cuthbert Bennett, because Caim knows where *he's* been all the while.

"What'd he look like?" asks Caim.

She sighs. "A beautyful lookin' man, barely more than a boy."

"Did he look like a Viking?"

"Well, yeah, I s'pose he did. Tall and young, long blond 'air, blue eyes. A real *looker*."

He takes another swig. "Yeah, I know 'im," he says. "Well, don't *know* 'im exactly, but I know who he is. He don't work for the Tower, neither. He's a student ... at Oxford."

Nan's eyes grow all dreamy. "Is he wed?"

"Not yet, but the girl he took out of 'ere is the one he wants." He laughs quietly. "Nan, yer old enough to be his gammer!"

She half-smiles. "I can dream, can't I?"

"I s'pose so," he says, "and it's still free o' charge."

She points to his ale. "That's not," she says, and he hands her a coin in payment.

———⋅∘◁⧓▷∘⋅———

DARKNESS HAS OVERTAKEN THE SKY.

As Caim draws up to Essex House, he can barely believe what he's seeing. There are so many men stuffed into the place, some are literally backed up against the window glass.

"Caim," says the stableman keeping the gate, "the earls have missed ye, but I have most of all. Where've you been since the theater let out? I've been keeping the—"

"Shut up, John," says Caim firmly.

"Caim, you got no call talkin' to me—"

Caim slaps the stableman across the face, then realizes how misdirected his anger is. "I'm sorry, John," he says sincerely. "Since the theater let out, I've been chasing ghosts. Every blessed thing I've done today has gone cock up. I've made things much more dangerous for everyone here, and I'm worse than worthless. But I've got no call ventin' it on you. Now I have to go tell the earls how I screwed matters up. If you'd like to slap me face, I got it comin' and I won't come back at ye."

The stableman, whose face is burning from the affront, very nearly strikes Caim in the chin with his fist. But he controls himself. "Don't ever do that again, Caim, or there'll be more than a slap in it for ye. Meantime, I dunno what you gotta tell the earls, but you better think twice. There's pryin' eyes and ears everywhere, and this 'ouse is so crowded there's no place for you to tell 'em where you won't be overheard. Before you start givin' these men bad news, best think of the effect it'll have on all of 'em."

Caim realizes that, for purposes of Essex's attempt to gain an audience with the Queen, tomorrow is the end of the world. It's time for these men to do or die. What are the chances Tadson will break before tomorrow afternoon and spill his guts? As for the abduction, responsibility rests principally with Caim, and he'll likely swing alone.

"You're right, John. I suppose it's a talent I got that I can *always* make matters worse, and I *woulda* done that right now, but for your good advice. Have they started discussions?"

John nods sadly. "I heard some of it before. The guard at Whitehall's been doubled. Sheriff Smyth sent Essex a note sayin' he'd have a thousand trained men at the ready tomorrow mornin'."

Caim stares at the stableman in wonderment. "A thousand men? What good would havin' a thousand men do ye, if all you're lookin' for is an audience with the Queen?"

"Essex is plannin' on enterin' the city with two hundred of the lot he's got here at Essex House before church service at Whitehall. He'll tell them lot that his life's been threatened by Raleigh and ask for the support of the 'citizens of London', if ye can believe it. Keeps talkin' about how beloved he is by the citizens. Dunno 'bout you, but I ain't never seen nobuddy ask the citizens of London for their opinion on *anything*."

Caim stares at John incredulously.

"Ye doubt me? Go in!" says John. "See fer yerself."

Caim heeds John's advice yet again, enters the house, and slowly makes his way to the rear where Essex is still carrying on in the vein John mentioned.

Essex is standing on a chair, so he can be seen by all.

"We may not have a set plan, we may not even know whether to address our forces to the Tower of London or Whitehall. But we know these things: The citizenry is on our side. The most worthy noblemen of the realm are on our side. And *Almighty God* is on our side." The applause and cheers are deafening within the house, but Caim can only imagine how small and seditious they must sound from Westminster, where someone's surely listening. "Finally, as I might say to you the night before battle, gentlemen. Get what sleep you can tonight, that you may live to see many a dawn."

CHAPTER 32

ONE OF THE FORTUNATE FEW, Sir Ferdinando Gorges has a small room of his own upstairs at Essex House. At dawn, he's awakened by a crisp knock on his door and a note being slipped under it. Though he's tempted to return to sleep, he recalls what day this is, as well as what tribulations he's likely to suffer, and all thought of sleep departs.

He unfolds the note. It's from his distant kinsman, Sir Walter Raleigh:

> *While I appreciate the difficulty of your situation, I shall, as you suggested a few days ago, meet you in a wherry at midstream on the Thames within sight of Essex House at 8 of the clock this morning. I shall be alone (except for the wherryman) and unarmed, as I expect you shall be, as well. Time is short, so I shall be punctual and expect the same of you.*

Eight o'clock doesn't leave much time. Perhaps the immediacy was designed to deprive Ferdinando of time for discussion. Still, he feels he must at least mention it to Lord Essex. He puts on his boots and descends into the large salon.

Though a few elders have been given places of repose on one of the three couches, the floor of the salon is littered with men asleep with their weapons either nearby or grasped in their slumbering hands. The stench of tobacco smoke nearly overwhelms Ferdinando, though emitted by no more than a handful of "smokers" clustered in a remote corner.

Essex walks into the salon from the dining room, preoccupied by a letter in his hands. When he spies Ferdinando, he says, "So, you're going to meet him?"

Ferdinando is at a momentary loss for words, surprised that Sir Walter's note was read before it reached him.

Reading his thoughts, Essex shakes his head. "Everyone's on edge, Ferdinando. A half-dozen men read every message that comes into the house before I see it. They report to me only those that seem of some significance."

Ferdinando sizes up Essex's appearance. He's a wreck. His clothes sit askew on his shrinking frame. His vest is unbuttoned, his belly swollen, and his eyes bloodshot and sunken in dark circles.

"I must meet with Sir Walter, m'lord," says Ferdinando. "I have no choice. Besides, what loss could we suffer by a parley?"

"We could lose *you*," says Essex gravely.

Sir Ferdinando shakes his head. "No, m'lord. I shall remain true to your cause."

Essex waves away his concern. "I wasn't even considering that. I was thinking Raleigh might take a potshot at you. If you wouldn't deem it dishonorable, I could disguise a pistolier and send him out as your wherryman. In fact, I'd recommend it."

Sir Ferdinando finds the idea absurd. "I don't think he'll *shoot* me, m'lord."

Essex shakes his head almost imperceptibly and shrugs. "Well," he says, "he'd shoot *me*. I've been sending out notices all night that Raleigh, along with his friend Lord Cobham, is planning to assassinate me presently, and that I shall go to court today to so inform Her Majesty." With that, he returns to the dining room and the letter he was reading.

Sir Ferdinando swallows a splash of wine to wash down some bread left over from the previous night's meal. He dons an extra layer under his heaviest cloak, and walks out into the crisp morning to descend the steps from Essex House to the Thames.

There's a race among the wherries to carry him. The first to arrive is a burly young fellow with rosy cheeks. "To Southwark, suh?"

Sir Ferdinando shakes his head and points to the middle of the river. "Just take me to midstream, straight out from here. Stay with me a few minutes, then bring me back."

"That's all, suh? Midstream?"

"That's all. I'm meeting someone there to talk. It won't take long."

"It'll be a full crossin' fare all the same, suh," says the wherryman tentatively, obviously expecting a tongue-lashing.

But Sir Ferdinando absentmindedly tosses him a coin well in excess of the fare.

"Yes, *suh*," says the relieved wherryman. "Midstream is just the place to be on a nippy mornin' like this. It'll be a bit of a fight to keep from bein' dragged every which way by the shiftin' currents, though."

"I know it," mutters Sir Ferdinando, stepping into the boat. "I know it well."

AT THE AMES RESIDENCE, Noah sleeps in his best chair, his head lolling about occasionally, ever seeking a more perfect posture for snoring.

David's so exhausted he's fallen asleep lying face down on the bed in the back servants' quarters that was occupied by Stephen the night before. David found saving Esther from certain murder to be stressful enough for one day, but compounding that was the heart-wrenching exercise of watching her drawn away by cart—even if only as far as Sheffield House.

In a spare bedroom upstairs, Francis has fallen asleep to the shuffling of women's feet alternately entering and leaving Lady Jessica's room.

Ever ready for trouble, Chester is asleep in a sitting position with his back against the front door and a dagger in his hand. After he's been asleep in this uncomfortable posture a long while, someone tries to slip a note under the door, but it bumps into Chester's bottom and he opens one eye. The note, having failed to make it all the way into the house, stealthily withdraws. In a moment, it tries to slip under the door at a different point. Chester stops it with his hand. Again it slinks away.

He rises and waits for the note's third attempt to force its way in, when he can be certain the messenger will be crouched down and off-balance, leaning in toward the door.

A moment later, a corner of the note slithers slowly under the door. In one silent motion, Chester turns the doorknob, opens it inward, and pulls the messenger into the house by the hood. The messenger collapses on the floor with an *oof*, and Chester rests his knee heavily on the small of his back.

"Please, suh," says the messenger in the high notes of an adolescent boy. "Don't hurt me. I'm here on Queen's business."

"Oh?" says Chester suspiciously. "And what business would that be?"

"Deliverin' messages, suh."

"Give it over," says Chester.

The boy, his face still pressed against the floor, twists his arm back and offers Chester the note. It's folded and sealed. On it is written, *To Chester of the Tower Guard.* The seal says *ER.*

Chester's mortified that he greeted the messenger so harshly. Not only is the note for him *personally*, but it's from the Queen—or one of her principal ministers. He breaks the seal and opens the note. *At dawn, you shall escort Serjeant Noah Ames and Master Cheerful Killigrew to the Presence Chamber at Whitehall Palace. Present this note at the Holbein Gate, where you will be required to surrender all weapons. Remain outside the Presence Chamber and await further instructions.* The signature is that of "Robert Cecil, First Secretary of State."

Chester picks the messenger up from the floor and dusts him off. "Where you off to next?" he asks.

The boy's face reddens with outrage, but he keeps his voice down for fear of waking the house. "Ye throw me on the floor for deliverin' the Queen's message, and next y'ask me where I'm goin'?"

Chester concedes the young man's point. "I'm sorry fer that. Been on edge these past couple nights." Fishing in his pocket, he's surprised to find a half groat, which he gladly hands the young fellow.

The young man regards the coin with tempered disappointment, and glances at the next letter in his pouch. "Goin' to Sheffield House."

"To Gardner?" asks Chester.

"Aye."

"Do me a good turn, lad. Tell him Chester's been called to Whitehall."

The boy seems to be awaiting more. "That's all? Chester's called to Whitehall?"

"That's it."

The boy nods, pockets the coin, and rides off.

Before closing the door, Chester steps out into the night and inhales the cold air deeply. There's a steely, indifferent quality to it, and he wonders how much English blood will be spilled on the cold ground today.

Looking eastward to tell the time by the most familiar constellations, he realizes he'll need no subtle celestial cues, for the stars on the horizon are already beginning to fade. What little time he has is fast passing. He returns indoors, closes the door behind him and goes to wake Master Cheerful.

———————◦∘◦————————

WHEN LADY SHEFFIELD AND ESTHER arrive at the Ames residence, the sun hasn't yet attained the horizon. They dismount and the driver begins his return trip to Sheffield House.

The front door opens and a sleepy Serjeant Ames steps out, still donning his gloves.

He looks up and bows to Lady Sheffield. "Thank you so much, m'lady. Your assistance is most welcome. I'm told Lady Jessica has asked to see you several times."

"God bless you, Serjeant Ames," she replies. "We'll do everything possible for her, and I'm sure she'll be fine."

Serjeant Ames inhales deeply, momentarily uplifted by Lady Sheffield's comforting words. Spying Esther, he opens his arms to her.

Esther rushes forward and buries her face in his shoulder. "Oh, Serjeant Ames, I don't know why I'm so upset."

He takes her gently by the shoulders and looks into her eyes. "Dear, it takes *time* to get over a horrible incident such as you suffered yesterday."

"But it's not having been abducted that's upsetting me," she says. "I fear ... I fear I shall lose you or David and that my coming here may prove the end of this happy home ... or ... or my place in it."

He looks at her skeptically. "That will not happen, dear. You'll see. All will be well with us quite soon. And your place here is assured."

As Esther calms down, David emerges, dressed like a wayfarer or a soldier, she can never decide. He's wearing a sword and a dagger in a scabbard. Though she can't see it, she's sure he has a pistol hidden in his clothing. He bows to Lady Sheffield, who smiles upon him.

Esther favors David with a smile and draws him aside. "David, please return to me safely."

When he looks down into her eyes, his face is downcast, as though he's lost all hope of her love, and regards her attempts to cheer him as mere prolongation of the agony. Chester appears, leading Bucklebury and two other horses around from the stables.

"I'll do my best," David assures Esther impassively and walks to his mount. He turns to Serjeant Ames. "We're due at court by dawn, sir. It's time."

Serjeant Ames bows to Lady Sheffield and leaps onto Bucklebury.

The three riders turn and canter off west toward Saint Martin's Lane, no doubt to give the widest possible berth to Essex House and Drury House to the south. *Good*, thinks Esther, *they're also staying far from Bowyer's Row.*

Esther opens the front door for Lady Sheffield, who walks toward Serjeant Ames's study as though she's been there many times.

"We'll be out of the way here," says Lady Sheffield. "You wait here, dear. I'll go and speak with Aunt Beth."

"Yes, madam," says Esther absently.

Lady Sheffield evidently notices the pain in her voice. "What's got into you, dear?" she asks. "Is it your Cornish Viking?"

Esther nods morosely.

"Well," says Lady Sheffield, "please pardon my jutting my nose in where it has no place, but I think you've driven him to despair, my dear."

Esther looks up at her plaintively. Lady Sheffield is one of very few people who could actually tell her where David was during his two-day absence. Overwhelmed by her feelings, she can hold back no longer. "M'lady, do you know what David was doing those few days when he was gone this past autumn?"

Lady Sheffield's face falls into the guiltiest, most embarrassed expression Esther's ever seen. She seats Esther on the settee, and draws up a chair. "Where to begin?" she says to herself.

"M'lady, perhaps we should find out the condition of Lady Jessica first."

Lady Sheffield shakes her head. "Not necessary, dear. I've seen many deliveries, and when they become urgent they get quite … noisy." She gestures toward the staircase. "At the moment, all seems to be at peace."

Lady Sheffield removes her elegant gloves, holds them in one hand, and drops her hands to her lap. "Please don't say anything until I've quite done, dear. I know that, to you, Lord Sheffield and I probably appear the picture of marital bliss." She shakes her head. "While things have been much better lately, it was not always so." She purses her lips. "Between you and me, last autumn, when I was missing and believed by some to have been abducted, in fact I had decided to leave his lordship."

Esther's jaw drops in horror. "For … for David?"

Lady Sheffield smiles to realize how her halting storytelling has led Esther's imagination astray. "No. I was not leaving him for David, dear. Nor was David on a tryst with Constance, though that wicked girl has undoubtedly done her level best to make you think he was."

"If I may, madam," says Esther quietly. "For whom were you leaving your husband?"

Lady Sheffield sighs. "For no one. I suppose I had a vague notion that another gentleman might be interested in me. I was prepared to do *anything* to escape what I thought a loveless marriage."

"What changed your mind?" asks Esther.

"Not *what*, dear, but *who*," says Lady Sheffield. "'Twas David."

"David?" says Esther with quiet astonishment.

"Yes. I was running away, you see. Lord Saint Ives got wind of it—

how, I'll never know, for I took great pains to make it seem an abduction. But he sent David and his clumsy friend Chester to fetch me. At first I resisted being returned to Sheffield House, but David is such a persuasive fellow, he'd hear none of it. He dispatched the men I'd hired to help me—"

"He *killed* them?" asks Esther, wide-eyed.

Lady Sheffield regards her incredulously. "Why, *no,* dear. My word, what you must think of this young fellow! He's neither a barbarian nor a murderer, I assure you. Anyway, David and Chester brought me home."

"And Constance?"

Lady Sheffield looks at Esther skeptically. "Constance? What *of* her?" She places her hands comfortingly over Esther's. "She's a pretty *idiot*, my dear, and David knows it. No gentleman takes a pretty idiot seriously ... unless she's of high station, of course. Even then, she's a mere bauble"—she tilts her head in equivocation—"unless she's wealthy *indeed*." She looks at Esther, who seems to have lost the thread of her tale. "But I digress. David was *courteous* to Constance, but no more than courteous. Would you have wished him to be rude?"

Esther equivocates. "Well—"

"Nonsense, my dear," says Lady Sheffield. "David is a most polite and respectful young man."

"But, upon your return, after you and Lord Sheffield went indoors, I saw her kiss him ardently."

"Were you *spying* on him, my dear?" asks Lady Sheffield with a raised eyebrow.

"No. Well, no, not exactly, but she took him aside and kissed him."

Lady Sheffield's face reddens and she suppresses a laugh. "Dear, I assume that you, having known David for several months, have had occasion ... at least once or twice ... to look upon his face and form."

Esther nods, evidently not quite sure where Lady Sheffield is going with this.

"And it makes you wish to kiss him, does it not?" asks Lady Sheffield.

"Oh, yes."

"Well, then," says the lady, "there you are. That's what *every* woman sees, isn't it? I expect David's been showered with kisses since the first few wisps of beard sprouted from his chin. What's he supposed to do when an attractive young woman hurls herself at him? *Hmmm?* If you're expecting him to shove her onto her rear, you're expecting too much. He is a man, after all. It's for *you* to make sure he has no reason to wander, isn't it?"

Out in the hallway, the footsteps of an older woman can be heard shuffling down the stairs. In a moment, Beth enters the study in her nightgown. She curtseys. "M'lady, I was hoping it was you I heard. And thanks for bringing Esther, too. We can always use an extra pair of hands."

As Beth speaks, a blast of chill air wafts through the study, as though someone left a window open, and Esther glimpses a lady's maid silently traversing the hallway toward the stairs with a covered pot in her hands, steam rising from it.

AS CHESTER LEADS THEM ROUND the bend to the Holbein Gate at Whitehall, they find a queue of some of the most powerful men in England. While they're strangers to David and Chester, Noah has met them all before. A few have close ties to the Earl of Essex.

First in line is Popham, the Lord Chief Justice, who's just attained his biblical three score years and ten. Noah knows him well, as he also serves as Chief Justice of Queen's Bench, where Noah practiced before attending upon the Queen. But Noah likes him less than fully, for Popham served as a commissioner on the Court of Oyer and Terminer that convicted Noah's client, Doctor Lopez and, when that conviction proved inadequate, presided over his retrial at Queen's Bench, resulting in Lopez's dying an unwarranted traitor's death at Tyburn.

Second is Egerton, Lord Keeper of the Great Seal, who recently served as keeper of the Earl of Essex, while the earl awaited trial and then, after conviction, Her Majesty's pleasure. He wasn't a commissioner in the Lopez case; his predecessor was. Egerton is known to be a friend of the Earl of Essex, and it was at his doorstep that Noah last saw the Bennett brothers together, still alive and well.

Third is Essex's uncle, William Knollys, whose claim to the Queen's affection comes to him through his sister Lettice, a lifelong friend of the Queen's until she married the Queen's favorite, the Earl of Leicester. That same Lettice is Essex's mother. Evidently, Knollys has remained in the Queen's good graces despite his recent humiliation for openly lusting after a woman less than half his age nicknamed "Mal," and being roundly humiliated for it in the character of Malvolio in Shakespeare's *Twelfth Night*.

Last is the Earl of Worcester, a highly respected peer. Although least well known to Noah, the earl is known to value Noah as a trustworthy attendant to the Queen.

All those gentlemen having been admitted upon surrendering their weapons, Noah and his party have moved to the head of the queue. Looking behind him, Noah is surprised to see that there's someone behind his party.

It's a gentleman in his mid-forties, who's looking at him rather intently. "Are you the Queen's Jew?" he asks without evidence of rancor.

Noah smirks. "I have been referred to in that manner."

The man extends his hand. When Noah reaches out his own hand, it's taken and warmly shaken. "You're a good friend of my cousin. Sir Henry."

"Neville?" asks Noah.

"The same, sir. I'm Sir John Leveson. It's a privilege to make your acquaintance."

"And my privilege to make yours, sir," replies Noah. "I received a note some days ago saying that Sir Henry had got his money at last from the Exchequer and was returning to France forthwith."

There's a flicker of doubt in Leveson's eyes, when there's a small commotion at the guard's station.

"Serjeant Ames?" shouts the guard. "Is it your intention to keep Her Majesty waiting while you socialize?"

Noah shoots an embarrassed smile at Leveson and proceeds to the gate.

Seeing that Chester and David have surrendered considerable arms to the guard, Noah is a little embarrassed to surrender nothing more impressive than Uncle Avram's ancient dagger. They're waved onto the palace grounds where they see that the four men ahead of them have been held up, waiting for Noah. Evidently, they're all going to the same place, namely, the Presence Chamber.

The guide accompanies them past a few buildings. Through the open door of one of them, in what appears to be a waiting area garishly lit by the rising sun, sits a corpulent man alone on a bench. For the few moments that he spies the man in passing, Noah becomes increasingly convinced that the seated man is Sir Henry Neville. His features appear to be somewhat darkened, slightly altered in indefinable ways, and his gown is more maroon than the somber black most often worn by Sir Henry, but the masterly attitude and form is Sir Henry's.

But Sir Henry has been on his way to Dover for the past several days, at least that was the impression given by Sir Henry's latest letter. He must have encountered an unexpected delay in getting his money from the Exchequer, as he couldn't leave without it. But why the secrecy? Why the disguise? And the man he met on the way into the palace—Sir Henry's cousin Leveson—is he coming to the palace to *meet* with Sir Henry?

Noah's struck with an alarming possibility: Could *Sir Henry* be the one who's betrayed the Queen? *Is he the spy in our midst?*

Noah decides there was a reason the man on the bench didn't look precisely like Sir Henry. It simply *wasn't* Sir Henry. And, anyway, it's too late to investigate now. Noah's on his way to the Presence Chamber.

The guide leads them into the most impressive building of them all. At the entrance to the Presence Chamber, Chester is told to wait outside while the rest of the company enters.

There, already seated on her Throne, is Her Majesty. Beside her stands his lordship Robert Cecil.

Noah and David stand a little apart from the four dignitaries, as the importance of those four to the realm so far exceeds Noah and David's that it would be presumptuous to assume they've all been called on the same business.

"Welcome, gentlemen," says the Queen wearily. "Let's get right to important matters. By now, all London knows that Lord Essex has gathered a large group of armed malcontents to his house, which is nearly bursting at the seams." She turns to Sir William. "Knollys, have you heard from your wayward nephew in the past few weeks?"

"No, madam. Not a word."

"I'm unsurprised," says the Queen, turning to Egerton. "And you, Lord Keeper, has the earl consulted you?"

Egerton hangs his head and shakes it. "He has not, Your Majesty."

And then the Queen turns in a direction that Noah would never have anticipated. She turns to *him*.

"And you, Serjeant Ames, when did you last have speech with Lord Essex?"

Noah is shocked to be included in those canvassed about recent contact with Essex, and to be queried *prior* to the two remaining dignitaries, although in truth the Queen probably expects (with some justification) that Noah is more likely to have been contacted by Essex.

"I have not met with his lordship," says Noah, "nor been contacted by him since attending a sermon at Essex House several months ago, Your Majesty. That was the day after Your Majesty kindly encouraged me to do so."

"We recall, Serjeant," says the Queen, glancing sidelong at Robert Cecil. "And what was the topic of that sermon?"

"It was a lecture about *Utopia*, Majesty, a book by Thomas More."

"Did you discourage him from convening men to hear such seditious rubbish?"

"Most assuredly, madam," says Noah. "In speaking to his lordship, I referred to the work by that same word, "seditious." I suggested that his lordship ought not to be filling heads with such rubbish, especially the heads of men privileged to carry swords in London, and told him it would be madness for him to think that such activities would go unnoticed by the government."

"And how did he respond?" asks the Queen.

"He dismissed me from his presence, Majesty."

"Very well," she says, turning to the four dignitaries. "You gentlemen shall visit the earl at Essex House immediately." To a man, their eyes drop to the floor, as though they'd been dispatched to hell to chat with the devil. "Find out, in his lordship's own words, the cause of this assembly. You may assure the earl that we—personally—shall patiently hear the causes of his distemper and satisfy them individually, that he may instruct his followers to disperse peacefully."

"And if he will not tell us, Majesty?" asks Popham.

She sighs. "I have no ultimatum for you to pass along, m'Lord Chief Justice. Just find out his grievances and relate them to me."

"Madam," says the ever-sensible Earl of Worcester, "he surrounds himself with rabid supporters, who will implore him to detain us, or worse."

The Queen's face falls into a cold anger reminding one and all that she is a daughter of Henry the Eighth, though the object of her anger is unclear. "To detain you? To what end?" she demands.

Worcester shrugs. "To gain time, if nothing else."

"Do you *fear* his lordship, Worcester?"

"Nay, madam," he replies. "I fear only the failure of this little expedition, which could render us unable to assist in putting down the coming … unrest."

"Leave that to me," she replies, "for I have just now instructed the Lord Mayor to place everyone under his authority at the ready awaiting our orders, and our ministers are assembling a 'little army' for that purpose." She turns to Noah. "Serjeant, you shall follow these gentlemen, mixed into their retinue. If they are taken and you escape, you shall report to me personally at once."

Noah swallows hard and bows.

"May I accompany Serjeant Ames, Majesty?" comes a young voice.

Noah can barely believe that David has had the temerity to speak to the Queen before being spoken to. And he most assuredly does not wish David to be endangered by coming along on this hopeless entreaty.

"David!" says Noah angrily.

The Queen sits up, amused. "That's quite all right, Serjeant. Master Cheerful was summoned here no less than you. If he wishes to go along, then so he shall."

Noah's jaw hangs open incredulously at this state of affairs. "But madam," he says, "David is my charge. I am responsible for him."

The Queen lets go a long, clear, healthy laugh without a bit of rancor. "Cheerful may be your charge, Serjeant Ames, but he's *our* subject. And, as for responsibility"—a weariness overcomes her aspect—"well, we are responsible for *all* of you."

Noah bows, embarrassed.

The Queen beckons Noah and Robert Cecil to approach for a private conference. They huddle closely, and only the Queen speaks. "I have decided to take your advice, Serjeant Ames. As soon as you leave here, I shall secretly move to the Tower, where I will await the outcome of this gambit. Seek me out in my private chamber. No one knows of this but you two. Be sure to keep it that way."

Noah and Robert Cecil bow silently and return to their former places.

The Queen addresses the whole company. "Gentlemen, Lord Robert has had the guard clean and sharpen your weapons. They will be returned to you at the gate.

"Go now, and Godspeed!"

CHAPTER 33

GORGES ARRIVES AT MIDSTREAM on the Thames before there's any sign of Sir Walter. The wind blows steadily, but the currents are not excessive, so the wherryman lifts his sculls out of the oarlocks and lowers them onto the deck. Almost immediately, the boat begins rocking from side to side in the currents, and the higher whitecaps spray froth into the boat.

The wherryman seems wholly unperturbed. "I'll spot Essex House stairs as me reference," says the wherryman. "It'll tell us pretty quick if we're driftin', and which way."

Gorges nods and continues scanning the river for any boat coming his way. There's a small group of wherries by Durham House, which is where Raleigh is reputedly staying. At last, one breaks from the group and heads straight for him.

When it comes within a hundred yards, Raleigh waves. Sir Ferdinando waves back and signals for him to move to the stern so they can speak without being overheard. Raleigh's wherry passes Gorges', turns about, and comes alongside till they're nearly touching.

"Sir Ferdinando," says Raleigh, "how is that band of brigands treating you?"

"It's crowded, Sir Walter, but I have my own room, and the board is ample."

Raleigh chortles. "You know he can't pay for it, don't you? *Any* of it."

"I'm sure Lord Essex has his ways and means," says Gorges, when in fact he's unsure of any such thing.

"He hasn't a *pot*, Sir Ferdinando," says Sir Walter. "His creditors are in for a rough ride, but not as rough as you lot."

"How d'ye mean?"

Raleigh leans forward. "Sir Ferdinando, your brother is worried sick about you. He knows, as I do, that the Queen will not issue a general pardon in the coming riot. She regards it as an insurrection. *High treason.* You know what that means?"

"Which coming riot, Sir Walter?"

"Sir Ferdinando, the plot's been discovered," says Raleigh, "and it's happening this morning. The Queen's men know everything Essex will do before he does it. Best get out of there right now. Come with me."

Sir Ferdinando shakes his head.

Sir Walter shakes his head in disbelief. "How in good conscience can you support him?"

"Essex was good to his men in Ireland," says Gorges tepidly.

"Because he didn't want them to fight the rebels," says Sir Walter. "He'd made a deal with Tyrone, who promised to help him become King of England."

"Rubbish," says Gorges. *Is it possible Raleigh's right?*

A tall whitecap sprays both men with foam, not enough to drench them, but enough to remind them how cold the water is. They chafe their sides to keep warm. The next wave shoves the wherries together, and the resulting clatter combines with the wind to drown out Raleigh's next words. Raleigh's wherryman skillfully rows him back into position.

"And there's another thing, Sir Ferdinando. How could you just leave your post as Governor of Plymouth without the required leave of the Crown?"

Ferdinando shrugs. "I expected my absence to last for an inconsequential time," he says.

"I'd suggest you come with me, or you'll end up in the Fleet Prison for it."

"Will you turn me in, Sir Walter?" asks Sir Ferdinando angrily.

"Don't be silly. By now, *everyone* knows you're absent without leave, because they're all watching Essex and you're rather foolishly standing right beside him."

Sir Ferdinando's anger only grows. "Essex is heavily guarded at his house, Sir Walter. If you assail him, you're like to have a bloody day of it. Instead of talking about how *I'll* end up in the Fleet, best you return to court." He kicks the boats apart and orders his wherryman to return to Essex House.

While Sir Walter appears loath to end the conversation, he peers over at the Essex House stairs where four of Essex's men have boarded rowboats. They're loading muskets; some are practicing aiming in his direction. As an experienced soldier, he knows that the likelihood of being hit at this range is small, but not non-existent. He orders his wherryman to proceed due west as fast as he can row before returning north to the Durham House stairs.

In a moment, several booms come in rapid succession from the direction of Essex House, followed in short order by the plunk of several balls falling into the water. Though all the shots have fallen short and behind Raleigh, they're still too close for comfort.

From his wherry, Sir Ferdinando can make out the figure of Sir Walter as he fades into the west, thrusting his hands heavenward, as if to say, "You've chosen your fate. You're in the hands of the gods now." Sir Ferdinando shakes his head. Sir Walter's right.

What the devil have I got myself into?

———————⊸∘⟡∘⊶———————

A FEW MINUTES LATER, a large group of barons and knights have assembled on the courtyard within the Essex House gate. Milling about with them from time to time are the Earls of Essex, Southampton, and Rutland.

Caim is quietly seated near the gate on the Strand, envisioning different ways to dispatch Cuthbert Bennett and the blond Tower guard who released the girl, when a rather distinguished group of four men with a small entourage appears on the Strand traveling on foot from the direction of Whitehall. They stop outside the gate and wait to be attended.

"Chase them away," shouts one baron.

"Tell 'em his lordship's not at home!" shouts another.

In a moment, the hectoring erupts into a general uproar.

Caim rises and goes to the gate. One of these men is obviously an earl, bedecked as he is with an elaborate coat of arms. One's the Lord Chief Justice, whom he recognizes from a few scrapes with the law. The other two are friends of Essex, namely, the Lord Keeper, who provided Essex with room and board till he was released, and Essex's uncle Knollys.

Caim bows, but before addressing the four, he turns back and addresses those already on the grounds. "These gentlemen are come to see Lord Essex. Let's show some respect and *pipe down*!"

To his surprise, from the center of the assemblage emerge Southampton, Rutland, and Essex himself, who beckons Caim over.

Essex leans in to speak privately with him, his eyes never wavering from the four dignitaries. "I know them all. Let all four in through the wicket. Keep their servants out, except for the Lord Keeper's purse-bearer, who carries the seal. And—" Now that his eyes have shifted to the servants, he sees a familiar face. "And invite in Serjeant Ames—he's the drably dressed fellow trying to be invisible."

Southampton hastens to add, "And also admit the tall blond fellow beside him." He turns to Essex. "He was staying with Raleigh when I was attacked by Lord Grey and his servants. He acquitted himself admirably."

Essex turns to Southampton, a bit confused. "Why should that earn him admittance today?"

Southampton smiles cleverly. "I believe he's a member of the Serjeant's household. Perhaps we can hold him to force the Serjeant's cooperation."

Caim berates himself for failing to recognize the Queen's Jew. After all, he admitted him by this very gate only a few months ago in the company of the girl that he abducted yesterday and was rescued out from under his nose. The blond fellow is likely her rescuer; he certainly fits Nancy's description.

Caim returns to the gate and opens the wicket to the four dignitaries. "Please come in, gentlemen," he says. After they've filed in, he reaches his big hand in among the servants, takes both Serjeant Ames and David by the elbow, and leads them through the wicket. He turns to the others. "You lot'll have to wait out there." He waves them away from the gate. "Please stay where you won't block anyone."

As the gate closes, the barons and knights in the courtyard assemble behind Essex with folded arms, looking very much a well-dressed, well-armed rabble.

The Lord Keeper Egerton leans in to have a private word with Essex.

"Lord Essex, on the way here, we heard gunfire on the Thames. We trust this does not betoken a commencement of hostilities."

Essex scoffs. "It does not, m'lord," he says. "It was a private matter."

The Lord Keeper Egerton stands apart and addresses Essex in a public voice: "We four have been sent by the Queen to know the cause of so great a concourse of men, and to bring to Lord Essex Her Majesty's assurance that, if injury has been done to his lordship by any man, his lordship shall receive equitable justice."

Essex looks to Southampton, as though to suggest these men know full well the many injuries he's suffered. He draws himself up to reply in equally public tones.

"There is a plot laid against my life," he shouts. "Some are set on to stab me in my bed. We are perfidiously dealt withal. Letters are counterfeited under my name in false hand. We are met here together to defend ourselves and save our lives, seeing neither my patience nor misery can assuage the malice of my adversaries unless they may also suck my blood."

The Lord Chief Justice then says virtually the same thing as the Lord Keeper did, asking Essex for specifics of the incidents to which he's referred. He assures Essex that he will report everything faithfully to the Queen and that Essex's case will be justly and duly heard.

Southampton replies this time. "I was assaulted by Lord Grey some weeks ago, who drew his sword upon me and cut off my servant's hand. Is that not specific enough?"

"But, my lord," says the Chief Justice, "Lord Grey languished in the Fleet Prison for weeks on account of that damnable wrong."

The Lord Keeper says to Essex in a moderate tone, "Perhaps, my lord, you might feel more at ease elaborating upon such grievances privately."

Essex beckons Southampton, and the two of them retire to the library at the rear of the house.

"Leave them, m'lord," shouts one firebrand as they go. "They abuse your patience!"

"They betray you and undo you," cries another. "They're *delaying* you."

The Lord Keeper turns to the firebrands. "On your allegiance to Her Majesty Queen Elizabeth, it is time for you to lay down your arms, and *I command* you to do so!"

The four gentlemen are bidden to join Essex and Southampton in the library, while the curses of the assembled still echo in their ears. "Kill them! Destroy the Great Seal! Shut them up in m'lord's custody!"

Noah and David, not having been separately beckoned, wait outside the library door. Though they remain within view of Essex's angry supporters, they seem to be of little interest to anyone except Caim, who glares at Noah as though trying to read his mind and determine how he was outsmarted.

Being closely watched doesn't bother Noah, and he's careful not to respond with so much as a change of expression. But what *does* concern Noah is the occasional shift in Caim's stare to David, who's been careful to avoid so much as looking at Caim. David apparently wishes to avoid confirming in Caim's mind that, *yes*, he is indeed the one who pulled Esther out of Caim's clutches. *There are plenty of other fair-haired men about,* David's thinking must be. *Let Caim retain some doubt that I'm*

Esther's rescuing hero.

The library door opens a few inches. Essex can be heard saying, "Have patience a while. I must presently go into the city to advise with m'Lord Mayor and the sheriffs. I will return again by and by, within the hour most likely." He opens the door and Noah can see the four are crestfallen and have been left in the custody of Sir Ferdinando Gorges and a few others.

Essex closes the door behind him and invites Noah and David to the gate on the Strand. He beckons Lord Southampton and Sir Gelly Meyrick to follow.

"Serjeant Ames," says Essex, "you continue your custom of appearing at the most consequential of times. While I am inclined to release you, I need your sworn oath that you shall neither go to Westminster today, nor tell anyone at Westminster, or who may go or send there today, that those gentlemen are detained."

Noah shakes his head. "This is madness, m'lord. If you were a foreign power, the detention of such high ministers against their will would be an act of war, *casus belli*. Being but Her Majesty's subject, your actions are high treason against the Crown. And yet you will require me to keep this a secret?"

Lord Southampton intercedes. "His lordship knows nothing of the madness of which you speak," he says. "His demand is your oath that you shall neither go to Westminster today, nor tell anyone at Westminster or who may go or send there today, that those gentlemen are detained. Do you so swear?"

Noah points to David. "Will no oath be required of Master Killigrew?"

Southampton throws his hands up and nods to Meyrick. "Add these two to the captives."

"No, wait!" says Noah urgently. "I shall swear."

"*Do* you so swear?" demands Essex.

Noah's trapped. He nods gravely. "You turn me against myself, m'lord. Nevertheless … I so swear."

"Good," says Southampton. "You may go. Master Killigrew shall remain here as your surety."

Sir Gelly immediately lays hands on David, whose face is unreadable.

Noah protests. "You've now proposed a material change to the arrangement *ex post facto*."

Southampton sneers. "No, we haven't," he insists. "You still have a choice. You may go or stay. Either way," he says, indicating David, "*he stays.*"

"I withdraw my oath, unless—"

"Unless what?" asks Essex.

"Unless you swear to keep your footman Caim away from him, and keep Master Killigrew in the sole custody of Sir Gelly Meyrick."

Meyrick is about to protest, when Southampton says, "I give you my word that we shall keep Caim away from Master Killigrew, and that he shall remain at all times in ... either *my* personal custody or Sir Gelly's. Now get out before we change our minds."

Noah takes a parting look at David's stoic face, and vows in his heart to see him set free, should it cost him his own life. "You shall see me again, David." Noah looks to Meyrick, whose eyes are downcast. "Sir Gelly?" he says, seeking unspoken assurance of humane treatment for David.

Without meeting Noah's gaze, Meyrick nods.

"Very well," says Noah, and marches out to the wicket, where Caim lets him out with a contemptuous sneer. As soon as the wicket's closed behind him, Noah turns and locks eyes with Caim, leaving no doubt what will happen to Caim should David come to harm. Noah turns and walks north toward his home.

Inside Essex House, Meyrick takes David out of the sight and hearing of the others. He leans into him and asks, "One way or another, this crowd's gonna end up on the Thames. If I tie your hands tightly, and you get tossed overboard, you'll drown. I'd rather not have that on me conscience. You swear ye won't raise a hand to Lord Essex or Southampton?"

David nods solemnly. "I swear."

Meyrick proceeds to tie his hands, leaving his right hand loose enough to escape at need, and marches him into the library to the astonishment of the other captives. He's the only one manacled.

Outside the library, Southampton is beside himself with glee. "*Did you see that?* He made it so easy. As there are only two readily guarded sites in the area about London, the Queen must be either at Whitehall or the Tower. So, Ames has given us a pretty good idea where Her Majesty is."

Essex looks at him, puzzled. "How so?"

"You've said it yourself more than once, Robert. Ames is too proud to violate an oath. And the only way for him to keep this oath is either not to report our captives to anyone, which is beyond the capabilities of someone with even *his* self-control, or to report it to someone who's neither at Westminster nor headed there, which means he can't tell the Queen, unless ..."

Essex smiles wickedly. "Unless she's at the Tower."

Essex beckons Sir Gelly and gives him instructions. "Please *discreetly* follow Ames," he says. "We believe he's headed to the Tower, and we need to know Her Majesty's location so we can direct our forces there."

"How am I to get into the Tower, m'lord, if he's let in through the main gate?" asks Sir Gelly.

"Do you remember the secret entrance the old Italian showed us?" "Aye," says Sir Gelly, "but I expect the Tower'll be crawlin' with guards."

"Not if our intelligence is accurate," says Essex. "We've heard they've doubled the guard at Whitehall. To do that, they would've had to deplete the Tower Guard badly."

"I'll go and fetch me mount," says Sir Gelly.

"I doubt you'll need a horse," says Essex. "He left on foot not a moment ago."

Sir Gelly shakes his head. "I saw him, m'lord. He was headin' for his house at Holborn, where he's got one of the fastest horses in the kingdom." He looks to Southampton. "What about young Killigrew?" he asks.

"Leave Killigrew to me," says Southampton, "and before you go, tell *Caim* that if he so much as touches Killigrew while he's in our custody, I'll have his head."

CHAPTER 34

"SIR FERDINANDO," says Essex, "together with Davies, you shall take charge of Essex House during our absence. I had intended to leave Sir Gelly in charge, but he's been called away on an errand and his return is not to be expected for some time. In the meantime, see to the comfort of our guests in the library. By all means treat them hospitably, and invite the ladies to come down from upstairs to entertain them." He turns to Southampton. "Let's go now. I need to go and see the sheriff and the Lord Mayor, and gather my many supporters in town."

Essex and Southampton don their elegant cloaks, hats, and gloves, and lead a disorderly crowd of some one hundred young noblemen and soldiers through Essex House gate into the frosty afternoon.

"A plot is laid for my life!" shouts Essex. "For the Queen!"

Loud and strong, his followers echo his sentiments. On they march to the Strand, where Essex leads them east toward the Tower of London through Ludgate, the oldest gate into the walled city.

Unbeknownst to any of them, they're being watched from a few hundred yards to the rear by Sir John Leveson, the cousin of Sir Henry Neville who followed Noah's party into Whitehall this morning.

Sir John shakes his head in disapproval. If this is rebellion, where's the discipline? Where are the weapons? As far as he can see, each man carries his own sword, and a few of *those* are purely ceremonial, by the look of them. Very few of Essex's followers carry pistols. And no man … *not one* … has a horse.

As the last of Essex's stragglers pass through Ludgate and turn left into London proper, Sir John calls up the vanguard of his foot soldiers, a dozen men weighed down by a massive chain formerly used to block shipping from an inlet on the Thames, and orders the chain firmly suspended across Ludgate.

The remaining men of his contingent, about fifty pikemen and a dozen musketeers in all, move up to the chain, set themselves behind it, and prepare to thwart any move by Essex to return through Ludgate, which he must do either to advance to Whitehall or return to Essex House. The only alternative is by wherry, with which his party is not equipped.

The pikemen are mostly active or retired soldiers or constables. Though some are a bit long in the tooth, they seem a sturdy bunch … even the puritan sent over by the archdiocese ostensibly to protect Saint Paul's and Saint Gregory's from looting, although how anyone could protect either the cathedral or the church from this side of the chain is a mystery.

Sir John sits atop his mount peering over the chain onto Bowyer's Row.

Even after all these years of command, he finds waiting difficult. He recalls from other battles how difficult it can be to persuade even the best of soldiers to man stationary positions in cold weather. His own mount's breath steams in the cold. Well, it may be cold for a little while, but things will surely heat up soon.

Two faded bloodstains on the Bowyer's Row pavement remind him that this was the site of two murders some months ago, and he wonders idly if they had anything to do with Essex's uprising. Though he hopes no such stains will be added today, he doubts that the outcome of this affair will be entirely peaceful.

For one thing, it's just too poorly organized.

FORTUNATELY FOR SIR GELLY, Serjeant Ames has no occasion to bring his horse up to speed, restricting his moderately paced ride through London to busy streets where Sir Gelly can lose himself in traffic to the Serjeant's rear. Even if Sir Gelly were to lose sight of Ames, it's obvious he's headed to the Tower. So, Lord Southampton was right about where Ames was going. Whether Southampton was also correct in concluding that the Queen is at the Tower remains to be seen.

Approaching the Tower, Sir Gelly realizes that all his efforts at stealth have proven unnecessary, as the good Serjeant never turned about once. How careless!

Serjeant Ames reaches the Tower and veers off to the stables, no doubt to avail himself of the secret passage into the residence.

To pass through such a confined space so soon after the Serjeant would make Sir Gelly's discovery inevitable, so he rides instead to the main gate, where a bustle of guards and tradesmen suggests that the gate will soon open.

Sir Gelly dismounts and ties off his horse a little ways from the gate. In short order, the large, heavy Tower gate opens to let out two peers on horseback, each accompanied by a herald holding what appears to be a copy of a freshly minted proclamation.

At the edge of the gateway, several provisioners, obviously with the cooperation of the Guard, take the opportunity to roll out empty barrels of ale and provender, and roll in fresh ones. In the midst of the general business, Sir Gelly enters using his most reliable disguise, which is simply to act as though he belongs there.

The moment he steps inside the gate, he hops up the steps leading to the dormitory of the support staff serving the royal residence, and admits himself through an unlocked door he's passed through during happier times in the company of Lord Essex.

He slips into an anteroom he's seen used as a drying room for wet cloaks. As there's been no snow or rain for days, there should be no reason for anyone to peek into the anteroom, and it's in an opportune location directly in the path leading from the secret passage by which Ames is entering the royal residence. It's the perfect place to keep an eye on Ames, so he resolves to wait here until the good Serjeant approaches.

As Sir Gelly waits, it occurs to him that Essex was also right: The guard here is severely depleted. But it's *so* depleted that Sir Gelly begins to doubt the Queen is here—until he reminds himself that Serjeant Ames would have little reason to come here if the Queen were at Whitehall. He sits on the floor and pretends to be asleep, which should give him a moment to bluster up some excuse in case he's discovered.

LORD THOMAS BURGHLEY, son of the late Lord Treasurer and elder brother of the current Secretary of State Lord Robert, waits on horseback for the Tower Gate to rise. It's a creaky task, requiring numerous men, ropes, and pulleys. Before the gate's been lifted high enough for him to exit with his herald, already the provisioners are rolling barrels in and out, in what appears to be barely organized chaos.

Lord Thomas views the encroachment of petty commerce into a momentous state occasion such as this as undignified, and he makes no pretense about his views, glowering down at the merchants disdainfully.

His herald, the Garter Principal King of Arms William Dethick, obviously agrees with him in full, adding a set of angry eyes and flared nostrils to his protest against the commercial profanation of a grave state occasion such as this. On the other hand, Dethick's having stabbed both his brother and another man at a funeral at Westminster Abbey tends to diminish whatever moral support Lord Thomas might otherwise draw from Dethick's indignation.

Also ready to leave through the gate is another pairing of an earl and a herald who have been assigned to read the same proclamation all along Thames Street. When the gate has risen far enough, all four men shake their horses' reins and ride out of the Tower.

Lord Thomas and Dethick proceed to Cheapside Street, where Lord Thomas asks Dethick to hold forth with the Queen's proclamation. Glancing about after pronouncing the full scope of the Queen's titles, Dethick is pleased to see that he's gathered quite a crowd, due in large part, no doubt, to his stentorian tones.

"Her Majesty hereby declares," he continues, "the Earl of Essex and all who have conspired with him, or shall hereafter act at his behest, to be *traitors to the Crown,* the earl having disobeyed and conspired to betray Her Majesty on numerous occasions in Ireland and elsewhere, having acted with contumely and malice against her, and having now sought to raise an army against her, designed to deprive Her Majesty of her God-given right to govern this realm as its rightful Queen."

The crowd is amazed and confused by the pronouncement, as they've just heard rumors that Essex is heading this way from the opposite end of Cheapside for the purpose of *saving* the Queen, repeatedly announcing that a plot has been laid against his life by a group of treacherous counselors conspiring against not only himself but Her Majesty, as well.

The Garter Principal King of Arms clears his illustrious throat and continues his reading of the proclamation. "Her Majesty commands and implores her subjects to prove their loyalty to the Crown by abandoning the earl and his current devices, and by instead capturing his lordship and all who support him, and bringing them under restraint to the lawful authorities at Whitehall, where they shall be arraigned for their miscon-duct, and where his lordship's grievances shall be heard by the Crown's ministers in the fullness of time."

With that, the herald rolls up his scroll, and clops away with Lord Burghley to spread the word to other corners of the town. As they depart, one or two mutters of complaint are heard from the crowd.

"Essex didn't betray anybuddy, in Ireland or anyplace else," says one.

But such words fall on deaf ears, as a clear consensus of self-interest has instantly arisen. However much a citizen might be inclined to assist the earl, to support him is hardly worth losing one's own wealth, one's own station, or one's own head. After all, Essex is seeking support for the airing of *private* grievances. His problems, however grave, are *his*, and there seems to be no question of the *public* welfare underlying his mysterious fears and accusations. Moreover, it's not every day the Queen declares someone a traitor to the Crown. Nor has she ever done so without good reason. And she has ever been famously merciful to Lord Essex in the past.

Those who were once inspired by the earnest call of their beloved Essex now think better of their former enthusiasm, and return to their homes to await the outcome with some little regret—but no further thought of taking up arms.

———⸺◦⟨⟨⟩⟩◦⸺———

"RALEIGH DESIGNS TO TAKE MY LIFE," shouts Essex as he storms eastward on Cheapside. "To arms, my fellow countrymen. For the Queen!"

Essex's hundred followers are quickly doubled by men who dart out of their homes weaponless, and mingle with the crowd behind him. When they've nearly reached the Royal Exchange, Essex turns and orders a halt.

"I must see Sheriff Smyth here," he shouts. "Please await my return. I shan't be long. But in the meantime, I would ask those of you who came without weapons to return to your homes and retrieve them. This is no petty bunch with whom we stand to tangle, gentlemen."

Essex climbs the steps to the sheriff's house.

Sheriff Smyth opens the door, his mouth hanging open in wonder, and admits Essex only to save him the embarrassment of publicly turning him away. He closes the front door.

"My lord," says the sheriff in amazement, "what in heaven's name are you doing here? What can I do for your lordship?"

Essex smiles. "Hah! Smyth! You jest, yet this is no time for jocularity. I come about the hundreds of men promised me by your note of yesternight."

Smyth is genuinely stunned. "Note? Hundreds of men? What can your lordship be thinking? I sent your lordship no note. Why, your lordship and I have neither corresponded nor spoken these *nine year*! As for hundreds of men, I don't think I've ever had more than a few dozen, and those only part-time. For what purpose do you need so many men, m'lord? And who are all those gathered outside?"

Essex is crestfallen. Smyth is obviously not having him on; he has no knowledge of any of this.

"You know nothing of doings at Essex House, Master Smyth?" he asks.

"Nothing, m'lord," says Smyth. "And just a few minutes ago, Lord Burghley appeared outside this very house, where his herald read aloud a proclamation declaring your lordship *a traitor to the Crown*! But I didn't believe it, and I don't believe it now." He peeks through a window at the waiting throng. "But who are those men, m'lord? And what is the import of this assemblage?"

Without a word or change of expression, Essex turns, lets himself out, and descends the stairs as though thunderstruck. Even with so many watching, he finds himself unable to dissemble, though he knows he should do so. Southampton rushes up to him, followed at a respectful distance by Essex's page leading the manacled David Killigrew by the arm.

"What is it, Robert?" asks Southampton. "What's happened? Why, you look as though you've had the rug pulled out from under your feet!"

"There *are* no men," says Essex. "And the Queen has declared us traitors."

Though Essex spoke the words quietly, apparently it was not quietly enough. A murmur of fear bruits through the crowd like a rifleshot. All at once men begin to split off from the main body like so many papery peels off an onion.

The sheriff's footman flies down the stairs behind Essex and offers him and a dozen of his followers the run of the sheriff's home.

Essex nods. "Yes, that's what we need. A moment's respite."

With that, a dozen men enter the sheriff's house, leaving a main body of fewer than a hundred men. The servants pour ale for those fortunate enough to be admitted, and send some out in cups to those waiting on Cheapside.

AS SOON AS SHERIFF SMYTH has instructed his servant to admit Essex and a few followers to his home, he grabs his cloak and runs out of the back door to the Lord Mayor's house, where he finds the Lord Mayor ordering a lockdown of the city, with chains to be laid across major streets and armed men to be placed at strategic points.

"Stay with us, Master Smyth," says the Lord Mayor. "I've heard that Essex has told others that I promised him material support." He turns to him, offended. "Can you imagine that? I, whose principal assignment is to protect the city from all threats? Needless to say, I haven't spoken or written to him in many a year."

"I fear he has been deceived, Lord Mayor—in fact *goaded*—and not by his supporters."

"God help him," says the Lord Mayor, "as you and I cannot do on peril of our lives."

A HALF HOUR LATER, Essex remains unsure what to do. He accepts the servants' offer of a few of the sheriff's halberds for his men, and descends the front steps again onto Cheapside, this time heading back the way he came.

Though he still shouts for assistance to each house he passes, precious few join him, and not one brings a weapon. His numbers have dwindled to a few dozen, a stalwart group, but not nearly enough for any kind of effort.

Reaching the north side of Saint Paul's, he gathers his men in the churchyard, and walks a half hour alone in the woods. At last he decides it's time to regroup at Essex House, but first he wishes to know that the path is clear. He orders his men to stay where they are until his return and, as he rounds the cathedral alone, he sees that Ludgate is blocked by a heavy chain and a few dozen men armed with pikes and muskets.

BY FOUR IN THE AFTERNOON at Ludgate, Leveson is nearly asleep on his horse waiting for something—anything—to happen. One of his pikemen escorts a man to him, a knight, by his dress and demeanor.

"I saw this gentleman walking behind us, sir," says the pikeman. "I'd decided to bring him to you to be questioned, when he suddenly walked up to me and asked to speak with you." The pikeman takes a step back and, unsure how to introduce two gentlemen to each other properly, reverts to military form. "Captain Sir John Leveson, permit me to introduce Sir Ferdinando Gorges, Governor of Plymouth."

Leveson is shocked. "*Plymouth,* sir? What brings you all the way to

London?"

Gorges sighs. "I hesitate to say, Sir John, that I came at the call of my former commander in Ireland, Lord Essex."

Sir John scowls skeptically. "Seemed like a good idea at the time, eh?"

Gorges shrugs. "Old loyalties, Sir John. They die hard."

Sir John nods reluctantly. "Indeed they do," he says. "But if you're looking to surrender, I haven't the men to—"

"Not surrender, Sir John," says Gorges, "but to renounce my role in this affair and make such amends as I may." He gestures with his head that he'd like to speak with Sir John alone.

Sir John dismounts and takes Gorges aside. "What can you do for us?" he asks.

More than a bit embarrassed, Sir Ferdinando begins slowly. "I don't know whether you're aware of how this whole business began this morning."

"Enlighten me, sir," says Leveson, "but I pray you be quick about it, as I'm in charge here and have no idea when we shall be called to action."

"Certainly, sir," says Sir Ferdinando. "This morning four dignitaries came to speak with Lord Essex at Essex House. They were the Lord Chief Justice, the Lord Keeper of the Great Seal, an earl, and Lord Essex's uncle, who's in charge of the Queen's household."

Sir John is concerned. "Where have they gone to now?" he asks.

"That's just it, sir. They're still there."

"Still th—Don't tell me they've joined Essex's side!"

Sir Ferdinando shakes his head emphatically. "To be sure, they have not, sir. They're being held very much against their will."

"Ah, I see," says Leveson. "Well—and I very much regret saying this—but I cannot spare the men to free them. I simply can't help them now."

"No, sir," says Sir Ferdinando, "but I can. You see, they're in my custody."

"Your—?"

"Aye, sir. Well, mine and a few others, but for all practical purposes I have the key in my pocket."

"Jesu!" says Sir John. "Then let them go!"

"I plan to do so, sir, but I need to obtain some assurance of three things: First, as I see you will not permit Lord Essex to pass west through Ludgate, I need for you to allow me to pass east, the other way. I expect I know where Lord Essex may be found, and I shall urge him to provide me with a written order to release the Lord Chief Justice. I need a written order to that effect so that I may persuade the others in charge."

"Just the Lord Chief Justice?" asks Leveson.

"Well, the Lord Chief Justice has made it emphatically clear that he shan't leave without the others. This will give me an opportunity to let them *all* go."

"So, you're just seeking leave to enter London here?" asks Leveson.

Gorges nods.

"How will you get back to Essex House?"

"By wherry, sir," replies Gorges.

"Very well, on your first request," says Leveson. "What of your remaining two?"

"I need assurance that I shall be permitted to depart with the former captives by boat. We have the necessary boat at Essex House stairs on the Thames."

"Well, I won't stop you. I couldn't if I wanted to. And your final request?"

"I need you to vouch for me, at need, as having renounced my participation in Lord Essex's present actions by acting in voluntary cooperation with the Queen's men."

"That's all?" asks Sir John suspiciously. "To what place will you row the hostages?"

"To Whitehall, sir. That's where they've asked to go."

"And you'll accompany them, and surrender yourself when you arrive?"

"I will, sir."

"Then I'll bloody well vouch for you, for what good it'll do. I'm not so well-known that my say-so will get you off, but I suppose it'll help." He shrugs. "Can't hurt."

"Indeed it cannot, sir," says Sir Ferdinando, extending his hand, one knight to another. "Farewell and Godspeed."

"Sir Ferdinando Gorges? Did I get that right?"

"Yes, sir."

Sir John takes Ferdinando's hand. "Farewell, sir. And Godspeed."

Ferdinando salutes, and Sir John follows suit. Ferdinando turns in crisp military fashion and marches up to the chain. Before letting Ferdinando pass, the pikemen turn to Sir John, who waves him on and watches him enter London in search of Essex.

"Extraordinary," mutters Sir John.

CHAPTER 35

FOLLOWING LORD ROBERT'S INSTRUCTIONS, Noah strides into the royal residence and advances to the threshold of Her Majesty's private chambers, where he hesitates.

He's never entered Her Majesty's private quarters at the Tower of London before, and the prospect gives him butterflies. Though he's been summoned to her sick room at other palaces a few times, there's something forbidding about her regular dressing quarters, such that entering them feels … disrespectful. This is likely the very threshold, after all, that Essex crossed on his return from Ireland against the Queen's orders only to discover her partially dressed, a transgression for which he's paid dearly. Perhaps only men are meant to feel this way as, on an ordinary evening, there seem to be innumerable ladies-in-waiting comfortably entering and leaving the quarters without a second thought.

Firming up his resolve, he crosses the threshold and wends his way to the sleeping quarters, counting every change of direction on his fingers to ensure adherence to the path prescribed by Lord Robert. At last, he comes to the little room appointed for his meeting with Queen Elizabeth.

It's deathly quiet. There's no one here. Evidently, he's arrived before she has. He assumes a chair by a modest shrine in a corner of the room. Mounted on the wall are a Latin Cross and a portrait of Her Majesty's father, Henry the Eighth. Sitting atop a chest on the floor beneath them is a well-worn Bible. Should he read it? After all, Bibles are all the same. It's not as though this one will reveal some state secret for which his life will be forfeit.

In an act of faith in both Her Majesty's reason and her mercy, he picks it up and begins to read in the Old Testament.

"I wonder," says Her Majesty's disembodied voice, "whether you've ever read beyond the midpoint of that book."

So shocked is he by the sound of her voice, he rises suddenly, heart pounding, and nearly drops the Bible. At the last moment he manages to grasp it by the binding.

"Your Majesty?" he says. "I ... cannot see you."

"Nor are you intended to, Noah. Nor shall you see me go. I come to hear your news and to assure you that, when the hurly-burly's done, I shall go where I first appeared to you so many years ago. Understand, Noah, that in my current position, I distrust nearly everyone—especially mine own family, who have the most to gain by my undoing—and I will not reveal myself unless I'm quite sure you are there, and under no compulsion. I will be confident of your safety if you will sing the song I first heard you sing."

He opens his mouth to clarify her meaning, but she silences him before he can speak by saying, "Don't say it aloud! As you can see, the walls have ears," she says. "Say no more on the topic—now or ever again. Now, what is your news?"

"First, Majesty, in my defense permit me to say that I have read the Bible many a time, and both testaments. As for my more pertinent news: It is as I expected, Majesty," says Noah into the ether, for he's unable to locate her. "All four of your emissaries have been locked in Lord Essex's study. His lordship ordered them confined there while he went into town to muster from Sheriff Smyth and the Lord Mayor the support of which they assured him in their letters of last evening—letters they never wrote and know nothing of. In this respect, Sir Walter's false messages have had their desired result."

"If only we could be there to see his lordship's face when the good sheriff and Lord Mayor look at him as though he's gone mad," says the Queen, with a smile in her voice.

Noah considers her words. "Indeed, Majesty, I expect he is afflicted with the same madness as Narcissus."

"No doubt," she says. "I know you well, Noah, and I can hear in your voice that you are burdened by a heavy weight. What's the matter?"

"It's Master Killigrew, madam. He's being held by Lord Southampton as surety for my oath that I will tell no one at Whitehall, or who might send to Whitehall, of Lord Essex's captives."

"And well you have kept your oath, for I shall neither go nor send to Whitehall until this rebellion is quite put down. Tell that to Southampton, so he will release Master Killigrew."

"I am leery that his lordship will see it that way, Majesty. I rather fear for Master Killigrew's life."

After a moment's hesitation, she says, "Master Arden is here at the Tower, Serjeant. Bring him with you to aid in Master Killigrew's recovery, together with whichever other commoners you deem wise. But leave the noblemen here with Raleigh, as I have other plans for them all."

"Yes, Majesty. And thank you," he says, bowing to her voice.

"Godspeed, Serjeant Ames."

For a few moments, he stands by, listening attentively. But there's no bustle of clothing or slippers, no opening or closing of doors. She has simply … disappeared. Still, he's comforted to know that no one else can reach her, either.

He returns the Bible to its perch on the chest below the cross, and leaves the room. Using his fingers to count off each turn, he reverses his earlier path, moving toward the threshold that he hesitated to cross earlier.

Noah assumes that Arthur is meeting with, or at least has sought out, Sir Walter Raleigh, so he takes a shortcut leading down the hall to the staff's quarters and down into the yard. As he turns the corner, he spies someone at the opposite end of the hallway that he never expected to see here: Sir Gelly Meyrick.

Noah darts into an ornate room lined with some of the Tower's textile treasures, such as tapestries, arrases, and the like, but he's fairly certain he wasn't quick enough, for he saw a distinct sign of recognition on Sir Gelly's face. Bracing himself for confrontation, he strikes his sternest posture.

Sir Gelly turns the corner into the tapestry room, sees Noah glowering at him with his hands on his hips, and freezes in the doorway.

"And where is your charge, Sir Gelly?" demands Noah in a voice so steely, he almost convinces *himself* of his superior strength.

"Yer little blond boy is in Southampton's care, as promised. Speakin' o' whereabouts: Where is she?"

"Is Master Killigrew well, Sir Gelly? Has Caim been kept away from him?"

"Yes, and yes," says Sir Gelly, obviously losing patience. "Now, *where is she*?"

"'She,' Sir Gelly? Whom do you mean by 'she'?"

"As if you don't know," says Sir Gelly with disgust. "Where is the Queen? Look, Serjeant Ames, I ain't got time for yer lawyer's games."

"Oh, I'm well aware that you're short of time, Sir Gelly. Lord Burghley and the herald were dispatched a short time ago to proclaim Lord Essex a traitor to the Crown, as well as everyone who helps him. I should think that, after trial, you'll be found to fall into that category."

With the mention of "traitors" and "trials," Sir Gelly's eyes open wide with horror.

"Why me?" he demands. "I been tryin' to talk sense into 'im since you come to Essex House that day last summer."

"And yet your talk seems to have had no effect at all. More importantly, you've made no move toward leaving his lordship's service. I'd say you're pretty well in the soup about now."

Sir Gelly takes a threatening step forward and places his hand on the hilt of his sword. "I didn't come to parley with barristers. I came to fetch the Queen, and I know you just left her. Now tell me where I can find 'er."

"Her Majesty is nowhere *you* can find her, Sir Gelly," Noah says. "Lay down your sword, renounce your allegiance to Lord Essex, and I'll help you to survive this affair. There can be no assurance it will have the desired effect, but I'll do the best I can. But you must lay down your sword *at once*."

Noah can now see visible manifestations of a war that's been waged in Sir Gelly's heart for quite a long time. He's sweating. He wishes to relent, but with each refusal to reconsider his staunch support for Essex, his face hardens further until at last it resembles pale stone.

"I'll kill ye, so help me God," says Sir Gelly, evidently at the end of his tether.

"And what good would my death do you, Sir Gelly? It wouldn't get you the information you seek. You'd be killing such information along with me. Besides ... would you kill someone who saved your own life barely a year ago?"

Meyrick can dispense with that easily. "That's the tides o' war, Serjeant. One day you're my friend, the next the very devil. If killin' ye won't make ye tell what I want, mebbe *pain* will serve."

At last, Sir Gelly draws his sword. Immediately, a voice comes from behind him, one he's dreaded hearing for nearly a decade. And there's a tickle of cold steel at the back of his neck.

"Drop your sword, Meyrick!" says Lord Saint Ives. "'Tis I, Jon Hawking."

Meyrick could kick himself. Wasn't it less than hour ago he scoffed at Ames for failing to look behind? For a moment, Meyrick considers turning about regardless, but it would avail him nothing. Hawking is the better swordsman and has placed himself to the rear of his adversary. He's younger, lighter, and quicker. With all those advantages, he could put Meyrick down before he completes the turn. Besides that, as Meyrick himself has observed before, Hawking *wants* to kill him. Why provide him the excuse?

Meyrick drops his sword with a clang and turns about with his hands up. All at once, the weight he's been carrying on his shoulders presses him to his knees, where he covers his face with his hands in despair. If only he'd renounced his participation in this idiotic plan a moment ago, he'd have a fiery advocate to defend him. But, as it is, he has no hope. Nothing awaits him now.

Nothing but Tyburn.

WHAT CHOICE HAVE I, but to fight my way back to Essex House? Essex asks himself. There are no other gates near Ludgate that could provide a practical exit from the walled city.

He turns and tallies his strengths. He has perhaps three dozen men in all. All have swords, fewer daggers. Fewer still have firearms, and those seem mainly to be old-style pistols, long and ungainly, good for no more than a single shot in close-in fighting because of the time it takes to reload. One or two muskets.

Many of these men he doesn't even know. Most are at least a bit aged, as well. Comparing them to the company manning the chained gate, well, *both* sides are more seasoned than befits a street fight such as this. And his favored page is burdened with a prisoner, Killigrew, whose hands are still bound as Sir Gelly left them.

In assaying his strength, Essex fails to recognize one heavily armed and thinly disguised fellow who joined his company on the return trip through Cheapside.

One Cuthbert Bennett.

TO THE ASTONISHMENT of the captives, Sir Ferdinando storms into the back library at Essex House waving a note written in Essex's hand.

"Lord Chief Justice," he says, "does your refusal to leave this place without these other three gentlemen still stand?"

"It most certainly does," says the Lord Chief Justice stoutly.

Ferdinando smiles inside. "Then all of you fortunate gentlemen are about to experience Lord Essex's mercy and courtesy," he pronounces, "and I beg you not to forget it. He has ordered me personally to return you to Whitehall stairs by boat without awaiting his return to Essex House. His lordship begs forgiveness for your brief detention, but hopes that your afternoon with the ladies of the house was not without good conversation."

Sir Ferdinando's astonished fellow captors ask to see Essex's note. Sir Ferdinando exhibits it to them briefly and shoves it back in his pocket, giving them no opportunity to detect his skillful interlineation of a few words. He makes it clear he will brook no delay.

"Prepare an outsize wherry for launch," he commands Essex's servants, "big enough for five. The Queen's forces are presently holding Ludgate against Lord Essex's return, and Lord Essex wishes to ensure that no harm of any kind befalls his distinguished guests."

"But is that Lord Essex's command, sir?" asks one of the servants sheepishly.

"Do you doubt me, you dog?" shouts Ferdinando, reaching for the hilt of his sword—just clumsily enough to be restrained by those of calmer temperament. The cheeky servant bows perfunctorily and runs to the steps to prepare the boat.

As the captives step down into the boat, Caim appears at the riverside door, and asks, "Did m'Lord Southampton concur in this order, Sir Ferdinando?"

Ferdinando glares at him ferociously. "He was standing next to Lord Essex when the order was given, and expressed no reservation. Lord Southampton is not far away, Caim." He thrusts the note into Caim's face, being careful not to release it. "Why don't you go and ask him? Of course, you'll be arrested before you can reach him."

Though the written order closely resembles Essex's handwriting, Caim doesn't trust its authenticity. There seems to have been some modification in some of the words. Still, he can do nothing to stop the prisoners' release. After all, Essex entrusted the captives to Gorges, who's a knight and Governor of Plymouth, rather than Caim, a mere footman.

As the captives' little boat shoves off toward Whitehall with Sir Ferdinando at the helm, Caim takes it upon himself to order a half-dozen of his allies on Essex's staff to arm themselves with sword and pistol.

"The rest of you stay here," he says to the remaining staff. "I'm taking these men to assist Lord Essex in taking Ludgate, to speed his return home."

A short time later, Caim and his small contingent dock at Puddle Wharf, by Blackfriars. According to Caim's reckoning, this is the nearest dock within the walled city, and will leave them off on the side of Ludgate where Gorges told him he could find Southampton.

They leave the boat tied off and unattended, and rush north up Saint Andrew's Hill in aid of Lord Essex.

CHAPTER 36

SIR JOHN LEVESON rides up to the chain across Ludgate and peers down the lane on the south side of Saint Paul's. A lone man looks back at him about three hundred yards away. He squints to get a better look.

"That's Lord Essex, boys," he says, gritting his teeth. "We're in it now. Time to look sharp."

As Essex turns away and disappears behind the cathedral, two barristers in a cart approach from the direction of the Tower.

———————⊶∘⫷⫸∘⊶———————

"IS THAT LORD ESSEX UP AHEAD?" asks Arthur, though Noah can barely hear him over the clopping hooves and clattering cart.

Noah squints. "I believe it is," he says. Looking past Essex, he sees that Ludgate is heavily chained and defended by pikemen and musketeers led by an imposing-looking horseman. "And I see his dilemma. The Queen's men have chained and barred the gate."

"Good for them," says Arthur. "What do you suppose Essex will do now?"

"Arthur," says Noah, "if I understood what motivates that gentleman to do *anything*, I might have avoided his arriving at this pass."

They watch Essex walk up the east side of Saint Paul's churchyard toward a sparse band of men concealing themselves from view.

"If they've kept their word and Southampton is with them," says Noah, "then David must be there, too."

"He shouldn't be hard to pick out," says Arthur. "His hair and mine are about the same length and color."

Not that Noah generally notices such things, but he sees that Arthur has begun emulating David's somewhat romantic appearance. They're both a bit shaggy. While that may be fine for a pupil at Oxford, it's unlikely to inspire confidence in a practicing barrister. He makes a mental note to speak with Arthur about it later.

Noah glances down Creed Lane toward the river and sees half a dozen well-armed men in the distance rapidly approaching up Saint Andrew's Hill on foot.

"Stop the cart," says Noah, the conviction growing in his mind that he and Arthur have arrived here at precisely the *wrong* time. Arthur pulls the cart to a halt and turns to him expectantly. "We obviously can't reach Essex House any more than Essex can."

"We could take a wherry," suggests Arthur.

"We could," says Noah, "but that would take time, and we'd have to stable the horse and cart, as I'm answerable to Sir Walter for them. On the other hand, we were going to Essex House only to fetch David, who's not there, but rather *here* ... somewhere. And I've sworn not to go to Whitehall today."

"So, what need have we to pass through the gate?" asks Arthur.

"True," says Noah contemplatively. "But we can't even return to Marie's house at Holborn unless we can get out of the walled city."

"If that's where you want to go," says Arthur, "we could pass through Newgate. It's but a quarter-mile north."

"But why hasn't *Essex* passed through Newgate?" mutters Noah. "He seems to have come from that direction. He may have found it barred the same as Ludgate."

Noah turns anxiously to his young friend. "Arthur," he says, "I can't leave here without David, but you can. Return to the Tower. Take the cart."

Arthur digs in his heels. "I shan't leave you, sir. Who's in charge here at Ludgate, do you suppose? Perhaps he can be persuaded to let us pass. You're Queen's barrister, after all."

Noah sighs. "It's remarkable how little that matters when it ought to matter most," he says. "All right, I'll find out who's in charge. Perhaps he knows conditions at Newgate." He gets down from the cart and turns back sternly. "But this place is rife with the threat of immediate violence. I can feel it in the air. You must promise me that, at the first sign of it, you'll return straight to the Tower *without awaiting me*."

"Very well," says Arthur, a bit too breezily.

Noah steps down from the cart, a feeling in his gut telling him this is perhaps the worst decision he's ever made. He crosses Bowyer's Row to the chained gate with his arms raised and his hands open. The men in the first row behind the chain watch his approach warily with their eyes wide, clearly frightened half to death.

"I am Serjeant Noah Ames, Queen's barrister," he says conversationally. "Who's in charge here?"

A voice comes from the mounted officer at the rear. "Good after-noon, Serjeant. 'Tis I. Sir John Leveson. We met early this morning."

Was it just this morning? It seems weeks ago now, so much has changed. Noah's about to return the greeting when a musket is fired somewhere well behind this contingent of men.

"Hold your fire!" shouts Leveson furiously, looking behind. "*Who bloody fired?*" he demands, awaiting an answer that never comes.

A bearded man in the first rank behind the chain, a few feet from Noah, points in the direction of Saint Paul's and shouts, "They're comin', sir!" A musket fires somewhere behind Noah, and a ball whizzes past his ear, thwacking into the man's forehead. The man's head jerks back, and he falls dead at Noah's feet, leaving the face of the man behind him covered in blood and brains.

When Noah turns to order Arthur back to the Tower, several things happen, seemingly all at once.

In the distance, Essex's band begins its slow advance toward the chained gate. In its first rank, one of Essex's pages pushes the manacled David Killigrew along as a shield.

Between Noah and Essex's main body, the men he saw walking up from the river have reached Bowyer's Row and turned toward Ludgate, effectively becoming Essex's vanguard. Noah's heart sinks as he sees Caim at the head of it.

Nearest Noah is Arthur Arden, who's left the Tower's horse tied off and begun running toward the chained gate with his hands up in supplication.

"Don't fire!" Arthur shouts as he approaches. "They have a hostage!"

Caim draws his sword and races ahead of his group, straight toward Arthur.

Someone breaks ranks with the Queen's men, clambers under the chain, and rushes forward with his sword drawn in defense of the helpless Arthur, who's plainly unaware that Caim's behind him. To Noah's amazement, it's the puritan Knott.

Knott parries Caim's first thrust at Arthur's back, but he's thrown off balance. Caim cuts him deeply in the shoulder, and Knott falls to the ground clutching his wound.

Heedless of what has happened behind him, Arthur has nearly reached the chained gate, when Caim plunges his sword through Arthur's back with such force that it emerges through his chest. His eyes go wide as he struggles to breathe. Caim puts a boot to Arthur's back and pulls out his bloody sword, kicking Arthur to the pavement like a despised cur.

Caim smiles cruelly at Noah. "Is this your Master Killigrew, Serjeant?"

Noah makes no reply, but drags Arthur and Knott off Bowyer's Row. He calls over a young pikeman. "Get these two brave men to a surgeon," he commands.

"But, sir," says the pikeman, "we cannot go to the surgeon until the fight's over."

Noah looks at him angrily. "You're not on some remote battlefield, boy. You're in London, where surgeons are a ha'penny apiece."

The young man looks over at Sir John, who's seen the whole exchange from his mount. He nods to the young man. "Take them on one of the weapons carts," he says. Turning to Noah, he adds, "I'm sorry for your loss, Serjeant Ames."

Especially in light of Sir John's extraordinary act of kindness, Noah hasn't the heart to express reciprocal condolences, as Sir John is evidently unaware that Arthur is—or was—a relative of his.

"Thank you, Sir John," is all he can think to say.

———————o○◁▱▷○⟵———————

LORD ESSEX'S FAVORITE PAGE Peter pushes David slowly toward Ludgate at the head of the disorganized crew. As David's hands are only loosely tied, and as he might be shot at any moment, his eyes dart about for a sword the right size for his own hand. He finds a shiny gold-handled one conveniently situated in Peter's scabbard.

When David sees Arthur interpose himself between the warring factions and Caim come up from behind, he knows Arthur's risked his life for *him*, and decides the time has come to show his true colors. Though he promised Meyrick he wouldn't turn his sword against Essex or Southampton, he never promised the same of Caim.

David shakes off the rope, draws Peter's sword, and knocks the page down with a heavy boot. Before anyone can react, he runs to Arthur's aid but, in the few moments it takes for him to reach Arthur, Caim has fought off one defender, run Arthur through, and kicked him to the ground. By the looks of the wound, Arthur is gone.

David stops and raises his sword. His eyes red with anger, he waits for Caim to turn about.

———————o○◁▱▷○⟵———————

NOAH IS POWERLESS to intercede in the confrontation between David and Caim, just as he was powerless to prevent Arthur's death. David is in God's hands now, just as Arthur was but a few moments ago, a fact Noah finds less than comforting. Esther's dream of a blond man being run through at Bowyers' Row has now come true, though the man turns out to have been Arthur, not David.

That gives him at least some hope that at least David will live out the day.

CAIM'S MEN BACK OFF and join Essex's main body, which halts its advance in view of David's challenge to individual combat. Suddenly, Bowyer's Row and Ludgate are motionless and silent but for the soft whir of the cold breeze.

Caim senses the stillness. He turns and comes face to face with the estimable David Killigrew who, in the cold light of day, seems to have been transformed into one of his Viking forbears. He seems taller than usual, his shoulders broad, and his feet set wide.

In David's mind, a single intention is fixed: Caim's bloody death.

Caim's sword hangs in his hand, dripping Arthur's blood onto the pavement.

"Who the devil are you?" he grunts.

"David Killigrew, at your service," replies David, seething with anger.

"What kinda 'service' you providin'?" asks Caim, attempting to enlist his friends in jeering this saucy fellow. But the jest falls flat.

"Executioner's services. I'm *your* executioner," says David mirthlessly.

"Well, if you're Killigrew," says Caim, pointing to Arthur's lifeless body being loaded onto the cart, "then, who's that?"

"Someone whose name you were too stupid to learn and you'll shortly die without knowing. Suffice it to say you were unfit to shine his boots whilst he lived," says David with contempt, shifting his weight threateningly. He sees that his adversary is sweating. "Oh, now I see the poison seeping through your leprous skin. Have at me, venomous toad! And *I* shan't turn my back till you're squashed on the pavement."

"Then, feel my sting, Squire Lackbeard!" The enraged Caim lunges at David with his sword straight out.

Barely moving out of the way, David dodges Caim's thrust and kicks him as he passes. Caim is thrown off-balance by force of his own weight and lands on his shoulder. In obvious pain, he rises, red-faced. "You'll have to lock horns to get the better o' *this* toad!" he shouts, raises his sword, and begins circling David, who circles opposite him.

Since Caim's reach is shorter than David's, he has no choice but to step in close to score a hit. If he tries to stay outside David's reach, all he'll ensure is that David will remain outside *his*. And once David learns that Caim prefers to fight defensively, David can cut him to ribbons with the point of his sword with little risk of injury to himself.

Caim thrusts once more, testing David's reflexes, which seem extraordinarily quick. Twice, three times, Caim swings at David, his steel being met by David's each time.

David begins to admire the gold-handled sword he filched from Essex's page. Its blade is nimble, but its hilt heavy as a bludgeon. The clang of the blades is barely sensible to his hand, while he can see it rattle Caim's sword-hand badly.

Caim is sweating hard now, while David is barely exercised.

Caim comes in with a hard swing. Instead of parrying it, David deliberately meets it with a hard swing of his own and sparks fly from the point of impact. Caim, who can barely hold onto his sword, withdraws a step, his blade visibly notched.

David uses the occasion for a thrust of his own. His point sweeps across Caim's chest. The spectators gasp, forgetting their own peril.

Caim looks down at his chest. The wound is not deep, but it's bloody. He lunges at David recklessly. While he fails to score a hit, his sheer determination throws David backward.

Caim rushes in for the kill, but realizes he's succeeded only in thrusting his belly onto the point of David's outstretched sword. The wound hurts like the very devil, and his belly begins bleeding profusely.

Not one to delay matters, Caim draws a dagger with his opposite hand and lunges at David, cutting him in the upper arm, but David grabs Caim's hand and holds him still as he brings his swordpoint to the base of Caim's neck.

"Drop your sword," David commands him.

"Eat my dagger!" responds Caim, and takes another stab at him. David avoids the blade.

As they tussle, Caim drops his sword inadvertently. David flips his own sword in his hand and bludgeons Caim's face with its golden hilt. The contact is solid, and Caim's eyes roll up into his head. David strikes him once more, harder, in the same place, and Caim's nose bleeds profusely.

David shoves him away, and Caim falls to the pavement, barely conscious. David finds Caim's dropped sword and places it next to his right hand.

"Pick it up!" David shouts at the top of his lungs.

Caim fails to respond, in fact he shows no sign of having heard David's command.

"Pick it up," David repeats, "or I'll kill you where you sit, you sack of shit!"

Caim's eyes are barely open, and his head lolls back and forth without purpose.

"Very well," says David as he raises his sword and prepares to run Caim through at the throat.

"Stop!" Noah commands. "David, you may not kill an unarmed man. You're not an animal!"

But David surely *feels* like an animal, and wants very much to kill the beast that killed his friend and abducted his lady love. As long as this beast lives, he's a danger to her. David spies the dagger in Caim's hand.

"Look!" he shouts. "He still has a dagger!"

"You have subdued him quite, David," says Noah, "and he is unable to respond." Noah approaches David and looks him in the eye. "Please knock the dagger out of his hand," he quietly commands.

"Why? What are you going to do?" shouts David, the blood still pounding in his ears.

"I'm going to arrest him on grounds of high treason against the Crown," says Noah. "Indictments for other crimes will follow."

David nods and appears about to relent when the matter is taken out of their hands.

A madman in black bearing a long dagger runs between them, knocking them apart like a pair of bowling pins and running straight at Caim's seated figure.

"This is for Tobias!" shouts the unmistakable voice of Cuthbert Bennett, as he jams the dagger into Caim's cheek, slicing it open. "No arrest for you, you bastard!" The prone figure of Caim reacts with what appears to be no more than a reflexive effort at avoidance.

Cuthbert stabs Caim in the neck repeatedly, until there's nothing visible holding up his head and he collapses onto his back, his unseeing eyes fixed on the indifferent sky.

Suddenly, Cuthbert sucks in a breath and staggers backward. As he turns toward Noah with a stunned expression, his hands are holding his belly. Black blood flows over them onto the pavement. Apparently, Caim had more of his senses about him than anyone realized.

David seizes Cuthbert in a hug to keep him from falling. But Cuthbert's eyes are locked on Noah's.

"I'm sorry, Serjeant Ames," says Cuthbert weakly, offering Noah a deathly rictus, breathing heavily. "I did my best. I suppose I've … just … never been much … for the law." He coughs convulsively and his face goes white.

Cuthbert looks quizzically at the figure holding him up, as though he's forgot who it is. David turns his tearful face to Cuthbert, so he can see it. "No, don't weep, David," says Cuthbert pathetically. "It's your lot in life … to be … Cheerful." Cuthbert's head falls backward and death overtakes him, peace blossoming on his face as has not been seen there in many a year.

David carries Cuthbert's body to the same weapons cart that left a few minutes ago and has just now returned. He puts the body down and closes the eyes gently. Turning away from those looking on, he prays over his friend's body.

The young pikeman who drove the cart away and then back again, seeing what's transpired, walks meekly up to Noah and says, "I'm sorry, sir. Your young barrister friend has … passed. The surgeon said he surely died before he hit the ground. His remains are dispatched to the Tower. The other one, the puritan, is gravely injured but he should recover." He bows deeply and, seeing there may be more bodies for carting, returns to the weapons cart to await orders.

Bowyer's Row is silent, the opposing factions overcome with the intensely personal violence they just witnessed. Noah takes the gold-handled sword from David and, holding the hilt to the fore to show he has no violent intentions, returns it to Essex's page. The page accepts it and bows deeply to Noah.

Lord Essex himself stands erect beside his page. Noah whispers in the earl's ear so quietly that not even the page can hear.

"*You* summoned the butcher, m'lord. Is it not madness that *others* must pay so much of his bill?" He waits a moment for the point to sink in, then destroys any remaining hope Essex may have that help could yet arrive from another quarter. "Meyrick is *arrested* at the Tower."

As all eyes are on Essex, he maintains his erect posture, but his eyes drop to the ground and he holds his advance in respectful abeyance until Noah and David have moved Cuthbert's body to the cart formerly driven by Arthur, and clop away back toward the Tower.

Caim's body will lie a long time where he fell.

CHAPTER 37

CUTHBERT'S BODY LIES in the rear of the cart, covered with an oilcloth. It bounces with every bump in the street, and Noah and David cringe each time it falls back to the cart with a macabre thump.

The Tower comes into view, and with it the end of their brief but mournful journey. At last, they break their somber silence.

"The fellowship of the jesters was further broken today," says David.

Noah nods pensively. "Doubly. Two jesters lost in one afternoon."

I suppose," says David, "you're grieving for all the wonderful times you and Arthur would have had, in and out of court, had he lived."

"Yes," says Noah equivocally, "that's the selfish kind of grief, though, pitying oneself for the loss of a dear friend. The *unselfish* part is even more difficult to come to terms with, for it requires contemplation of all that an energetic, wise young man will never experience because his life has been cut short.

"No more summer days with his lady fair, no icy swims in the sunshine. No meals fit for a king. No more victories of his own, nor the precious vicarious victories of his children. Never a wife shall he have, nor a family, nor his own barrister's practice, although he'd begun to make good headway on that score. It makes you take stock of everything that comprises a whole life, and then it makes you knack off everything he'll miss. Such butchery, though figurative only, is almost too painful to contemplate." He shakes his head mournfully. "Oh, I should *never* have let him come with me from the Tower."

"You couldn't foresee," offers David, "that he would disobey your order to return to the safety of the Tower once trouble began."

There's a long silence as they approach the Tower gate. "*Couldn't* I foresee it, though?" asks Noah. "It's foreseeable that men will make mistakes. Young men make *many*, some foolish." He turns to David. "Such as grabbing someone else's sword and fighting a known killer to the death. Well, I shall make no more such mistakes with young men today. You shall remain at the Tower until I call or send for you in writing."

"Oh, but sir …" says David.

Noah avoids looking David in the eye to remove some of the bite from his stern tone. "David, there shall be no discussion of this. Unless I have your oath to await my instructions before leaving the Tower, I shall personally toss you into a cell and hand the key to Sir Walter." He stamps his foot emphatically on the rail, and tears come to his eyes. "By God, *you* shall have those days in the sunshine with your lady fair, and all the rest life can give you." His stridency wanes. "And you'll remember Arthur from time to time, and only wish he could share those days with you. Cuthbert, too, though he had a hard, *hard* life."

"But shall my halcyon days be spent with *Esther*?" muses David.

Noah looks at him sidelong. "Yes, David. *With* Esther. Do not doubt it. You two love each other so strongly that watching you argue is equally agonizing and humorous. I'll not let a misunderstanding over where you spent a few days stand between you two and happiness. Jonathan would have resolved this himself had he not been so distracted with Jessica, and then Essex."

The Tower Guard admits them, and they pass through the portcullis. As they enter the yard, Noah says, "Let's go straight to Sir Walter's office. Perhaps he'll have more news."

As they tie off the cart outside Raleigh's office, they find him asleep in his chair.

"I don't think I've ever seen him asleep before," whispers Noah. "He must have been up for days."

Sir Walter evidently hears him, for he sputters and coughs himself awake. "Good evening, gentlemen," he says. "What news?"

"We left Ludgate a few minutes ago," says Noah, "which had been chained by Her Majesty's men, blocking Essex's way home. When we left, Essex's diminishing band was preparing to storm the chained gate. We barristers suffered several casualties before the fighting began in earnest."

"The gate was chained? Bloody good idea! Who's in charge there?"

"Sir John Leveson."

"Who put *him* in charge?" asks Sir Walter. "Ordinarily, he would act only by command of the Bishop of London. And you mentioned casualties?"

Noah bites his lip, and his voice breaks slightly. "Arthur Arden was slain without provocation by Essex's footman Caim."

"*Young Arthur?*" says Sir Walter in disbelief. "He was here at the

Tower this afternoon."

Noah sighs. "Her Majesty suggested I bring him with me to Essex House. While we sought leave to cross through Ludgate, Essex's contingent began a slow advance on the gate with *this* young man as prisoner"—he points to David—"being pushed along at the fore, when a musket was fired on each side. At the same moment, Caim arrived with a few of his thugs—by way of the Thames, I believe. Instead of returning to the Tower as I'd instructed, Arthur interceded, trying to dissuade the Queen's men from firing on David. Caim—may his vile name never be heard again—ran Arthur through from the rear. A young fellow deflected Caim's first thrust on Arthur, but he was off-balance and was himself hurt and put out of commission."

"Was this brave fellow a puritan?" asks Sir Walter.

"Yes," replies Noah with surprise.

"I may be mistaken," says Sir Walter, "but I expect he's in the infirmary here at the Tower. The Warders told me that a wounded puritan was brought in at the same time as a ... a body. I expect that's Arthur. Oh, my. This is awful. Has Arthur kin?"

Noah nods. "He's a cousin of Sir Henry Neville. Also, of Leveson, though I haven't calculated degrees of kinship among them."

"Well, we can pay our respects to Leveson later. As for Sir Henry, I suppose we could send someone after him, as he only just left for Dover this morning."

Noah freezes, barely able to breathe. So that *was* Sir Henry at Whitehall early this morning!

"I suppose Sir Henry only got his money from the Exchequer this morning," says Noah, testing Sir Walter's knowledge.

"No, in fact he got it some days ago, but only *left* this morning."

Noah's heart sinks with dread. Sir Henry appears indeed to be the Queen's 'enemy' of which she spoke in Noah's awful dream. He expels the thought from his mind once again, lest something be read in his expression that could incriminate Sir Henry.

"But our tale is not done yet," says Noah. "David subdued Caim in a sword fight, in fact beat him nearly to death. As Caim was unable to answer further challenge, however, I forbade David to finish him off."

"You *what?*" exclaims Sir Walter in disbelief, looking to David. David shrugs, as though to say, *You see what I have to put up with?* "God save us from these meddlesome lawyers!" says Sir Walter. "So, what happened then?"

"Then, Cuthbert Bennett," resumes Noah, "whose twin brother had been murdered by Caim at the same place some months ago, took it upon himself to rush forward and stab Caim to death. Unfortunately, Caim was not too disabled before dying to administer a fatal wound to Cuthbert, whose body now lies in the cart outside. If I may, Sir Walter, I wish to entrust those remains to you. The horse and cart belong to the Tower. I wish to entrust David also to your care, as I seem to be doing poorly today protecting fine young men. If he tries to leave, please lock him up. Meanwhile, I need to speak with Lord Saint Ives. Is he at the Tower?"

"Last I saw his lordship, he was at the Warder's mess." He regards Noah skeptically. "Did you say earlier that you spoke to the Queen before leaving the Tower?"

Noah realizes he's put his foot in the punch. "Aye. Very briefly."

"But the Queen's been at Whitehall this whole time."

"I would love to stay, Sir Walter, but I really must go now." With that Noah rises, and leaves Sir Walter and David wondering what his sudden departure was all about.

A short time later, Noah finds Jonathan at the infirmary holding an open prayer book, praying silently over Arthur's body.

Noah stands at the door without bringing attention to his arrival. His heart goes out to Jonathan, especially in light of the close relationship he had with Arthur at Eton.

Jonathan looks up tearfully from his prayer book and sees Noah watching him. "Oh, Father!" he says, running to Noah's arms. "Arthur is dead! Oh, it's just so hard."

"It's hard beyond words," says Noah, nearly choking.

Jonathan looks at Noah. "Did you know?"

Noah nods. "I was there, Jonathan. He had no chance. He was trying to stop the Queen's men from firing on David, who was Essex's captive at the time."

"Damn that man!" cries Jonathan.

"Keep your voice down, m'lord," he says. "However we feel about Lord Essex, he's not the one who killed Arthur. That was Caim."

Jonathan looks at him with a smoking fury in his eyes.

Noah shakes his head. "Caim is already dead, Jon."

"Who killed him?" asks Jonathan.

"David Killigrew cut him badly with sword, and knocked him cold."

A look approaching laughter crosses Jon's face. "Little Cheerful?"

"I don't know if you've noticed it, Jon, but 'Little Cheerful' is taller and broader than you are. And he's a hell of a swordsman. But I wouldn't allow him to execute Caim once he'd incapacitated him."

"So how did Caim die?" asks Jonathan.

"He was 'executed,' for lack of a better word, by Cuthbert Bennett."

"And how are David and Cuthbert?"

"David is fine, Jonathan. He's here at the Tower and shall remain here for the remainder of the day."

"And Cuthbert?" asks Jonathan warily.

"His body will be brought here in a few minutes."

"Caim killed *him*, too?" asks Jonathan.

Noah nods sadly.

"I wonder how Cuthbert escaped from Jacob. In any event, I shall have to notify Jacob that he's dead."

Noah nods. "Summon Jacob here, Jonathan, please. I don't wish either you or David to leave here for the moment."

WITH ONLY CAIM'S BODY SEPARATING the two sides, Essex and his men advance on the chain blocking their path across Ludgate.

On the Queen's side, Leveson orders his pikemen to thrust their pikes forward in formation. With so few firearms on Essex's side, Leveson hopes to hold them off with pikes alone. If a few of Essex's men are deeply cut, that's all it should take to halt their advance.

But Essex changes tack, summoning his few pistoliers to assemble and take aim at the pikemen.

Before Essex's order can be obeyed, Leveson orders *his* pikemen to part, so that two rows of five musketeers can advance to the chain, and prepare to engage by dropping to one knee. By standing order, the first volley is to go over the heads of Essex's men. "Ready!" Leveson shouts. The rearmost rank stands and takes aim. "Fire!" he shouts.

Five muskets fire at once. The noise is staggering. Leveson is shocked to see that one of the shots has gone low and knocked Essex's tall hat straight off his head, making a clean hole through it at a point not much higher than the brim.

The musketeers who fired drop to one knee to reload while the other rank rises and prepares to fire into the meat of the uprising. As Essex's pistoliers have scattered, however, Leveson hesitates. His orders are to arrest these men, not slaughter them *en masse*.

"To sword!" shouts Essex, drawing his sword for the first time today.

"Pikemen to the sword!" shouts Leveson in immediate reply. "Ranks One, Two, and Three, advance under the chain!"

What follows is a furious melée on Bowyer's Row.

Surprisingly few are hurt or killed. One 'Waite' is killed by Essex's stepfather Blount, but in truth that's a grudge murder based on real or imagined sins of long ago.

In Leveson's command, the only men killed in the actual fighting are three of the Queen's pikemen.

Two of Essex's favorites are also killed in the fighting. One is a civilian named 'Henry Tracy,' whom Essex loved dearly and whose death is a grave blow to his spirit. The other is Essex's page Peter who unwittingly lent his sword to David Killigrew.

As Essex calls a general retreat, Peter lies splayed, face-down on the pavement. Near his motionless right hand lies his gold-handled sword, its blade broken in two.

Leveson forbears from ordering pursuit.

As Essex's diminishing contingent scrambles away west down Watling Street, Essex can be seen stopping at every corner to peer south down each street until at last he finds one unblocked by the Queen's men that will lead him to the Thames. He ultimately escapes with his men down Bow Lane to Queenhythe Wharf.

Leveson shakes his head in wonderment. *Who the devil is this Essex?* Is it possible he's a *peer*, yet unable to foresee that an uprising against the Crown will be resisted? Could he be an *Englishman* who expects the Crown's resistance to be so perfunctory that he fails to plan for it? Could Essex be a *general* whose retreating soldiers are about to hire *wherries* to return them to Essex House stairs, like so many gentlemen returning from an afternoon play at Bankside? He shakes his head in dismay. How could any such man ever have been placed at the head of an army?

"Madness," he mutters.

A dozen voracious birds descend on Caim's trampled corpse.

JACOB IS BROUGHT TO JONATHAN in a private room at the Tower. Considering that Jacob knew Cuthbert only a few weeks before his death, his grief at the news seems disproportionate.

Jacob blows his nose in his handkerchief. "I thank you, m'lord, for having me come here before I was told of Cuthbert's passing. He was a fine young man. Finer—and *sharper*—I've never encountered. I kinda got used to him helpin' me with record keepin'. That's very important for somebody in my position, y'see, handlin' dear and delicate goods all day, every day. He never failed to account for so much as a farthin'. And he treated the missus with great respect and care. She needs so *much* care," he says, "it's gettin' to be more than I can manage."

"What is her affliction," asks Jonathan, "if I may ask?"

"Well," says Jacob, "the physicians say they've seen it before, but no one's given it a name. About ten years after we got married, she started complainin' she couldn't see, even when she could. I had no idea what to make of that. Then, one very long, hot summer she started to complain that there was a tinglin' run down her spine. Since then, she's lost more and more control of her hands, her balance. She's 'slowly failing,' is all they can say. I just feel lucky she's with me still. We live ... day to day, y'know."

"I suppose as long as you can work, you'll do fine," suggests Jonathan.

"You'd think so, m'lord, but those drapers can be very demandin'. That's one reason it was such a relief to have Master Cuthbert around to help." He looks down sadly. "If they needed somethin' on the spot and I couldn't get away from the missus, he'd be right there. And they'd be happy to see 'im, too. I know I shouldn't be surprised by that, him bein' a trained barrister and all. He told me all about his life, and it was a tough one, I'll say. Mebbe someday you'll want to hear it."

"I will," says Jonathan, "very much."

"So, m'lord," says Jacob, "have they finally put down this rebellion I been hearin' about all day?"

"I think matters will shortly be in hand," says Jonathan. "I was involved in an arrest of one of the rebels right here at the Tower."

Jacob's eyes go wide. "Really? Who was it?"

"Well, I'm not sure I should say."

Jacob smiles. "If he was arrested, m'lord, there's bound to be an appearance in court, and all that information'll be public soon."

"I suppose it will," says Jonathan. "Okay, I'll tell, but let's keep it between us, shall we?"

"Who'm I gonna tell?" says Jacob, looking as old and innocent as possible.

"It was Sir Gelly Meyrick," says Jonathan.

Jacob's mouth hangs open, as though he's being put on. "No. Not Gelly Meyrick?"

"I assure you, Jacob, it was he. I've known him a long time. The first time I saw him, I was but a small child, when he knocked over Goodwife Graves' selling booth on the street."

Jacob regards him askance. "Tell me, m'lord. Did ye see that happen?"

"No, I was—"

"Did it happen more than once?" asks Jacob.

"No, I'm fairly certain it didn't. Why?"

"Well, I don't know how to tell ye this, m'lord, but he's not the one who knocked her over. I remember it like it was yesterday. Some drunken officer in Her Majesty's Navy. I recognized him 'cause I'd seen him a few times before at the docks. He was two sheets to the wind and rode through the little marketplace like he was ridin' a bull. Knocked over Goodwife Graves' and a half-dozen other booths."

"Gelly Meyrick?"

"No, m'lord," Jacob says. "Meyrick was a *customer* at the market. He was buyin' some vegetables. Anyway, after doin' all this damage, this drunkard's horse stops right in front of Meyrick. He falls off his horse *onto* Meyrick, leavin' im with plenty o' scrapes and bruises, and *takes a swing* at 'im!"

"At Meyrick?" asks Jonathan incredulously. "You *saw* this?"

"Saw the whole thing, m'lord. Meyrick beat 'em good. When he was done with this officer, a bunch o' men, mostly 'usbands of the women whose goods had been ruined, hustled 'im off to another part o' town, tied off his horse, and put 'im back in the saddle, sound asleep. They left him there. By the time he was found—or come to his senses—he 'ad no idea how he'd gotten all black and blue. But I expect it wasn't his first time. He was no good to nobody when he was drunk, which was most o' the time."

Jonathan is amazed at the inaccuracy of his own recollection. "What happened to Meyrick?" he asks.

"He got fixed up by a local woman. She was a—waddya call?— midwife. She gave him some whiskey and bound up his wounds. He was still cussin' that drunk when she was all finished with him, prob'ly an hour later."

"But I have a distinct recollection of him shouting a denunciation of the local people."

Jacob smiles. "Sure! He got drunk. He 'denounced,' as you say, everybody on this earth. I think Her Majesty even got in there a coupla times. I'm sure *I* was on the list. Sort of a dishonorable mention, if ye take my meanin'. But he never raised a hand to nobuddy but that officer, nor confronted nobuddy else face-to-face."

"So, he did us a good turn?" asks Jonathan.

Jacob nods equivocally. "*Graves* thought so."

CHAPTER 38

AS ESSEX CLIMBS OUT of the wherry onto Essex House stairs, he's alarmed to find that one of his larger boats is missing. He storms into the house apprehensively and barges into the rear study where he left the hostages.

A few friends mill about, reading books. Otherwise, the study's vacant.

"Where's Gorges?" asks Essex.

The browsers look up him curiously. "Good e'en, your lordship," they say, bowing. Essex is too dismayed to return the greeting.

Lord Sands, a white-haired gentleman, approaches Essex just as Southampton comes in. "Pardon me, your lordship," says the old man, "but we thought you were aware that Sir Ferdinando left with your guests."

"Guests?" says Essex blankly.

"Yes, m'lord," says Sands, "your guests ... from Whitehall. The Lord Chief Justice, the Lord Keeper, and the other two gentlemen."

Southampton moans miserably. "Do you mean to say Gorges released them contrary to my orders?" demands Essex.

"No, m'lord, rather in *conformity* with your written order," says the old fellow, glancing about the library. "Oh, where is it?" he asks himself. Turning back to Essex, he says, "Well, Sir Ferdinando showed us your written order calling for the release of the gentlemen. I suppose he took it with him when he rowed them to Whitehall."

Essex places both hands on his head in dismay and turns to Southampton, who takes charge. "Lord Sands," says Southampton, "please escort these gentlemen to the parlor so that his lordship and I may be alone for a while."

But the old fellow is too deaf to hear the request fully. "Certainly, m'lord," he says nonetheless. He turns away, but then turns back as though he'd forgot something. "How did things pass in Cheapside, m'lord?"

Southampton takes the old man gently by the elbow and escorts him toward the door. "All in good time, m'lord. All in good time."

The old fellow smiles and leans into Southampton as though to give him some confidential advice. "Remember this, m'lord: The most resolute counsels are the safest. 'Tis more honorable for a nobleman to die fighting than at the hand of the executioner."

Southampton glances discreetly at Essex and sees that, unfortunately, he overheard this aged prophet of doom. Southampton bows to Sands. "Thank you, m'lord, for your words of encouragement," he says drily.

Sands dodders up the hall. Seeing him escorted out, the other browsers follow, bowing silently as they leave.

Essex is dismal. "My God, Wriothesley, what have I done? Without hostages, we have no bargaining chips to use with the Queen." He covers his eyes with his hands. "We're at her mercy."

Southampton compounds Essex's lament. "We've created the worst conceivable conditions, Robert, for justice in our own case. We'll stand accused of assembling a rump rebellion against the Queen and taking hostage the highest judicial officer in the land. And before whom shall we be haled? Why, the selfsame Queen and the selfsame judge!" He shakes his head. "We'll be lucky to get out of this alive. We can forget about mercy."

"Piss on mercy!" says Essex angrily. "The most I'm guilty of is riot ... and there were mitigating circumstances."

"Oh?" says Southampton. "And what were those? That the Queen cut off your income? Be earnest, Robert. A half-dozen men lie dead on Bowyer's Row."

"Meanwhile," replies Essex, "we must prepare for the worst, to the extent we can. Please have all my papers on the top floor thrown in the fire and burned thoroughly, and prepare the house for assault. Have the men stack the books before the windows, and have every man arm himself as best he may."

Southampton leaves for only as long as necessary to relay Essex's orders, and returns to his side.

A considerable time later, John the stableman knocks at the library door and enters. "M'lords, will Caim be returning soon? He's gone a long time, and my hands are full with the horses, let alone the door."

Southampton responds in measured tones. "Master Caim will not be returning. He has ... passed."

The stableman shakes his head. "More awful news."

"Did you have someone to announce?" asks Southampton.

"Yes, m'lord. There's a little army out front. They've asked to speak with m'Lord Essex."

"How many men?" demands Essex.

The stableman shrugs. "I can see about fifty, m'lord, but it's dark outside and I can't see 'em all."

The earls failed to notice how late they arrived or how long they'd remained in the library, but a glance at the clock confirms that it's very nearly nine o'clock.

"Who's at the head of this little army?" asks Essex.

"Lord Grey, m'lord."

"Lord Grey!" Southampton exclaims. "Lord Grey, who cut off my servant's hand and got himself tossed into the Fleet for it? *That* Lord Grey?"

The stableman blushes, apparently uncertain whether he's been admonished, and says tentatively, "I ... believe so, m'lord."

Essex intervenes with the stableman. "If you can manage it, please avoid speaking with Lord Grey. Ask if we can speak with the Lord Admiral instead."

The stableman bows and heads toward the gate, leaving the two earls alone again.

Essex pats Southampton on the shoulder comfortingly. "Don't be too fearful of what these people have in store for us, Wriothesley. They're all relatives of ours."

"That's what most *concerns* me," mutters Southampton.

The stableman returns, hesitant to speak, his face ashen.

"Speak, man!" says Essex.

"M'lord, Lord Grey asks you to commend him to the Lord Admiral. He says you'll find the Lord Admiral in the garden."

"Which garden?" asks Essex.

The stableman points to the river door. "Your own garden, m'lord."

Though momentarily confused, Essex and Southampton quickly realize what Lord Grey intended to convey, namely, that Essex House is already surrounded, besieged by both land and water.

To confirm their suspicion, with his fingers Southampton draws aside a few inches of the heavy curtain that hangs on the rear window in winter to suppress the draft from the Thames. There on the river, no more than fifty yards away, loom two river craft, perhaps not seaworthy, but each armed with two large cannon.

"There are four cannon on the river aimed at the house," says Southampton to Essex. "In your garden, the Lord Admiral is calmly conversing with a man in his late thirties having curly blond hair."

"Is it Sir Robert Sidney?" asks Essex.

Southampton opens his eyes wide for a better look. "Aye," he says.

"Let's see if we can talk to him," suggests Essex.

"I'm quite certain we can," replies Southampton.

"That's uncharacteristically optimistic of you, Wriothesley. What makes you so sure?"

There's a firm but polite knock on the river door.

"That's his servant," says Southampton. He shouts for the stableman minding the gate. "A servant of Sir Robert Sidney is at the river door," he tells the stableman. "He's about to request a parley. Tell him that we consent to a parley at which Sir Robert remains in the garden, and we speak with him from the balcony."

In a few minutes, a parley has been sounded and the Lord Admiral has been rowed by wherry to one of the gunships in the river. Essex and Southampton peer down at Sidney from the balcony.

"Dear Cousin Sidney," says Southampton, "to whom would you have us yield? To our enemies?"

"No," replies Sidney, "you must yield yourselves to Her Majesty."

All the while, the ladies within Essex House can be heard weeping and crying out.

Southampton confers privately with Essex. "That would we willingly," says Southampton to Sidney, "unless by doing so we confess ourselves guilty without having offended. Yet, if the Lord Admiral will yield us honorable hostages to assure our safe return to this place, we will go and present ourselves before Her Majesty, to whom (God knows) we never intended the least harm and whose royal disposition we know to be such that we might but freely declare our minds to her, she would pardon us, and blame those at court who plotted against us. Is it likely that *we*, who have often risked our lives for Her Majesty and her realm, should now turn traitors? No, cousin, we detest all traitorous actions."

Sidney shakes his head. "You must not bargain with your prince, my lord. And you must know that m'Lord Admiral will not yield to any such condition of hostages."

"But cousin," says Southampton, "if we yield ourselves to you, we'll be placing ourselves in the mouths of those very wolves who would eat us before we can make our case to Her Majesty. Tell me, cousin, what would you do in our position?"

Sidney sighs. "Good cousin, I would not be in your position. I think you're best off yielding *now*. The Lord Admiral has already sent for powder and ordnance enough to blow Essex House to the moon, and you know the house is not made to survive such warlike measures."

"How could the Lord Admiral do so, to men who've fought so hard for Her Majesty?"

"M'lord," says Sidney, "your past deeds on Her Majesty's behalf are well known and will surely be pleaded in the appropriate forum. This parley is no place for such considerations. And, as you know, I am no judge."

"Will you take our proposal of hostages to the Lord Admiral? We would accept as such a hostage even so lowly a person as the Queen's Jew."

Sidney, making no pretense that such an entreaty might have a chance of success, agrees to take their proposal to the Lord Admiral. A short while later, he returns and calls the earls out to the balcony again. The ladies inside the house are crying ever more stridently.

"The Lord Admiral," he shouts, "will not hear of hostages for 'rebels,' which is the word he uses for my lords. Having spent the day at Whitehall, the Lord Admiral assures my lords, of his own knowledge, that the good Serjeant has been neither seen nor heard from there since quite early this morning—"

Southampton nods to Essex. Essex was right; Ames *is* too proud to violate an oath.

"—and that he knows not the present whereabouts of Serjeant Ames. The Lord Admiral said that he would not give any hostage to rebels: Not the Queen's Jew, nor the Queen's jester, nor her cat, nor the clippings of her royal fingernails. He has humanely authorized me, however, to offer to allow the ladies promptly to leave the house before pressing his advantage."

Southampton confers with Essex. "Please thank the Lord Admiral for his kind offer and return him thusly: We have now fortified our doors, which took us a long while. If we are to *unfortify* them to set our ladies forth, we shall thereby make an open passage for your forces to enter, which we are confident is not the Lord Admiral's purpose in making this humane proposal. If the Lord Admiral would grant us an hour to open the passage for our ladies, and another hour when they're gone to *refortify* it, we will willingly suffer our ladies to depart."

A short time later, Sidney returns with the Lord Admiral's acceptance of such terms.

Essex and Southampton breathe a sigh of relief. At least they won't be required to sacrifice their ladies' lives. And the extra hours will provide more time to consider whether, should they choose to go down fighting, it would be just and fitting to drag their remaining followers along to their doom.

JONATHAN WISHES JACOB FAREWELL, with a well-intentioned promise to find a way for Jacob to serve at the new house in Holborn, once finished. As Jacob walks across the yard to the small gate, his gait seems more somber than when he arrived. That much was to be expected. But he also seems—older somehow.

Noah walks in, breaking Jonathan's reverie. "How did Jacob take the news of Cuthbert's passing?" he asks.

"About as well as can be expected, I suppose," says Jonathan. "Do you know what he told me—of my own past, I mean?"

"Well," says Noah, dubious of the vagueness of the question. "I know a good deal of what he's told you in the past. But what he told you just now? I haven't a clue."

Jonathan plops down in his chair. "He said that Gelly Meyrick was entirely innocent of knocking down Goodwife Graves, and that instead Meyrick badly beat the drunk who did it."

Noah sits to get a better look at Jonathan's face. "Then what of your recollection that he berated the victims, saying they got what they deserved?"

"Well, I never said he berated them *to their faces*. As it turns out, when he said those things, he was under the care of a local midwife who was attending to his wounds and who'd given him plenty of spirits to cover the pain. He was simply railing at all and sundry—regardless whether they were at fault—or even *involved*."

Noah sees that Jonathan has learned a great deal about the limits of memory, as well as of his tendency to judge harshly where the interests of loved ones are concerned.

"Are you glad you didn't need to kill Meyrick today?" asks Noah flippantly.

"Don't think I didn't consider doing it before he surrendered," says Jonathan, "but at this moment I'm quite relieved he never gave me cause either today—"

"Or at the ferry in Oxfordshire?" says Noah. "Don't forget you nearly killed him at the Boar's Head in Cheapside."

Jonathan looks at him, chagrined. "Here I am, being contrite, and you throw those incidents up in my face?"

Noah smiles wanly, though he's truly exhausted. It occurs to him that there's someone else here at the Tower who might be taught not to judge others too harshly.

WHILE ESSEX VACILLATES numerous times between the alternatives of fighting to the death and yielding, at last he decides to yield.
Although the choice is painful, the loss to be occasioned by the death of
all these good men is simply too great to be justified by an act of what
may be called honor, but may in fact be little more than personal pique.

It's full dark by the time Essex's wife and the other ladies are led
downstairs into the cold. The lawn is full of men's faces lit by the greasy
light of smoky torches. Torches light the Strand and a Westminster
church.

To one side kneel Essex and Southampton, their hands tied and heads
lowered.

Lady Essex speaks to the Lord Admiral. "M'lord, have you agreed to
report my husband's testimony to Her Majesty, and to assure him the
company of a divine in his confinement?"

The Lord Admiral bows. "I have, m'lady, and I reaffirm my agreement now." Lady Essex nods and proceeds to a waiting carriage that
clops off at once.

M'lord Admiral," says Essex, "I remind you that not all the men
indoors have agreed to yield. I commend your men to prepare to defend
themselves if they proceed into the house."

Troops chosen for the occasion step forward and enter the house. Not
a minute later, a dozen muffled gunshots are heard coming from the
bedrooms, while accompanying flashes of light penetrate the windows
into the night.

Southampton shakes his head. "That will be Owen Salisbury."

A moment later, four dead men are carried out, two defenders and
two besiegers.

The Lord Admiral summons one of his officers. "It's too dark to pass
under the bridge reliably. Take m'Lords of Essex and Southampton and
this lot to Lambeth House," he says, pointing to a half-dozen high-level
conspirators. "The Archbishop has rooms and guards waiting. At sunrise,
bring them all to the Tower by boat." He points to the remaining men.
"Take these to the Newgate and Fleet prisons, however many they can
each take, but keep them separate from the rest of the prisoners. I won't
have you lose track of any of them."

And thus was the rebellion quashed.

CHAPTER 39

NOAH AND JONATHAN sit asleep on their chairs in the room where Jacob was informed of Cuthbert's death. While they sleep, David joins them on a third chair and promptly falls asleep, as well.

Noah's awakened by a wild cheer from the Tower Guard. One of the smaller alarum bells begins to ring. Jonathan and David are so exhausted, they merely shift uncomfortably in their chairs.

A young member of the Tower Guard knocks on the open door.

"The Earls of Essex and Southampton have surrendered, Serjeant Ames," says the guard. "They're at the Archbishop's in Lambeth, and they'll be brought here by boat at sunrise. The Lord Admiral has arrived here at the Tower."

"Praised be the Lord," mutters Noah. He looks at Jonathan's and David's sleepy young faces and thinks fondly that they'll be retelling the tale of this day for the rest of their lives. Then the memory of the day's losses occurs to him and his relief is overshadowed by grief once more. "Why did the Lord Admiral come to the Tower?" he asks.

"That's just it, suh," says the young man. "Her Majesty is evidently gone from Whitehall, and his lordship's not quite sure *where* she is." He regards Noah tentatively. "Sir Walter said you might know where she can be found. Is that so?"

"Oh, that's right," says Noah, remembering his audience with Her Majesty earlier today. "I'll go and fetch Her Majesty."

"*You'll* go and fetch her, suh?"

Noah shrugs. "I don't think anyone else knows how to reach her, except Lord Robert. Where's he?"

"At Whitehall. So says the Lord Admiral. Stay here, suh. I'll be right back."

In a few minutes, a small platoon marches up to the door, awakening Jonathan and David at last.

Lord Grey—the very Lord Grey who intruded into Noah's meeting with the Knights Percy at the Saracen's Head, who recklessly cut off the hand of Southampton's boy and was tossed into the Fleet for it, and who led the "little army" out of Whitehall this afternoon—marches in and orders Noah to come out to speak to the Lord Admiral.

The Lord Admiral looks askance at Noah. "This young Warder informs me, Serjeant, that you know Her Majesty's location. Is that correct?"

"Not precisely, Lord Admiral," says Noah. "I—"

The young Warder interrupts him. "It's what he told me, Lord Admiral."

"It's not quite," says Noah. "I said I'd go and fetch her."

"From where?" asks the Lord Admiral skeptically.

"From the place of safety where Her Majesty has chosen to conceal herself."

"And where is *that*?"

"I don't rightly know, m'lord."

"Then how can you fetch her?" The Lord Admiral is losing patience, and Noah realizes that if he simply continues to answer questions, he'll soon be severely punished.

"M'lord, I ask that you follow me to a place on the grounds appointed by Her Majesty for me to fetch her. Haven't I earned that much credibility?"

"Go. We'll follow."

Noah begins the walk to the little kitchen cottage where first he met the Queen. He finds the jangling of swords and buckles behind him unnerving, as though he's being marched off to a cell, or worse. He stops before the cottage and waits for the soldiers to stop, which they do smartly.

"Very well, Serjeant," says the Lord Admiral impatiently. "What must be done now?"

"A song must be sung," says Noah, realizing how ridiculous that must sound. There's a general muttering from the soldiers who, until now, had been admirably behaved.

"And what song shall we sing, Serjeant?"

"Your *men* can sing all night long if they wish," says Noah with a shrug, "but Her Majesty will ignore them."

The Lord Admiral grabs Noah by the collar. "Listen, Serjeant. Today, these brave men and I besieged Essex House, which was occupied by a force hostile to Her Majesty's reign. Several of them have lost compatriots. We've all been up since dawn, and we're fresh out of patience. You, on the other hand, woke up whenever you felt fit and floated through the day—"

"Pardon me, Lord Admiral," replies Noah testily, still in his hostile grasp. "Today, I stood between two opposing factions who were ready to rip each other apart. I lost two of my most helpful young barristers to Lord Essex's footman, and they were murdered at a distance no greater than you are from me now. They both now lie in cerements in the Tower infirmary. If you choose to hang me or beat me, that is m'lord's prerogative … but please don't tell me I had an easy day."

The Lord Admiral softens, and he releases Noah.

Noah continues. "I have been ordered not to disclose the location at which Her Majesty will appear, nor the song which *I* must sing for Her Majesty to bring her forward."

The Lord Admiral looks at him sternly. "I countermand that order. You shall tell me right now."

"Lord Admiral, most respectfully," says Noah, "there is one person in this realm whose order my lord is powerless to countermand. I cannot disobey the order on your say-so."

The Lord Admiral walks apart from his troops and beckons Noah calmly over. He speaks very quietly. "Go and do what you must to cause Her Majesty to appear, but do not leave this cottage. You'd better hope it works, or I'll hang you *regardless* of the day you've had. Now, go."

Noah bows deeply. He lights a taper off one of the torches and walks in through the same door he used more than forty years ago. He closes it behind him. *Please God this had better work,* he thinks. "Please be there, Majesty," he mutters.

And then in the purest and loudest voice he can muster, he sings in the tune of *Greensleeves*:

Alas my love you do me wrong
To cast me off discourteously;
And I have loved you oh so long
Delighting in your company.

Nothing happens.

He glances sidelong out the window at the Lord Admiral. *Oh, God, I'm going to hang.* Perhaps she was too far away to hear. He begins again:

Alas my love you do me wrong
To cast me off discourteously—

Her Majesty's voice comes from an impossibly long way off, but the distance seems to diminish with each line:

Greensleeves was my delight,
Greensleeves my heart of gold
Greensleeves was my heart of joy
And who but my lady Greensleeves.

Noah falls to his knees with his back to the fireplace and, from the opposite hallway, in walks Queen Elizabeth, the Red Lady. She stops as soon as she spies him.

"Noah, you look as though you've seen a ghost. Did you think I would abandon you?"

"Never, Majesty, but the Lord Admiral was losing patience, and—"

She interrupts him, frowning. "Where is Essex?"

"He yielded and was taken at Essex House, Majesty. He is disarmed, toothless, and in the custody of the Archbishop at Lambeth. He'll be brought here tomorrow morning ... and that's all I know."

"And all one *need* know," adds the Queen. "The Lord Admiral will surely know more. Open the door and announce me, Noah. I want to see who hesitates to bend the knee."

Noah stands, bows, opens the door behind him, and moves backward through the doorway. He turns toward the Lord Admiral.

"Gentlemen, your full attention, please!" he says in his broadest and loudest tones, which is entirely unnecessary, as every man is standing at attention and all eyes are already upon him, including the Warders on every parapet and walkway.

"I give you Her Majesty Elizabeth, by the Grace of God, Queen of England, France, and Ireland!"

He steps back, bows nearly to the ground in his most courtly manner, and moves backward out of the walkway.

There follows the loudest communal gasp Noah's ever heard, as Her Majesty appears at the doorway and steps out into the cold night, illuminated by a dozen smoky torches. In a moment, every man is on his knees, his head bowed.

"God save the Queen!" shouts an impetuous Warder across the yard, and his shout is echoed by hundreds of voices throughout the Tower yard. Noah's is easily loudest. The crowd cheers and hats are tossed.

Noah gazes at the Queen. She seems as happy as she once was. Tomorrow she'll learn of Arthur's death and hear all the names of those who died in her service today. Then, she'll need to face the question of what to do with Essex and Southampton, and their minions. But that's tomorrow.

For tonight, she's glad.

———————⟶∘⟨✐⟩∘⟵———————

ESTHER SHIVERS AND SLEEPILY PULLS the shawl up around her shoulders. When she sleeps on the soft chair in Serjeant Ames's study, it's usually so warm that she has no need to pile the wood high before settling down. But tonight it's especially cold.

Suddenly, the front door opens.

Good heavens! It must be after two in the morning. She hears the shifting of Francis's heavy feet as he goes to ensure that the new arrival belongs here. Then she hears men's low voices and many heavy footsteps, of at least four or five men. *David!* It might be David! She gets up, hastily finds the looking glass over the Serjeant's fireplace and brushes her hair back. She runs to the front door, which closes on a blast of frigid air just as she arrives.

"Essex has surrendered and Her Majesty is well," she hears Serjeant Ames say to Francis.

"David!" Esther cries, and falls on his neck, kissing him. He smells like sweat and a little bit like … blood? No matter. She's just so happy to see him.

He smiles back at her wearily. "Well, that's an unexpected welcome," he says. "Has hell frozen over?"

"Lady Sheffield *told* me where you were, David. You're so heroic, and I'm so sorry for being bullheaded! I shall never doubt you again."

Lord Jonathan speaks in hushed tones, his expression full of worry. "Keep your voice down, Esther. Is all well with Lady Jessica?"

Esther's response is to run to Jonathan and hug him unashamedly. "Oh, Papa!" she exclaims just the way Jessica says it, with the accent on the latter syllable. He regards her quizzically. "Are *you* our new addition, Esther? Am I *your* papa?"

She points toward Jessica's room. Like magic, a baby cries. "No. *His* papa. Go upstairs and see your beautiful healthy *son*, m'lord." Jonathan runs up the steps three at a time.

David says to Esther, "Did you just—?"

Esther runs to Noah next and hugs him tightly. "Oh, Grandpapa! Can you believe it?" She takes his hands in hers and dances about. "You're a grandfather! And he's *so* beautiful!"

Noah has tears in his eyes. Is it possible that he, a Jew from another country, another world, has survived so long and had such success in life that he'll live to know his grandchild? He's ineffably happy but, as always, his happiness is tinged by the losses of his early life and those of yesterday. "And how is Jessica?" he asks.

"She's wonderful, Serjeant Ames! 'Strong as an ox' is what Aunt Beth says of her. She just gave birth yesterday, and we can barely get her to lie down." She leans in as though to speak confidentially. "But Aunt Beth says it's good for her to walk about with the baby. Here comes Lady Jessica to see *her* papa!"

But Jessica is not present. David counts. One. Two. Three. Four. Five. Jessica's door opens and the new mother emerges with the baby in her arms, looking sleepy and quite pleased.

Oh, Esther is going to make some wife, thinks David. He has no idea whether Esther even knows she's doing anything unusual. Did *she* cause the baby to awaken and cry, or was it all the noise at the front door? How did she know Jessica was about to come out of her room? Jessica walks down the stairs under her own steam and proudly presents her newborn son to her father.

Noah's hesitant to accept him into his arms. It's been so long since he held a baby, and he was never confident about it. Perhaps he's forgot how to do it. Women are so much better at these things. Before he knows it, he's holding the lad, who's promptly returned to sleep.

"Jessica," says Noah tearfully. "I … I don't know what to say."

"That's a *first!*" says Jessica with a broad smile, her voice a bit scratchy.

"You've made me so happy!" says Noah. "God bless you and Jonathan. God bless this family!"

Beth appears at the top of the stairs. "He's already blessed it," she says. "It's for us not to wear out His patience!"

Noah hands the child back to Jessica. "Thank you, Beth! You're a major blessing yourself. You appeared just in time to ensure that an awful history would not repeat itself."

Beth nods appreciatively, but says modestly, "It was just a matter of Epsom salt."

Esther turns proudly to Noah. "And Beth thought to hire a girl to continually bathe Jessica in the salt. Even when everyone else was asleep, she'd go upstairs with a steaming solution in a little pot and I could hear her humming so beautifully as she bathed Jessica." She turns to Beth, who's looking at her oddly.

"Oh, dear," says Beth quietly.

Esther is silent a moment, as everyone looks at her strangely. "Did I say something … inappropriate?"

Beth looks as though she's not sure *what* to say. She's not angry, and that's good.

"*Which* girl, dear?" asks Beth. "Was it one of Jessica's two maids or the midwife?"

"No, I know who the midwife was. And Jessica's maids wear flaxen-colored smocks. This one was wearing black with white trim, like—" She stops in midsentence.

Noah speaks to her kindly. "Was she redolent of clove, dear?"

Esther knows precisely why he's asking. Jessica's mother wore clove all the time. And the girl *did* smell of clove. She's mortified. "I … must have dreamt it," she says. "I wish to sleep now." She turns back to Noah's study, and David follows her like a puppy.

Noah turns to Francis, whose eyes have been tearing up along with everyone else's, as he's undoubtedly thinking of his own lost happiness with the girl he fancied who was cruelly drowned at the Tower in a barrel of wine. Noah places his hand reassuringly on Francis's arm but makes no mention of it.

"None of Essex's men has been seen lurking about the place?" asks Noah, bringing Francis back to the present.

Francis shakes his head reassuringly. "No, suh. And things are fine at Sheffield House, as well. I was there at eight o'clock this past evening."

Noah turns to Jessica, having forgot a very important question. "Have you thought of a name?"

"We were thinking 'Arthur.' Arthur Hawking," she pronounces. "How does that sound?"

"It sounds wonderful, dear," he replies. "Which of you thought of the name?" He's certain he's going to hear it was suggested by Esther.

"'Twas I," says Jessica, leaning into Noah. "His Hebrew name shall be 'Avram,' after Mother's father."

Noah smiles and kisses his daughter, then his grandson, on the forehead. He's so tired he could sleep standing up. He rubs his eyes. "Is … er … is my bedroom vacant?" he asks.

"'Tis, Father."

"Beth," he says, "please tell the servants I'm not to be disturbed by anyone—but Her Majesty."

"Don't you think you should go now to Marie at Sheffield House?" suggests Beth rather imperiously.

Noah moans. "I'm not going to wake that whole house, Beth. Francis, would you mind going to Sheffield House, and telling Gardner and Mistress Ames that we're all right and Essex is in Crown custody?"

"Right away, sir. Is it all right for me to wake her, sir?"

"Please do. I've known her long enough to know that, if her family had a coat of arms, the motto would be Latin for 'Wake me, or I'll never forgive you.'"

Francis grabs a cloak and heads to the stables.

"Do you wish to be disturbed only by Her Majesty *personally*," asks Beth, "or shall I wake you for her writing, as well?"

"Surprise me," he says flippantly. "To think better of it: her *writing*, as well. And also Lord Robert … and *his* writing."

Noah starts upstairs, but stops midway and, without so much as turning around, says, "And Beth, as you brought Esther here, please tell her: *No more dreams!*"

He staggers up the rest of the stairs and into his room, plops onto the bed, removes one boot, and falls back sound asleep.

CHAPTER 40

EARLY THE NEXT MORNING, Noah finds Sir Walter at the Tower near a row of cells.

"Are they all here?" he asks.

"Yes," says Raleigh. "Each in a separate cell. We don't want them concocting false tales in their common defense. Essex and Southampton are in the two commoner's cells at opposite ends of this row. They're furious at being treated like commoners. Very touching, really," he says sardonically. "Who're you here to see?"

"I received a note from one of Essex's divines telling me his lordship wishes to speak with me privately. Do you suppose he wishes to apologize?"

Sir Walters scoffs. "I'd give odds against it." He points to the end of the hallway. "Turn right at the end. Essex's cell is last on the right. You might wish to leave, and return in a bit. Cuffe's in there now. 'Course, he's been there a while and might be finished soon."

"You're letting prisoners talk to each other?" asks Noah with surprise.

"The divines are there," says Sir Walter. "The prisoners are not likely to fabricate anything with men of the cloth present, are they?" Sir Walter leans in toward Noah. "I said they were divines. Not angels. They give a full report to Robert Cecil twice a day."

"God save us from such ministers," mutters Noah. "I'll go there now, in case they're finishing up."

"Francis Bacon's waiting outside, too," says Sir Walter. "Good luck," he says and leaves the cell block.

Noah turns right at the end of the hallway and stops. He can hear an intense confrontation taking place in Essex's cell. Just outside it, Francis Bacon waits with his eyes down, evidently unaware of Noah's presence. There's nowhere for Noah to conceal himself, so he steps into a shadow, expecting the noise to subside fairly quickly. Cuffe is evidently attempting to wheedle some form of forgiveness out of a resistant Essex.

Essex's voice is sufficiently loud that Noah can hear the words. "Oh, Cuffe!" says Essex with evident disgust. "Ask pardon of *God and the Queen's Majesty*, and see you deserve it. For my part, my mind is now wholly fixed upon the afterlife. I have resolved to deal sincerely before God and man; and I cannot but tell you this plainly: *You were the principal man that moved me to this disloyalty!*"

A moment later, the cell door is opened and Cuffe emerges weeping. The door clangs shut behind him. Seeing Bacon there, he rushes to his arms.

"Oh, Francis!" Cuffe moans as he embraces Bacon. "Did you hear what he said? He has *killed* me!"

Bacon says something in comforting tones, but Noah cannot make out the words.

"No, Francis," insists Cuffe. "He needn't repeat it. Those divines report to Cecil. Oh, I'm going to be torn to shreds at Tyburn!"

Francis returns the embrace and they stand there in that dank piss-smelling hallway for a long time. Noah's heart goes out to them, and he suddenly feels as though he's spying.

Cuffe draws his face away from Bacon and says, "Oh, Francis, if only we could relive those blessed weeks, I would go willingly to the executioner. As it is, I don't know how I shall drag myself to the end."

Bacon pats Cuffe's back comfortingly, and Cuffe buries his face in Bacon's shoulder, his cries muffled by the lawyer's robes.

Tears come to Noah's eyes. This is simply too painful to watch. He darts away in the shadows, down the long hallway, and out into the sunshine. But even in the clear winter air, he finds it difficult to breathe. Everything still smells like piss. His breaths are short, as though there's a heavy belt around his chest.

Noah struggles to make sense of what he just saw. Just this morning, he was told that Francis Bacon will serve as a chief prosecutor in the whole Essex case. Cuffe will be an *accused*, so what the devil does this mean?

In an epiphany, he realizes that Francis Bacon and Henry Cuffe are the "Romeo and Juliet" described by Sir Henry all those months ago at Lothbury. They're the two who occupied Anthony Bacon's rooms just before his return to England, who loved each other ideally, but whose love was forbidden. And who, after skulking about secretly for some months, grew frustrated with the futility of it all and turned against each other on the pretext of their radically … differing … *politics*.

Bacon has a conflict of interest in Cuffe's case, but it can readily be resolved by the appointment of another prosecutor. It will probably be Coke. Still, Bacon will have no choice but to sit at counsel table and watch Cuffe's case being torn apart. And after his conviction, Bacon will be expected to watch dispassionately as Cuffe is forced to watch himself torn to pieces at Tyburn.

The world is a cruel place. A mad place. Perhaps it shall remain mad, he supposes, but must it ever remain so cruel? *And what I saw just now, was not that love?*

He remembers someone he's resolved to see before leaving the Tower, and tramps off to the infirmary.

Essex can wait. He's not going anywhere.

⟶∘⟨◯⟩∘⟵

THE PURITAN KNOTT lies on a bed in the Tower infirmary. They've finally removed the corpses that lay there all night. The smell was becoming overwhelming. Knott wonders how long they'll allow him to stay. His shoulder is painful and inflamed, and his right arm useless for the time being.

He's lifted a cup of small beer in his left hand and brought it to his mouth, when Serjeant Ames walks in. As Knott drinks, Ames looks about to see who else is there. At the moment, that's no one. Even the attendant has left on a break.

The Serjeant takes a chair and places it by his bed.

"Constable Knott," says Ames, "that was a brave and noble thing you did yesterday in trying to save my young friend from Essex's footman. I thank you for your effort. How are you faring?" he asks, pointing to Knott's right shoulder. "How is the wound?"

"Thank you, Serjeant. I'd feel better if your friend were still living. I'd also feel less of a fool, having been injured quite badly without managing to accomplish a thing. It hurts badly, but I thank you for asking."

"Life is hard," says Noah, "but it would be harder still were it not for young men such as yourself who will place themselves at risk for the protection of others. Tell me, Constable, did you hear of what happened after you were wounded and Arthur was killed?"

Knott takes another sip from the cup and struggles to put it back on the little table by his bed. Noah gently takes it from his hand and puts it down. "I heard that Caim was killed by a tall, strapping young blond man. I believe the gentleman came here to pray over the body of his friend yesterday, though I was in no condition to speak with him."

"Did you know Caim before the incident?" asks Serjeant Ames.

"I had met him once or twice. I can't recall the context."

"The man who bested Caim at sword is named 'David Killigrew,'" says the Serjeant, "but he didn't finish Caim off. That was accomplished by another barrister of Gray's Inn, named 'Cuthbert Bennett,' who was himself slain in the tussle. Did you know Cuthbert?"

Knott squirms in the bed, which tugs at his wound, causing him to groan.

"That looks very painful," says Serjeant Ames. "Would you like me to get you some more water?"

"No, sir," says Knott. "Thank you." What he'd truly like is for the good Serjeant to stop asking questions and go away.

"About Cuthbert Bennett then," says the persistent Serjeant. "Did you know him?"

"I don't believe I did," says Knott.

The Serjeant nods skeptically. "But you know that he lay here in the infirmary all night, not six feet from you."

"I heard that was he," says Knott.

Serjeant Ames sighs. "I knew Cuthbert well. His twin brother, may he rest in peace, was murdered by Caim on nearly the same spot some months before."

"I'd heard that, as well."

"Did you know that his twin brother Tobias was a catamite?" asks Noah.

Knott squirms. "There's no point in speaking ill of the dead, Serjeant."

"No, of course not," says the Serjeant. "It's just that you seem to have an interest in finding out such things. Cuthbert used to settle up Tobias's bills at an inn just outside Queenhythe where many catamites gather. Do you know the place?"

"I ... I believe my constabulary responsibilities have brought me there on one or another occasion."

"Did anyone ever break into your room there and announce that you were being robbed?"

Knott sits up and regards the Serjeant suspiciously. "What are you getting at?"

"Cuthbert told me and others," says the Serjeant, "weeks before he was killed that he had broken into a room there one night, subdued Caim with a knock on the head, and freed two catamites from Caim's menace.

I was just curious whether you knew anything about it."

Knott says nothing, but just looks at the Serjeant.

"You know," says the Serjeant rising and beginning to pace, "everyone—*everyone* looks for love in this mad, mad world. Some do so in a manner approved by the church, the state, and society. And some do so in a different manner. You will agree with me, will you not, that some men seek the pleasure of other men without meaning them any harm or violence? Hmm?"

Knott feels quite deflated. "I suppose they do."

"Yet you seem to take an overweening interest in their sexual proclivities and crimes, do you not?"

"There is often violence or extortion involved," says Knott, with a gulp.

"But, when there is *not*, there's no particular reason to trouble men who simply go about looking for love, but have no interest in women. Now, is there?"

Knott is trapped. This man can expose him at whim. Knott's mouth is almost too dry to speak. "No, there's no particular reason to trouble men about sexual matters when they show no intention of committing violent acts or extortion."

"Then you won't be doing that any more, will you?" asks the Serjeant.

Knott frowns. After a long time, he responds. "I think I shall not bother with such things, where no violence or extortion has been threatened."

The Serjeant nods. "Nor I," he says agreeably. "By the way, I've arranged with the Bishop of London for you to remain as his guest at his private infirmary until you've quite healed. It's the least he can do, as you were injured in service of his church." He glances about critically at Knott's surroundings. "I think you'll find *those* accommodations more to your liking."

Knott nods his thanks.

The Serjeant smiles and says, "And the food's *much* better. I'll see you sometime when you're feeling quite yourself. In the meantime, I wish you a quick and complete recovery. Good day."

<hr />

THE JAILER ESCORTS Noah to Essex's cell and unlocks the door.

"Serjeant Ames has come to visit, m'lord," says the jailer.

"Please come in," says Essex in a surprisingly self-possessed tone. "Thank you for coming, Serjeant. I was beginning to think you wanted no more to do with me."

"I expect your lordship has more to concern yourself with than my affections," replies Noah, "but I have no less concern for your well-being today than I did before this latest unpleasantness." He smooths his robe. "I do feel I have personally lost two dear young friends to the maelstrom your lordship began, however."

"You're speaking of Arden, I assume. And that *is* a loss I will confess, one for which I am sorely sorry. Who is the other one?"

"Cuthbert Bennett," Noah replies.

"The one who finished off Caim?"

"Aye, m'lord."

"His case is a bit more equivocal, I should think, as he appears to have killed at least two of my servants himself."

Noah shakes his head. "Only after they murdered his brother, m'lord. Under the circumstances, I think his actions were at least understandable, though not condonable."

"And have you no reservations about his willingness to join my retinue?"

"I don't know what to make of it, m'lord," says Noah, "but I suppose it no longer matters. The man is dead."

"He is that," says Essex. "Both he and his brother are."

"May I ask, m'lord, your reason for summoning me here?"

"Yes, Serjeant," says Essex, rising and leaning against a wall. "For one thing, I wanted to tell you myself that I've found you to be true to your word, honorable, and somehow loyal to both Her Majesty and myself. These are admirable and remarkable qualities in you."

"I care for you both, m'lord," says Noah, bowing humbly.

"And you've given advice to both of us."

"In every case, m'lord, the advice I gave was the best I could come up with for each of you. Unfortunately, my advice in this dispute was never taken. My inability to persuade either of you to heed my advice I consider to be a singular failing of mine, which I will regret to the end of my days."

"Looking back," asks Essex, "do you think that, had your advice been taken, it might have prevented this current pass?"

"I've no doubt of it, m'lord. The problem was not my advice, but my inability to persuade those most concerned of its wisdom."

"Well," says Essex in good humor, "at least your confidence has not been abated by this affair."

Noah doesn't wish to be disrespectful, but he's tired of being criticized by a man who's done almost nothing right. "Your reason for summoning me, my lord?"

"I have two things to tell you. One will likely please you, the other certainly not. First, as you may have suspected, your friend—and to some extent mine—Sir Henry Neville is the greatest playwright to write in our English language. He (with some small collaboration) has penned all the plays attributed to William Shakespeare, a capital dunce if ever there was one."

Noah had long suspected a connection between Neville and the plays, but to hear this confirmed so categorically by a patron of the art is amazing.

"Why does he write under a pen name, m'lord?" asks Noah.

Essex shakes his head. "You may ask him when you see him."

"That will be a long time from now," says Noah. "Sir Henry left only yesterday morning to return to his embassage in Paris."

"I expect," says Essex dourly, "that he will be brought back to London before he ever reaches Dover."

"M'lord?"

"But that pertains more to my second point. Have you any questions about my *first*?"

"Yes, m'lord," says Noah. "Who else knows he wrote these plays?"

Essex searches the ceiling as though the answer is written there. "Let's see. Sir Henry's wife, Lady Anne, surely knows. Lord Southampton certainly; 'Shakespeare' has publicly dedicated epic poems to him. Perhaps one or two playwrights, as well. But few more."

"Does Her Majesty know?" asks Noah.

"That's a good question to which I'm unsure of the answer. I've never discussed it with her, but she's as sharp a dagger as there's ever been, and I've heard her remark upon Sir Henry's writing and Shakespeare's in the same breath."

"What about Robert Cecil?" asks Noah.

Essex shrugs. "I don't know. Needless to say, Sir Henry keeps this secret closely held indeed, and would regard it as a betrayal of the worst sort for either you or me to tell anyone else. Which brings me to my second reason for summoning you here today … which is also my reason for telling you about Sir Henry's authorship. Until this moment, I expect you've felt your crisis was resolved and that there is no urgency left to my plight, at least for you. You could not be more wrong."

At this point, Noah's confused. These words are portentous.

Essex says, "Sir Henry has known of the conspiracy to invade the Queen's privy chamber for some time, and did nothing to oppose it."

Noah rises in shock.

Essex continues. "In fact, Sir Henry agreed that, should the Queen agree to the appointment of a regent, or should she abdicate the Throne, Sir Henry himself would become Secretary of State in place of Cecil."

Noah's head is spinning and his stomach turning. He places his hands on either side of his head. "Who else knows this, m'lord?"

"Well, Sir Henry wore a disguise and went under a false name. Although neither would fool anyone who already knew him, it's possible he fooled others."

"So, m'Lord Southampton knows?"

Essex nods confidently.

"Who else knows?" asks Noah.

"Cuffe, certainly. Which others? I could only speculate."

"Why are you telling *me* about Sir Henry's cooperation with the conspiracy?"

"Simple. I want you to save Southampton and Sir Henry from the hangman."

Noah's mind is all a rush. "Southampton is under arrest, m'lord. Is he going to inform on Sir Henry to the authorities?"

Essex shakes his head. "No, nor have I heard that anyone else will."

"Then how will the authorities learn of this?"

"*I'm* going to tell them."

Noah is shocked at Essex's cruelty. "*You,* m'lord? But *why?*"

"I do not expect to survive long. I believe the Queen wants my head and she shall *have* it. I have been persuaded by the divines that I cannot enter the Kingdom of Heaven unless I have unburdened my soul of the full and accurate truth of all I know concerning my crimes."

"*When* will you tell them?" asks Noah, bewildered.

"Not until I'm convicted and sentenced. Then, I must confess everything. That may be no more than a week from now, but I wanted you to have as much time as possible, should it be of any use to you."

Noah is too stunned to speak.

"You see," continues Essex, "Her Majesty is aware of the recent staging of *Richard the Second* and I expect she'll investigate thoroughly who commissioned the staging ... and who actually wrote the play. As I doubt Master Shakespeare will voluntarily submit himself to be four-and-quartered in his cousin's stead, I expect you'll need time to prepare to defend against such an investigation. Well ... do you agree to my request?"

"I don't know that *anyone* can do *anything* to save them, m'lord," says Noah, feeling cannon-shocked.

"If anyone can help them, Serjeant, it's you."

"If I'm to undertake this thankless task, m'lord, I must have free rein to impeach even your lordship's veracity and cause damage to your case. Are you agreeable to *this*?"

"I am," says Essex. "In fact, I *expect* it. Give no thought to me. Think of your new charges only. Do you accept?"

Noah wishes earnestly to think it over. "And if Her Majesty objects?" he says.

Essex smiles wanly. "Once again, I'm a step ahead of you. Her Majesty has already consented in respect of Southampton. But, of course, she knows nothing yet of Neville's complicity."

Noah's eyes go wide and he turns about, facing the bars. For a moment, he grabs them as though he's the one imprisoned here, so little choice is left to him. He fights for breath, as a man drowning.

"Jailer!" Noah shouts with what little breath he can muster. "Jailer!" he shouts a little louder.

He turns back to Essex.

"I accept your charge, m'lord. God help me!"

"God *bless* you!" says Essex.

The jailer appears and lets Noah out, but when he tries to make friendly conversation, Noah ignores him and strides down the hallway and out of the building into the sunshine, where his mind races and his breath begins to return at last.

THE END

HISTORICAL NOTE

The series *In the Den of the English Lion* is a work of historical fiction, a sort of "what if" winter's tale, written for the reader's amusement. A great deal of research went into it, but it should not be relied upon for scholarly purposes, other than to excite further inquiry. Book 1, entitled *A Second Daniel,* and Book 3, *A Dragon in the Ashes,* contained historical notes which, between them, covered the story through the end of Book 3. This note is intended to cover events in Book 4, *All the Men as Mad as He.* To the extent feasible, the author has tried to avoid spoilers of Book 5 in this historical note.

Many characters in the story thus far are fictitious, including all who are portrayed as being (or as having once been) Jews or of Jewish descent. Jonathan Hawking (now Jonathan, Lord Saint Ives), Arthur Arden, the Bennetts, and all other barristers formerly resident at Gray's Inn are likewise fictitious, except for Francis Bacon, whose position is more or less accurately portrayed. Mistress Marie Ames is fictitious, as are the individual Yeoman Warders in the book. David "Cheerful" Killigrew is a fictitious member of the real Killigrew family; he is putatively a nephew of Lady Anne Neville, born Killigrew, who was a real person married to the equally real Sir Henry Neville. Caim and his henchmen are fictitious.

Most of the historical figures are more or less accurately portrayed, for example: Anthony Bacon was a real person, and he's accurately, if incompletely, described in the story. The Percy brothers were real knights. Lord Grey did in fact cut off the hand of Southampton's servant and later lead the "little army" to Essex House. Augustine Phillips would likely have been involved in quoting and collecting a fee on behalf of the Chamberlain's Men to stage *Richard the Second* at the Globe Theater on the eve of the rebellion; in any event, he would later be questioned by the authorities about those activities.

Many of the lines spoken in the story during the negotiations leading to Essex's surrender, including those of Lord Essex, Lord Southampton, and Sir Robert Sidney, have been lifted nearly verbatim (with a little modernization) from secondary sources relying directly upon primary sources. To the extent that there is disagreement among the sources on a few trivial questions, it is hoped that the reader will defer to the author's need to decide such questions for narrative purposes.

Readers who would like to visualize the streets and other locations on a map are strongly urged to examine the invaluable interactive copy of the Agas Map operated online under the designation "Map of Early Modern London." It will give the reader some idea of not only the locations, but also the distances between various places.

The remainder of this note will roughly follow the progress of the story in Book 4.

In 1600-1601, there was indeed a Saint Gregory by Saint Paul's; it was a parish church attached to Saint Paul's Cathedral. Both Saint Gregory's and Saint Paul's would be destroyed by the Great Fire of London in 1666. Saint Gregory's would not form any part of Christopher Wren's plan of reconstruction but, while it stood, it indeed overlooked Ludgate. The path from Saint Gregory's to Ludgate was in fact called "Bowyers' Row." Bowyers' Row was later to be renamed Ludgate Street, but The Worshipful Company of Bowyers fortunately lives on, and now maintains a website. There's no reason to believe that there was a double murder committed on Bowyer's Row at the end of August 1600.

By the end of August 1600, as depicted in the book, Sir Henry Neville had temporarily returned home from his French embassage, and occupied his house at Lothbury, together with Lady Anne.

The Inn of Glaucus was indeed the jocular name of Anthony Bacon's rooms at Gray's Inn. See Daphne DuMaurier, *Golden Lads* (1975). The mythological tale of Glaucus is accurately described by Sir Henry in the story. The Romeo and Juliet-like tale of the Inn of Glaucus told by Sir Henry is the author's fabrication, although there is some reason to believe that Henry Cuffe was a homosexual, see Casson & Rubinstein, *Sir Henry Neville Was Shakespeare,* at 135 (2016), and the same has long been said of Francis Bacon. There is no reason to believe, however, that the two were ever an "item." Although Essex did denounce Cuffe in the words provided in the story, such denunciation did not take place until a point in the legal process later than that depicted, and it was much more public and even more devastating.

As described in the story, the Queen allowed Essex's patent on sweet wines to expire of its own terms, and issued a new sweet-wines patent to the Crown, appointing Sir Henry Billingsley to collect royalties. The

Queen's remark likening Essex to an unruly horse was as stated in the story, verbatim or nearly so. In fact, Essex had no other income of any significance when his patent expired.

The sermon at Essex House attended by Noah and Esther pertaining to Thomas More's *Utopia* is not as farfetched as one might think. The possibility of republican government was much discussed in those days, and such sermons were one way Essex attracted non-conformists of every stripe to his cause.

While several of Sir Henry Neville's formative years were spent at Blackfriars, Sir Henry would not necessarily have been greeted at the Wardrobe as a returning journeyman. Although Sir Henry was known to have disguised himself to pay his respects at one politically sensitive funeral, see Brenda James & William D. Rubinstein, *The Truth Will Out* 133 (U.S. ed. 2006), it is unknown whether he donned a disguise or used a pseudonym during his appearances at Ewelme or Drury House. It would have made sense for him to do so, however.

Sir Henry Neville's attitude toward his role in the coming uprising appears to have been much as observed by Southampton in the story, that is, as a fellow traveler having no direct involvement in the plot but standing to gain by its success.

Lord and Lady Sheffield are fictitious, as is the indolent Lord Swindon. Lady Sheffield's picaresque scheme is fictitious, as well. Chester's interrogation of Lady Sheffield's "ruffians" was, of course, inspired by Shakespeare's comical portrayal of constables. In speaking to David Killigrew, Lady Sheffield is careful to specify that much of Lord Swindon's property is "unentailed." At that time, much real property was held only for the owner's life and, upon his death, would pass not in accordance with his own will, but rather in accordance with conditions imposed either by his grantor or by law, called "entailments." The importance to Lady Sheffield that much of Lord Swindon's property be unentailed was that she could inherit such property upon his death.

There was a Cathedral Constable at Saint Paul's in 1600-1601 though, to the author's knowledge, such office was not occupied by a puritan named "What-God-Will Knott." Puritans did have some very odd names, however.

The laws making buggery a capital offense, imposed during the reign of Henry the Eighth, were later abrogated and then, as observed by Noah, reinstated by Queen Elizabeth early in her reign.

As stated in the story, items in the care of the Queen's Wardrobe consisted of much more than just clothing, and included substantial armaments at the Tower of London and other royal locations. The wardrobe at Blackfriar's was the "Wardrobe of Wardrobes," in that it was devoted to certain clothing in the Wardrobe's charge.

Drapers' Hall was real, and evidently remains at or near the location indicated.

Although Jonathan Hawking and Jacob are fictitious, Sir Francis Drake and the powerful Hawkins family were quite real, as was the Golden Hind's circumnavigation of the earth, as described by Jacob.

There is indeed (and was, at the time) an old church at the location where Cuthbert is depicted killing Meriton. It's Saint Margaret's. The location and description of the graveyard and the well are imaginary.

The illness suffered by Jessica during pregnancy was pre-eclampsia, a principal symptom of which is extraordinarily high blood pressure with resultant severe headaches. While the illness was unnamed in Elizabethan England, its symptoms would have been familiar to midwives, who would undoubtedly have treated it with such folk remedies as seemed to work in the past. If untreated, pre-eclampsia can progress to eclampsia, which runs the regrettable course described in the case of Jessica's mother Rachel, and can often be fatal to the mother.

As Beth indicates in the story, Dead Sea salt would have little or no beneficial effect in the treatment of pre-eclampsia, as such salt lacks a significant concentration of magnesium sulfate (though it contains some magnesium). By contrast, as Beth accurately observes, Epsom salt properly refined, measured, and administered by trained medical personnel can have a major beneficial effect in preventing pre-eclampsia from developing into eclampsia. Epsom salt consists of magnesium sulfate in heptahydrate form which, administered incorrectly, could result in hypermagnesemia, a dangerous, sometimes fatal condition. Epsom is a town in Surrey, England, and is the source of the original Epsom salt. Whether, in Elizabethan England, Epsom salt was recognized as a midwife's remedy for pre-eclampsia is unknown.

As Jessica tells Jonathan, Essex did say that Queen Elizabeth was "an old woman whose mind is as twisted as her carcass," and it cannot have endeared him to the Queen when his words eventually reached her.

Queenhythe was a real place that was about as rough as depicted in the story. Its name is now spelled Queenhithe, and the neighborhood is now perfectly respectable. Perhaps it was reformed on account of the re-spelling of its name.

Sir John Fortescue was indeed Chancellor of the Exchequer at the time. A patent licensee generally had (then, as now) a financial incentive to understate his or her sales of licensed items, in order to pay less to the patent owner in royalties. The particulars of the scam set out by Sir John in the story were designed based upon the author's forty years' experience representing actual intellectual property licensors and licensees, and years of reading and seeing entirely too much David Mamet.

Shortly before the Essex Rebellion, as described in the book, Lord Grey, with a few of his attendants, attacked Southampton on horseback, costing Southampton's servant a hand, and resulting in Lord Grey's being lodged in the Fleet Prison for several weeks.

Sir Ferdinando Gorges did in fact depart without leave his Governorship at the Fort of Plymouth to attend upon Lord Essex. Other than the intuited inner workings of Sir Ferdinando's mind, his actions are fairly depicted.

The progression of events leading up to and comprising the Essex Rebellion is depicted in a manner quite close to known fact, although it's compressed, and narrative detail (with fictitious characters) has been supplied by the author. The written assurances of support that Essex received from Sheriff Smyth and the Lord Mayor in the days leading up to the rebellion were unauthorized forgeries, and Essex's attempt to obtain help from the Sheriff and Lord Mayor was futile, and unfolded pretty much as described in the story.

The relative merits of various claims to the Succession are as framed (albeit one-sidedly) by Lord Southampton in the story. Sir Henry accurately relates to Cuffe the process of revision undergone by Magna Carta in the early years.

The several visitors received by Essex on the day before (and the day of) the rebellion were as described in the story, including the extra note that dropped onto Essex's lap, warning him to see to his own safety.

The mid-Thames meeting between Raleigh and Gorges is as accurate as it could be made, given the conflicting testimony of Raleigh and Gorges at the trial of Essex and Southampton.

As depicted in the story, Sir Henry Neville was indeed seen at court on the morning of the rebellion.

Sir John Leveson's actions at Ludgate are more or less accurately portrayed in the story, as is his family relation to Sir Henry Neville.

The following material changes were made for narrative purposes:

During the day of the rebellion, the Queen was likely at Whitehall, not the Tower of London, although Essex and Southampton were unsure where she'd be. Consequently, they did in fact spend a fair amount of time and debate deciding whether it would be sufficient to overcome

Whitehall or it would be necessary to take the Tower, as well.

Together with Sir Ferdinando Gorges, Sir Gelly Meyrick was put in charge of the councillors detained at Essex House. Meyrick did not leave Essex House to go to the Tower as he does in the story, nor was he captured at the Tower. There's no reason to believe Meyrick was inwardly tortured by misgivings over his participation in the plot to invade the Queen's court.

There is no reason to believe that the vessels placed by the Lord Admiral in the Thames by Essex House had a total of four cannon, but it was obviously the Lord Admiral's strategy to threaten Essex with overwhelming force from all sides.

Sneak Peek at Book 5 of
In the Den of the English Lion

SHAKESPEARE IN THE TOWER
by Neal Roberts

CHAPTER 1

THE SUPPRESSION OF ESSEX'S REBELLION, far from putting matters to rest, marks the beginning of the most harrowing few months in the life of Noah Ames, when a single slip on his part can result in his dearest friend being torn to shreds and left to rot before completing the greatest testament to humankind ever written.

At mid-afternoon on the thirteenth day of February in the year 1601, Noah is called to the office of Lord Robert Cecil at Whitehall Palace. He quickly takes to his horse, the invaluable Bucklebury, and begins the wintry journey to Westminster from his wife's house in Holborn.

As Noah rides into Whitehall stables, he's surprised to find the diminutive Lord Robert awaiting him in a fretful mood. Mere days earlier, Lord Robert guided the government through Essex's rebellion—a difficult challenge to Her Majesty's reign—but now his face is pallid and fatigued, as though he's been up for days.

"To what do I owe this courtesy, m'lord?" asks Noah. "I was expecting to meet you at your office."

"Something's come up," replies Lord Robert uncomfortably, "and I need your immediate help."

"Then you shall have it," replies Noah, having no idea what will be asked of him. He dismounts, hands off Bucklebury's reins to a familiar stableman, and brushes the dust of the road off his silk Serjeant's robes.

"Walk with me, Noah," says Lord Robert, leading him into Whitehall Palace.

Noah has always found that walking beside the diminutive Lord Robert presents no problem. Speaking with him privately while doing so is always a tribulation, however, owing to the difference between Noah's height and Lord Robert's. Somehow, Noah always ends up bowing forward to lower his head, and turning his face toward his small companion. In this awkward posture, Noah's always at risk of bumping his head into someone or something, as he cannot see directly ahead. Fortunately, Lord Robert, through long experience, has become the watcher of the way for both himself and his companion.

"Even before my urgent business," says his lordship, "permit me to ask how the ... interment of Master Arden went."

"There is no sadder event, Lord Robert," laments Noah, "than the interment of a young person who's been robbed of such a rewarding future. Few of his family were able to come to London on such short notice. Some live as far away as Stratford. Fortunately, Arthur's (and Sir Henry's) cousin Sir John Leveson attended, which was reassuring to us all."

Sir John Leveson is one of very few people Noah intends to speak to without delay concerning Sir Henry Neville's complicity in the abortive rebellion, as it was Sir John who spoke with Sir Henry before reinforcing and defending the most important military position of the rebellion, namely, Ludgate.

Noah continues. "Arthur's friends attended the interment *en masse*— even Andres Salazar, who had to ride all the way from Cambridge. All of them being barristers and long-time friends of Arthur's, each held forth with a mirthful story of their youth together. The merrier each memory, of course, the more it cut like a knife. 'Twas difficult, Lord Robert, quite difficult."

"I can imagine," says Lord Robert. "Arden was an able and welcome presence in Her Majesty's service. Keep his remaining friends together, Noah, and, as my father was wont to say, 'grapple them to your soul with hoops of steel.'"

"I shall," Noah assures him. "And what is your urgent business, m'lord?"

"Two naval officers came to see me a few hours ago," Lord Robert begins. "One was Robert Crofts ... or Cross ... I couldn't make it out clearly. He's a ship's captain. He told me that another officer, one Sir Thomas Lea, had told him last evening that 'it would be a glorious thing for six courageous, brave fellows to go together to the Queen and compel her by force to deliver Essex and Southampton out of custody.' When

Lea was unable to enlist any of his preferred six men for the job, he announced he'd do it himself."

"And where is this Sir Thomas Lea now?" asks Noah.

"That's just it," replies Lord Robert. "No one knows. He could be anywhere, especially as he's likely to be alone. For all we know, he could be in Westminster"—Lord Robert's eyes dart about the hallway—"why, even here at the Palace of Whitehall." He sighs with fatigue. "It's one of my persistent nightmares that the Queen might be the object of a lone assailant having no care for his own safety. There's no way to be certain of protecting her from that."

"Lord Robert," says Noah, "I know it will be cold comfort to hear, but any notion that Her Majesty is ever completely safe is illusory. We do the best we can by exercising eternal vigilance—which no one does better than your lordship. How may I be of service in this?"

Lord Robert snorts and looks up at Noah.

"You can find the bastard."

———————⊸๐⊂⊘⊃๐⊂———————

BEFORE PROCEEDING FURTHER with our narrative, perhaps it would be well to remind the reader of the prevailing political and legal waters in which Noah finds himself immersed.

By said February 13, Lord Essex has been incarcerated in the Tower of London these five days in connection with the late uprising bearing his name. Lord Southampton has been imprisoned there for as long. A few of their subordinate conspirators have also been imprisoned for such time at the Tower, but the more mundane sort has been spread about the local prisons of somewhat lesser security, such as the Fleet in London and the Clink in Southwark.

For Noah's part, a mere three days have passed since Lord Essex secretly imparted to him two explosive facts and assigned him a Herculean task to which he reluctantly agreed. As for the facts imparted by his lordship: First, Essex identified their mutual friend Sir Henry Neville as the author of the works publicly attributed to William Shakespeare, confirming Noah's suspicion of many years; second, Essex told Noah that his lordship would soon publicly accuse Sir Henry of complicity in the late uprising.

As yet, however, no accusation has been lodged against Sir Henry by anyone. As Sir Henry departed London on the morning of the uprising to resume his French embassage, hope still lives within Noah's breast that

Sir Henry will reach the South Sea and set sail for Paris before Her Majesty's men can overtake him. A foolish hope perhaps, in light of the impediments encountered in moving one's entire household to a foreign land, but one seizes on foolish hopes when reason sees no hope for a happy resolution.

The Herculean task that Noah accepted from Lord Essex was to do everything possible to avoid Sir Henry Neville and the Earl of Southampton coming to serious harm on grounds of their involvement in the uprising. As no one else is yet aware that Sir Henry will be accused, Noah is severely hampered in his investigation by the need to avoid arousing suspicion, for as soon as Sir Henry falls under a cloud, his escape will be cut off and his capture a certainty.

As for helping Southampton, there seems little Noah can do, as he knows Southampton to have encouraged Essex's insubordination. What's more, Southampton tried to enlist Noah's own cooperation, though in which capacity never became clear, as Noah declined the invitation as soon as he heard it.

"WHERE DO YOU SUPPOSE this rebellious Captain Lea is likeliest to be?" asks Lord Robert as he and Noah walk the corridor toward his office.

Noah's mind races to put himself in the shoes of a naval officer preparing to assail the Queen's person, a difficult turnabout for Noah's brain. He stops walking and stands still.

Lord Robert stops beside him. "I'll get you as many men as you need," he assures Noah.

Noah shakes his head. "As for the judicious application of force, m'lord, I'll have to leave that to you. You are far more practiced in it than I, and you haven't time to teach me now. What I could use is more information. You said Thomas Lea is a naval officer?"

"Aye."

"What does he look like?"

"Crofts proffered nothing in that regard," says Lord Robert, "and I was so alarmed, I'm ashamed to say ... I didn't think to ask."

"Is this Lea presently assigned to a ship?"

"Aye," says Lord Robert.

"Has he any social contact who might gain him admittance to Her Majesty's court?"

"Perhaps," replies Lord Robert. "The traitorous Sir Thomas Lea is a kinsman to the loyal Sir Henry Lea, a Knight of the Garter well known to me, and well regarded."

Noah cannot conceive of a Knight of the Garter—so few and so loyal—seeking a rebellious cousin's admittance to court.

"Would Sir Henry Lea ever—?" Noah begins.

Lord Robert interrupts, shaking his head vigorously. "Never in a thousand years. More likely he'd slay his traitorous cousin on sight."

Noah's mollified on that score. Lord Robert is as good a judge of character as his father before him, who was unerring.

An idea occurs to Noah. "Those rooms outside the Queen's Privy Chamber ..."

"With the benches?" asks Lord Robert.

"Yes," says Noah. "I can't quite recall whether any of them has a balcony onto the open air."

Lord Robert searches his memory. "Two of them do," he says. "You don't suppose—Well, shall we go and look?"

Noah gives it some thought, but declines. "I don't think your lordship should be there with me. If we find Thomas Lea, and he's desperate enough, he might try to make a hostage of someone of such high place as your lordship."

Lord Robert regards him skeptically. "What of yourself?"

"The Queen's Jew?" Noah scoffs. "To those unfamiliar with the court, Lord Robert, I expect I'm no more than an oddity, an amusement for Her Majesty."

Lord Robert shakes his head emphatically. "You're not going without accompaniment. I'll send two guards there wearing plain doublets. They'll keep away from you unless you beckon them."

AFTER MEETING WITH Lord Roberts' plainclothes guards, Noah slips out of his office and assumes a place on a short queue before the guards stationed at the entrance to Her Majesty's Privy Chamber.

At the head of the queue stand two older women who appear to be of some note, being extraordinarily well-dressed and -mannered, here no doubt to beg the Queen's mercy for husbands caught up in Essex's rebellion. Each carries a small box, surely containing the customary "small gift" for Her Majesty meant to soften her regard toward their erring husbands.

The ladies, who evidently arrived together, ask the guard when Her Majesty might appear, but their inquiry is greeted with little more than a shrug.

A few minutes later, a supercilious clerk appears. Seeing noblewomen present, he emerges to address them. "Her Majesty has not yet supped," says the clerk, bowing formally. "Unfortunately, there can be no assurance that she will emerge this evening. As you can imagine, her time is quite taken up with matters arising out of the late unpleasantness."

While Noah is unable to hear the ladies' reply, the clerk makes no effort to keep his voice down. "If you have letters for Her Majesty," he pronounces, "I can relieve you of them now—with assurances that she will receive them at a time of her convenience."

Once more the ladies murmur, and once more the clerk bows and holds forth. "I am not at liberty to accept any parcels intended for Her Majesty. I'm sorry, ladies, but accepting your letters is all I'm authorized to do this e'en."

Another feminine murmur.

"No, madam," replies the clerk to the next unheard question, and for the first time the sheer persistence of these women makes Noah appreciate the clerk's plight and the reason for his haughty manner, "there can be no assurance that others will not read anything you give me before Her Majesty sees it. There are ... procedures for such things in the palace of which I have little knowledge, and over which I've no control. Now I really must be returning to my other duties." At last the ladies relent and hand him their letters.

But before the clerk can recede into the palace, a man strides toward him out of one of the siderooms. "Hoy!" the man shouts, gesticulating with his arms. "A moment, young man!"

The clerk, whose back is already turned, stops, and brings his shoulders up in an evident cringe, as though this same fellow has already tried his patience more than once this evening.

As the man approaches, Noah gets a good look at him. He's dressed in a doublet of some quality, but other aspects of his appearance distinguish him from those indolent gentlemen who seem to make it their practice to loiter at various points about the palace where they might be seen by Her Majesty.

Although the man's weapons have necessarily been left at the gate, he yet wears the scabbards and other leather items that carried them, and they bear blemishes unmistakably left by exposure to salt water. Leather wears differently at sea than on land, and his leathers all bear the telltale white streaks made by repeated exposure to seawater. His boots, though recently polished, bear similar markings. The skin of his face and hands are weathered and dark, marking him beyond doubt as one who spends most of his time out of doors.

The man's countenance is stern and impatient, as one would expect of someone accustomed to command, but there's also great anxiety on his face. He's pallid and sweaty, as though uncomfortable with the tenuousness of his position.

As he approaches, he speaks as loudly as the clerk did earlier. "Can you tell me, at least, whether Her Majesty is about to go to dinner and, if so, whether she will be accompanied by the Privy Council?"

Before the clerk can reply, Noah steps forward. "Pardon me, sir. I am Serjeant Noah Ames. I couldn't help but overhear your interest in speaking with the Queen and her Privy Council. I personally know several gentlemen who might be of interest to you, but it's unlikely you'll be admitted to see them tonight. However, if you would care to accompany me into one of these anterooms and give me your message, I can assure you I'll relay it no later than tomorrow morning."

At first, the man and the clerk both regard Noah with great surprise, but a look of appreciation gradually dawns on the clerk's face.

The clerk turns to the man and says, "My suggestion would be that you avail yourself of this gentleman's acquaintance, sir. He is no doubt correct that neither Her Majesty nor the Privy Council will admit you tonight."

Though clearly reluctant, the man relents, bowing perfunctorily to the clerk. As he approaches Noah, he nods to the clerk, who bows in turn—plainly grateful to be relieved of this persistent fellow—and quickly escapes into the palace before anyone else can call out to him.

IT TAKES NO MORE than a minute to deduce that this seaman is indeed Thomas Lea. He asks Noah to accompany him onto the balcony so he can smoke tobacco, a filthy habit which Noah has long known signifies exposure either directly to the Americas or to men who've visited there and afflicted themselves with the habit. Noah's assumption that Lea is a smoker is the only intuition he's exercised this evening, and he feels vaguely vindicated when it turns out to be correct. The weather-beaten fellow, being a gentleman, has no doubt heard that the Queen finds smoking obnoxious and will not suffer to have it about her; hence his attraction to a balcony on the open air.

Before the man identifies himself, he casually mentions that he gained entry by invoking the name of a cousin who's a Knight of the Garter. Noah catches the eye of one of the two plainclothes guards and beckons them over.

"Captain Lea?" one asks the seaman.

"I'm Thomas Lea," confirms the man, plainly a bit surprised at being recognized by this stranger.

"Please come with us, Captain," says the guard. "The Privy Council has heard you were here, and has instructed us to bring you forthwith to the First Secretary, Lord Robert Cecil."

"Well," says Lea, turning to Noah with evident satisfaction, "I see you were in earnest when you said you knew men on the council." He reaches out his hand to Noah in friendship. "I'll be sure to mention your name, Serjeant—?"

"Ames," replies Noah, accepting his handshake a bit queasily. Although he bears the man no ill will, he's morally certain the man will not be received by Lord Robert in the tenor he hopes. "Best of good fortune to you, sir."

<hr />

WHEN NOAH STOPS by Lord Robert's office an hour later, Lord Robert is alone and answers his own door.

"Good evening, Noah," he says with some surprise. "I would have thought you'd gone home by now, you did your job with such elegant dispatch."

"So," says Noah, "did you meet with Captain Lea, m'lord, and hear him out?"

Lord Robert goes to his desk and triumphantly holds up a paper with a great red seal at its foot. "I heard him out and have his full confession right here."

"What did he confess to?" asks Noah.

"High treason!" says Lord Robert.

"Did he intend to take Her Majesty captive?"

"Of course."

"He admitted that?" Noah asks with some surprise. "Did he say he'd come alone to Whitehall for that purpose, even without confederates? Seems foolhardy."

"No," says Lord Robert, "Lea said that after his preferred confederates declined to join him, he came here alone to speak with a member of the Privy Council or, barring that, to lock Her Majesty up in her rooms until she were to sign an order releasing Essex and Southampton."

"And," says Noah, "having spoken to a member of the Privy Council, namely, your lordship, he abandoned his plan. So ... is that nonetheless high treason, Lord Robert?"

Lord Robert gapes at Noah in disbelief. "I'm shocked to hear that question coming from the learned Serjeant. As you know, it is high treason merely to mentally conceive of using force against the Sovereign. He confessed to much more, namely, attempting to enlist confederates in such a cause a few days ago. That was quite sufficient. His coming here alone with the same intention, contingent only upon his success in seeking out a member of the Privy Council, would itself have been quite sufficient. Do you doubt it?"

"No," Noah admits, "but what penalty will the Crown exact?"

At this Lord Robert is quite exasperated. "What's today, Thursday? He'll be questioned again tomorrow, arraigned on Monday on the basis of his confession, and face a traitor's execution at Tyburn on Tuesday."

Noah's perplexed by Lord Robert's certainty and the anticipated pace of the proceedings. "But even Essex and Southampton may not meet such a bitter end, m'lord, and they led the uprising. There are many abroad who still speak of it in terms of mere riot."

"Well," says Lord Robert, "I don't know whom you've been speaking with, but I've been speaking with Her Majesty and the Privy Council. The charge is to be open rebellion against the Crown, and the penalties will be ... severe."

Evidently dissatisfied with Noah's dour expression, Lord Robert sighs, shows him to the door, and lets him out. "Noah," he says, "you were right to leave the bloody matters to me. You haven't the stomach for it. You did an excellent job today. Go home and enjoy your growing family. Good e'en."

After Lord Robert closes his door, Noah stands a long time in the hallway wondering what he can do to prevent—or even delay—the likely execution of Sir Henry Neville and the Earl of Southampton.

And not a bloody thing is occurring to him.

END OF THE SNEAK PEEK

Visit www.authornealroberts.com
to learn more.

ABOUT THE AUTHOR

Neal Roberts and his wife live on Long Island, New York, where they have two grown children. Neal is a practicing attorney and adjunct law professor, and spends as much time as possible researching his next novel while enhancing his lawyer's pallor. When he's not writing Elizabethan politico-legal novels, practicing law, or teaching, he's an editor of an international peer-reviewed publication in the field of intellectual property law. Neal is also an avid student of Elizabethan literature and politics, which subjects form the basis of his first novel, A Second Daniel. His analysis of Shakespeare's Sonnet 121 has been extensively cited by some of the most important authorities seeking to identify the true author of the poems and plays attributed to William Shakespeare. Connect with Neal at his website (authornealroberts.com) or on Facebook (Facebook.com/authornealroberts) and join his mailing list (bitly.com/FreeHistorical) to know when upcoming books release and to grab your free short.

ALSO BY NEAL ROBERTS

A Second Daniel, In the Den of the English Lion, Book 1 (Historical Mystery): London 1558. An orphan from a far-off land is renamed "Noah Ames," and given every advantage the English Crown can bestow.

London 1592. Now an experienced barrister, Noah witnesses what appears to be a botched robbery outside the Rose Theater, a crime he soon suspects to be part of a plot against Queen Elizabeth herself. Steadfast in his loyalty to the Queen, Noah must use every bit of his knowledge and skill to lure her most disloyal subject onto the only battlefield where Noah has the advantage ... a court of law – though in doing so he risks public exposure of his darkest secret, a secret so shocking that its revelation could cost him everything: the love of the only woman who can offer him happiness, his livelihood ... even his life.

The Impress of Heaven, In the Den of the English Lion, Book 2 (Historical Mystery): LONDON 1600. When the Earl of Essex is removed from command and placed under arrest for reaching a forbidden truce with the Irish rebels, Serjeant Noah Ames reluctantly accepts a commission to investigate the earl's fitness for command, and the two are pitted against each other once again. Meanwhile, Noah's beautiful daughter, Lady Jessica, has sought to remarry into the nobility, but events have thus far frustrated her plans. One day, Noah attends a briefing where the Queen's new commander displays maps of English military positions in Ireland. Noah's suspicions are aroused when he sees that one map is missing a watermark appearing on all the others. When he informs his young barrister friend Jonathan of his concern, he inadvertently sets in motion events that throw Jonathan and Lady Jessica together on a journey across England into ever greater peril.

A Dragon in the Ashes, In the Den of the English Lion, Book 3 (Historical Mystery): LONDON 1600. When an attempt is made on Queen Elizabeth's life, Serjeant Noah Ames races to her rescue, then sets out to identify the culprit among a band of foreigners who've newly arrived from the Continent to join with the seditious Lord Essex. In the course of his investigation, Noah uncloaks an unmitigated rein of evil that has resulted in the murders of kings, queens, and religious minorities ... and which now threatens Noah's life for reasons no one would ever suspect. Will Noah pay the ultimate price for forgetting that the past is never past?

All the Men as Mad as He, In the Den of the English Lion, Book 4 (Historical Mystery): LONDON 1600. Though Queen Elizabeth has ordered the Earl of Essex's release from confinement, she's thwarted his return to social and military grace by barring him from court for an indefinite term. Unsatisfied with this humiliation, the Queen considers whether to cut off his sole remaining income, as well. Noah Ames strongly advises against it on grounds that the Queen will thereby lose any remaining influence over Essex's conduct and also place him in desperate financial straits. When several seemingly unrelated men are found murdered, Noah begins to suspect that such murders reveal Essex's treasonous intention to return to court in bloody defiance of the Queen's order.